FORGIVENESS ROAD

Center Point
Large Print

Also by Mandy Mikulencak and available from Center Point Large Print:

The Last Suppers

FORGIVENESS ROAD

Mandy Mikulencak

CENTER POINT LARGE PRINT
THORNDIKE, MAINE

This Center Point Large Print edition
is published in the year 2019 by arrangement with
Kensington Publishing Corp.

The text of this Large Print edition is unabridged.
In other aspects, this book may vary
from the original edition.
Printed in the United States of America
on permanent paper.
Set in 16-point Times New Roman type.

ISBN: 978-1-64358-148-4

Library of Congress Cataloging-in-Publication Data

Library of Congress Cataloging in Publication
Control Number: 2019002482

*For the Southern women
whose voices sing to me —
Katrina, Wendi, Jane, and Annelle*

Before

I was born in the spring of 1960 and for several years held the record as the longest baby ever delivered at Biloxi Hospital. When I was young, I didn't have a clear idea of who or what I'd be; just that I'd be in Mississippi. Probably in Biloxi. Near my mama. Near my baby sisters. Like none of us would ever age, or go to college, or get married and move away.

It wasn't until I was sixteen that I learned how far an open road and a grandmother's love would take me.

Chapter 1

Cissy stood in the exact center of the bedroom, chewing her bottom lip and staring at the dark oak flooring. The morning sun streamed through the east windows, illuminating scratches from her recent failed attempt to move the bed against a different wall. She'd get holy hell for that later, but she couldn't be bothered with worrying now. Cissy was too busy appreciating how the light made it easier to count the number of six-inch-wide boards that stretched from one side of the room to the other. There were always twenty-three, unless of course she decided to count the half board at one end as a full board or disregard it altogether.

Since it was summer and she knew she'd not be late for the bus, Cissy counted a second time, allowing the numbers to wash over her like a warm rain shower.

Jessie, the youngest of the three Pickering sisters, flung open the door. "Eleven twenty, sixteen eighty!"

Cissy turned and pulled her baby sister into a hug. She smelled of children's sleep and Ivory soap and all comforting things. "Silly goose, those are made-up numbers. Now I have to start over. And if you don't hightail it to breakfast,

9

Mama will start ranting about our lollygagging. Or she'll make an excuse not to drive us to the library."

The sisters had already consumed an impressive stack of books since school let out, reading long into the sticky June nights, even under threat of punishment. Jessie still preferred picture books, but Lily had progressed to Nancy Drew mysteries. For the past week, Cissy had needled her mama until she finally agreed to take the three of them to the Biloxi library that morning. Her chief argument against getting more books—and a flimsy one at that—was that the girls read too fast and the books they had should have lasted all summer. Cissy chose to ignore her complaining, something her grandmother once remarked took a special talent.

"Get your butts downstairs this instant. Your cornflakes are getting soggy!" Her mama's voice carried easily from the kitchen, down a long hallway, and up the flight of stairs. Cissy believed scolding to be one of *her* special talents, as was pouring milk into their cereal before they got to the table to punish them for their tardiness or some other transgression.

Her mama could have avoided much of her aggravation this summer, including multiple trips to the library, if she had just agreed to teach Cissy how to drive. Her excuse had been that Cissy didn't exhibit the maturity necessary to operate a vehicle, and until she gave up her childish ways, a license was off-limits. Cissy vowed to wear her down, though. It had been providence that she earn her license this year: it was 1976, she was sixteen years old, and it was twenty-six miles to the Department of Motor Vehicles office. You couldn't ignore that many sixes.

After Jessie scurried off to brush her teeth, Cissy slipped into a plaid cotton sundress and pink plastic sandals that squeaked when she walked and rubbed blisters on her little toes. The sound irritated her mama just enough to make those blisters worthwhile.

As Cissy left her room, she noticed Jessie across the hall, her ear pressed to the closed door of the bedroom she shared with Lily.

"What's going on?" Cissy asked.

"Daddy's talking to Lily and they don't want to be disturbed. But I need my shoes." The six-year-old squirmed with indecision.

Cissy had made her sisters promise never to be alone with him and to always keep their door open. Her hand hovered over the porcelain doorknob, hopelessness squeezing her heart into a tight mass. Her breath began to escape in short bursts. She put her hands to the sides of her head to stop the rush of thoughts tumbling up and down and sideways. When that didn't work, her hands curled into tight fists at her sides and she stood as stiff as a board.

Jessie tugged at her sister's dress, anxious fingers twirling the cloth. "What's wrong? You having a spell?"

Cissy unclenched her fists and looked at the marks her fingernails had dug into her palms, half-moons that looked like the birds Lily drew in pictures of the sky.

She counted to twenty to steady her breath. "I'm fine," she finally said. "Head on down to breakfast."

But she wasn't fine. She'd made a deal with her daddy, one that protected her sisters if Cissy agreed to keep their secret. She didn't know why she felt he'd one day go back on his word, but that's what her churning gut told her. It was rarely wrong, and to ignore it now could jeopardize the two beings in the whole wide world who still made it worthwhile to get up each day.

With Jessie out of sight, Cissy turned the knob and the door swung open easily. She shuddered to realize it made no noise, not even a halfhearted squeak from the metal hinges to alert someone, just like her own door.

"You can't be in here!" Lily snatched the piece of orange construction paper that lay across their father's lap and shoved it under a pillow. Bits of gold glitter clung to his slacks. "I was showing Daddy a birthday surprise for Jessie. Now get before Jessie barges in and ruins everything."

Her father stood. He adjusted his tie with his

right hand. His left clenched his favorite gray fedora. It was the one he wore on mornings he had to be in court. He said it brought him luck.

Cissy looked at her feet, then to the flowers on the wallpaper, an atrocious pink not found anywhere in nature. There were too many blooms to count and she doubted anything could calm her stomach in that moment anyway. When he slid past her in the doorway, the lingering scent of shaving soap clung to him.

"You got something on your mind, girl?" His whisper was just a breath, warm and disquieting.

"No, sir." She turned her head to the side, desperate to escape their proximity. "Mama wants us down at breakfast. I came for Lily."

"Well, you know better than to keep her waiting."

He laughed to himself and left them be. Cissy couldn't help but watch him until she could no longer hear his footfalls on the stairs. The ghost of him remained, though, almost a solid thing rendering her fixed to the spot.

"You're a hot mess. You better brush that hair before Mama sees it." Lily's command seemed to break the spell.

"I'll be right down," Cissy said. "Go on without me."

She waited a few seconds before walking into her parents' room. Something wholly outside herself compelled her forward. She headed straight to the old bureau where her daddy hid his revolver in the bottom drawer under his socks, neat little bundles grouped according to color. He kept the thing loaded because he said an empty gun wasn't much use when it came down to needing it. Today, she agreed with him. She wouldn't have known how to load the bullets, but was hopeful she could pull a trigger.

She heard her mama berating their housekeeper, Bess, for using too much dish soap, but it was Lily's voice that dominated the kitchen conversation. She asked Jessie what kind of picture books she wanted from the library and told her it was time she tried some big-girl readers. Cissy smiled to think she'd imparted a love of reading to her baby sisters. Books would never fail them. And she wouldn't either.

While the girls finished up breakfast, Cissy tiptoed down the hall and out the front door, following her daddy to the detached garage. With the gun behind her back, she walked in sync with his steps, although several paces behind. Her eyes were riveted on the heels of his shoes, ink black and shiny. There was a time when the sisters fell over themselves begging to help him shine those shoes, eager for just a crumb of approval, even if it meant extra time in the bath to scrub the polish from beneath their nails. Cissy couldn't remember the last time she wanted his attention.

When he whipped around, she almost dropped

the gun. "What do you want, Cissy? I'm going to be late for work."

She soaked in every detail of how he looked: his light gray suit, which set off his freckled skin better than his other suits; the maroon and navy striped tie and white dress shirt starched just so; the silver cuff links that cast tiny globes of light against the window panes of the garage door; the red hair they'd both inherited from his own mama.

"Good God, girl, cat got your tongue?"

Her wrist shook from the weight of the gun, still behind her back. She didn't know what she could possibly say to make things any different.

"I don't have time for your foolishness, Ciss. Go back inside."

He pulled up on the handle of the garage door. The steel springs sang out their displeasure, causing goose bumps to travel the length of her body. He walked inside and opened the back door to his new Lincoln. With the sun in her eyes, he became just a shadow in a dark garage. Not even a person really.

She steadied the gun with both hands and pulled the trigger until no bullets were left. Her arms jerked upward with every shot, making it difficult to stay centered. More than one bullet made an ear-splitting ding when hitting the metal of the car. She'd aimed at his back so he wouldn't realize what was happening to him. It was an odd feeling not to want your daddy to be disappointed in you, even for killing him. It was an even odder feeling to love him despite his lack of good boundaries.

Her aim had been good enough. A pool of blood crept beyond his body and the briefcase he'd dropped. In the shadows, it looked black as oil, and Cissy figured it'd stain the concrete just as bad. She stood there, not knowing what else to do.

It seemed an eternity before her mama and Bess ran past her and into the garage. Screams twisted their faces into horrible masks. Bess scanned the scene for a second before her gaze settled on the gun still in Cissy's hand. Her screaming stopped abruptly.

"Please, girl, don't shoot. Please. Think of your sisters."

Cissy didn't understand Bess's pleas. She *had* been thinking of her sisters. She wasn't going to hurt anyone else. When Lily and Jessie appeared on the porch, Bess ran for the house, yelling for the girls to hide upstairs.

Her mama's wailing continued as she knelt over her husband's body, desperately trying to squelch the flow of blood. For a second, Cissy panicked that her daddy would open his eyes, sit up, and demand to know what all the fuss was about.

She shook the image from her head and dropped the gun. A cool breeze nipped at her neck even though the summer sun was already showing its strength. She slipped off her sandals, letting the cool grass soothe the sting of her blisters, and made her way to the tire swing hanging from the big magnolia.

Chapter 2

Janelle Clayton hung up the phone without saying goodbye and walked down the hall. The stairs loomed before her unwilling legs. She pulled herself up the banister, hand over hand, until the landing mercifully appeared. When she opened her armoire, she blinked in confusion, its contents foreign and disorienting.

"Mrs. Clayton, let me help you. You're not yourself." Ruth darted around her, grabbing a pair of slacks, her knee-high hosiery, a blouse and light sweater.

"I'd like a scarf," Janelle said, moving a hand to her throat. "This sweater demands a scarf."

"Should I drive you to your daughter's? You're talking nonsense and sure don't look in any state to drive yourself." Worry was always most apparent in her housekeeper's eyes, which glazed with emotion when she was upset. Ruth used the edge of her apron to wipe the perspiration from her upper lip and sat on the edge of the bed.

"Don't tell me what I can and cannot do. You're treating me like an infirm old lady." Janelle sat down next to her. She grabbed Ruth's hand, a gesture to soften the sharpness of her words.

She wasn't good at apologies, although if anyone deserved one, it was Ruth. Many times over. They'd been raised side by side, the judge's and housekeeper's daughters. One was rarely seen without the other, causing Janelle's mother to comment on the inappropriateness of her attachment to a house servant. When Janelle married in 1924, it was a given that Ruth would follow and manage her household. On the first day of work, she'd called her Mrs. Clayton. Janelle laughed and said, "That's my mother-in-law's name." Ruth had smiled weakly. Not a real smile, but one suffused with sadness and memory and longing that things could have been different if they'd both been black or both been white.

"I wish Mr. Beau was still with us," Ruth said.

Janelle had been thinking the same thing. Her husband died of a heart attack five years ago. They'd just celebrated his seventieth birthday with a barbecue on a stifling August evening. Dozens of well-wishers surrounded them. After dark, when the fireworks lit up the Mississippi sky, she remembered thinking they still had twenty good years left in them and plenty of celebrations to come. She and Beau had been on the front porch, waving goodbye to the last of the guests, when he said he didn't feel quite right. Janelle chalked it up to the heat and too much bourbon. She showed him to his rocker and went inside to get an antacid. When she'd returned to the porch, Beau's chin was tucked to his chest as if he'd just nodded off.

"Well, my husband's dead," Janelle said. "And now, so is my son-in-law."

She headed down the stairs and out to her car. Ruth shuffled after her, insisting with each step that she call someone, anyone.

"Who, Ruth? Tell me who I can call?" She'd barked the words, unable to contain her rising panic. "My granddaughter has just . . . Caroline's husband is dead."

Ruth's mournful mouth twisted. "I just want to be of help. You know that I love those girls, too."

"I do know that. I shouldn't have raised my voice," Janelle said, and got into the car. "I just need to get going."

Within twenty minutes, she drove through the arch over Caroline's driveway and down the gravel path to the freshly painted Georgian-style mansion. Bess sat on the front stoop, holding Caroline against her breast. She was hysterical, one second clawing to get away and the next holding on for dear life. Cissy sat motionless on the tire swing under the largest magnolia in the front yard.

"What happened here?" Janelle shouted to no one in particular. "Tell me this instant what happened."

"Like I told you on the phone, Miss Cissy shot her daddy!" Bess wailed. "Lord save us all!"

"Don't be ridiculous. Calm yourself and tell me what happened."

21

"She did, Mother! She did!" Caroline directed her voice at Janelle, but pointed violently toward Cissy.

Her granddaughter stared at her with soft, haunted eyes and moved her head up and down slowly. The blood drained from Janelle's limbs, and the truth she refused to believe earlier now gut-punched her.

"Where are the police? Did you call someone?" she demanded. The nearest neighbor was a half mile away, but gunshots weren't uncommon out in the country. They'd have no reason to call the sheriff's office. It seemed clear now that Caroline hadn't called either.

Without waiting for an answer, Janelle ordered her rubbery legs to carry her to the garage. Richard's body lay facedown on the cement floor, his briefcase at his side, two islands surrounded by the ever-widening sea of blood. She gagged back her breakfast and wrapped both arms around her middle trying to hold the world together.

The gun lay on the grass right outside the garage next to a pair of pink plastic sandals. Why hadn't Caroline or Bess thought to pick it up? She considered wiping Cissy's fingerprints off the gun and throwing it out into the oat field next to the house to rid themselves of at least one piece of a horrific puzzle. Or she could tell the police she shot Richard.

"Janelle, pull yourself together." She spoke the

22

words out loud, needing the sound to awaken her brain and legs. She ran toward the house, shouting for Bess to help Caroline inside. Then she changed course and headed for Cissy.

"Child, what have you done?" She shook her granddaughter's shoulders, but Cissy remained placid, a pitiful slackness in her face and body. "What happened?"

"Don't worry, Grandmother," she whispered, and cast her vacant eyes toward the sky as if watching the clouds. "It'll all be okay. Lily and Jessie are safe now."

Janelle couldn't deal with her gibberish. "Stay put. Don't you go anywhere."

"Of course not, Grandmother." She kicked her bare feet in the dirt beneath the swing.

Janelle ran into the house to look for Lily and Jessie. She explored the first floor, room by room, calling out their names until her voice grew raspy and inadequate. She heard nothing. Where were those babies? At least Bess had managed to stop Caroline's screaming.

When she reached the second-floor landing, muffled cries escaped Cissy's room. Janelle opened the closet door to find Lily with her hand over her sister's mouth to stifle the whimpers that had already given them away.

"Oh, children. Come out of there this instant. Don't be afraid."

Lily, only twelve but the protector, shook her

head no. Janelle had offered no proof that the girl's world was once again safe or normal, so her hesitancy was expected. Jessie, however, busted loose from her older sister's grasp and shot out on her knees. She threw her arms around the lower part of Janelle's legs, knocking her off-kilter. Within seconds, Lily also emerged and squeezed her stooped shoulders. The girl stood almost as tall as Janelle.

"Bess said Cissy killed Daddy." Lily's tone implored her to contradict those words.

She embraced the girls. "Well, I'll go find out exactly what happened if you promise not to worry. Now, go to your room and wait until Bess or I come for you." She pushed them down the hallway and waited to hear the click of the door. Then she made her way downstairs and to the phone. Someone had to call the sheriff.

On the phone, Sheriff Roe had promised her that he'd not make a scene, yet the first of two cruisers arrived with lights flashing. When two young deputies emerged from the first car with guns drawn, Janelle marched toward them ready to unleash a fury the likes of which they'd never seen.

The sheriff exited the second car quickly. His booming voice instructed the men to stand down and he rushed over, taking liberties to place his arm around her shoulder. The deputies milled about uncomfortably, waiting for orders.

"Mrs. Clayton, I'm terribly sorry. The dispatcher leaked word Richard had been murdered." He towered over Janelle. "They ain't seen this much action before. Getting a little too excited, I suspect."

"*Shot,*" she said. "No one said anything about murder."

"Ma'am, I'll need to speak to your granddaughter. May I?" He nodded toward the swing, where Cissy waited in her limbo. Janelle shooed him over with both hands.

At the same time, Caroline couldn't be contained by the house or Bess, and raced about the side yard, her arms and legs out of sync. "I wish you'd never been born!" she howled, and pounded her gut as if expunging Cissy from her womb.

Cissy's expression never changed, a still pond not yet disturbed by a skipping stone. She nodded once, maybe twice while the sheriff spoke to her, yet seemed deaf to her mother's anguish.

The deputies retrieved yellow tape from the cruiser's trunk and cordoned off the front of the garage. The men stood in front of the crime scene, awaiting instructions. *Crime scene.* Janelle stood, useless, listening to the hum of a horsefly and noting the brutish Mississippi humidity.

A few minutes passed before Sheriff Roe took Cissy's upper arm and pulled her from the swing.

He led her back to his car, a gentle hand around her elbow. Without any instruction Cissy opened the back door herself, crawled in, and folded her lanky legs in front of her. Grasping her knees, she seemed to sway to a lullaby only she could hear.

Sheriff Roe instructed his men to stay by the garage until the coroner arrived. He said Cissy would be detained at the county jail in a small room he used when staying overnight.

"Don't worry, Mrs. Clayton. She'll be treated well," the sheriff said. "I'll see to it myself."

Janelle had no choice but to believe him.

"Ma'am, you should get a lawyer for that gal right away. I can put off questioning her officially only for so long before it appears I'm not doing my job."

"Yes, of course you're right." She handed him Cissy's sandals, although she wasn't sure how they got into her hands.

"I'm sure you can find yourself a good one," he said. "Folks remember your husband fondly. Judge Clayton made more friends than anyone I'd ever seen preside over a circuit court."

Beau had been a good man and an even better judge. He built a fine reputation over thirty years, and the Clayton name meant something in Mississippi. Janelle also had the financial means to hire the best attorney in the state, or elsewhere for that matter, but there'd be challenges.

"My son-in-law is . . . *was* a highly regarded attorney," she told the sheriff. "He'll garner sympathy in some circles."

"Don't you be worrying about Richard." He wiped the sweat from his brow and fanned his face with his hat. "You need to focus your energy on helping Cissy now."

Her granddaughter had always been an unusual child, with peculiar notions about the world that often made Janelle's head spin or her blood boil, sometimes at the same time. She questioned authority relentlessly, but with a genuine curiosity rather than rebelliousness. Her odd behaviors caused family and strangers alike to shake their heads in wonderment. Janelle refused to believe Cissy capable of premeditated murder, yet failed to ask her the reason for changing their lives so irrevocably. And what did she mean when she said Lily and Jessie were now safe? Why hadn't Janelle asked?

When the sheriff started the car, she pressed a hand to the backseat window. Cissy's enormous blue eyes, glistening and distant, revealed no clues. Her lips, upturned in a strange little smile, mouthed, "Don't worry about me, Grandmother."

Janelle watched the car drive away, her eyes fixed on Cissy's ginger curls. Her granddaughter didn't turn around, so she returned to the house to see about Caroline and the girls.

• • •

"Miss Caroline, you need to tell Mrs. Clayton what your daughter told you," Bess pleaded, but Caroline stayed mute. The three of them stood in the parlor.

"Miss Cissy said her daddy touched her in the wrong way," Bess said, her hand over her mouth. "Said she'd not let him do the same to her baby sisters."

"She's a lying bitch," Caroline shouted.

Janelle hit her daughter with all the force she could muster. "Why would she lie? She's a good girl. She's never told a lie in her short life."

Janelle recalled the many rules that governed her granddaughter's odd behaviors. Topping her list of things she vowed never to do was lying. Even as a very small child, she'd stride up to her parents and grandparents to confess any wrongdoing, even when it would have likely gone unnoticed. Once, when Cissy was just six or seven years old, Janelle asked her why she didn't just keep the deed to herself. Cissy had said, "If we can't trust each other to tell the truth, Grandmother, what's to become of us?"

Bess stepped between them, perhaps to stop Janelle from striking Caroline again. Janelle steadied herself by placing a hand on the back of a wing chair. She shuddered to imagine Cissy speaking her horrors aloud, trusting that Caroline would believe the unthinkable of her husband.

"How could you not know?" Janelle asked. "She's your daughter."

"She's not my daughter any longer!" Caroline spit her words. "She's telling horrible, disgusting lies about Richard. Why are you taking her side?"

"Because I'm her grandmother and I believe she'd never do something like this without reason." Janelle pondered what other motive Cissy might have had if she wasn't telling the truth about her father. Why today? She'd been so calm, sitting under the magnolia. Shouldn't a sixteen-year-old who'd killed a person be distraught? If anything, the girl looked at peace.

"She murdered him, Mother. Murdered!"

Anyone could understand Caroline's anguish and her primal hope that Richard was not capable of such monstrous acts. But Cissy needed her mother more than anyone right now. She needed to be believed.

Bess grew alarmed by their shouting and put an arm around Caroline's shoulders.

"You'll frighten the little ones, Miss Caroline," she whispered. "Please lie down. Rest a spell."

The wildness in Caroline's eyes dimmed in response to the soothing tone of Bess's instructions. Caroline curled up on the sofa. Bess touched her hair lovingly, something a mother would do; something Janelle couldn't imagine being able to do again.

"Bess, why don't you go check on the girls. I need to speak to my daughter."

"I don't have anything to say to you, Mother. You can believe Cissy, but I want that girl put away for good, someplace where she can't hurt any of us ever again."

Bess locked eyes with Janelle. Sympathy flooded her dark features.

"I don't care how you treat me, Caroline, but I expect you to pull yourself together and be there for your child," she said.

"That's rich coming from you," Caroline said. "And today of all days, when I've lost my husband, you're going to believe a girl who's never been in her right mind."

Janelle bristled at the unfair assessment. "Don't say that about your daughter. There's nothing wrong with her mind."

"Oh, Mother, don't try to rewrite history. You've told me on more than one occasion that I needed to do something about Cissy's 'eccentricities,'" Caroline said. "What possesses an eccentric child to retrieve her father's loaded gun from a drawer, follow him out to his car, and kill him in cold blood?"

"I can't begin to understand the depth of your pain right now, but please reserve your judgment about Cissy until we know more."

"What more do I need to know? Isn't a dead body enough for you?" Caroline demanded. "You know Richard was a good man. There's no way he'd harm a child, much less his own daughter."

Janelle found it hard to argue with that. Over the years, he rarely attracted Janelle's attention at all. She thought him a vain sort of man, wrapped up in his career, but harmless. If he was guilty of anything, it was neglecting his wife and family. The law appeared to be his whole world.

"But, Caroline, why distrust Cissy? Has she given you any reason?"

"She's not right in the head, and Richard can't defend himself, can he? I don't know what's going on, and neither do you. Now, please. Just leave me alone." Caroline grabbed a chenille throw from the foot of the sofa and pulled it up around her head.

Janelle had always worried that Caroline loved the *idea* of being a mother more than the actual responsibility. All she'd ever wanted was to marry the "right sort" of man, someone who could provide her with a large, exquisitely furnished home where she could entertain his colleagues and their wives. She'd envisioned three perfectly obedient children that others would envy. Instead, the couple never developed a close circle of friends, they never had enough money in Caroline's opinion, and the three girls? Well, they were rambunctious and independent— nothing that Caroline expected.

Janelle moved toward the front door, unable

31

to summon an ounce of compassion to comfort her daughter. "I'm going to find legal counsel and then we'll figure out where to go from here. Perhaps you'll feel differently tomorrow."

From the beginning, Janelle's relationship with Caroline had been a rough patch of road that ceased to end. As a baby, Caroline bucked and kicked, refusing to be held by anyone but Ruth or Beau. It didn't take long before Janelle decided she just wasn't mother material and left the caregiving to Ruth. Of course, Ruth chastised her for not trying hard enough and pushed Caroline onto her day after day. One afternoon, they got in such a row that Beau stepped in to grab the screaming child and told the women to take their argument outside.

"I know your mama had a vicious streak in her," Ruth had said to Janelle more than thirty years ago. "She didn't exactly set a good example, but you can't go on ignoring the fact that you have a child who needs you."

Those words came rushing back to Janelle as she drove home from Caroline's. Janelle had just said the same words to her daughter. Had three generations of women failed their children so completely?

When she pulled into her own driveway and killed the ignition, Janelle had no memory of her route or speed. Ruth stood on the front porch, wringing her hands. She managed a tired nod.

All Janelle wanted was her wicker rocker. She sank down into the cushions long faded by summer sun and winter rains, feeling the heartache pressed against her chest. Looking over at Beau's empty chair magnified the ache, and Janelle reached over to touch the arm of his rocker. She slipped off her shoes and waved Ruth away, wanting nothing more than to disappear into the muggy June night.

"Beau, how I wish you were still alive," she whispered.

A familiar sense of abandonment overtook her. Many evenings she'd sit on this porch, imagining her husband next to her. She usually spoke of mundane matters—the peach trees that needed pruning, the leak under the kitchen sink, the drought ravaging the crops tended by the tenant farmers. Tonight, she talked instead of their family torn apart; how she needed him here, now, with her.

Janelle closed her eyes and tried to fathom the depth of Caroline's loss. A heart attack had claimed Beau at age seventy. Caroline's Richard had only been forty-four. Her grief bubbled up memories of the long and full life Beau and she had enjoyed, and of the resolute bond that held them together for half a century. Caroline's grief would be divided between the overwhelming sadness of a loved one wrenched away too soon and the agony over how Richard had died, *why* he had died. Caroline's memories would be rewritten, never to be accurate or comforting again.

Sleep nipped at the edge of Janelle's consciousness but never took hold. Her waking nightmare would not allow respite. She couldn't help but think how they'd all serve a sentence for Cissy's crime.

In the early morning, Ruth found her in the same spot, covered in mosquito bites and joints protesting the night spent upright in a chair. Her hand was still around a tumbler of Old Grand-Dad. Knowing Janelle rarely took to the drink, Ruth gave her wide berth. Around seven, she set out toast and black coffee on the wicker table next to Janelle's rocker.

"Are you all right?" Ruth asked, sitting down.

"None of us will ever be all right again."

"Lord knows that's the truth," Ruth said. "Bess called and told me why Cissy done what she did. My heart is torn open for that girl and her sisters, for Miss Caroline."

"Did Bess also tell you that Caroline doesn't believe her own daughter?"

"But you believe Cissy?" Ruth asked.

Janelle leaned forward. "Why shouldn't I? She's a child. Why would a child concoct such a horrific tale? Where would she even get those ideas?"

"You can settle back down, Mrs. Clayton. I believe her, too. I just know this must be about the worst thing that will ever happen to Miss Caroline in her entire life."

"She worshipped that man," Janelle said. "If Beau or I said anything the slightest bit negative about him, Caroline would start listing his many virtues and how lucky we were that he was our son-in-law. It almost drove Beau to drink more."

"Mr. Beau liked that boy," Ruth reminded her. "Thought he came from a fine family, that he was smart and educated and could take care of his little girl. He seemed relieved she'd found such a man. *You* seemed relieved."

"But why did Caroline turn a blind eye?"

"A person capable of the things Mr. Pickering did . . . well, you get good at keeping secrets. The fact that Miss Caroline didn't recognize that in a man she thought she knew so well . . . it's probably driving her mad. She won't be in her right mind for a long time."

Janelle couldn't worry about Caroline's state of mind now. Her greater fear was that no one would believe Cissy or, like Caroline, they would just assume she'd gone mad.

Janelle may have failed her daughter, but she wouldn't fail Cissy.

Chapter 3

The metal fan and open window did nothing to ease the stifling heat in the dank, paneled cave Charles Whitney called his office. Janelle should have known by his address he'd be in an older building without air-conditioning.

The lawyer melted before her eyes, perspiration sliding off his high forehead and nose, and landing on his paper desk blotter, his dress shirt pasted against his undershirt. Janelle fanned herself with a folded newspaper, trying to ignore the smell of cigarettes and mold. She'd had some dizzy spells lately, a crippling vertigo that demanded she sit down or risk a fall. She hoped she wouldn't faint and end up facedown on the matted shag carpeting.

Mr. Whitney wouldn't have been her first choice, but Janelle trusted the advice of Judge Rick Berry, who had recommended him. The judge, an old friend of her husband's, said Mr. Whitney had a distinguished career as a prosecutor before going into private practice. A few years back, he'd won a number of difficult cases, including the conviction of a KKK member who murdered a black teen. That case alone gave her reason to hire him. Anyone who could convince a jury in south Mississippi to convict a Klansman must be a snake charmer or indebted to the devil himself. She didn't care which as long as her granddaughter didn't go to prison.

He thanked Janelle for allowing him to take the case, then settled into the legalities of Cissy's situation and the next steps before them. Juvenile proceedings moved quickly, he said. Their first challenge would be convincing the judge Cissy shouldn't be tried as an adult.

"Mrs. Clayton, I know you have some reservations. But Cissy's best option is to be declared mentally ill and sent to a state hospital for observation."

"I've wasted your time." Janelle rose from her chair. He'd given her no indication of his expertise, and his appearance was far from professional. She'd wasted a morning.

"Mrs. Clayton, have I offended you?"

"Everything about this place offends me, Mr. Whitney," she shot back at him. "You don't exactly inspire confidence."

"Then why are you here?" His face was blank, as if untroubled by her insult.

"Judge Berry said I should trust you. That you had what it'd take to make sure Cissy didn't go to prison."

"Would you like to call the judge right now? Tell him about your misgivings? I'm sure he could go into more detail about my record of success in the courtroom and put your mind at ease. As for my office, it's what I can afford, and I'm usually in court or meeting with clients elsewhere anyway."

Janelle sat back down, surprised at the sudden confidence in his words.

"Mr. Whitney, you can imagine what a difficult time this is for me and my family. I am unsure about everything right now. Forgive me. Let's continue."

They spoke for more than an hour. He asked the impossible of her—whether she thought Cissy would be better off at a psychiatric hospital for evaluation or at the Columbia Training School for Girls until the district attorney decided his next step. Judge Berry had mentioned the school's reputation for discipline included rumors of abuse and neglect. He, like Mr. Whitney, advised her to think hard whether or not Cissy could handle that environment.

The day after the shooting, Janelle had spoken with the lawyer briefly on the phone. He'd arranged for a pediatrician from Mobile to drive up immediately and examine Cissy for physical signs of abuse. The clinical details confirmed the worst. Next, she'd meet with a psychiatrist who could testify as to her state of mind the day she shot Richard. Mr. Whitney wanted to hire a psychiatrist he knew in Baton Rouge, a man he trusted but one who'd stay impartial. He'd ask him to clear his schedule and make the three-hour drive the next day.

"Is that necessary? Isn't there another way?"

"Ma'am, she killed her own daddy. The court's gonna have to render some judgment. She can't just go scot-free."

He explained that in the best-case scenario, the judge would call for Cissy to be evaluated over a specific period of time at a psychiatric facility. After that, the district attorney would decide whether to prosecute or enter a plea agreement based on the findings from the evaluation.

"She could be prosecuted for murder?" Janelle asked.

"Unlikely. No DA in his right mind would want a case like this, considering the abuse she's suffered. And she's the granddaughter of one of the state's most respected judges. She could go free after her stay at the hospital if we play our cards right. Our challenge is that the girl keeps saying she knew what she was doing."

The magnitude of Cissy's action hadn't escaped Janelle, but that didn't mean she liked the recommendations before her. The physical exam had proved too much for Cissy to bear. The doctor's report said that Cissy had to be sedated; that she thrashed about, screaming at the top of her lungs for the doctor not to touch her. How much more could that child handle without her mind breaking in two? Cissy had already been at the jail three days. Although she appeared in good spirits, Janelle worried what horrors played out in Cissy's mind when she was completely alone.

When Janelle asked if the public would be allowed in the courtroom, Mr. Whitney assured her the hearing would be closed except for those presenting testimony. There'd be no jury or trial if Cissy's case remained in juvenile court. She closed her eyes, thankful her granddaughter might be spared a circus of media and Biloxi busybodies.

"Mr. Whitney, there's one other thing. I'd like a judge to appoint me as Cissy's temporary guardian," she said. The idea had just occurred to her, but once it took hold, she wasn't about to back down. Janelle didn't trust her own daughter, whose own pain and loss were all-consuming.

"On what grounds? Her mama's still in the picture," he said.

"Neglect."

In her conversation with Judge Berry, he'd said Caroline could be found negligent for not having protected Cissy from the assaults. Janelle dug deep within herself for some compassion for Caroline. She barely recognized her daughter in the woman so ravaged with pain. When they spoke briefly on the phone the day before and Caroline admitted she wanted Cissy in a correctional facility, it was the last straw. Janelle wouldn't let Cissy be hurt any more than she'd already been. She would protect her at any cost and from anyone, including her own mother.

Mr. Whitney hemmed and hawed through an explanation of what that would entail, that courts almost always ruled in a parent's favor.

"Just prepare the petition, Mr. Whitney. Remember you work for me," Janelle said, getting up from the chair. "And by the way, should you need any information, you are to call me. Do not contact Cissy without my permission. I'll be at the jail the rest of the afternoon, then at my home."

She left Mr. Whitney standing with his sweating hand outstretched. She hoped she'd not made the biggest mistake of her life in trusting him.

The county held Cissy in a sparse ten-by-ten-foot room that looked nothing like a jail cell. There were no metal bars or cot with creaky springs, or even a lock on the door for that matter. She had a simple twin bed with an adequate mattress, a wooden desk and chair, and a stainless-steel toilet, sink, and shower behind a cement block partition. The room served double duty: the sheriff and his deputies used the room as a place to bunk down when working late shifts, and the county met the requirement to have a detention area set aside for juvenile offenders. Cissy was the first official detainee. Most offenses were so minor—vandalism, shoplifting—that children were released into the custody of their parents until a hearing could be held.

Sheriff Roe allowed Janelle to visit Cissy as often and for as long as she liked. She brought her granddaughter an extra quilt because she forever complained about being cold. She also brought her lunch and dinner each day, sometimes prepared by Ruth and other times picked up from C.J.'s Diner near the courthouse. The diner's fried chicken and okra were voted best in the state, and Cissy requested those dishes more than any other.

Deputy Parks, the youngest of those on the day shift, brought her a donut and glass of milk each morning. Each time he'd bring a different variety, making a game of it by asking Cissy to guess maple or plain, chocolate with sprinkles or jelly-filled. That child would eat sweets three times a day if allowed.

Janelle believed Cissy liked the young man's company, too. Fred Parks had kind eyes and spoke of things not associated with death or hearings or lawyers, like the new hunting pup he and his father were training, or the promotion he hoped to get by year's end. Sometimes he'd stay a few extra minutes and read to her from the paper, even though she was capable of reading the day's news all on her own. Janelle thought he did it to spare Cissy from reading any articles about the killing.

This morning, shards of maple glaze rimmed the edges of her lips. "Grandmother, thank you for still loving me," she said.

"That's what kin do, child. No need to thank me."

"Mama doesn't love me anymore," Cissy said in an even voice. "That's okay, though. I knew things had to change between us."

"Her grief prevents her from acting like a normal mother. You needn't worry about anything or anyone but yourself."

"I'm not worried," Cissy said. "I know what I've done. I'm ready to go to prison now."

Janelle shook her head at her granddaughter's naïveté. Yes, she was correct to assume her mother would be devastated by her actions, but she had no idea what it would mean to be tried as an adult, to be housed in a Mississippi prison or a youth correctional facility. Janelle shuddered.

"You're not going to prison, Cissy. I want no more talk like that."

They sat in silence for a while as Cissy fingered the two library books Janelle had brought—*The Adventures of Huckleberry Finn* and *Gulliver's Travels*. She'd looked for books to transport Cissy's mind to faraway lands. Happy books; books for children.

To keep her hands busy, Janelle took a brush

and worked it through Cissy's tangled mane while she read. Sitting behind her, she took the errant strands and wove them in and around each other, forming tight braids against Cissy's scalp. She didn't complain once.

"Grandmother, thank you for believing me," she said.

Janelle patted her shoulders, letting her hands rest there. She was ashamed she'd not paid more attention to her granddaughters. Why had it taken a tragedy like this? Even if she'd given up on her relationship with Caroline, she could have had a role in the girls' lives. Maybe Janelle thought she couldn't have one without the other. Had garden parties and library boards and attending functions with Beau really mattered more than her family? Cissy had made attempts to win her affection over the years: working on her manners, wearing dresses more often, learning about art and music that Janelle liked. Her absence from Cissy's life meant no one had been there to recognize a cry for help. They'd spoken of her daddy's actions just once and Janelle's heart had fractured, never to be mended. Sitting there with her granddaughter, she feared coming undone.

"Do you think Lily and Jessie could visit me?" Cissy turned and looked her straight in the eyes.

"Soon," she lied, holding her gaze.

"Good," Cissy said, returning to the books.

"Mama doesn't like reading aloud to them. They'll be sad."

Janelle changed the subject to keep from breaking down completely. She'd managed to keep her emotions in check until late in the evenings when she was home with Ruth.

"I saw Mr. Whitney," she said. "He's busy working on your case. He'll take good care of us."

"That's good, Grandmother," she said. "It'd be nice if I didn't have to meet with him anymore, though. It's not that I don't like him. It's that I don't yet *know* if I like him. He asks too many questions."

When the three of them met earlier in the week, Cissy had said she shot her daddy to protect her baby sisters. Janelle hadn't understood a love so boundless until her feelings for Cissy took hold. She'd do anything for her and knew Cissy had had no other choice the day she shot Richard. Janelle knew it in her gut. Nothing Caroline could say would change her mind.

"I'm sorry about the doctor's exam, Cissy. I really am." Janelle failed to keep her voice steady. "You won't have to go through anything like that again."

"Change the subject, please." Cissy rose and paced about the cramped room, her eyes cast downward, her lips barely moving as she counted each tile and each step.

pacing and asked her to sit on the bed. They held hands for a few moments without speaking. Janelle's apple-red manicured nails looked garish next to Cissy's healthy pink unpolished ones, so she curled them into her palms.

After a while, Cissy brought her hand up to Janelle's cheek and let it rest there. "Shooting Daddy wasn't crazy, Grandmother."

Janelle took Cissy's hand and kissed her palm, remembering sixteen years ago when Caroline first brought home that skinny, long baby with the bright red tuft of hair. They'd all laughed that she'd be the spitting image of her father.

"I know, sweet child. I know."

Back at home, Janelle was in the kitchen with Ruth, arguing over whether Ruth should bake Cissy a coconut cream or peach pie when they heard Caroline knocking on the screen door, shouting obscenities that echoed through the foyer. They almost collided in their foot race to reach the door. Janelle suspected Ruth wanted to spare her the verbal assault by reaching Caroline first.

"What in the goddamn hell do you think you're doing?" Caroline shouted through the locked screen. "Open the door now!"

Her words shot through the wire mesh as she pulled at the handle. Janelle refused to unfasten the latch.

"I won't talk to you at all, child, if you continue to use language like that around me and Ruth."

Caroline paced to and fro. Her splotchy face bore no makeup, normally a cardinal sin for her daughter. When Janelle still refused to open the door, Caroline pulled out a pack of Salem Lights from her purse and lit one, blowing the smoke through the screen into her mother's face.

"I'm ashamed of you, girl," Ruth called out from behind Janelle. "Your mama and daddy raised you better. *I* raised you better!"

Janelle held up her hand, signaling Ruth to be quiet. She told Caroline if she was going to smoke, then they'd sit outside on the porch. To exit, she had to push the screen door out, forcing Caroline to step backward. Agitated, Caroline took a long draw on her cigarette and rocked on her heels.

"How dare you try to gain custody of Cissy!" she howled.

"Please sit and we can talk." Janelle motioned to the wicker rockers.

A stinging slap across Janelle's face electrified her limbs. She wanted to knock the cigarette from Caroline's angry mouth. Instead, they stood staring at each other in silence. Neither of them cried; perhaps there'd already been too many tears over things more painful than a slap.

"I'm willing to forgive a lot because you're going through a horrific time, but if you ever strike me again, we will not speak from that day forward," Janelle said, ignoring her own hypocrisy in striking her daughter the day of the shooting.

Caroline's chest heaved. She dropped to her knees, arms outstretched feeling her way to the steps. Janelle knelt beside her daughter, pressing Caroline's face to her chest. Her quaking body became slack in Janelle's arms and she rocked her, telling her everything would be fine even though she knew no such thing. She couldn't recall the last time she'd comforted her daughter.

Caroline's sandy blond hair, slicked back in a tight ponytail, made her look fifteen years younger. Her small frame, clothed in clam diggers and a plain white tee, added to the illusion Janelle held a girl, not a woman.

"I'm not a bad mother." She pressed her face into Janelle's chest, and hot tears soaked the thin cotton blouse.

"No, you're not. And Cissy's not a bad girl." Her words made Caroline cry harder.

"Then why are you trying to take her away from me?"

"It isn't like that," Janelle said. "You're going through a lot of turmoil. Your feelings are rightly conflicted. Your husband is dead. Your daughter killed him. It makes things easier for an impartial party to make medical and legal decisions for the girl right now."

"You're impartial?"

"To the best of my ability," Janelle said. Even though her petition for custody was made in the heat of the moment, she didn't regret it. She did regret the additional pain it brought her daughter.

"How could I not have known?"

She had no answers for Caroline, but shared her guilt that no one suspected, that no one stepped in to rescue Cissy. They all shared the blame.

"I can't go to his funeral tomorrow, Mother."

"That makes two of us," Janelle said. "Mimi will just have to understand."

Richard's mother had called Janelle once since her son's death. She'd raged that Janelle was protecting a murderer. She listened a minute or two to Mimi without speaking and then hung up. On some level, Janelle understood why Mimi had to blame Cissy. The alternative was to admit her son was a monster who killed the very spirit of his own child.

"What if I can't ever forgive Cissy?" Caroline looked to Janelle's face, perhaps for reassurance that forgiveness was even possible.

"I'm not asking you to forgive Cissy. I'm asking you to help me protect what's left of that child's mind and body."

She told Caroline a medical doctor would testify Cissy had been sexually assaulted, and a psychiatrist would recommend she be remitted to a state psychiatric facility. Janelle asked Caroline not to fight the recommendation. She agreed and allowed Janelle to hold her until the sun dipped behind the weeping willows shading the porch.

"You should go home, Caroline," she said as the sun set, its unrelenting heat shielded by the horizon. "I'm sure Bess will have dinner waiting for you and the girls."

There were just the two girls now—Lily and Jessie. What did their young minds make of the hushed conversations, the shouting matches, and their mother's anguish? They couldn't be allowed to know the details of the case. The thought of three very broken girls drove a stake of panic deep in Janelle's heart.

"How are the girls doing?" she asked.

"I don't know, Mother. Bess is so good with them and they love her. I just can't be around them." Caroline ran her palms over the front of her tee, smoothing imaginary wrinkles.

"They need you." Janelle touched Caroline's back, but let her hand drop when she stiffened.

"They need someone who can keep it together," Caroline said. "I can't take any more of their questions. I don't know how to act around them. I don't know how to act period."

Janelle suggested Caroline sleep over to give her the time she needed before facing her children again. Bess could take care of Lily and Jessie just for tonight.

"Thank you, Mother," Caroline said, and got up to go inside the house.

The comforting scent of potatoes frying wafted out onto the porch. Janelle suspected that Ruth would be serving roast chicken, Caroline's favorite, although she wondered how any of them had an appetite to speak of.

Chapter 4

The house now seemed a monstrous thing to Caroline, dark and menacing and eager to swallow her alive. The day after Richard's death, she'd instructed Bess to shut the doors to all the upstairs rooms and to bring some linens and a quilt downstairs. Caroline now slept on the sofa, unable to enter the bedroom she'd shared with her husband for seventeen years.

The last two mornings, she woke to find Lily and Jessie asleep on the floor next to the sofa, huddled together under one blanket and sharing a pillow. They needed her. She knew that without her mother having to tell her. But she couldn't find the words—any words—to comfort or explain or apologize. After all, she was the only one who could have prevented the nightmare they were all now living. Or, at least that's what her mother claimed.

It was morning already, but probably only six or six-thirty. She faced the back of the sofa, the quilt pulled up to her ears. If Caroline could turn off her thoughts, she'd stay in that same position rather than wake to another day of unknowns.

"Miss Caroline?" Bess nudged her shoulder. "The hearing is today. Do you remember?"

"Is there any way I could forget?" Caroline rose

reluctantly, staring at her housekeeper. "Where are the girls? Did they sleep down here again?"

"Yes, ma'am. But I carried them up to their room an hour ago," she said. "I drew you a hot bath and set out a fresh change of clothes so you wouldn't have to . . ."

Bess's eyes were glassy, but her face remained neutral. She'd stopped her crying bouts the day after the shooting, but emotion threatened to overtake her every time she spoke. Caroline felt this made her choose her words carefully and to speak only when necessary. Except to the children. Bess drew strength from some deep, maternal place so that she could fill Lily's and Jessie's lives with what passed as normalcy. She cooked their favorite foods, helped them catch grasshoppers, turned the dining room table into a craft area, and sat beside their beds until they dropped off to sleep. Caroline wondered what words of comfort Bess imparted to the girls, but asking outright would have just stirred the bitterness she already felt because no one had thought to comfort her.

"Thank you, Bess," Caroline said. "I'll go up right now."

"And, ma'am, I washed and ironed some things for Miss Cissy. Your mama called yesterday and said she would be needing some things if the judge decides to send our girl to that hospital up in Meridian. Do you want me to pack a suitcase?"

Caroline's first thought was to allow Bess to continue taking care of things, but she knew it was something a mother should want to do. She couldn't shake the feeling of being judged: for her action or non-action; things she said or failed to say. But she was no longer a normal mother. How could she be expected to go through the motions? Today, though, it was required of her.

"I'll take care of it, Bess. But thank you just the same."

Caroline sat in the tub until the water cooled. Time moved more slowly now. She was sure of it. Only the sound of the girls in the kitchen having breakfast prompted Caroline to dry off and dress.

She hated being upstairs alone, near the bedrooms. Cissy's was at the far end of the hall, far enough that Caroline and Richard didn't have to listen to her god-awful counting; far enough that Caroline failed to hear anything, especially the nights she took sleeping pills or her nerve medicine.

Her and Richard's room was at the opposite end of the hall, across from the bathroom and staircase. Sandwiched in between were an empty bedroom and one that the younger girls shared. Although Lily was old enough to have her own room, Cissy had convinced her sisters that if they separated, they'd have to divvy up their shared toys. Caroline suddenly understood Cissy's motivation in keeping them together: protection.

Standing in front of Cissy's door, she steeled herself and entered.

The weather outside was stormy and unsettling. She didn't know why she wished for sunlight to fill the space. Caroline had always thought the light was garish in this room while Cissy remarked how lucky she was to get the morning sun on her side of the house because it was better than an alarm clock.

Her eldest daughter's room was the largest bedroom, but spare. A bed neatly made. A small desk with a chess board on top. A map of the United States tacked to the wall. Two bookcases filled with Cissy's favorite novels, a dictionary, and an atlas. Cissy didn't care for dolls or knickknacks. She seemed to only have room in her life for reading, writing in her notebooks, and persisting with the counting nonsense.

Bess had left an open suitcase on the bed and already laid out socks, undergarments, and pink slippers.

Caroline gravitated toward Cissy's orderly closet to guess which items her daughter would want her to pack, those that might bring her some comfort and sense of routine. When Caroline spoke to her mother the day before, Janelle was overly confident that Cissy would be placed in a mental hospital for observation and treatment, and not a correctional facility. Caroline wasn't as certain, but she couldn't allow her thoughts to drift to the latter option. She already found it unbearable that Cissy was confined to one room in the county jail. No matter what Cissy had done, Caroline hated to think that she felt alone and afraid.

"Ma'am? May I help you?" Bess stood in the doorway.

"Where are the girls?"

"With their paper dolls at the dining table," she said. "Is that all right?"

Caroline nodded and waved Bess in. They worked in unison, pulling slacks and dresses and blouses from the closet and folding them neatly.

"We need more pants." Caroline pointed to the dresser. "You know she doesn't like dresses nearly as much."

After a few minutes, Caroline walked over to the window. The winds kicked up so forcefully that raindrops pelted the panes.

"What is it?" Bess asked.

"No one understands what I'm going through. I cannot survive this. I'm all alone." Caroline coughed to cover a sob, gaining her composure quickly.

Bess stood beside her, their shoulders not touching. "Ma'am, may I speak frankly?"

Caroline wiped her face with her sleeve and

nodded. She hadn't meant to break down in front of Bess. And now she was shocked that Bess was ready to talk to her again.

"We were wrong, the way we acted that day," Bess said. "Not believing Cissy. Not stopping to listen to what she tried to tell us."

Caroline's cheeks burned with fury. "She killed my husband," she said. "If those things really happened . . . if Richard . . . why didn't she tell someone?"

"Miss Cissy said she couldn't, to protect her sisters," Bess said. "Dig down deep, Miss Caroline. Think about that girl. Would she ever harm someone without there being a good reason?"

Caroline went back to the suitcase and continued packing, but Bess seemed emboldened to continue, like she'd been biding her time the last few days, waiting for the right moment to speak her mind.

"If we was honest," Bess said, "we'd admit that we knew. Not the full story, mind you. But we saw how different Miss Cissy was. How she acted around Mr. Pickering."

Caroline flinched. "I knew *nothing* of the sort! You overstep."

"The light went out in that girl a long time ago," Bess continued. "I'm to blame, too. I saw how she pulled away from his hugs, kept her distance when she could."

"You should go now, Bess. I'll finish packing," Caroline said, trying to keep her anger in check. She was dangerously close to firing her housekeeper for impertinence, but knew the girls didn't need any more upset at this time.

Bess stood silent for a moment, then said, "Don't forget to pack her notebooks. The ones with all those lists. They're under her bed."

"How did you know—"

"I dust mop this room once a week, ma'am, so if anyone would know, it'd be me. She asked me to be careful of them when I'm cleaning."

"I won't have any more of your smart mouth, Bess," Caroline said.

"I'm sorry, ma'am. I wasn't trying to be smart," she said. "I'll leave you alone and bring up a cardboard box in a few minutes."

"The notebooks will fit in her suitcase just fine."

"I meant a box to hold some of her favorite books. I think she'd like to have them to pass the time. Don't you suppose?"

"Close the door on your way out." Caroline didn't need her housekeeper telling her what to do, as if she knew Cissy better than her own mother did.

God, she needed more time to pull herself together. The hearing started in two hours. She hadn't seen Cissy since the sheriff took her away. Caroline didn't know what to say or how to say

61

it. Perhaps it wasn't the best time for them to speak. Not just yet.

Even though Caroline knew she should go downstairs and be with the girls for a while, she couldn't resist reaching for the box under the bed. She opened up the first spiral notebook and began reading, hoping against all hope that she'd find a way to forgive Cissy. Her eye stopped at a page listing the things that Cissy was most afraid of. The last word was written in large, block letters: *DADDY.*

Chapter 5

A hellacious rain storm pounded Biloxi the morning of Cissy's hearing. Like water from floodgates, Janelle's grief poured forth whenever she stopped to contemplate what would become of her granddaughter, or any of them for that matter.

Cissy's time in the jail had become a limbo of sorts. It was devastating to think of the girl alone for most of each day except for the deputy on shift. Yet, she was safe. No father to violate her body. No mother to blame her for taking control of her world. Janelle no longer censored the daydreams she had of Cissy remaining indefinitely in that room, never being charged with a crime, never having to be punished, never seeing the inside of a psychiatric hospital. Cissy had been right when she said killing her father wasn't crazy. If Janelle had known about the abuse, she'd have taken care of Richard herself and gladly spent her remaining years in a prison for it.

When she arrived at the jail, she found Cissy sitting on the bed, hands folded in her lap, her eyebrows knitted with just a hint of worry. She'd dressed in a muted, floral cotton dress and white sandals, and looked ready for church or a Sunday social. Deputy Parks had told Janelle that Caroline dropped off the clothes but didn't stay to see Cissy. He hadn't known what to say when Cissy asked why her mother left without saying anything, especially since she had already been in the building.

"Fred, I mean Deputy Parks, brought me a jelly donut today," Cissy said when Janelle sat down next to her. "Well, three actually."

"I could have guessed." Janelle licked her thumb and rubbed away a sticky red spot at the corner of Cissy's mouth.

"Jessie would've just licked my face."

"Well, I'm not Jessie and no one should be licking anyone's face." Janelle appreciated the levity that Cissy managed to bring to any moment that started to feel heavy. She wondered if that was a natural talent or something Cissy had developed in order to soothe those around her.

Janelle motioned for her to turn slightly. She twisted her locks into two neat rows down the back of her scalp, freeing her freckled face. Her granddaughter looked much younger than sixteen, not a teenager at all.

"Is everything all right?" Janelle asked.

"As rain," she answered. "Let's go soon or we'll be late. I expect a judge wouldn't look too kindly on tardiness."

Deputy Parks led them out of the jail and

toward the rear door of the courthouse less than a block away. He didn't put handcuffs on Cissy. Over the past ten days, Janelle suspected he'd come to know the gentleness in her. No one need fear this child. The storm had passed, but a quiet rain still fell. Deputy Parks struggled to keep an umbrella over the three of them until Cissy wrestled it away saying she was the tallest and it made more sense for her to carry it.

As they entered the cavernous halls of the courthouse, the clicking of Janelle's heels echoed and she tried walking on the balls of her feet to silence the aggravation. Cissy hooked her arm through Janelle's and stomped her feet in unison, adding to the noise. She patted Cissy's hand.

Sheriff Roe had cleared the building earlier and locked the doors so the newspaper reporters couldn't accost them in the public areas of the courthouse. Janelle said a prayer of thanks that the sheriff was such a good man.

The setup of the actual courtroom made her think of weddings, where one side of the church was designated for the bride and her family, and the other for the groom and his. That morning, the aisle divided those who wanted Cissy to pay for a crime and those who accepted Cissy's act as a cry for help.

"Will Mama be here?" Cissy whispered, her hand cupped against Janelle's ear, as if her question was a secret. "When she dropped off my clothes, she didn't stay to say hello or anything."

There as a witness, Caroline had been instructed to wait in a room down the corridor until her time to speak. She acquiesced to Mr. Whitney's recommendation they push for Cissy to be committed. But emotionally, Caroline was in no shape to show any other support. It was best she wasn't allowed in the courtroom.

"Yes, dear, she'll be here," Janelle said. "When the judge asks her in."

"She doesn't want to see me, does she?"

"Cissy, I just said she can't be in the courtroom until she's called to the witness stand. Plus, she's just very sad by all that's happened. She's lost both a husband and daughter, and she'll need some time to work through the bigness of it all."

"She hasn't lost me," Cissy said.

"I meant that figuratively, child, meaning you'll be apart if you go stay at the hospital in Meridian for a while."

Cissy tapped the toes of her sandals against the wooden floor.

"Meridian's far away, Grandmother. Deputy Parks told me."

The judge approached the bench and Janelle shushed her granddaughter, delaying an explanation of why they'd chosen the facility in Meridian, 160 long miles from Biloxi. Mr. Whitney had explained the Greater Mississippi State Hospital was the best choice as it had a separate ward for young women aged fifteen to twenty-one and a few private rooms. Janelle would address Cissy's concern about distance if the judge granted their wishes.

Mimi had sought her own legal counsel. The woman had the idiotic idea that they could convince the judge Cissy should be tried as an adult, that the killing of her son was premeditated. She and her lawyer looked straight ahead, refusing to meet Janelle's eye as she and Cissy took their places on the first of several wooden benches, akin to those in church and just as unkind to the bones.

In Janelle's opinion, Mimi had never been a pleasant woman. Her face was pinched in a permanent scowl, as if the entire world offended her in some way. Caroline had battled to gain her approval for most of her marriage, but gave up on her mother-in-law a couple of years ago when she'd overheard Mimi telling Richard that his wife didn't know how to run a proper household or discipline her unruly daughters.

Mr. Whitney already sat at a small wooden table a few feet away, furiously scribbling notes. Janelle hoped Judge Berry had advised her well. Witnesses and other concerned parties sat or milled about outside in the hallway. Assembled that morning were a representative from the State Department of Health, someone from the youth corrections board, a youth advocate assigned to

Cissy's case, the psychiatrist and pediatrician Mr. Whitney would call for expert testimony, and Caroline. Those in the courtroom included the court stenographer and Sheriff Roe and his deputies, who answered the call about Richard's shooting.

Sheriff Roe relayed the basic facts of the shooting first. He'd kept his tone even and non-judgmental, even expressing his sadness that a decent young woman felt compelled to commit such a crime. Mimi's lawyer had objected to his sympathetic tone, but the judge informed him it wasn't a trial and to keep his mouth buttoned until it was his turn to speak.

Mr. Whitney presented his case next. He seemed a different person before the judge, articulate and confident despite his disheveled appearance. The courtroom door clicked open and shut, and Janelle turned to see Judge Berry had quietly taken a seat at the very back. He winked his support and she nodded in return, her admission she'd misjudged Mr. Whitney.

The next witness called was the pediatrician from Mobile. He used explicit medical terms to describe how Cissy's body had been harmed by the abuse and the evidence that would be presented should the case go to trial.

Janelle stood and motioned at the bench. "Judge Harper, please! There's no reason for the girl to be in the courtroom for this."

She glared at Mr. Whitney for not preparing them for what might be said, or thinking far enough ahead to request that Cissy not be present. Janelle turned her worry to Cissy, whose eyes, lost and dreamy, seemed to focus on a world wholly different than the one the rest of them occupied.

"Deputy Parks, please escort Miss Pickering to one of the holding rooms down the hall," the judge boomed. "We'll send for her after the rest of the testimony."

When Fred rested a hand on Cissy's shoulder, she flinched. Orienting herself back to the present, she smoothed the front of her dress and rose to follow him out of the courtroom. Janelle placed one hand over her heart and nodded for Cissy to go.

Out of the corner of her eye, Janelle saw Mimi rise and push past the deputy. "All of you are liars. No one cares that my son is dead!" she shouted, then spat at Cissy.

The judge slammed his gavel and barked for another deputy to restrain Mimi.

"It's all right, Grandma Mimi. I understand," Cissy said, never taking her eyes off her. She didn't move until Fred nudged her along.

Janelle scooted across the bench, ready to attack Richard's mother, but the judge put up his hand. She sat down, fuming. She'd deal with Mimi later, though, on her own terms. And she'd dress down the judge for not having Mimi barred from the proceeding after such a display.

When the courtroom settled down, the pediatrician quickly finished his testimony. More important was the testimony from the psychiatrist who'd interviewed Cissy twice since the shooting.

"Miss Pickering exhibits signs of obsessive-compulsive disorder." He spoke mostly to the judge. "She uses the lists and counting games to make sense of her world. She had no control over her body for many years. It was natural to seek external ways to find order."

None of the psychiatrist's findings surprised Janelle. He noted that Cissy seemed dissociative, or detached from her actions. She had blocked the most painful memories, he said, and had developed techniques to keep those memories buried. He said the act was not premeditated. She had simply snapped the morning of the shooting, and the loaded firearm had been readily accessible.

When Janelle was another person, before the hearing and before the killing, she'd not given psychiatry much credence. She believed depression could be overcome with a little hard work and a better attitude. She'd never looked on Cissy's peculiar habits as *symptoms;* Cissy was Cissy. Janelle sat, mesmerized, when the psychiatrist described the calming effects of those habits and how critical they were to managing Cissy's anxiety and fear. Janelle's face flushed remembering the times she told her granddaughter to stop the child's play; the times she grew irritated with the counting and admonished her. In hindsight, each instance now seemed a cry for help gone unanswered.

"Then, what is your recommendation, sir?" The judge leaned forward.

"I'd say Miss Pickering would benefit from some time under psychiatric care and evaluation. I recommend a year, six months at the minimum. She is not a danger to society, but she is in need of professional help. The DA will need to take into account any evaluation made by the state hospital's psychiatrist. But I do not believe it's in her best interests to remand her to the Columbia Training School at this stage."

Janelle was shocked that Mimi and her lawyer hadn't hired their own psychiatrist to interview Cissy. It went against all reason if they'd hoped to sway the judge toward some form of punishment. Was it Mimi's subconscious admission that Richard wasn't the only victim? Even more shocking was that Mimi's lawyer had no prepared remarks; he said he was there strictly as an advisor to Mrs. Pickering.

She glanced in Mimi's direction and saw her dab away tears for the first time that day.

• • •

After a small break, Deputy Parks escorted Cissy back into the courtroom. Caroline had entered just moments before. Mother and daughter stood just a few feet apart. Each turned her head to face the other, but neither spoke. Time stood still for those few seconds and Janelle held her breath. She thought she saw Caroline's face soften, but the softness disappeared as quickly as it had appeared. Janelle's stoic daughter approached the front of the courtroom, resigned to follow through on her promise to go along with Mr. Whitney's recommendations.

After Caroline's testimony, Mimi grew agitated and implored the judge to let her speak next. Her lawyer whispered his protests, but Mimi held her hand up for him to be quiet. Cissy put on a brave front as if Mimi's outburst had happened lifetimes ago or perhaps to someone else altogether. She calmly watched her paternal grandmother take the stand.

"Mrs. Pickering, I'll allow it, but be fore-warned. I'll not have you upsetting the girl or these proceedings, or you'll be asked to leave," the judge said.

Mimi sat in the witness box, her gloved hands clutching a purse on her lap. "I have new evidence that should be noted in the record," she said. "Although my daughter-in-law is sure to deny it, I have reason to believe that Cissy was fathered by someone other than my son. She is no blood relation to Richard. I think the sheriff should have investigated whether their . . . their relationship was consensual."

Caroline bounded up the aisle of the courtroom, but Mr. Whitney grabbed her from behind, stopping her from reaching her mother-in-law. Mimi shrieked and covered her face as if she was already being attacked.

"Sit down, Mrs. Pickering!" the judge bellowed. "Both Mrs. Pickerings! Stop this nonsense right now!"

Although Cissy didn't stare directly at the exchange, the corner of her mouth turned up slightly. Janelle wondered how she could find levity in the circus around her. But perhaps she was just pleased to see her mother's protective instincts finally kick in.

When the room had settled down, Judge Harper wiped the sweat from his brow. "Mrs. Pickering, your unfounded accusations are not pertinent to this case and I question your motives in declaring them. If you speak again, I'll throw you in a jail cell myself."

He then pointed at Caroline. "And you . . . settle down or you'll share her cell."

Mimi sat down and Caroline moved to a bench near the back of the courtroom. The hearing ended quite abruptly after that. The judge didn't seem interested in Mimi's petition to have Cissy tried as an adult, particularly after Mimi's two outbursts. Actually, the morning seemed to cause him a great deal of discomfort. Emancipated from his assignment, he scurried to his chambers.

Janelle assumed she'd feel some measure of relief when the judge agreed to send Cissy to a state psychiatric hospital for observation. Her fear of Cissy going to a correctional facility had been all-consuming, and she hadn't thought through what hospitalization would mean. Her primary goal had been to get Cissy through the hearing. She could tackle only one obstacle at a time, and now another reared its insurmountable head.

As the room emptied, Cissy appeared distracted, eyes darting to the doors.

"What are you looking at?" Janelle asked.

"I thought maybe Mama would stay behind and speak to me. She must have left."

Janelle's heart broke for the girl. No matter how hard Janelle tried to make things better, she couldn't give Cissy what she longed for most: her mother's love and forgiveness.

"She had to go. I'm sure she'll visit soon." Janelle found it easier and easier to lie to protect Cissy's feelings, especially where Caroline was concerned. "How about some fried chicken from C.J.'s?"

"May I also have a thick slice of coconut cream pie?" she asked.

"You may have two if you like."

Sheriff Roe smiled at the exchange and waited close by to escort Cissy back to the room at the county jail where she'd been sequestered.

"Will you stay and eat with me, Grandmother? We could pull the desk and chair up to the bed and pretend we're having Sunday dinner. And then you can tell me all about the hospital in Meridian."

Janelle nodded, refusing to cry until her granddaughter was out of sight.

Caroline packed a suitcase with clothing she thought Cissy would need. When she arrived at Janelle's home, she set the suitcase down on the edge of the porch, laying it on its side. Knowing Caroline, Janelle suspected each item would be laundered, pressed, and folded meticulously. She'd probably set the case on its side so the clothes wouldn't bunch and wrinkle.

"Your daughter wants to see you," Janelle said.

Caroline looked down and shook her head no before retreating to her car to grab a cardboard box. She walked it over to Janelle's car and hoisted it into the trunk.

"I thought she'd like to take some books with her. Well, Bess suggested it," Caroline said. "You know Cissy. Always reading. Always nagging me to take her to the library."

Her voice trailed off and she stood staring

down into the trunk. Janelle walked over and laid a hand on her shoulder, but Caroline dipped away, avoiding the touch.

"Mother, don't. I can't—"

"I'm sorry, Caroline," Janelle said.

"Aren't we all."

"No, I mean, I haven't been there for you, for my granddaughters. It's been—"

"Let's not do this now." Caroline pushed past and got into her car, driving away without looking back. Janelle let the dust from the gravel subside before she walked over to the porch to grab her purse and Cissy's suitcase.

When she showed up at the jail, Janelle asked Deputy Parks to retrieve the books and suitcase from her car and bring them into the room where Cissy was held.

"But, ma'am, why don't I just load them into the cruiser?" he asked. "We'll be leaving soon."

"Because she'll want to see them first," she said with no other explanation. He rolled his eyes and marched away in sullen stomps.

Janelle guessed Cissy would want to inventory the suitcase's contents in the new spiral notebooks she'd asked her to purchase. She had stacks and stacks of notebooks hidden in boxes in her room, detailed inventories of the past several years of her life, and Caroline had placed those at the bottom of the suitcase. As soon as Deputy

Parks brought the suitcase and box into the room, Cissy's face lit up and he no longer seemed put out.

"Thank you, Fred!" she said, and hugged him.

"Deputy Parks," he whispered. Red-faced, he pushed her away. "You should call me Deputy Parks."

"Oh, Fred, it's just my grandmother." She laughed like a much younger girl and dove into the suitcase. Janelle sat at the foot of the bed and watched as one by one, her blouses, slacks, socks, and undergarments found their way onto neat little piles on the bed. Cissy and her lists.

"Mama did a good job packing," she said. "She knows just how I like my things."

Janelle smiled at the girl's innocence and the things that brought her comfort.

"Did you know your mother was a messy child?" she asked.

Cissy snorted. "I find that hard to believe. You've seen the way she makes Bess keep the house."

"No, really. Her room was always in such a state, especially when she was a teenager. She'd try on two or three different outfits each morning before school and leave them in piles on the floor," Janelle said. "Ruth would have fits about it."

"There'd be holy hell if *we* did that," Cissy said.

She continued her sorting and repacking, not looking up. "Say, Grandmother, why don't you drive me to Meridian today?"

"The court has to be certain you arrive at the hospital," Janelle explained. "What if I decided to just keep driving until we hit New York?"

"Would you do that?" Hope strained Cissy's features. "I've always wanted to see the Empire State Building to see if it's just like in the movies. We could go shopping on Fifth Avenue. I know how you like fancy clothes."

"Dear God, child, I wasn't being serious," Janelle stammered, explaining that it was law enforcement's job to check her in; they had the court's order.

Stupid old woman. Why had she made that offhanded comment? Those words added to Cissy's hurt. She couldn't forgive herself for speaking out loud a daydream she turned to time and time again for solace.

"You'll be just fine," Janelle assured her. "I'll visit you as often as I can."

"That's a long way for an old lady to drive," Cissy said, eyes down, hands still busy. When she grinned and cut her eyes at Janelle, they both laughed.

Janelle asked if she could help Cissy repack her things. When her granddaughter said she'd rather do it herself, Janelle leaned over and rummaged through the box of books. Inside each cover,

Cissy had printed: *Property of Cissy Pickering. Please ask nicely before borrowing.*

"I guess Mama should've left some of my books for Lily. She's getting to be an excellent reader," Cissy said.

"I suspect Lily knows you need them more than she does. It'll be good to have your books to pass the time."

Cissy nodded and then began alphabetizing the books, aligning each spine in the same direction.

"They won't be coming to say goodbye," she said.

"No, no, they won't," Janelle admitted. "Does that make you sad?"

"Not seeing my baby sisters is on my List of Very Sad Things. But I understand they don't want to see me after I killed our daddy."

"They're too young to understand all this. But they miss you so very much." Each time Janelle had visited her two other granddaughters, they'd clamored for information: whether Cissy liked her room at the jail, if she enjoyed the art supplies they'd sent, if the guards were nice to her, and most importantly, when she'd return home. Dodging the questions and struggling to find appropriate answers had worn Janelle's nerves raw.

"They miss me?"

"Absolutely. Things are just too complicated

for a visit just yet," Janelle said. "I bet they'll write you very soon."

Caroline had kept Lily and Jessie clear of town and any gossip they might hear, but the girls resented being homebound in the summer. They clamored for friends and swimming parties and family picnics—the normalcy of summers past. Bess did her best to keep them occupied and shielded from Caroline as she tried to find some sort of routine in her life now.

At least the break gave them respite from the cruelties they were bound to face once September rolled around. Caroline spoke about moving, but Janelle advised her to take her time before making any major decisions. The house had been in Richard's family for many years and it was an asset she should safeguard for now, especially from Mimi.

Janelle closed her eyes and breathed in deeply. Their family was buried under an avalanche of unspoken heartache that threatened to suffocate everyone, including Richard's mother. Each of them would have to find her own way through this dark time, even Cissy.

"Grandmother, I see you're fretting."

"No, child. I'm fine." Janelle bit her tongue to focus on something besides the incomprehensible goodbye she was facing.

"I'm not scared and you shouldn't be either," Cissy said.

Deputy Parks appeared in the doorway, looking for assurance he could enter and get the journey to Meridian under way. Janelle nodded, so he placed the box of books under one arm and picked up the suitcase with his other hand.

Cissy hugged Janelle one last time and kissed the top of her head. "Grandmother," she whispered, "please don't remember me for what my daddy did."

When Cissy had gone, Janelle pulled the quilt from the bed and folded it in a bundle. She turned out the light in the room and walked down the hall, wondering if a human being could survive this much sorrow.

Chapter 6

Deputy Parks agreed to crack the window in the backseat of the police car so Cissy could feel the wind on her face during the long ride to the state psychiatric hospital in Meridian. She begged him to roll it down all the way so she could stick her entire head out like a dog lapping up the humid July breeze. He said it was childproof and not meant to roll down past halfway, but she failed to see the risk. Were children, criminals, and crazy people known for throwing themselves out of moving cars? He probably just wanted to follow the rules to a T since he was the youngest of the deputies at the sheriff's office.

They'd become friends in the last two weeks, or at least Cissy thought of him that way. Before his shift started each morning, he'd bring her a donut. As much as she enjoyed that deep-fried dough, she liked his company more. She'd asked him to call her Cissy instead of Miss Pickering, but he said they should keep things on a professional level and he preferred to be called Deputy Parks. He still seemed more like a Fred.

Cissy turned her attention to the parched fields that rushed by in a dismal brown blur. In stark contrast were the red, white, and blue decorations on every farmhouse, barn, and small-town Main

Street. U.S. flags of all sizes and yards and yards of bunting jumped out in all their glory. Mississippi may have suffered from a lack of rain that summer, but its citizens had a surplus of bicentennial spirit. It struck Cissy that she'd always equate the killing of her daddy with the summer the country turned two hundred.

Fred had a pleasant smell, perspiration and Ivory soap tangled together, and it was something Cissy thought she'd miss about her time in jail. Today, his uniform stayed crisp while her cotton dress wilted and the backs of her thighs stuck to the vinyl seats. She lifted the hair off her neck and wished she had a ribbon or rubber band for a ponytail. He looked in the rearview mirror and turned away red-faced when she caught his eye.

"Let's count the number of flags, Fred. Just to pass the time." Cissy hoped counting might keep her mind off the god-awful heat and lack of air-conditioning in the police car. She was usually cold, even in summer, so being hot was a strange and uncomfortable change.

The deputy sighed and shook his head. "Doubt either of us can count that high. Plus, I have to keep my eye on the road."

Cissy stayed quiet, thinking he'd rather not talk. It was upsetting considering they'd spent hours over the past week talking about everything and nothing. She really wanted to know more about his hunting pup. She and her sisters had always wanted a dog or cat, but their parents wouldn't allow pets. They said animals were filthy and carried disease, although both her mama and daddy had dogs and cats growing up. About a year ago, Cissy had benignly pointed out their hypocrisy, which resulted in a severe grounding and two weeks without books.

Fred must have found the silence just as uncomfortable as talking. He looked at her in the rearview again and asked if he could ask a question.

"You just did," she said.

"Did what?"

"You asked if you could ask a question, and that was a question."

"I'm trying to be serious." His face flamed and suddenly she worried she'd jeopardized their friendship in some way.

"I apologize. I'm guessing you have a serious question, then?" She wanted to give him her undivided attention, so she settled back into the seat and drew her legs up, careful to tuck her dress underneath. Her stomach cautioned that serious questions usually had something to do with her daddy, and she wasn't about to answer those questions, not even for Fred.

"Are you scared, Miss Pickering?" He choked back the emotion that accompanied the simple words that everyone seemed to ask lately. The sound of the tires through the open window almost drowned it out, but Cissy had heard it.

"No, I'm not." It was the truth. And the truth was a gift she wanted to give Fred for making the last two weeks bearable.

"Not even a little? Being away from your family?"

She hadn't thought of the separation from family as something to fear. It made her sad. But she also knew that the word *family* meant something wholly different now. Even if she were home in her bed, nothing about the house or her sisters or her mama would ever feel the same. She remembered how terrified Bess had looked the morning of the shooting, as if Cissy had it in her to harm any one of them; as if she was a danger to others and the act of killing her daddy had been senseless. How would any of them even act around her? No, she wasn't afraid of living at the hospital. It would just have to become a different kind of normal.

"Would I be out of line if I said I worried for you?" he asked.

"No," she said. "But I wish you wouldn't. And I wish very much that you'd call me Cissy."

Fred said he'd try, but he remained silent for the rest of the drive, not sharing anything else that occupied his thoughts. She didn't bother him further. He'd given her a gift as well—a connection with someone who cared about her, someone besides her grandmother.

When they reached the hospital, Cissy couldn't help but be disappointed. The building looked so ordinary; just a homely, two-story brick box with bars on the windows like eyelashes closed for a long rest. The grounds, however, were something to behold. They must have been immune to the drought because the grass glowed as green as a traffic light. She probably wouldn't be spending much time outdoors, and the most she could hope for was a room on the second floor so she could watch the gardener caretake the fine expanse of lawn.

Cissy couldn't fathom what it'd be like living at the hospital, but it had to be better than the little room at the county jail. The room had been terribly small and windowless, and she could hear the drunks and ne'er-do-wells shouting from their cells on the other side of the building. Even books wouldn't have been able to keep her mind occupied for much longer. She appreciated the court's speediness in making its decision.

When Fred turned off the ignition, he didn't move or say anything for a minute. She broke the silence by telling him she'd carry her own suitcase.

"I'm not a little girl. I need to start taking care of myself."

He walked around the car and opened her door. "Careful. Don't hit your head as you get out."

At five foot nine, she stood as tall as Fred and

he arched his back a little straighter when she got out of the backseat. He allowed her to walk a few steps ahead of him until they entered the building, where he took her elbow and led her over to the nurse at the front reception desk. The temperature dropped a good twenty degrees in the cavernous hall.

"Ma'am, this here is Miss Pickering. *Cissy*. You should be expecting her." His voice cracked like a young boy's.

Cissy knew it was time for goodbye and hoped their parting would ease his discomfort somewhat. "Nice knowing you, Deputy Parks." She held out her hand professional-like, which he shook.

He whispered, "Just Fred is fine," before turning and walking down the hall and back out into the heat for the return trip to Biloxi. She regretted not hugging him goodbye, but understood he was a reserved sort of person who embarrassed easily.

The pudgy nurse behind the desk had eyes as black as a possum's and deep furrows around her mouth that indicated she didn't like her job very much. The unhappy woman introduced herself as Nurse Brown and then remarked how tall Cissy was for a young lady.

"Thank you," she said, not knowing what else to say. She wanted to say everyone must seem tall to such a squat person, but Grandmother had warned that her smart mouth could open up a world of hurt.

Nurse Brown led Cissy up a flight of stairs straight out of *Gone with the Wind*, then down a hall and through several locked doors. She shifted her considerable weight from side to side and made low, puffing noises. Cissy struggled to keep her steps slow and small. Every corridor was sorely in need of a new coat of white paint, yet the tile floor glistened. It reminded her of St. John's Parochial School, right down to the pine disinfectant tickling her nostrils.

The final locked door led to a spacious room with tall, multipaned windows with thick wire mesh in front of them instead of plain old window screens. Dusty streams of sunlight spilled onto a handful of girls sitting at wooden tables covered with paper and crayons. Cissy's lawyer had said there'd be patients as young as fifteen and as old as twenty-one in the ward. Seeing the other patients for the first time, she could only guess their stay at the hospital gave them the appearance of being very young and just a little lost.

Two other patients lounged on a brown and orange plaid sofa watching a rerun of *The Andy Griffith Show*. Nurse Possum Eyes said the recreation area would be where Cissy would spend most of her time except for meals and meetings with the hospital's psychiatrist, Dr. Guttman. Cissy guessed he'd been tasked with making broken girls whole again, and this made her think of the story about Humpty Dumpty, which didn't have a happy ending.

Unlike the rest of the hospital, the white floor tiles in this room suffered from a sad dinginess that matched the walls. Her mama said painting a wall white was telling the world you had no imagination, so the rooms at home were bright yellows, greens, and blues, colors of the Old South, she'd say. Cissy guessed that if her mama ever decided to visit, those hideous walls would be the first thing she'd comment on. In contrast, the uniforms of the hospital staff were bleached bright white and stiff with too much starch, creating an illusion of good posture among the whole lot.

It didn't take long for the patients to realize someone new was being admitted. Most of the girls in the room rushed toward Cissy, talking over each other excitedly. They formed a stifling circle around her, offering their names and asking hers. One touched her hair and she flinched away. She suspected that her red hair, whipped wildly into knots from the drive, drew the girls' attention, or maybe it was the pink sandals, which she regretted wearing on her first day. The utter lack of color at the hospital was making Cissy even more self-conscious.

She noticed that a small girl with raven black hair sat on the sofa, completely disinterested.

Cissy thought to herself only a deaf person could ignore the commotion.

"Girls, girls," Nurse Brown shouted. "Go sit down. You can introduce yourselves later."

The nurse motioned for Cissy to follow. They shuffled down a narrow hall that reminded her of those in dreams, the kind that get longer and longer no matter how fast a person tried to run down them.

Her room was at the end of this nightmarish hall, the sixth door on the left and the one closest to the bathroom she'd be sharing with all the other patients in the ward.

Cissy was startled to see a young man in her room. His black hair was slicked back, although long pieces kept flicking down across his face. His cheeks had a bluish shadow left from missing a day's shave. He was in an all-white uniform, except for his black shoes, so she knew he was part of the staff.

"Ma'am," he said, and nodded her way. And to Nurse Brown, "I was just finishing up. Had to move the desk and chair from another ward."

"I'm Cissy Pickering." She extended a hand and it hung in the air. He looked at Nurse Brown for permission to shake.

"Lucien. Pleased to meet you," he said.

"I know you have some other work you should be doing, Mr. Thibodeaux," the nurse said sternly.

The orderly gave a little bow as he left, which

made Cissy smile. That is, until Nurse Brown coughed to get her attention.

"Dinner's at five-thirty in the cafeteria. One of the girls will show you the way. Oh, and no bringing food back to your room," she said, leaving Cissy to unpack her suitcase.

She assessed her meager belongings and realized Fred had forgotten about the cardboard box of books. Perhaps he'd done it on purpose so he'd have a reason to visit her. At least that's what she hoped.

"What's your name?" asked a girl in the doorway. It was the dark-haired patient who'd been watching TV earlier. She couldn't have been much over five feet tall. Cissy wondered how many times she'd be startled by strangers before day's end.

"I'm Cissy Pickering. You look just like Elizabeth Taylor in *National Velvet*."

"I'm Martha," she said, not offering a last name, and sat on the floor instead of on the wooden chair in the corner.

Her skirt rode up when she hugged her knees, revealing her panties. Cissy turned away and started transferring her clothes to the small dresser, the sole piece of furniture in the room except the bed and desk and chair.

"I was looking out the window just as you drove up." Martha didn't mention the sheriff's department car. Just as well. Cissy wasn't ready to share anything of herself, particularly with a stranger. "I could help you unpack."

Cissy considered carefully how to handle this first request without seeming rude. But having someone touch her things made her anxious, so she said, "Thank you very much, but I'm all right."

When Martha grew sullen, Cissy worried that she'd offended someone in her first thirty minutes at the hospital. "I do appreciate your kind offer, but I like things just so."

"Suit yourself." Martha hopped up on the desk and squatted. "They look brand-new."

"My mama is a particular sort of person," Cissy said. "She doesn't believe in hand-me-downs and buys us new outfits each season. I think she liked the look on Daddy's face when he saw how much she'd spent."

"Well, you have an awful lot of pink clothes."

"Mama said redheads look good in pink, although purple is my favorite color. But since she packed my suitcase, I guess I shouldn't be surprised."

Martha let out a small snort that put Cissy at ease. "Mothers have a way of getting their way," she said.

Cissy didn't want to talk anymore about mothers, so she didn't ask Martha about hers. She also didn't feel right asking why Martha had been admitted to the hospital and for how long.

Those types of conversations demanded time and small talk first. While Cissy didn't know any crazy people personally, she had a good feeling about Martha. At least the girl made her smile on this very strange day. And it couldn't hurt to have a friend.

"Best to avoid Lucien," Martha said, chewing a thumbnail. "The orderly who was just in here."

"Why is that?" Cissy asked.

Martha seemed surprised that she'd not just agreed and carried on with the unpacking. "Well, first, he's staff. And we don't make friends with staff. I'll be your friend while you get the lay of the land."

When Martha didn't follow up with a second or third point, Cissy was relieved not to hear another warning. The orderly seemed nice enough and she liked to make her own judgments about people.

"Your mama packed an awful lot of sweaters." Martha craned her neck as Cissy closed the bottom drawer of the bureau. "It's July and, believe you me, this place is never cool enough."

Cissy paused before deciding it was safe to discuss her temperature regulation problem.

"When I was little, I sometimes wore two sets of clothes at the same time. The problem was I couldn't wear multiple pairs of socks and still fit in my shoes. I tried wearing several pairs of socks *without* shoes, but my feet were still cold."

"You're a hoot." Martha shook her head and laughed. "My guess is you'll be stripping off your clothes the first time you sit in that hot recreation room."

Cissy knew that wouldn't be true in her case. Her daddy had made her cold from the inside, and no amount of warmth on the outside was going to change that. She felt she could blame her daddy for this because he didn't have good boundaries, and people without good boundaries had to take responsibility for it in some fashion. What made her most angry was that he had seemed like a normal daddy in most respects. Before she turned nine, he was always working late. On the rare evenings he was home, they'd read the paper together, or look through the atlas, discussing all the places that Phileas Fogg and Passepartout traveled to in Jules Verne's *Around the World in Eighty Days.* His hugs were normal hugs, like the ones TV daddies gave their little girls.

Then later, when Mama or Bess wasn't looking, he let his hands go to places they shouldn't have gone. When he started coming to her room at night, he'd ask her to touch him back, that it was as harmless as giving a hug. If he had to ask her to pinky swear not to tell anyone, Cissy sensed it was a long way from harmless.

"My sisters made a game of it," Cissy said, shaking off the memory. "For my birthday and Christmas, they'd give me stuff to warm me up, like flannel pajamas, wool slippers, even some very thin nylon socks with so-called amazing warming properties that you're supposed to wear underneath regular socks."

"And did they work?"

Martha seemed overly interested in something as boring as socks, but Cissy continued.

"Nah, but I told them they worked. While someone might classify this as a lie, I think words used to protect the feelings of people you love aren't really lies." Cissy suspected this type of reasoning was one of those things that made her peculiar. She didn't worry about it too much since they were *her* rules and didn't have to make sense to other people.

"I like that rule," Martha said. "I'll remember that if you ask me a question and I think my answer will hurt you."

"How's the food here?" Cissy asked, changing the subject. Martha's directness gave her a funny feeling in her stomach. In fact, she didn't think she'd be hungry for supper at all.

Chapter 7

All patients were given light green cotton pants and smocks, a cross between pajamas and a uniform, but they could wear regular clothes if they wanted, and that's what Cissy did most days. No matter how many times she asked, no one would tell her why they weren't allowed to wear street shoes. She felt silly wearing slippers, but since her mama packed mostly pink clothes, at least the pink wool slippers from her sisters matched somewhat.

At breakfast a few days later, Martha walked in wearing Cissy's yellow gingham dress. When Cissy wore it, the hem hit right below her knees, but on Martha, it touched the floor.

"You didn't ask to wear my things." She tapped her fork against her tray, first five times in a row, then four, then three.

"Are you mad?" Martha asked.

Cissy sensed she didn't care about her answer. "I guess not." They were just starting to become friends and she didn't want to risk sounding selfish. The girl's friendship made long days seem shorter, and for that Cissy was grateful.

"You *seem* mad," Martha said.

"Well, I'm just not used to anyone touching my

things without permission, and it's too long for you," Cissy said. "It's dragging on the floor. It might get dirty."

"Then I'll walk on my tippy-toes." Martha dug into her scrambled eggs like she hadn't eaten in a week.

"Did you move around any of the clothes in the drawer where you found the dress?"

When Martha stared at Cissy's tapping, she put down the fork and sat on her hands.

"After breakfast, I'll go straight to your room and return the dress," Martha said. "I didn't know it'd be such a big deal."

Bess and Mama had known how she liked her clothes folded and put in her dresser. She trusted them to place the socks in order of color, from lightest to darkest. Cissy's pants were always pressed with a light crease, just enough to act as a guide for folding them. Her blouses and dresses were placed on wooden hangers, all facing to the right and ordered from shortest to longest.

At the hospital, there wasn't a closet, so she had to find a way to store her clothes without hangers. To find Cissy's yellow gingham dress, Martha would have had to move several things in the bottom drawer of the dresser. Cissy had a long morning ahead of her rearranging anything that had been misplaced. She wondered if the laundry room would rewash and press her clothes if she asked nicely.

"Are you going to eat your bacon?" Martha asked.

"You go ahead," she said. No use causing a ruckus.

Martha took to sitting with Cissy in the game room for a few minutes prior to her appointments with Dr. Guttman, the hospital's psychiatrist. She said it was for moral support.

"You don't have to talk to him. I don't." Martha flipped through an old issue of *Seventeen* magazine because she said books didn't hold much appeal; that they felt too much like assigned reading at school. "At least try it today. Just sit there and nod your head, or stare out the window. It works for me."

"What if he starts thinking I'm not crazy any-more?" Cissy pulled down the magazine so Martha would listen more closely. "They might transfer me to that reform school for criminal girls."

"I'm not crazy and they keep me here," Martha said. "And like you said, you're peculiar. That should work well enough."

She was right. Peculiar was just this side of crazy. For those who didn't know better, like Dr. Guttman, it was a good enough reason to keep both of them here.

Cissy used to think Dr. Guttman didn't have good boundaries because he asked straight out about what her daddy did. She came to understand that's what psychiatrists do. It was probably one of the few jobs, other than being a lawyer, where someone could ask you to talk about memories that are yours to keep to yourself.

This posed a danger to Cissy because, as a child, she'd vowed not to lie except when absolutely warranted and had kept that vow most of her life. Luckily, she'd always been able to turn off a part of her brain when pulled into a deep, dark place. When she told Dr. Guttman she didn't remember details, it wasn't a lie. What Cissy didn't tell him, though, was sometimes—when she was drawing or watching TV or playing chess with Martha— she got a glimpse of the shut-off parts of her brain and thought she might faint with fright. It was like waking up from a terrible nightmare and not being able to remember all the details. A person's just grateful to be awake, even though the pieces of the nightmare linger and threaten to come together like a solved puzzle.

Dr. Guttman walked into the recreation area, interrupting the girls' discussion. "Cissy, ready for our appointment?" While he directed the question to her, he kept his eyes on Martha, like he didn't trust her somehow.

Cissy followed him into his office and sat in the leather chair, her usual spot. The grown-up part of her brain knew Dr. Guttman was extra smart because he had several diplomas with his name in fancy script hanging on his walls in thick gold frames.

"I see you and Martha have become friends," he said, settling into his chair.

"Nurse Edna said the same thing, but both of you seem to want to say more on that than you're letting on," she said.

"Not really, Cissy. It's just that when there's a new patient in the ward, Martha tends to monopolize her time."

"I've got a lot of time to spare, so that's not a big deal." Cissy sensed caution in Dr. Guttman's voice. Did he guess that Martha had been coaching her to remain silent in their sessions? It got Cissy to thinking what advice Martha had given other new patients.

"Would you prefer I not spend time with Martha?" she continued.

"Not at all," he said. "It's just that Martha doesn't think her sessions with me provide any value. I'd like you to give therapy a chance and make those decisions on your own."

She hadn't been at the hospital long enough to know if there was any benefit to her time with Dr. Guttman, but she had become increasingly alarmed at his expertise in getting her to talk about things she'd rather not talk about. What if he eventually found a way to open up the shut-off parts for good? The thing about deep, dark places in a person's mind was that you never knew what it might be like there. It could be just dark enough you'd never find your way out again. Some of the girls at the hospital lived in that dark place. Cissy figured it was safer to talk about them than about Martha.

"I noticed some patients never laugh, not even when we watch *Happy Days* or *Laverne & Shirley*. Sometimes they scare me, shuffling through the halls, arms hanging heavy at their sides."

"What scares you about that?" he asked.

"They don't seem awake. It looks like they're trapped inside themselves."

"Some of the patients here are taking powerful medications," Dr. Guttman explained. "It can make them appear without emotion, but they're not being harmed in any way. It's for their own good."

He seemed pretty sure of himself, but the way they hollered out in their sleep made Cissy think they weren't getting any better either.

"They have lots of nightmares," she said. "I hear them. We all hear them."

"Do you have nightmares?"

"I thought we agreed that you'd tell me things about New York and in exchange, I'd answer your particularly hard questions."

"I didn't say I'd do that each and every session," he said.

"That's what you implied."

He smiled while rubbing his nose. Cissy had seen that move a time or two. It meant she was testing his patience, but that he'd eventually give in.

"Okay. What do you want to know today?"

"What's the tallest building?"

"You already know that. It's the World Trade Center," Dr. Guttman said.

"Yup. Thirteen hundred and sixty-eight feet."

"You're stalling," he said. "Answer my question."

"Wait," she said. "Tell me about the elevators. Is it thrilling to go to the top? A magazine article I read said you can see fifty miles away on a clear day."

"Actually, Cissy, I've never been to the top. Not many people know this, but I'm afraid of heights. I've shared something with you. Now let's talk about whether you have nightmares."

Since he'd been so honest with her, Cissy thought it'd be all right to admit she'd had nightmares since she was a little girl. Most were about the devil, but she called him Old Scratch because the D word was on her List of Banned Words. "Old Scratch just sounds like a mangy old dog looking for scraps in an alley, don't you think? That's what Bess always said."

"Do you think maybe Old Scratch is symbolic for your father?" he asked.

Dr. Guttman readied his pen as if she was about

to say something profound, but he should have known better than to sneak the conversation back to her daddy. "I don't want to talk about that right now."

Surely it was being brought up in the Catholic Church that solidified her fear of Old Scratch. From an early age, she thought religion should be about uplifting people's spirits and not scaring them to death. The nuns made religion ugly by concentrating on sin and hell, and how to avoid both. They even had students sprinkle holy water over their beds at night so Old Scratch wouldn't stop on his rounds.

Cissy would have rather heard Bible stories about Moses or Noah or Abraham. She liked going to Saturday night mass best. Father Isadore wasn't a fire and brimstone sort of priest, so she didn't mind his preaching. She did find it strange, however, that priests could come across as loving and kind while nuns were mean. Did their schooling differ that much? Or did kind and loving nuns exist outside her parish and she had the misfortune to be born in Biloxi? Cissy told Dr. Guttman she was still forming opinions on how the Catholic Church shaped who she was today, and he said it'd be an excellent idea to discuss it in future sessions.

"I've been meaning to ask you something," she said, changing the subject in case he started in again about her daddy or Old Scratch.

"Sure, go ahead."

"I'd like us to agree not to use the word *murder* during our visits, because it's also a banned word. I usually just say I shot my daddy." She didn't like to use the word *kill* either, but there was no getting around that. Killing was killing even if done for the right reasons.

"If you wish, Cissy," he said. "But you've got to trust that you can talk about anything in our sessions. You're safe here."

When Cissy didn't want to pay attention to Dr. Guttman, she thought about how many things in the room begged to be touched—the sheet of thick glass that covered his cherry desk, the rough pile of the carpet beneath her slippers, the sleek coolness of the black leather couch. Although smell was her favorite sense, touch was a close second because the surfaces of things sometimes spoke louder than words. A porcupine's quills said, "Back off!" while rabbit fur said, "Squeeze me carefully."

Her favorite part of the office was the wall behind his desk, which was covered from top to bottom with books—even more books than the library in the recreation room. She hadn't asked him if he'd read them all, but she suspected someone so smart had read at least most of them. Some must have been very old because old books put off a special odor, a cross between cigar smoke and tree bark. While she'd always had an especially keen sense of smell, the summer humidity likely coaxed the scent out into the open.

"Cissy? Are you paying attention?"

"Of course," she said, looking into his face. "I can talk about anything in our sessions because I am safe here."

He stared at her for so long that she thought they might be having a contest.

"You have an awful lot of books." She began counting, starting with the very top row and going right to left, just to mix things up.

"Cissy, you're welcome to count my books another time," he said. "But I'd like you to be brave and share something that's been on your mind. Would you do that?"

She thought about the thing that kept entering her mind over and over recently. "I've been missing the beach. Something fierce."

Growing up in Biloxi meant Cissy could smell salt in the air all the time, and it became a part of every other scent. She smelled lots of things at the hospital. The strongest odor was of people who'd messed their pants on days the nurses were too busy to clean them up right away. When the hallways were freshly mopped, they smelled of stale water and pine cleaner. When the sheets were washed, they smelled of hot water and bleach. Nothing compared to the smell of the ocean, though.

"Tell me about the beach, then," Dr. Guttman said.

"A few times each summer, Mama takes us to the beach even though she doesn't like what she calls the hordes of vacationers who should keep driving until they hit Pensacola."

Dr. Guttman chuckled, which put Cissy at ease. She told him how she and her sisters were made to wear wide-brimmed straw hats while they played in the sand and water because all three were freckled and fair-skinned. She told him she was often embarrassed that her mama made Bess carry their picnic basket and set up their beach umbrella when other families didn't have their housekeepers along. Some of her classmates' families didn't even keep house help at all anymore.

"Did your father ever join you?"

"Not once," she said. "He was always working. Mama didn't work, so she had plenty of time to take us to the shore, even though she never seemed to enjoy it as much as us kids did."

Cissy was grateful her daddy wasn't part of her beach memories. Too many other memories— like birthday parties and Christmas mornings— had him attached to them. On those days, she wore her happiness on the outside. She did like looking at old photographs, though, because she could sometimes trick her mind into believing other parts of her childhood were happy.

"Are you okay, Cissy? You look very sad," Dr. Guttman said.

"I was just thinking it's hard to enjoy anything when you think you're at least partly to blame for the bad things that happened in your life."

He put down his pen and notepad, and leaned forward. "It's normal to think there was something you did or didn't do to deserve what happened. I'm hoping our work here together will convince you that just isn't so."

She wanted to believe that was possible because Dr. Guttman seemed especially smart and he'd worked with lots of people who were crazy, and perhaps some who were just peculiar like she was.

Cissy's mind went back to a time when she was younger, sometime before her tenth birthday. For a very short time, she decided to stop being sarcastic and be the best daughter she could be. She studied her schoolwork day and night. She took on so many extra chores that Bess asked if she was trying to take over her job. She acted so polite sometimes she felt her smile would freeze on her face. Her mama probably thought she was going through a phase, while Mimi and Grandmother probably thought God had answered their prayers and she'd finally become a civil child with good manners.

Cissy didn't care what anyone thought except her daddy because she did all those things for him, to show him she was a good girl. She thought that it'd put an end to their secret special time.

Later, when she suggested he stop coming to her room—that her mama would probably not like it—he turned mean. He no longer called it their special time. He said she deserved the bad touching because she was a bad girl. She should've had him clarify what he meant by *bad*. Instead, Cissy tried being good at everything. When none of that worked, and her circumstances didn't change, it messed up her idea of how the world should be. She dropped into what her mama called a blue funk. She stopped trying to be the perfect student and the perfect daughter. She just stopped trying in general. Cissy didn't feel up to being around her friends. After school, she would come home and lie on her bed with the covers up to her ears. Lily tried everything in her power to coax Cissy out to play. But even she gave up after a while and decided to ride out the blue funk like one rides out a hurricane. Lily tiptoed around Cissy, not knowing if she was the calm before the storm or the storm itself.

While Lily might have noticed a change in Cissy, her mama did not because she was too busy with baby Jessie. She didn't even care when Cissy started getting bad grades except to tell her she was probably reading too many storybooks and needed to crack her school books open more often.

Then back in August of 1969, the winds of a real hurricane named Camille blew away Cissy's blue funk and most of South Mississippi. She guessed it took something that significant to wake her up again.

"Camille," she whispered.

"What was that, Cissy?"

"Nothing. Just a storm I was remembering."

"Would you like to stop for today?" Dr. Guttman asked.

Cissy nodded and left his office. She appreciated that one of Dr. Guttman's talents seemed to be in knowing how much questioning one person could take in an hour's time. It was one of the reasons she decided she could trust him no matter what Martha believed.

Later that afternoon, a thunderstorm rattled the hospital windows and lit the skies with angry lightning. The nurses warned patients to stay away from the windows, but Cissy thought they were exaggerating the danger. She found it strange that she was just thinking about Hurricane Camille in her session with Dr. Guttman and now the howling wind was dredging up even more memories she'd just as soon forget.

That was seven years ago, but the sound of that kind of wind couldn't be forgotten. It made the hair on her arms stand on end, and she couldn't imagine feeling more alive. While her parents argued about whether or not to evacuate, Cissy had stayed on the front porch watching the August sky turn dark as charcoal.

When the heavy rains and wind began, she begged her parents to let her stay outside. She wanted the storm to wash over her; to tear apart their proper Southern home and bury her former life in the debris that would later be carted away.

Bess's brother drove up in a spray of gravel and mad honking just as Cissy turned to go inside. "Bess, if we're gonna die in this storm, you ought to be with family instead of those white folks," he had screamed above the wind. "They don't need no damn housekeeper in a hurricane."

Cissy couldn't argue with his logic and she half thought about asking if she could join them.

Lily, who'd just turned five, and the newborn Jessie cried the entire time they were holed up in the pantry, and no amount of shushing from their mama eased their fear. Her inability to hug them in a soft and gentle manner made things worse. The saving grace was that the noise of the rain and wind often drowned out their wailing.

Cissy sat perfectly still in one corner with her eyes closed, imagining the destruction going on outside. She heard the crack of trees falling and shutters being blown open. They all screamed when they heard glass from the front windows crashing to the floors. They screamed in unison again when the electricity went out at around 8:30 p.m. Cissy hoped she was safe from her daddy's touching since her mama and sisters were trapped in the dark, too. It'd been going on for a little less than half a year, every few weeks or so. The visits to her room, though, had grown less frequent when the baby started disrupting everyone's sleep.

Four hours into Camille's rage, Cissy thought she'd suddenly gone deaf. No more howling wind or thunderous rain. Just silence. Her daddy had said the eye of the storm was overhead. He left the pantry to assess the damage to the house, garage, and yard. Cissy scrambled out after him.

She ran straight out the front door into the yard. The oldest magnolia had toppled, its giant roots exposed to the gentle rain that came down. If the wind had shifted direction to the east a bit, the tree would have smashed into the front porch, entry, and parlor. It would have wiped out the bedrooms on the second floor, including Cissy's.

She started to cry and her daddy told her to hush because the damage wasn't that bad and they'd have things fixed in no time. Cissy couldn't tell him she cried about the *lack* of damage.

Back in the pantry, she mumbled a prayer to a God she didn't know existed to allow Camille to continue her rampage. She begged the winds to uproot all of them like it had the old magnolia so they'd have to start fresh in some form or fashion.

Soon, Cissy fell into a deep sleep and dreamt she was walking through a pile of rubble—wood and glass mixed with bits of broken furniture, dishes, books, even clothing. She smiled at the destruction and twirled round and round in a circle, her eyes closed and her face turned up toward the blistering midday sun.

Her mama had shaken Cissy's shoulder to wake her. "We're all safe and our home is still standing, thank the Lord."

She resented being awakened from a good dream because she rarely had them, and she couldn't—she *wouldn't*—thank the Lord. He hadn't answered her prayers. Electricity was restored, broken shutters and windows were repaired, trees were replanted, life continued as if Camille had never visited the Gulf Coast. If the house had been destroyed, maybe they could have gone to live with her grandparents. She couldn't imagine either of them letting her daddy continue to get away with the things he did.

Some years later, Cissy became obsessed with Camille. In her notebook, she'd recorded facts about the storm instead of her feelings of disappointment over its inability to save her.

- Total area of destruction in Harrison County: 68 square miles
- Number of direct deaths: 143
- Number of related deaths: 153
- Number of injured: 8,931
- Number of homes destroyed: 5,662
- Number of homes damaged: 13,915
- Estimated damage: $1.42 billion

On her dark days, Cissy couldn't look back over those numbers because they filled her with a hot fury that her home wasn't one of the 5,662 destroyed and that her daddy wasn't one of the 296 killed.

She decided not to talk to Dr. Guttman about Hurricane Camille earlier because she was afraid of bringing up things that made her angry. Cissy could almost always handle sadness, but anger was a different story. Anger was on her List of Very Bad Things, and besides, what was the use of being angry at a dead father anyway?

Chapter 8

From time to time, Dr. Guttman asked what types of things Cissy wrote in her notebooks, but never prodded her for specifics. She figured he knew she needed something of her own. Patients in mental hospitals weren't allowed to keep many things private, so she appreciated having that one special privilege.

"What's been on your mind?" he asked.

She'd been at the hospital two weeks and hadn't had a visitor, so naturally, she wondered what her sisters were doing and if they were okay. Most days, Cissy tried not to think about her mama, though, because their relationship became complicated after the shooting. She wanted to believe in the deepest part of her heart that her mama knew nothing about the visits to Cissy's bedroom. If she had, Cissy didn't know what she'd do with that information. Just thinking about it made her sad to the bone. The good thing was that she was too afraid to ask outright; she'd never have to know her mama's truth.

When Cissy first arrived at the hospital, Dr. Guttman had suggested she write letters to her family. They could be about anything, he'd said. Cissy decided to write about what it was like to live in a mental hospital—what her room looked like, what she ate, the friends she'd made, like Martha and Lucien. Dr. Guttman had mailed the letters, but she had no way of knowing if they were read. He'd said the act of writing them was the important part and she agreed. Whether someone read those words was just gravy.

"I've been thinking about my grandma Mimi and whether I should write her, too," Cissy said.

"Why would you want to do that?" Dr. Guttman asked.

"I feel a little sorry for her. She told the judge that Daddy's actions were not so bad because I wasn't a blood relative. She must have been a little bit out of her mind to say that. Or she needed a way to make a terrible thing not so terrible. After all, her son is dead."

"Cissy, no one should hurt a child in the way you were hurt. Whether or not you are his biological daughter is not a pertinent fact in your case."

The judge had said the same thing in response to Mimi's outburst. Cissy wrote the word *pertinent* in her spiral notebook because she liked how powerful it sounded. Her notebooks came in handy because her head couldn't hold all the lists and everything else she wanted to remember.

As much as Cissy liked to think she controlled her thoughts, she didn't. Every day she was grateful her brain had shut-off parts, but she wondered how long they'd remain that way. For example, as much as she missed her sisters, she was worried what she could even say to them if they visited. Cissy figured it would be hard for Lily and Jessie to forgive her unless they knew the whole story. And since love was so complicated, they might not forgive her even if they did know.

"I have some good news," Dr. Guttman said. "Your grandmother is visiting soon. I mean your other grandmother, Mrs. Clayton."

The news was so huge, it barely sank in. People who won the lottery probably felt the same way.

"That's the best present you could have given me." She couldn't stop the tears that now ran down her chin. Cissy rarely cried during her sessions. That was on purpose to protect herself when the questions got too hard.

"She's special to you," he said.

"Very."

Grandmother was a formal sort of person, which was why the grandkids weren't allowed to call her Meemaw, Grammy, Mo-Mo, or any other nickname for grandmas. She was also one of the few people who still wore white gloves and thick tan hosiery all year-round, even in the hottest parts of summer.

She used to say Cissy was on the rude side of genteel, which was her way of commenting on her granddaughter's sarcastic nature. Cissy's grandmother grew up in a time when people didn't question their existence or what elders told them as fact. She also had old-fashioned ideas of what it meant to be a lady and tried her best to pass on this important knowledge to Cissy so she was prepared to live in the grown-up world.

Although her grandmother could be stern, Cissy liked how orderly the woman's life was, down to the proper way they ate dinner and only watched educational television programs that could enrich their minds. After one holiday dinner, when Cissy was thirteen, she had refused to sit on her daddy's lap for a group photo in front of Grandmother's Christmas tree. When her mama scolded her, she'd burst into tears and hid in the tiny room next to Ruth's that had been her mama's nursery when she was a baby. Only Grandmother and Ruth had come to check on her. It was the one time that Cissy considered telling her secret aloud. Recalling her daddy's threats, though, shut down that fleeting impulse. She said it was her monthly cycle that made her so emotional. The lie was something she considered adding to her List of Very Sad Things.

"I know I embarrass her sometimes," Cissy shared. "But she's never withheld her love."

Whenever she visited her grandmother, she'd try her best to keep her smart comments to a minimum because Grandmother's good opinion mattered so much. Others called her snobby, but Cissy just thought she had excellent boundaries and didn't want to share pieces of herself with people who didn't matter—meaning just about everybody outside family.

Cissy reminisced about the times she was allowed to stand in front of her grandmother's armoire and look at the clothes. They were mostly the color of Easter—yellows, greens, pinks—but that wasn't to say she didn't have excellent taste. Most of her purchases came from Lord & Taylor. She wore a lot of pale suits with matching hats and handbags, but always said a smart sweater or blazer could turn dungarees into an ensemble.

"My own wardrobe seemed drab and rumpled in comparison." Cissy looked down at the gray and lavender striped dress she had on, and smiled at the memories bubbling up. "Grandmother often remarked that my clothes and an ironing board weren't on a first-name basis."

"She seems like a very interesting woman," he said. "It will be nice to meet her in person."

"I wish you could meet Mama, too. She's not a bad person. I think her upbringing had a lot to do with her inability to show love in an outward way."

"What do you mean?" he asked.

"Well, Grandmother rarely showed any emotion, and I suspected she didn't show her love for Mama either and that made it even harder for Mama to show her love to us," Cissy said.

She often wondered if her grandmother

guarded her emotions even as a young girl. One day she asked Ruth. Cissy knew that the two of them grew up together, and friends know a lot about each other. Ruth seemed to grow sad at the question, but confided that Grandmother was quite different as a child, laughing so much that it brought on hiccups. She even peed her pants a few times. But Grandmother's own mother was relentless in "reforming" her into a proper lady, and did so by viciously pinching her arm until bruises were a common sight and long sleeves were necessary even in summer.

Cissy had asked Ruth if that's why her mama and grandmother didn't seem to get along, that perhaps Grandmother used the pinching technique herself. In response, Ruth had just asked if she wanted a slice of pie.

There was no one to tell Cissy happy stories about her mama's childhood, or that she, too, laughed until she got hiccups. In Cissy's memory, her mama had always been the same way. She remembered being very little and pushing against her mama's boundaries by trying to hug her every chance she got. And while her mama never pulled away, her body would get stiff as a fence post. It didn't take long before Cissy stopped trying. Instead, she loved on her baby sisters to the point that they would shriek for her to stop kissing them good night. She would pretend she was offended and leave their room; then they'd shriek for her to come back and kiss them some more.

"What are you smiling about?" Dr. Guttman asked.

"You got me to talk about some very hard things, but at the same time, here I am remembering some of the happiest times of my life."

The memories of those girls assured Cissy she'd done the right thing in protecting them.

Chapter 9

Janelle's husband used to say a name was worth something unless you got carried away and threw it around too much. She was sure she'd used "Do you know who you're talking to?" more than Beau would have liked, but affluence spoke louder than a whole string of lesser words and went a long way toward rectifying incompetence or poor customer service. She didn't think he'd mind that she intended to throw around the Clayton name with abandon when she reached the state hospital.

Cissy had been gone just two weeks when Janelle could no longer stand her own speculation about how the patients spent their days at the hospital. In Janelle's darkest moments she envisioned a madhouse, filthy and sinister, filled with neglected girls the world had forgotten. No matter how hard she tried, her imagination failed to conjure a Cissy who was safe, cared for, and unafraid. Even when Dr. Guttman assured her on the phone that Cissy was doing just fine.

Ruth and Caroline both chastised her when she announced her trip to Meridian.

"You're acting like I'm ninety years old." She had her sight and wits. Her reflexes were good.

She couldn't tell if they were more worried for her safety or the safety of others on the road.

"Caroline, if you're so worried, you can drive me," Janelle said.

"You know I can't," she whined.

"You *won't*. There's a difference. In any case, I'm a grown woman and I can go where I please."

Once Janelle was behind the wheel, her stomach felt more settled than it had since before the shooting. Action can do that to a person when everything else feels beyond one's control. She suspected that's why Ruth had rearranged the kitchen cupboards twice that week and baked seven pies for the church bazaar.

She wished she'd remembered to get gasoline on Saturday. Most stations were closed on Sunday except the Texaco station, which was in the opposite direction of where she was heading. Still, she needed gas and it wouldn't hurt to visit a bit with Joe Beard, the owner, who insisted on pumping gas and checking the oil himself. Cissy had nicknamed him Texaco Joe when she was just four years old and the name stuck.

When Janelle pulled up, the car's tires triggered the chime inside the mechanic's bay, which sent Joe running out to greet her. Only in his mid-sixties, Joe looked closer to ninety. The cancer had whittled away both meat and muscle, and he had to punch additional notches in his belt to cinch up his pants. He used to be a lightweight boxing champion, but illness seemed to be winning the fight now. Still, he was proud of the old days. Two cauliflower ears and a drooping eyelid were prized as much as his championship belt hanging over the station door.

"Mrs. Clayton, so good to see you, ma'am." He leaned against the Cadillac to open the gas cap. "Fill 'er up today?"

"Yes, Joe, please. I'm headed to Meridian and don't want to risk running out of gas," she said.

"Meridian? Isn't that where they put your granddaughter?" he asked. "I hope she's doing all right."

Good. A friend. Now that Janelle was out of the house again, she'd have to learn to face the awkward silence right before acquaintances or strangers offered their condolences, pity, or disgust. She'd perfected a visage of disdain that masked any hint at hopelessness or sorrow or panic. She longed for an iron gut to match. Maybe that would come with time and practice.

"I'm going to check on her today." Janelle handed over cash to pay for the gas. Beau never liked credit and she'd fallen into the same habit after he passed. "I'll tell her you said hello."

"Please do, ma'am. She's a good girl."

"Yes, she is." He'd given Janelle a treasure in

that simple assessment. She waved and pulled away.

On the drive, Janelle drew in bottomless breaths until her lungs burned from overuse. With every breath she savored a freedom Cissy no longer enjoyed. She pondered the other freedoms Cissy gave up to be rid of her father. Her granddaughter would have learned to drive this summer, perhaps accepted an invitation to a boy-girl social. She'd have walked down Main Street, browsed shops, and purchased an ice-cream sundae with her allowance. Only Cissy could decide if the exchange was fair.

The hospital seemed segregated from the city, its back to hayfields and low woods. Grateful to be done with the driving, Janelle still questioned whether it would be easier to turn and run. Cissy had no idea about her visit unless Dr. Guttman had mentioned it. Janelle could even rest a spell at a coffee shop. She idled for a minute at the oddly welcoming entrance, a stone wall covered with honeysuckle, before the guard in the gate house walked toward the car.

"Ma'am? Are you lost?" he asked.

"No, sir. I'm not. I'm here to see my grand-daughter," she said, and he waved her through the gate.

Even though Janelle had sat lost in her thoughts for the three-hour drive, she didn't feel collected, so she puttered down the drive as slowly as the car would go. The extensive grounds were verdant, even in the severest of droughts. Why waste taxpayer dollars watering a lawn so few people saw or walked on?

In the bright sunlight, the hospital wasn't sinister, and she felt somewhat embarrassed about the irrational fears that plagued her all week. The building looked more like a county courthouse with massive red granite bricks giving it a chiseled, stately air. The steps proved challenging given the stiffness of her muscles, but the coolness of the hall revived her.

The hallway led to a modest but tidy waiting area near a sweeping staircase. A nondescript nurse at the front desk greeted Janelle curtly as if she were an intruder.

"I'm Mrs. Beauregard Clayton from Biloxi. I'm here for a tour of the hospital." Beads of perspiration dotted her upper lip. She leaned across the nurse's desk and grabbed a tissue to blot it dry.

"I don't see anything in the schedule. Did you call ahead to arrange the visit?"

"No, I did not. But there shouldn't be a problem."

"Well, ma'am, there is a problem. We have rules, and you can't just walk right in and demand a tour." The nurse picked up the phone.

Janelle didn't wait to hear who she was calling. Bravado fueled a second wind. With a straight back, she ascended the staircase anchoring the building and proceeded down a hall to the right. She needed to find someone who had more authority than the uncooperative woman behind the desk. At the first locked door, she removed a glove so her knock could be heard on the metal. When no one answered, she pushed a button on the wall next to the door, which sounded a buzzer. A man in a white uniform opened the door a few inches.

"I'm here to see Cissy Pickering," she said. "She's in the women's ward."

Before he could answer, the front desk nurse bounded up behind Janelle and grabbed her elbow.

"Now, dear," Janelle said through clenched teeth. "You don't want to do that, I assure you." The nurse released her arm and backed away, panting her indignation, but unable to hide her fear.

Janelle walked down the opposite hallway, knocking on doors until someone had the good sense to call the head administrator. More astute than his subordinates, Mr. Carnell apologized for the nurse's behavior and cleared his schedule to personally give her a tour of the facility.

When Janelle entered the large recreational room where several girls watched television, Cissy sprinted to her side.

"Grandmother, I'm so happy you're here!

Everyone, this is my grandmother!" she called out to the other patients in the room. They ignored Cissy's jubilant introduction.

"I promised I'd come. After all, I want to be sure you're being treated well."

"I'm fine, Grandmother." Cissy held both of Janelle's hands in hers. "I'm making friends and I see a doctor every day. He's from New York and sort of odd, but I like him."

Dr. Guttman. Janelle had enjoyed her calls with him to check on Cissy's progress. Something in his words gave her great comfort, as if he cared personally for her granddaughter.

"And how is the food?" Janelle asked.

Cissy frowned and rolled her eyes. "I'm sure they do the best they can, but most meals would benefit from a splash or two of Tabasco."

Sensing Mr. Carnell wanted to continue, Janelle assured Cissy she'd be back to visit on her way out.

"Please don't go yet!"

"I must finish the tour." She moved her arms to unlock Cissy's embrace.

"You're not missing much," she said, and pouted.

"Cissy, please go sit down." Janelle hadn't known her to be a petulant child, but perhaps the rushed visit had pushed her limits.

Mr. Carnell managed a weak smile at the exchange before leading Janelle toward the sleeping rooms. The hospital prided itself on offering private rooms on this particular ward, but pride wasn't warranted in her opinion. While she could see a benefit to having some privacy, there wasn't much else the room offered. The space, devoid of color and light, seemed severe compared to someone as colorful as Cissy.

"Can the patients have personal items in their rooms? A picture frame, a stuffed animal perhaps?" Janelle already knew the answer from the barren rooms they'd passed.

"We like to limit personal items because we don't have the staff to ensure dangerous items aren't accidentally sent to a patient. We also can't be held responsible for theft among the young women." The administrator seemed frustrated, as if he'd answered that question a hundred times.

"I am going to bring Cissy some art paper and pastels the next time I'm here," she said. "Please inform the staff of the exception. And let them know I might need to visit outside of the scheduled visiting hours and days. I don't want there to be a scene."

Janelle turned away from Mr. Carnell to deny him an opportunity to answer. He had to scurry behind her to catch up to her efficient gait. When they reached the shared bathroom facility, he called out from the doorway to ensure no patients were inside.

After entering the cavernous space, Janelle was startled by the distorted image of herself in the stainless-steel rectangles impersonating as mirrors.

"For safety reasons," Mr. Carnell said. His tinny voice ricocheted off the porcelain and tile, magnifying in sound and intensity.

"Of course," she whispered, her heart as hollow as the bathroom's acoustics.

Rust stains marred the sinks and bathtubs, and she tried to ignore the steady drip from a leaky faucet.

"Why are there no stalls for the commodes?" She shuddered to think of Cissy's embarrassment, or any of the young women for that matter.

"Mrs. Clayton, the hospital wards are designed with the safety of the patients in mind," he said, and patted her forearm. "Believe me, they get used to the informality of a shared bathroom quite quickly. And even if we wanted to, the hospital has very limited resources that can be better spent elsewhere."

His condescension infuriated her. "How much do you need?" She withdrew a checkbook from her handbag.

"I . . . I don't know what you mean," he stuttered.

"I'm going to write you a check for whatever amount you deem necessary to have stalls built around the commodes. I will also hire the contractor myself if you don't believe you can make this a priority."

She and Mr. Carnell stood almost eye to eye. His beet-red face gave away his embarrassment but not his next move. Janelle braced for what she suspected would be the first of many battles with the man, and she expected to win them all.

"As you wish, Mrs. Clayton. Shall we look at the cafeteria now?" he asked, pointing to the door. She followed him out, grateful that he'd apparently given up any pretense of argument.

While the hospital was austere, it was far better than Janelle's nightmares. She couldn't deny that her granddaughter received adequate care. After the tour, she backtracked to the recreation room to find Cissy pacing near the far wall. Eyes down, lips moving, Cissy had turned to a counting game to pass the time until Janelle returned.

"You came back!" A wide smile overtook her face.

"Don't be silly, child. Of course I came back. I promised I would." She hadn't meant the words to sound harsh, but her mood had soured thinking of the tedious drive back to Biloxi. Plus, she felt flushed and slightly nauseated.

Disappointed that Janelle couldn't stay for supper, Cissy insisted on showing her all the books in the makeshift library in one corner of the recreation room. In just one week, she'd crafted a reading schedule, anticipating when she'd finish reading what was available. Apparently, Cissy already thought of her stay as long term. She'd even asked for school books so she wouldn't get behind in her studies in the fall.

Cissy prolonged their goodbye until Janelle shared her fear of driving on the highway after dark. She didn't turn around after she gave Cissy a last hug and kiss. At least Cissy was safe, but was that enough? Janelle thought of a brightly colored song bird locked away in a cage, a sheet draped over it to conceal all light.

"How did she look? What was her frame of mind?" Caroline's questions peppered Janelle the minute she entered the house.

"May I please have a chance to remove my gloves and have a drink before the inquisition?" she answered, weary from the return trip from Meridian.

Caroline followed a few steps behind her, imploring her to pay attention.

"Just stop already!" The vitriol in Janelle's voice startled them both. She was on edge from the long drive, exhausted by the monotonous landscape, drained by the effort it took to leave Cissy. The court had required that someone from the sheriff's office deposit Cissy at the hospital, sparing them the pain they'd feel leaving her there without family or friends or hope. Today, Janelle's heart had screamed for mercy when she loosened the girl's grip and said she had to leave.

Cissy had said she understood and quickly wiped a stray tear. She'd bucked up as she'd been instructed countless times by her parents and grandparents when something was difficult to bear. Janelle cringed remembering the number of times she'd told Caroline the same thing. *Don't show your emotion; it's not becoming of a lady.*

Immersed in her own hypocrisy, Janelle had wept with abandon as she pulled the car past the hospital's stone entrance. Blinded by the rainstorm of heartache, she had stayed on the side of the road until she could safely get back on the highway.

"Mother, you needn't bite my head off," Caroline admonished. "I'm just worried about Cissy."

"Are you? Really? You're worried about a lying bitch?" She flung her daughter's previous accusations at her.

"What's wrong with you?" Caroline wailed. "Why would you bring that up? We all said things that day we shouldn't have."

Janelle's hand began to shake so mightily that the stiff drink she'd just poured sloshed about in the heavy lead crystal highball glass. She set it on the coffee table with a loud clank and slumped into the sofa. Anger nipped at every nerve ending in her body. She had done nothing; nothing to spare her granddaughter the horrors at her daddy's hand, and now a different kind of horror, institutionalized with the feeble-minded and insane. Why had Janelle agreed to a psychiatric hospital? Perhaps Cissy could have won a jury trial. Then she'd be home with all of them. And if Caroline wouldn't have her, Cissy could have stayed with Janelle.

"What happened today, Mother?" Caroline sat on the sofa, holding her mother's hand even though she tried to pull away.

"She's well. She's taken care of. Where are Lily and Jessie?"

"They're with Ruth out back at the picnic table having supper. Tell me about the hospital. Please." Caroline's voice softened. Janelle guessed they were both trying to calm themselves.

"The hospital is fine. It's clean. The staff seems very professional," Janelle said. The balls of her feet burned with exhaustion. She removed her shoes and rubbed her swollen feet against the tight nap of the rug.

"And Cissy?"

"I don't know. Content, I guess. She was happy to see me and wished I could stay longer. She asked about you and the girls."

"Is she eating well?" Caroline asked, chewing the corner of her thumbnail.

Janelle relayed how Cissy had joked about the blandness of the food in front of the head administrator, and that brought a shadow of a smile to Caroline's face. Janelle worried more about Caroline's lack of appetite. She'd lost so much weight that her pants hung low on her hips, slack and awkward like a child in a grown woman's clothes.

Before Caroline could ask another question, the screen door to the kitchen swung open and Lily and Jessie raced into the living room. Sweaty ginger curls framed their sunburned faces and grape soda stains ringed their lips. When they saw Janelle, Lily jerked to a stop, then grabbed her sister by the collar to stop her dead in her tracks.

"Grandmother, you're home," Lily said, catching her breath. "We didn't mean to run in the house."

Her apologetic tone shouldn't have surprised Janelle. For most of the girls' lives, their grand-mother had been more likely to give a reprimand than a hug or kiss. She had always kept them at arm's length, thinking she was just respecting Caroline's place as their mother. The truth was that interacting with her granddaughters scared her. They were blank slates, impressionable. Janelle worried her hardness would affect them the way it had affected Caroline.

"Girls, why don't you give your grandmother a hug?" Caroline's request caught all three of them off guard. After a split second of hesitation, Lily and Jessie squeezed themselves between the coffee table and sofa and leaned down tentatively, not quite sure where to put their arms. They smelled of sunshine and perspiration. Janelle pulled them closer and lifted their blouses to tickle their rib cages.

A child's unbridled joy was a heady perfume, one now filling the entire room, pushing out the fear Janelle and Caroline had talked around. She wanted to bottle that laughter, to save it for the deepest part of night when black melancholy made its rounds.

"Tell me about your day," Janelle instructed. The uncharacteristic hug had put them at ease and they leaned against her sides, arms draped around her neck. There had been snail races, which were boring, and Ruth catching a dish rag on fire near the stove, which was exciting. They'd collected bouquets of dandelions in mason jars and lined the front stoop to welcome Janelle home. They saved her two chicken wings because Ruth told them those were her favorite.

"Miss Ruth said you went to visit Cissy," Jessie said.

Lily leaned across and pinched her sister so roughly, Jessie let out a yowl.

"Shut up, stupid! Mama said we're not supposed to talk about Cissy," Lily warned.

Caroline's eyes brimmed. Maybe she regretted the harsh mandate she'd given the girls. Janelle suspected she'd not known how to hold on to her anger at Cissy while the girls loved her so. Erasing Cissy from their conversations might have seemed the only answer a month ago. Two weeks ago, Janelle had asked Ruth to ask Bess how Caroline had been treating the girls. Ruth suggested she visit them more often to find out firsthand rather than enlisting Bess's help as a spy. Plus, Bess would have reported the request to Caroline and it would have been still another reason for conflict.

"Oh, girls, that's not exactly what your mama meant when she said not to talk about Cissy," Janelle said. "She's very sad about your sister and thought you'd all be less sad if you didn't say her name out loud."

"I don't know why Cissy would kill Daddy," Jessie said. "She was his favorite."

Caroline bristled visibly.

"Why do you say that?" Janelle asked.

"Daddy used to play chess with Cissy sometimes late at night," Jessie said, her tongue working to erase the sticky purple ring around her lips.

"What do you mean, Jessie?" Caroline spoke cautiously, as if her eagerness for an answer would render the child mute.

"I went to potty one night and saw Daddy coming from Cissy's room. I asked him what he was doing and he said Cissy and him were playing chess."

"Go on," Janelle urged. Jessie furrowed her brow, obviously confused by their interest.

"I asked if he'd play with me and he said Cissy was special because she was the oldest and that chess was their special time," Jessie said. "He said it was a secret and asked if I was a big girl who could keep secrets."

Caroline jumped up from the armchair, banging her shin against the coffee table before bolting out the front door. The screen door swung wide before slapping against the jamb.

Jessie's eyes opened wide to take in the scene. Her chest rose and fell, slowly at first, then faster until she was crying and hiccupping all at once.

"Shush now, girl. You'll make yourself sick," Janelle crooned into her ear. "What's wrong?"

"I made Mama mad because I didn't keep Daddy's secret," Jessie cried into her shoulder. "I *am* a big girl, I promise I am."

"Your mama isn't mad." Janelle looked up to see Ruth standing in the doorway to the dining room, a lemon meringue pie in one hand and a knife in the other. She'd heard the conversation and tears cut silver lines down her face. She looked at each of them in turn. Her lips parted, but she seemed to think twice about speaking. Janelle clung to Jessie even tighter.

"Lily, why don't you go help Ruth cut the pie and pour everyone a glass of cold milk," she suggested. "We'll let your mama go on home and you girls can sleep over."

Janelle heard Caroline's car start down the driveway. She'd already had the same idea. Janelle regretted she'd not run after her, offered some solace. Jessie's revelation stunned them all, but it had cut Caroline the deepest. As the weeks wore on, Janelle suspected clues like these chipped away at Caroline's tenuous belief in her husband's innocence.

"Grandmother, wake up."

Janelle felt hot breath on her face, then a gentle push on her shoulder.

"Caroline, go back to bed. You've just had a bad dream." She wanted to stay in the deep place she'd drifted off to after fitful hours of begging sleep to come. She hid her face under the coverlet.

"Grandmother, it's Lily, please wake up."

Janelle opened her eyes, but with difficulty. Lily stood illuminated by the moonlight that pierced through the lace curtains, a child specter in a white cotton shirt that swallowed her body.

"What is it? Is something wrong?" Switching on the lamp, she squinted against its glare, but could still make out Lily's wet cheeks and crimson eyes. "Did you have a nightmare?"

"Grandmother, may I please sleep with you?"

"Oh, honey, I don't know . . ." Her immediate

resistance had deep roots, seventy-plus years of fears and insecurities twisted and tangled as tightly as her nightgown around her legs. Yet, as Lily stood before her, hopeful and wanting, she relented.

"Just this once," Janelle said.

Instead of going to the other side of the bed, Lily pulled back the coverlet on Janelle's side, nudging her to the middle. Janelle curved her body around her granddaughter's and reached over to extinguish the light in their eyes. Her hand stayed lifted in the air just above Lily's head, unsure or unable to soothe her anxieties and fears. She rested it on her shoulder instead.

Not expecting the sleepover, the girls had no pajamas and had to make do with cotton dress shirts Janelle had kept even after she'd given most of Beau's clothing to the church thrift store. She wanted something to remember her husband by and now her grandchild lay next to her, where Beau should be, wearing a shirt she fooled herself still held his scent.

"I think I know why Cissy killed Daddy," she whispered deep into the pillow they shared, releasing the secret into the down. Lily's shoulders, wracked with dry weeping, bumped Janelle's hand off and she lost her breath as well. She didn't think she could bear to have this conversation with her twelve-year-old grand-daughter.

Lily told her that the week before, she'd been in the library restroom alone when two teenagers entered and began talking about Cissy. She'd lifted her feet up onto the toilet so they wouldn't know she was there. "I was so afraid, Grandmother. They said horrible things, but I couldn't leave or they'd know I was listening," she said.

The girls were from Cissy's class at St. John's High School and they would have started eleventh grade together this fall. Lily said they'd used some words she didn't know, but she understood enough to know her daddy had done something bad.

"They said the F word, Grandmother," she offered in a tiny voice. "Does that mean Daddy touched her private places?"

Janelle gasped. The child was too young to have to worry about boys much less incest. She had no comfort to offer Lily and lay in the dark, ashamed.

"Grandmother, please tell me it's not true," she implored.

"I wish I could, Lily. I wish I could," she whispered. "None of us can explain why your daddy did the things he did. He was a very sick man."

"What do you mean by sick?"

"Well, sometimes people have a sickness in their mind that makes them not know right from wrong."

"But why? Why did she have to shoot him? Why didn't Cissy tell Mama?"

"I suspect she was afraid. She didn't know if she could trust anyone." Janelle would never tell Lily that Cissy believed her silence was protecting her sisters.

The summer heat choked Biloxi long into the night and made the contact with Lily's body feel uncomfortable. Her sticky legs kicked and kicked to rid themselves of the sheet and coverlet, which now lay bunched up between them.

"So you believe Cissy?" Lily puffed the words, catching her breath after the battle with the sheets.

"I do."

"But why? Mama doesn't."

Janelle's first thought was to lie, to assure Lily her mama did believe Cissy. But Lily had soaked in every hushed conversation and everything that remained unspoken since the day Cissy had killed her father. Lily could probably read all of them, ferreting out what they thought they'd concealed so expertly.

"I see the truth in Cissy's eyes. I feel it in my heart," Janelle said. "Your mama knows the truth, but it hurts too much to admit it. She loved your daddy very much. It's hard for any of us to think he was capable of hurting anyone."

Lily's breathing grew steadier and her shoulders slacked. Janelle imagined her grateful to let go of at least some of the tension that had held her a silent prisoner.

"Will Cissy ever come home?" Lily asked, stifling a yawn.

"I hope so, dear."

A loose floor board in the hallway moaned.

"Jessie, is that you?" Janelle sat up and squinted into the dark. A shape stepped into the room; larger than a child, smaller than Ruth.

"It's me, Mother." Caroline's voice floated toward her.

"I thought you'd gone home," she said.

"I drove around for a while, but I was worried about the girls. Lily's not with Jessie in the guest room. Is she with you?"

"Yes, Mama, I'm here," Lily said. "I was scared, so Grandmother let me sleep with her."

"She did, huh?" Caroline's words hung accusingly.

Janelle's mind returned to those nights she'd turned away Caroline, instructing her to go back to her own bed and face her night terrors alone, or to call for Ruth when she needed comforting. She'd probably rekindled the pain that Caroline felt as a child.

"Grandmother, could Mama sleep with us, too?" Lily asked.

"If she'd like." Janelle held her breath, afraid of how her daughter would respond.

Caroline stood still, a statue with features

144

obscured by the black night no matter how much Janelle strained to make them out.

"I'd like you to," Janelle said. "Climb in."

Caroline padded across the floor and slipped off her clam diggers before getting into the bed from Beau's side. Clad in just a T-shirt and panties, she lay on top of the covers. Janelle reached for her daughter's hand and Caroline allowed it. Lily turned and grabbed Janelle's other hand, the three of them lined up like sardines in a can. This moment they shared was only possible because of Cissy's crime, but Janelle couldn't help but savor the intimacy she'd not been brave enough to ask for with her daughter and granddaughters.

"Before we fall asleep, could we play a game?" Lily asked. Nothing was normal about this evening and a game made as much sense as anything else.

"What kind of game?" Caroline asked. She tightened her fingers and Janelle squeezed back.

"Let's each say what we miss about Cissy," Lily said. "I'll go first! I miss her counting games. Oh, oh . . . and how she gave us slurpy kisses. You next, Grandmother."

"I miss watching that girl eat coconut cream pie," she said. "Lord, I've never seen another human being consume so much sugar and never gain an ounce."

The mattress bounced with Lily's giggles.

"What about you, Caroline?" Janelle knew how

145

difficult the interchange must be for her, but she prayed Caroline would answer, if only for Lily's sake.

"I miss being able to tell *all* my girls good night," she admitted in a tight voice.

They listened to each other's breathing, the cicadas that sang despite the late hour, and the cock that could not tell time and crooned in the distance.

"Let's all say good night to Cissy together," Lily pleaded. "On three, okay? One, two, three . . ."

"Good night, Cissy," they chimed.

Chapter 10

As soon as Caroline and the girls left the house, Janelle showered and dressed. Two important errands weighed on her mind: buying art supplies and some warmer clothing for Cissy. Ruth suggested she ask Caroline for some of Cissy's winter sweaters, but she wanted things that held no memories of her life in that house.

"You know you hate going out in public," Ruth reminded her sharply. "Folks are still talking, and you always return home upset and regretting you'd gone out."

Janelle stood in the foyer ready to leave while Ruth lingered in the doorway to the kitchen, her gingham apron covered in flour from her morning baking.

"Are my moods getting to you, Ruth?"

"No, ma'am. I've lived with them fifty-odd years, so we're all well acquainted."

Janelle laughed out loud, which startled both of them. They shared Ruth's joke a few more seconds until their giggles petered out.

"Nice to hear you laugh, Mrs. Clayton," she said, wiping her eyes with her apron. "It's been awful heavy in the house since . . . well, I just worry about you."

"Don't worry about me, old woman." Janelle

walked right up to Ruth and pretended to hug her. Ruth squealed to get away.

"I'm covered in flour," she chastised. "You'll mess up that fancy suit you're wearing."

Janelle used her clothes as armor for the battles she imagined waited outside her door, as if a Chanel pantsuit had the properties of steel. Preferential treatment was a given. The real value was in the distance it created between her and most of the world. Untouchable. Set apart. Strange that linen and cashmere and wool would give her a sense of self she had lacked before she took the Clayton name a lifetime ago.

Janelle remembered the first time she met Beau. He and a couple of law school buddies had been fishing on the pier when they witnessed a fight she'd foolishly picked with three high school boys. She'd been walking on the beach when she came upon the teens taunting a homeless man who tried to shield himself from their jabs with a large piece of cardboard he had been using as protection from the sun. Janelle ran up to them, kicking sand and yelling to high heaven. She stood chest-high to them, and the largest of the three put his hand on her forehead as she flailed her arms. Her leg, however, had a longer reach and made contact with the boy's groin. He fell to the ground clutching his injured pride. Although Janelle had taken him down, and was quite proud of herself in the moment, she hadn't given thought to the other two. Within seconds, a fist to her jaw spun her around. She fell flat on the wet sand, grit in her bloodied mouth.

Although a hundred yards away, Beau and his friends took off like Roman candles, chasing the nasty teens clear down Beach Boulevard. After a few minutes, Beau jogged back to where she sat on the sand, sniffling and rubbing her jaw. He sported a bloody nose, but assured Janelle the other guy would think twice before hitting a girl again.

"Thanks," she had mumbled, and dug her toes deep into the sand. He sat down next to her, their arms brushing together slightly. "I don't know my limits sometimes."

When Beau asked about the homeless man, she said she hadn't noticed him leave. Probably taking up residence closer to the fish vendors down the beach, where he wouldn't be so isolated.

Beau shook his head and laughed.

"What's so damn funny?" she'd asked.

"I don't mean to laugh, miss, but I've never seen so much fire in such a small package," he'd said. When he removed his T-shirt, Janelle had blushed to see his bare chest and the sparse patches of hair around his nipples.

Mesmerizing he'd called her as he wiped the blood and sand from her chin with his T-shirt. They sat for almost three hours, side by side, nursing their wounds, looking at the ocean, and telling the stories of their young lives. She never suspected that within the year she'd come to find out what money and power and a good name could do for her, or that they'd become the only things she could rely on now.

Except Ruth. Janelle could rely on Ruth.

"Are you having a seizure?" Ruth asked. "You look a thousand miles away."

"I expect I was at least a thousand miles away," she said, and changed the subject. "Does this outfit need a hat?"

Without waiting for agreement, Janelle turned and made her way up the stairs and to her room. The pale yellow felt Breton with navy grosgrain trim would match her yellow linen suit perfectly. She pulled the dresser chair up to the armoire so she could reach the familiar floral hat box, but felt light-headed and unstable on the chair. She knocked the hat box onto the floor trying to gain her equilibrium.

"Damn it." Janelle stepped down, picked up the hat, and perched it on her head, surveying the ensemble in the full-length mirror. Her mood didn't match the sunshine yellow of her outfit. She hoped the shopping trip to find Cissy a sweater would take her mind off things.

Janelle would have felt most comfortable shopping at Lord & Taylor—the selection was larger and the salesladies knowledgeable—but the Saturday morning crowds were off-putting under normal circumstances. With Richard's death so prominent in the newspapers, she had no desire to face the murmurs and stares of Biloxians who considered themselves Cissy's jury. Rosebuds, a small ladies boutique on Water Street, would be more private, although the prices were almost double those in a department store. At least Janelle knew Rosalie, the owner, who'd likely be sympathetic or at least closemouthed.

Janelle parked the Caddy at the curb right in front of the building's large glass window. SUMMER BLOWOUT SALE had been painted across it in bright orange, so she couldn't tell if anyone else was in the store. No matter, she'd be in and out in a few minutes. A tinkling bell announced her entry and she quickly scanned the store. Two women, possibly in their sixties, picked through a sales rack at the rear of the store, their faces too flushed with summer heat to be cooled by the weak window air-conditioning unit. Their voices dropped to a whisper and they turned their backs to Janelle.

"May I help you?" The young lady behind the counter announced Janelle's arrival too loudly and with false gaiety. Janelle didn't recognize the clerk, who obviously lacked the upbringing or class to carry off her role. Rosalie had always staffed the store herself, but didn't appear to be in the shop.

"I'm looking for a sweater, with large pockets, a woman's size small preferably," Janelle said.

"Ma'am, people just don't buy sweaters in August in Mississippi," she sneered as she finished up some paperwork. Her wide-set jaw moved side to side as she popped a wad of gum.

Once she got a good look at Janelle, though, stains of embarrassment crept up her neck. She'd worked retail long enough to surmise Janelle might be someone you worked your butt off to please. She stammered an offer to check the storeroom. A few fall and winter items had arrived, but were still boxed, she said. Janelle thanked her and said she'd browse in the meantime.

The store seemed chaotic in its bright colors and cramped racks. She hadn't remembered it feeling so intimate on other visits. In the past, Rosalie had grouped clothing by designer and allowed adequate space around displays. The upholstered settee was gone, as was the complimentary lemonade and cookies. Had the shop changed owners?

Janelle flipped through a rack of blouses, looking at everything and nothing at once, her eyes and hands uncoordinated, working independently. She moved closer to the other shoppers, hoping to overhear their conversation, or rather, hoping to disprove her suspicion they whispered about her.

Perspiration dotted Janelle's upper lip and she wiped it away with a handkerchief. She scanned the store for a chair, but none was to be found. Dizzy and a little nauseated, she thought of sitting on a bench in the fitting room when the clerk emerged from the storeroom, waving a garment above her head.

"I found something that might work," she said, out of breath.

Janelle wondered how the clerk could have become so exhausted in ten minutes of opening boxes, but she appreciated her industriousness. The sweater practically glowed on the counter, robin's egg blue with wide plastic buttons and deep pockets, perfect to hold the small notebook and pen Cissy carried with her everywhere. The clerk started to tell her the price, but Janelle interrupted. "I'll take it. And I need a gift box," she said. Janelle long ago stopped looking at price tags or feeling shocked at what things cost.

"Cash or credit, Mrs. Clayton?" The salesgirl's eyes widened and her mouth turned up in a slight smile as if she was the keeper of a secret.

"Do we know each other?" Janelle asked to be polite, but regretted extending the conversation.

"I've seen you in the paper recently," she said, and looked over at the two other shoppers who'd moved closer to the counter. "You're the grandmother of that little girl who killed her daddy."

"You're mistaken," Janelle said.

"I read about the murder, too," one of the shoppers said. "I heard the daddy was having relations with the girl and that made her crazy enough to kill. Isn't that right?"

"She's locked away in the nuthouse now," the other one added.

Janelle would have given anything to summon the courage she had on the beach as a twenty-year-old, to hit and pinch and bite and kick these women who distorted and mocked Cissy's suffering. Instead, she slapped a hundred-dollar bill on the counter and yanked the sweater from the clerk, not bothering with change or a box or bag. She bristled to remember Ruth's foreboding, but she could blame no one but herself.

Janelle replayed the incident in the boutique over and over on the drive home. The shame of inaction enveloped her. Should she have pushed over racks, screamed at the top of her lungs? She fooled herself into thinking she could have retaliated with something as outrageous as their remarks. No response would have been enough to shatter the kaleidoscope of laughing eyes and malevolent smiles overlapping and twisting out of control in Janelle's mind.

"Stupid, stupid, stupid old woman," she mumbled, and jammed the accelerator with the anger her limbs couldn't contain.

The siren and lights behind her broke her trance. She pulled over, not surprised her day spiraled in this direction. Janelle rolled down the window and the heat rushed in, displacing the cooler air pumped through the vents toward her face.

"Ma'am, please turn off the ignition," the officer said.

"I'm sorry, sir. Was I speeding?"

"Yes, ma'am, I'd call going fifty miles per hour in a thirty zone speeding, but I'm more concerned about the stop sign you just shot through."

Janelle rested her head on the steering wheel. She longed to shut out the voices of the women in the boutique, but their obscene faces still danced in her memory.

"Ma'am, are you feeling okay?" he asked.

"Oh, yes, young man, I'm fine. It's just . . . Well, I'm a little embarrassed. I've never been pulled over before," she said, even though she felt anything but fine.

"License please?"

The sun bounced off the liquid mercury of his sunglasses and her reflection stared back. Her tongue became cottony and useless. She handed him her purse. Janelle just wanted to get home to drink a seltzer to calm her upset stomach.

"I don't need your whole purse, ma'am. Please just remove your license," he instructed.

Her clumsy hands rifled past a lipstick tube

and tissues to find her wallet. Her gloves made it impossible to grab the thin plastic edge of the license, so she handed him the entire wallet hoping he could read it through the clear plastic sleeve.

"Mrs. Clayton, I didn't recognize you. I knew your husband, ma'am," he said. "Judge Clayton was a great man."

His words drifted out of her reach, muddled and foreign. She stared at his strange lips, thinking she should ask him to call Caroline or Ruth. Before she could say anything, the officer handed back the wallet and tipped his hat.

"Please be more careful, Mrs. Clayton," he said. "Or next time, you'll get more than just a friendly warning."

Confused, Janelle watched him return to his police car, start it, and pass her with a wave of his hand. No ticket? She rolled up the window, wishing the ringing in her ears would stop. Her eyes closed. She needed just a rest.

A loud rap on the window startled her awake. The teenage girl could have been Cissy's age, but she was petite and curvy, her skin browned from too much sunbathing.

"Excuse me, are you all right?" she shouted through the glass.

The molten pavement in front of Janelle resembled funhouse mirrors, wavy and distorted. The girl, too, appeared shapeless.

"You can't stay in a car in this heat with the windows rolled up," she said, tapping the glass harder now. "You don't look well. I have a car. Let me drive you to the hospital."

The young woman pointed to a faded blue Volkswagen, rusted by too many years at the shore, idling in front of Janelle's Cadillac. She rolled down the window and the outside air felt strangely cool, the exhaust of the engine pungent in her nostrils.

"Oh no, dear. I'm not ill," she said, but doubt buzzed in her ear.

"What's your name, ma'am? Could I call someone?"

Because Janelle didn't know the answer to either question, she left her car by the side of the road and allowed the girl to lead her away.

They circled around Janelle's hospital bed like mourners at a coffin—Ruth and Caroline with bloodshot eyes and wet cheeks; Lily and Jessie with confusion creasing their young foreheads.

"I'm fine," Janelle insisted. "I had a touch of heat stroke."

"The lady who brought you to the hospital said you didn't know your name, Grandmother." Lily seemed close to tears.

Janelle turned her palms upward, and each granddaughter took a hand. Jessie hesitated, though, worried about the IV.

"You won't hurt me, Jessie. Grab ahold."

"You know my name?" she asked, lip trembling.

"Why, of course I know your name. And hers and hers and hers," Janelle pointed. "Caroline, Ruth, and Lily."

"What's our dog's name?" she pressed.

"You don't have a dog." She smiled for their benefit. "Any other questions on today's quiz?"

"What's your name?"

"Janelle Eileen Clayton," she said.

"Then why didn't you know your name before?" Lily asked. "That's bad, right?"

"When you get overheated, your brain can start to act funny," she said, turning to face each of them in turn. "It's easy to get confused. But there's no need to worry now. I'm all better."

Her family took no solace in a lighthearted explanation of something that could have turned out much worse. Yet, how could Janelle add more chaos to their lives? Richard dead, Cissy at a psychiatric hospital, all of them trying to figure out how to live in an alternative universe where the bizarre is expected and pain commonplace.

"You've been in and out of consciousness for a whole day, Mother. Just how exactly should we feel? Relieved that you know our names?" Caroline moved to the window, her rigid back to the others.

"Actually, yes. Be relieved I know my name

because I obviously didn't at one point," Janelle said, biting back.

"You're infuriating," Caroline mumbled loud enough for them all to hear.

"Ruth, please take the girls to the hospital cafeteria," Janelle said. "I bet you can find some custard or tapioca." Ruth set her jaw and looked unwilling to budge. The girls' grip on her hands didn't lessen. "Go now. I need to talk to your mother."

Heads down, the girls followed Ruth reluctantly. Janelle asked Caroline to pull up a chair next to the bed and she complied. Her daughter looked exhausted. Her matted hair and wrinkled blouse told Janelle she'd slept in the hospital room last night.

"Caroline, those girls can't take any more upheaval in their lives. For their sake, let's try to keep conversations about my health between the two of us."

"I don't think I can take any more, Mother." Caroline rested her head against the metal bed railing.

"You bear so much every day, both in your waking hours and nightmares. I'm sorry this episode adds more pain."

"Episode? You call a stroke an episode?" Caroline's eyes mirrored the panic and anger in her voice. "You could have died if that girl hadn't seen you on the side of the road."

"What would you have me do? Stay at home? Quit driving just in case something might happen to me?" Janelle felt attacked and loved in the same moment and struggled to reconcile the turmoil she'd caused in everyone's lives.

"Actually, yes. Stay at home. Don't drive around Biloxi. Don't drive to Meridian!"

Caroline's objection to the visit with Cissy last week crept into the light, ready to take form. Janelle reminded her they were talking about her health; that she'd not entertain Caroline's annoyance over the trip to inspect the psychiatric hospital.

"I'm not talking about Cissy. I'm saying you could've had the stroke on the highway," she said.

Caroline was right. Janelle could have caused an accident had she been driving. She could've hurt others. Being pulled over for speeding probably saved her life because she fainted while the car engine was off.

Oh, how she wished Caroline would just leave. Her body longed to relinquish gravity's hold and drift unencumbered. She was only seventy-two. She shouldn't feel this way. Yet, Beau died of a heart attack at seventy. From the bench, he witnessed atrocities beyond comprehension. Perhaps the day he died, Beau felt as she did right now; that nothing felt as right as giving up. Death didn't frighten her. She'd be with Beau again. One last obligation tied her to this world, though: Cissy. What would become of her if Janelle died? She closed her eyes, summoning memories to help her fight the urge to give up.

"Mother, what's wrong?" Caroline touched Janelle's forehead and she opened her eyes.

"I'm tired," she said. "I didn't mean to alarm you."

"Oh, Mother, it's not your fault. We're just so worried." Caroline traced her finger over the tape that held the IV needle.

"Are you counting my age spots?"

"I guess I never noticed them before," Caroline said in a faraway voice. "They're the perfect caramel color, larger versions of freckles almost."

"I rarely pay them any mind," Janelle lied. Vanity, maybe the fear of lost youth, had her wearing gloves most of the time in recent years, even in summer. The sun only darkened the spotting.

"They're kind of lovely." Caroline kissed the top of Janelle's hand and then pulled away, robbing her of the chance to savor the intimacy.

"Please take the girls home, Caroline," she said, hoping to clear the room of their awkward emotions. "I'm sure I'll be released tomorrow. Get some rest. Just remember to tell Jessie and Lily I'm okay."

Her daughter wiped her face with the back of a

shirt sleeve and smoothed her tangled hair. She stopped at the door, head bowed.

"I love you, Mother," she said, keeping her back to the bed.

"I know."

Unable to sleep, Janelle pulled herself inside out wondering why she hadn't told Caroline she loved her. In truth, Janelle and Caroline rarely said the words aloud. When had Janelle stopped thinking it was important? She always assumed Caroline knew. But Janelle couldn't deny the jealousy she felt when Caroline, as a toddler, would call their housekeeper "Mama Ruth." As Caroline grew older, Janelle spanked her whenever she used the term of endearment. Years later, she'd overhear Caroline say the hushed words to Ruth when they thought Janelle was not around.

Today, by looking at her complicated feelings for her daughter, Janelle skirted a truth she'd hidden since the day Cissy killed her daddy. For a while she'd convinced herself that Caroline's refusal to comfort her own daughter, to believe her when it counted the most, triggered Janelle's anger.

Alone, in a dark hospital room, she couldn't hide from the truth. She blamed Caroline for not knowing about the abuse, for not stopping it. She blamed her for every single day, week, month, and year Cissy kept her father's dirty little secret to protect her sisters. Janelle allowed Caroline to become the target of all the emotion she could no longer contain, the horrors she could no longer allow to live within her. She couldn't attack a dead man, but she could hate Caroline. Janelle hugged her chest to stop it from bursting.

"Ma'am, are you in pain?" A nurse had entered the room unnoticed. She adjusted the IV and then refilled Janelle's water cup.

"No pain," she lied, and took the straw placed near her parched lips.

"You're soaked," the nurse said, wiping her brow. "I'll change your sheets and pillowcase. You'll feel refreshed. Let me help you sit up a while."

Janelle shook her head, certain that a simple change in position would bring on an exhaustion from which she'd never recover.

"I need to see the doctor," Janelle said.

"Ma'am, he's not making rounds until later. Is there something I can get you?"

"You can get me the doctor. I want to see a doctor!" The order didn't come out as the powerful shout Janelle intended.

The well-meaning shushes for Janelle to relax just spurred her to fight harder. She pulled the IV from her hand and blood trickled down onto the sheet. When she tried to get out of bed, the nurse pressed her shoulders back onto the sheets, holding her down for a few seconds.

"I'll get the doctor if you promise to calm down."

Janelle nodded her agreement and the nurse left her, IV unhooked and bedding disheveled. A half hour passed before an older man knocked and then entered the room. Janelle didn't recognize him. The last doctor she had seen didn't look a day over twelve years old. This man's maturity gave her some comfort.

"I'm Dr. Stone, Mrs. Clayton." He moved the chair down toward the foot of the bed so she wouldn't have to strain sideways to look in his face. "I'm an oncologist."

"Ah . . . Not a stroke, then."

"Not in the technical sense. You had a pretty severe bout of heat stroke and you're slightly anemic," he said. "However, we detected some abnormalities in your blood panel. I'm recommending we proceed with tests right away. Shouldn't take more than a couple of days."

"Cancer."

"We don't know with certainty."

His jaw sported a day's growth of white bristles, but everything else about him appeared impeccably groomed, laundered, and detached. In contrast, Janelle felt unkempt and soiled and unprepared for this conversation.

"No tests," she muttered.

"Mrs. Clayton, I advise you to rethink your decision," he said. "Treatment can extend life for some months, even with the most aggressive blood cancers."

The abnormalities he'd found must have told a more complete story than he chose to share at the beginning of their conversation. Perhaps too much for an old woman with heat stroke to absorb.

"Months, huh," she said. "My family isn't to know."

"But, Mrs. Clayton . . ."

"It's my right."

Fatigue softened his hard features, or maybe she wanted to imagine he was concerned.

"Yes, it's absolutely your right, as is your decision to refuse treatment," he said. "I'm going to leave my card with you just in case. We can schedule the tests anytime."

He placed the business card under the edge of the water pitcher and bid her good afternoon. She managed a weak smile of thanks.

The card he left, bright white with raised dark blue lettering, had absorbed moisture from the pitcher. She didn't bother to read it before tearing it in two and dropping the pieces to the floor. Janelle pushed the call button to get the nurse's attention. Tapioca sounded good for supper. Or maybe even chocolate ice cream, if they had it.

Chapter 11

Caroline found Lily and Jessie in the hospital's almost empty cafeteria, running from table to table, removing napkins from their dispensers and then stuffing them back in again. She didn't bother reprimanding her daughters. The interaction with her mother earlier left her raw. She feared any admonishment of her own girls would come out too harsh or too loud. The fact that they could laugh and play just minutes after being so frightened for their grandmother's health made Caroline jealous.

Ruth waved her over to a table in the corner. Caroline sat down gingerly. Spending all night in a hospital room chair created aches a woman her age shouldn't be feeling yet. "You're letting them run wild. What would Mother think?"

"I let you run wild and you turned out okay." Ruth reached over and patted Caroline's hand.

Ruth's words and touch ignited emotion that Caroline refused to give into. What made Ruth think she had turned out okay? Caroline had a dead husband with a reputation tarnished beyond repair, a daughter locked away in a psychiatric ward for killing him, a town that treated her with contempt, and a mother who blamed her for it all.

"Woman, don't make me cry in a public

cafeteria." She glanced at the elderly couple in the far corner of the room. They were deep in conversation and not paying a lick of attention to the girls, or Ruth and Caroline's conversation.

"Stop worrying what folks think of you," Ruth said. "Besides, there's a lot of heartache in a place like this. Perhaps if you need a big cry, this is exactly where you should be doing it."

"Crying won't help anybody or change anything," Caroline said. She pointed at the can of Tab on the table. "Is that for me?"

Ruth nodded. "I should have bought you a milkshake. You're skinnier than the bony teenager I used to try to fatten up. You don't want to end up in the hospital yourself. Serve you right if they put you in the same room as your mama."

Jessie's and Lily's shrieks rang out in the cavernous room. Caroline and Ruth turned simultaneously and shushed them. The elderly couple looked up and glared before leaving.

"Is your mama sleeping now?" Ruth took her spoon and finished up the last couple of bites of ice cream the girls had left. Her eyes were red. From lack of sleep or crying, Caroline didn't know. Surely she felt the strain as acutely as they all did. She was part of the family.

"Mother asked me to take the girls home and to tell you to head on out as well."

"Just like that ornery woman to think she can boss me around," Ruth said. "Well, she's in no

168

position to do so today. I plan on sitting with her for a spell once you leave. Whenever I read Bible verses to her, she gets all uppity and it gives us both a good laugh."

Caroline caught her reflection in the window behind Ruth and grimaced. Last night, she hadn't slept a wink, but instead listened to the steady beeps of the machines and the ever-constant noises in the hallway. She desperately needed a change of clothes. At the very least, her hair needed brushing.

"I've been pretty angry at Bess," Caroline admitted.

"She said as much."

It shouldn't have surprised her that Bess and Ruth confided in each other, but Caroline suddenly felt like an object of gossip. "So, she ran to you to tattle on her mean employer?"

"Oh, girl. It's not like that."

Ruth's heavy sigh made Caroline feel even worse. "What's it like, then?"

"Her heart's been heavy," Ruth said. "She's feeling the same guilt all of us feel. That we let our girl down. I told her there's no sense in laying blame."

"But Mother does blame me!"

Lily and Jessie stopped dead in their tracks at the sound of Caroline's raised voice and the crack of her palms against the table. A familiar dread flooded their sweet faces. Jessie's bottom

169

lip trembled, and Lily hugged her close. Lily had grown so tall. Almost as tall as Cissy at that age.

Ruth flicked her hands at the girls. "Pay us no mind," she said. "Go on, now. Those napkins won't put themselves back."

Caroline laid her cheek against the tabletop, its surface cooling the heat in her face. Ruth stroked her hair slowly. It reminded Caroline of days long past when she'd confide her worst hurts to Ruth: not making the cheerleading squad as a freshman, a broken heel on a new pair of pumps, a boyfriend who wasn't paying enough attention. The silly, stupid worries of youth.

"You and your mama have to get right again," Ruth said. "I'm not saying it will be easy. If you put your energy toward Cissy, that'd be a start."

Caroline lifted her head. "Were Mother and I ever right?"

"That's silly talk," Ruth said. "Your mama loves you. Always has and always will."

"She's never shown it," Caroline said, angrily.

"That's more silly talk. What did you want? More hugs? More attention? She showed her love in other ways. You always had the finest clothes, a brand-new car when you were just in high school. And that wedding? My Lord."

"Those are *things,* Ruth, not love."

"Jesus, girl, my blood pressure is rising. *You* wanted those things."

"I want her to love me the way she loves Cissy," Caroline said.

Ruth got up and moved to Caroline's side. She guided Caroline's head to the warm crook of her neck and held her tight.

"She does, sweet girl. How I wish you knew that," Ruth cooed. "But Cissy needs our love more than anybody right now."

"Mother is sick, isn't she?" Caroline spoke the words softly into Ruth's chest.

"I expect so."

Caroline had hoped Ruth would lie and provide words of hope or comfort to avoid worrying her further.

"I'm not ready to lose her in addition to Cissy."

"Why does everyone keep saying Cissy is lost to us?" Ruth gently pushed Caroline upright and touched her chin. "Cissy is going to be all right again. Just you see."

Caroline longed for Ruth's certainty, or at least faith that her fractured life could be repaired with time.

She kissed Ruth on the cheek and motioned the girls over. It was past time to go home. Bess would have supper ready any minute.

Chapter 12

The recreation room was divided into two unequal sections by a row of tall bookcases. On the larger side, patients played games at tables or watched television. The smaller side was a makeshift library with two worn leather chairs and ottomans reserved for reading only. A sign thumbtacked to the wall on the library side reminded readers to whisper even though the TV was situated just fifteen feet away and was almost always turned up too loud.

At the bottom of one bookcase was a stack of old *National Geographic* magazines with the mailing labels cut out. Cissy wondered who'd donated them and why they didn't want patients in a mental hospital to know their address. She'd read through them at least once and some issues more than once. Martha sat next to her with an issue on Antarctica, turning the pages too quickly to read the stories.

"Want to read this next?" Martha pointed to a picture of an iceberg.

Cissy shook her head no. Since she always felt on the cold side, she didn't like looking at photos of cold places.

"I'm tired of reading," Martha said. "Want to

watch TV?" She got up and left without waiting for an answer.

That's when Cissy noticed a woman sitting quietly over by the chess board. The bookcases were open on both sides, giving Cissy a good view. Short caramel-colored bangs swept across the woman's forehead and her tiny nose turned up at its end. She reminded Cissy of Julie Andrews in *The Sound of Music*, right down to the pale blue-green chiffon dress and flats she wore while dancing an Austrian folk dance with the Captain on the mansion's patio.

Usually staff introduced new patients. She wondered why Nurse Possum Eyes didn't this time. And why did they allow this woman to wear street shoes?

None of the other patients had bothered to introduce themselves to the woman, but she seemed quite content to stare at the board, her chin resting on one hand, as if contemplating a strategic move.

Since Cissy was good at chess and longed for someone to play with other than Martha, she made her way over to the table and sat down.

"My name is—"

"Cissy. Yes, I know. Nice to meet you." The woman, her smile wide and toothy, stared so deeply into her eyes that Cissy became uncomfortable. How had she known Cissy's name? Had one of the nurses pointed her out?

"What's your name?" Cissy asked, trying to control the agitation in her arms and legs. She'd never felt so nervous before. It was like when she'd wanted someone at school to be her friend especially bad, but she didn't want to risk scaring away the possible friend by being too needy.

"You may call me anything you like."

"Well, I'd like to call you by your given name."

"That's a little complicated."

The woman had smiled at Cissy with more sincerity than she'd ever seen before. Nervousness left her, and her whole body sank into a hot bath of love and goodness. She no longer felt ice cold from her temperature regulation problem.

"Shall we play a game of chess?" the woman asked. "I understand you're quite accomplished at the game."

Someone at the hospital must have told her. Maybe Dr. Guttman or Martha?

"I wouldn't say accomplished." Cissy blushed but felt a great sense of pride stir in her belly. "I like games that challenge my mind."

The woman set up the pieces on the board, giving Cissy the white pieces even though she hadn't asked. "It's important to keep your mind sharp," she said. "Especially here. Be sure to always stay in control of your thoughts. Don't let things get muddled. That's why your lists are so important."

"Who told you about my lists?"

Cissy's mind latched on to probably the most outrageous thought she ever had, but fear kept her from speaking it aloud.

"Yes," the woman said. "I am."

It was almost too much to fathom: having your mind read, meeting your God in person, and finding out He's a She. And yet, here was God, looking just like Cissy's favorite movie actress. She wondered why her first thought wasn't that she'd truly gone crazy. Honestly, she didn't have a first thought—just pure wonderment. Cissy didn't want to figure out the how and why of it all. She just surrendered to accepting maybe God could choose to take a form that human pea brains could understand.

Cissy's brain told her She was real. To think otherwise would mean she'd have to admit to seeing things that weren't really there, like the fairies that Olivia says land on her window sill those nights she spits out her medications. It could be awfully hard to keep this from Dr. Guttman and Martha. Would they believe that God Almighty could just appear at will? No, it seemed best to just keep this to herself, at least until she was absolutely sure she wasn't just going crazy.

"I'm not afraid," Cissy said.

"I knew you wouldn't be."

Cissy wondered why She decided to talk to her,

of all people, but she didn't want to ask. Maybe She thought it was safer to talk to crazy people if She wanted to keep Her visits on the down low. Appearing in the Vatican or on *The Carol Burnett Show* could upset the world order. Sitting in a game room at the Greater Mississippi State Hospital in Meridian wasn't going to cause much of a stir as they were all a bit out of the ordinary there.

"Will you tell me why you're here?" Cissy asked.

"There doesn't have to be a reason."

When She assured Cissy others couldn't see Her, she was grateful to have another special thing all to herself. Cissy's head began to fill with a thousand questions she could ask God, but not one question found its way to her tongue.

She considered contacting the nuns at St. John's to tell them they were right about there being a God, but wrong about Him being a He. But they'd never believe Cissy, and it might just give them a reason to say they suspected she was troubled from a very early age. The last thing Cissy wanted to do was give those nuns the upper hand.

"How about that game of chess?" Cissy asked. She hoped God wouldn't let her win just to be nice.

Chapter 13

Cissy knew it didn't take a whole lot of smarts to notice Dr. Guttman was different from the rest of the staff at the hospital. He was from New York City, which, according to the orderlies, was about as far away as you could get from Mississippi in terms of how people think and act.

The nurses and orderlies talked about him— sometimes joking and sometimes angry about the newfangled way he did things. Cissy wondered if New Yorkers in general were newfangled and made a note to ask Dr. Guttman for his thoughts on the matter.

He was the one person in the whole facility who didn't treat patients like inmates. Her lawyer said the hospital was better than prison, but some days, she pictured them exactly the same. Both patients and criminals were put away for doing something society didn't approve of, they lived in cramped quarters, people told them what to eat and when to sleep, and television privileges could be taken away.

It didn't help that Dr. Guttman *looked* so different. If a person wanted to introduce modern-day notions into a backward place, he should at least try to look like everyone else. Instead, he dressed in short-sleeved dress shirts that needed pressing and pants so short, you could see his threadbare socks where the shoe back rubbed. His thick, unruly black curls and his large-framed glasses perched on the end of his crooked nose gave him a mad scientist look. Cissy didn't mind Dr. Guttman's appearance because she appreciated people who were peculiar. To her, they were a lot more interesting than boring folks, like the orderlies and nurses who wore the same clothes and expressions every day.

Since her admission to the hospital a month ago, he'd been nicer to her than anyone else except Martha, which was more important than his looks. She found it curious in a good way that she trusted Dr. Guttman, because she didn't trust most folks until getting to know them better.

Today, when she was reading in the recreation room, she noticed Dr. Guttman moving his arms about wildly as he talked to Nurse Possum Eyes. She heard snatches of the conversation, including his rant about the patients being "over-medicated zombies." Nurse Brown yelled back that he was too young to know what he was doing and that he should have taken a job at an East Coast institution willing to try out his asinine ideas. Cissy wrote *asinine* in her notebook with a reminder to look it up in the dictionary. She figured it wasn't a compliment, though, by the way Nurse Brown's face flushed when she said it and the way Dr. Guttman's eyes popped out of his head.

Cissy wished he hadn't called them zombies. They took medicine to feel better, and it sometimes made them so tired they didn't want to paint or play chess or do anything but watch TV. But to Cissy, zombies had a horror movie quality about them. Still, the pills had made her feel less like herself. It was just a week ago that she decided not to take her medication. Other patients required so much supervision that the staff left Cissy alone for the most part—and her sweater had deep pockets that held the pills until she could hide them in a sock in her room.

As much as Cissy trusted Dr. Guttman, she didn't tell him about skipping her medication. Even though he seemed angry with the nurses about medicating patients, he was still a paid employee, and she suspected he had to obey some rules or he'd be fired. God wasn't too pleased about Cissy hiding her medication, either, and asked her to think about whether that was the best decision. Cissy had politely told God to mind Her own business.

After Dr. Guttman's earlier altercation with Nurse Brown, his mood seemed to permeate their session, which only made Cissy cranky.

"We're not zombies." She felt bold. Recently, he'd taken to questioning her relentlessly without giving her the option of ending their sessions early. She wanted to put him on the spot.

"I didn't mean for you to hear that," he said. "It was figurative. I just think patients benefit more from talking and sharing their feelings."

Cissy disagreed. At least talking with him didn't seem to make her feel better. But talking with God did.

It was the first part of September when they first talked about cornbread. She figured God wasn't from the South because She didn't like sweet cornbread. Cissy didn't feel she could argue with God, but she disagreed with Her strongly. She asked why God would give someone the idea to *add* sugar or molasses if She didn't prefer it that way herself? Couldn't She control people's actions? She laughed at Cissy, and it was the type of laugh that told her God was worn down by her assumptions about what She could and could not do.

"Do you think cornbread should be sweet or ordinary?" Cissy asked Dr. Guttman.

He took off his glasses and rubbed the bridge of his nose. "Why does it have to be one or the other?"

"That's a good point," she said. "Maybe people can feel anything they want about a particular thing without necessarily being right or wrong."

Cissy liked this line of thinking because she usually classified things as good or bad, right or wrong, when sometimes they just were what they were. "I'm going to start a List of Things That Just Are because that might make me feel a little better than keeping a List of Very Sad Things," she said.

"That's a good idea. Now back to what we started talking about in our last session. It's important."

She had important things to discuss, but wanted to talk to God about them. She wanted to ask if She really wrote the Bible, but maybe it was best to wait a while. It was one of the more important questions Cissy had, and she didn't want to spoil their visits with something that big yet. Perhaps she'd just ask God about New York City. God would know even more than Dr. Guttman.

"Tell me again about your Sunday mornings," Cissy pleaded. "First, you'd buy a copy of the *New York Times* on the corner, then walk ten blocks to the deli with the best onion bagels. Then you'd walk all the way to Central Park if the weather was warm."

"I had a favorite bench," he admitted, smiling.

"And sometimes it'd take all morning to finish the paper, right?"

"Cissy, we were talking about what makes you lovable," he said.

"I think most folks are lovable in some way," she said.

"What makes *you* lovable?"

"Is that a trick question?"

"What makes you think it's a trick question?" he asked.

"Because I've created a situation where my mama and daddy can't love me anymore, my Mimi doesn't love me anymore, and I don't know if my sisters love me because I shot our daddy. That doesn't leave anyone to love me except Grandmother."

"I asked what makes you lovable, not who loved you," Dr. Guttman said. "We can be lovable without anyone loving us. Do you understand that?"

Cissy struggled to stay present because that question made her brain hurt the way contemplating the boundary of the universe did. "Are you saying that there are things about me that could be lovable even if no one noticed them?" she asked.

"Exactly."

"Is this going to be another list?"

"It can be if you like," he said.

"I never lie. Well, almost never," Cissy said. "That makes me a good person."

"What else?"

"I appreciate little things other people don't, like smells and how they tie memories tightly to our hearts."

"Cissy, do you think you could be lovable for no reason at all?"

"That doesn't make sense to me."

"Do you think you could believe that you are deserving of love no matter who you are or what you do?" Dr. Guttman asked.

"I'd like to talk about something else," she said.

"Are you uncomfortable?"

"I'd like to talk about something else."

"Like what?" he asked.

"I know you don't wash your hair every day."

She thought he might bust out laughing, except doctors are probably taught not to do that when they're trying to get patients to talk about serious stuff.

"No, I don't. How did you guess that?"

She told him she had personal experience with wiry, curly hair. Washing it often made it straw-like and brittle. Her mama had said she needed to allow the natural oils to coat the hair to make it shiny and healthy looking. Dr. Guttman's curls had a raven sheen to them, indicating he'd heard the same advice at some point.

"Very astute, Cissy," he said. "Sherlock Holmes would be proud."

His praise made her forget his earlier questioning and she relaxed, feeling the worst was over for this session. Instead of returning to their talks on why she was lovable, she decided to discuss about how lonely she felt sometimes at the hospital because no one was her exact kind of peculiar, not even Martha.

"Let's talk about loneliness, then," Dr. Guttman said.

"Well, I know I can be in the middle of lots of people and still feel lonely."

"Many people feel that same way, Cissy," he said.

"I've been lonely all my life because no one knew my secret. And when I told my secret in the courtroom, I didn't feel so lonely anymore even though I knew I'd lost Mama's and Mimi's love."

"What would make you feel less lonely?" he asked.

She didn't know whether that was a trick question or just a hard question. She wanted to transport herself back to a time she and Lily and Jessie were playing in their yard in the spring before the damp, heavy air of summer moved in. She wanted to run in the grass in her bare feet without feeling cold. She wanted to hear her sisters howl with laughter.

"I'd like to see Lily and Jessie again," she said. "But I've done things that can't be undone, which means they'll never feel the same about me."

Cissy started to cry.

"What are you feeling right now?"

"Thinking about Lily and Jessie makes me lonelier than I've ever felt."

Dr. Guttman's face softened. Cissy thought it almost looked like he wanted to cry.

"I think if I ever leave the hospital and live out

in the grown-up world, I will still feel lonely," she continued. "What happened to me has marked me as different. People will sense that even without knowing the whole truth."

"There are many girls who have been hurt in the same way you've been hurt," he said.

Cissy had always believed Dr. Guttman to be smart, but he'd just said an especially dumb thing. She couldn't let that pass.

"No one has ever been hurt in the exact same way as I have because they are not me," Cissy said, her words firm and measured. "Pieces of my body and mind have been changed forever. While other girls may have been hurt in a *similar* way, their pieces are different than my pieces."

"You're correct, Cissy. I'm sorry," he said. "What I meant was that you might draw some comfort from knowing others have gone through *similar* experiences. It might make you feel less alone."

"Actually, that just makes me sad," she said. "Why would I draw any comfort knowing there are other girls out there whose pieces will never be the same?"

Chapter 14

"How long do you think you'll have to stay at the hospital?" Cissy tried to distract Martha, who was handing her a whooping at chess. As much as she liked to think she'd mastered the game, Cissy was beginning to feel like an amateur with every game that Martha or God won. And there'd been many lately. Perhaps Dr. Guttman would agree to check out a book on chess strategies for her from the local library.

Martha's mouth turned down slightly and she eyed the chessboard.

"Well, how long have you been here so far?" Cissy asked when she didn't answer her first question.

"Five years this December."

The shock on Cissy's face must have been apparent because Martha told her not to worry; that she was used to the place and it wasn't so bad. Cissy regretted pushing her, but she'd come to like Martha and wanted to know more about her.

"I killed my daddy," Cissy blurted out.

Martha's face remained calm as she took out Cissy's rook with her knight.

"Aren't you shocked or upset?" Cissy asked.

189

"Nope," Martha said, still looking at the board. "I'm sure you had a good reason."

"How can you be so calm? Are you used to having people tell you they killed someone?"

Martha smiled. "No, silly. Sometimes you have to sacrifice a knight or rook if it's the best strategy in the long run."

"Do you want to know why I did it?" Cissy's knee popped up and down.

Martha shrugged her shoulders. "Your move."

Cissy could no longer concentrate on the game. She got up from her chair and hugged Martha with all her might. Cissy was grateful that Martha didn't pull away after a few seconds the way most folks did.

"I'm glad you're here." Cissy sat back down. Her heart almost burst from the love she felt.

"I'm glad you're here, too," Martha replied. "It's been a long time since I made friends with anyone at the hospital."

Their conversation went on long into the afternoon. When Martha revealed she was twenty-one years old, you'd think she just told Cissy she was Santa Claus. Cissy's gaping mouth and wide eyes made Martha laugh so suddenly that they both laughed until they held their sides and struggled to catch their breath.

Not many of the secrets they revealed made them laugh, but they didn't necessarily make them cry either. Cissy felt as if the telling of those secrets loosened the chains that wrapped round and round their hearts.

Martha had no business being at the hospital. The thing that made her crazy in her family's eyes was loving a black boy and laying with him. Curtis and Martha had decided to elope, which Martha explained was running off and getting married in secret. They were halfway to Florida before the authorities tracked them down at a tiny motel in Gulf Shores, Alabama.

Separated from the love of her life, Martha's heart filled with a rage her family would not tolerate. When she learned Curtis hanged himself, Martha suspected her brothers had murdered him. She decided she could no longer go on living with that knowledge and without Curtis's love.

"Cissy, I did become a crazy person. I was a wild animal, caged up in my house. I wanted others to feel the pain I felt."

Martha said her family put her in the hospital more out of shame than concern, though. Seemed that society frowned upon taking a straight razor to your wrists as much as loving a person of another color.

Cissy wondered how Martha could live there, day in and day out, with people who deserved to be in a mental hospital, the so-called zombies whom Dr. Guttman had ranted about. "Why won't they let you go home?" she asked.

"I'm what you call an uncooperative patient,"

Martha said. "I refuse to talk to Guttman. I fight with the patients and nurses. Anyway, it's kind of like home now."

Cissy asked why Martha didn't just play by the rules so they'd believe she was better and let her go back to her family. Martha explained that when a person lives with anger for that long, the coals smolder so brightly it takes very little to ignite them into a roaring fire. And she didn't think her family wanted her back anyway.

After a while, Cissy told Martha her truths, skipping over the details she'd locked away to keep her mind safe. She knew Martha understood because she held her hand throughout the telling.

"I don't find you peculiar, Cissy," she said. "You're the most interesting person I've ever met."

Cissy blushed at her words. "Even though I'm just sixteen?"

"Age doesn't mean a thing," Martha said. "There's a goodness in you I don't see in myself. Maybe since we're friends, a little of that'll rub off on me."

"I'm not good. I killed someone."

"I'd say that's courageous."

Cissy had never thought of herself as courageous. Martha was brave enough to run away with her true love, but Cissy had just stayed silent, which seemed cowardly in hindsight.

Martha reminded her of the reason she stayed quiet, and that protecting Lily and Jessie counted as bravery in her book. She also said pulling the trigger was the most courageous thing Cissy would do in her lifetime.

Sometimes when Cissy couldn't sleep, guilt tried to wrap itself around her mind and heart. Had she let her daddy do the things he did? Would a boy, like the one Martha loved, ever love her if he knew what had happened?

"I don't want killing Daddy to be the most courageous thing I'll ever do," Cissy said. "It would be great if I could do something truly courageous—like fly across the ocean just as Amelia Earhart did, or climb Mount Everest. Perhaps those things would erase the shooting from my mind for good."

She felt hope as she'd not felt it before.

"Don't be so childish. Only pencil marks can be erased," Martha said. Meanness danced about her eyes and Cissy had to look away.

Some days, Cissy felt she'd figured out why Martha could go from being kindhearted to cruel so easily. Maybe that was the type of crazy Dr. Guttman saw in her.

The regularity of those shifts, however, caused Cissy a great deal of anxiety that even counting couldn't ease some days. It was the reason she decided not to tell Martha about God's visits.

Sharing wasn't a good idea when you didn't feel safe.

It was just yesterday that Martha stomped off in a huff because she thought it was a bad idea that Cissy spent so much time with Lucien, the orderly she'd met on her first day. Martha had called him a low-class dirty Cajun and made fun of his accent.

Cissy asked her why she disliked him so much, but Martha was always vague. It was almost as if she didn't want any of the girls to speak to Lucien; like she was jealous. Cissy ignored the name-calling and decided it was best to never mention Lucien in Martha's presence. Especially the part about him turning out to be a better friend than Martha had been recently.

The young orderly was short, but stout, and lumbered through the halls like the friendly circus bear Cissy had seen at the county fair-grounds last summer. He looked to be in his late teens or early twenties. He was among only a handful of staff who treated the patients with the utmost respect, as if they were all normal ladies out in the real world. Of course, Martha was right in that it was sometimes difficult to understand Lucien because of his accent, but Cissy loved the words of Lucien's French ancestors. She'd made a list of her favorites, such as: *canaille*, meaning "sneaky"; *couyon*, meaning "stupid person"; and *frissons*, meaning the "chills," which she always got. She had to write them out phonetically, though, since Lucien said he didn't know the exact spelling.

At bedtime, he always apologized for turning off the TV as if he'd taken away something special from a bunch of girls who didn't have much special in their lives anymore. Every so often, Cissy would touch him lightly on his hairy, bear-like arms and say it was okay, that they didn't mind going to bed. She doubted he believed her because of the ruckus some girls caused, as if each evening, Lucien's announcement came as a surprise.

She asked him if he liked to read, and he said he didn't have much time for it seeing as how he worked night shifts at the hospital and still tried to help his mama during the day. She took in laundry and Lucien would deliver the freshly pressed garments, bundled neatly with brown paper and string. He said some days the packages radiated a warmth from his mama's iron if she wrapped the clothing quickly and he'd hold the paper against his cheek.

Cissy guessed Lucien might not be able to read, or read very well, so she asked him one evening if he'd like her to read to him. Sensing his nervousness, she told him he should always lock her door last. That way he could stand near the door jamb and keep an eye out for the nurses while she read.

This evening, he seemed particularly happy to see her. "What are we reading tonight, Miss Cissy?" He checked the hallway one last time. "*Moby Dick*?"

"I was thinking another chapter or two of *Jane Eyre*."

"Oh, all right." He looked at his feet to hide his disappointment, but he didn't do a good job of it. He liked *Robinson Crusoe* and *Moby Dick* much more than *Jane Eyre*, but she wanted him to be a well-rounded reader. He never complained, but she could tell his favorites from the way his eyes lit up.

Cissy picked up where she'd left off the last time she read to him. She hadn't read two pages before Lucien shuffled from one foot to the other, agitated.

"What's wrong?" she asked.

"There's not a lot of happy in that story. I can't hardly bear how that girl's family treats her."

"It has a happy ending. Well, sort of," she said. "It just takes some time to get around to it."

"We might grow old waiting for that to happen," he said. "Can't you read some more about those *pischouettes*? I liked that."

He referred to the Lilliputians in *Gulliver's Travels*, although he'd used the Cajun word for runts or little people. Earlier, when he asked if they truly existed, Cissy said it was a possibility, because his question held such hope. His grins told her the stories would live on in his mind long after their visits and that's what books were meant to do.

On more than one occasion, he'd interrupt and ask a question as if she had the same knowledge the author had when writing the book. If Cissy didn't have an answer, she'd make one up so he wouldn't be disappointed.

Her grandmother had met Lucien briefly when she visited the hospital. The conversation was mostly one-sided with Lucien staring at his feet, which led her grandmother to declare the boy was simple-minded. Cissy disagreed. Just because someone didn't have book smarts didn't mean they didn't have interesting thoughts.

Some nights Lucien asked if Cissy would read from his prayer book. Before God visited her for the first time, she wouldn't have been able to force herself to read scripture after the atrocious treatment by the nuns at school. But knowing God personally these past few weeks had changed the way she thought about the Bible and most other things. She also knew that religion meant something to Lucien. As his friend, she had to respect that.

"Would you rather I just read from the Bible tonight?" Cissy asked.

"No," he said. "I'd better just get on about my job tonight. But could we still say the good night prayer?"

"Sure thing," she said. When their reading time was over, they'd say good night in the very same way and Cissy had grown to like it as well.

" 'Now I lay me down to sleep,' " she began.

" 'I pray the Lord your soul to keep,' " he said.

" 'But if I should die before I wake . . .' "

" 'I pray the Lord your soul to take.' But the Good Lord would never take someone as special as you," he said.

Cissy smiled and sank down in her blankets, listening to his key turn in the lock. The metal doors to their rooms locked from the outside, which caused some of the patients a good deal of discomfort. Martha likened it to being in jail, but Cissy thought of it as being tucked in snuggly—a safe place to be alone with her thoughts, her books, and with God on the nights She visited.

God was already in Cissy's room during the good night prayer that evening.

"I like Lucien," Cissy said. "He's on my List of Things That Make Me Happy."

"Some folks may not understand your special relationship." God had a worried look on Her face, which troubled Cissy because she figured God shouldn't have a worry in the world.

Cissy wanted to defend Lucien, defend their friendship. Her face burned hot, but she knew God was just stating the obvious—people would gossip about why she cared so much for the orderly.

Most of the patients chose to ignore the whispering among staff. Doctors complained about nurses and nurses complained about orderlies and orderlies complained about patients. Judgments flew right and left about who did their job and who didn't, as well as which patients received too much attention.

"They're just being busybodies," Cissy said. "I don't like when people talk bad about Lucien or Dr. Guttman. They're like the big brothers I never had."

God sat at the end of the bed near Cissy's feet. "Do you enjoy your visits with Dr. Guttman?"

She snorted. "I wouldn't use the word *enjoy.* But yes, I guess most days I look forward to our visits."

"What was that look you just gave me, Cissy?"

"I don't know what you mean." She made her expression as blank as possible so God would stop the questioning.

But God kept staring until Cissy threw up her hands.

"All right, all right already. I don't always like our visits. He has a way of making me talk about things I don't want to talk about. He might unlock things I'd just as soon keep locked up for good."

"Isn't that how you'll get well?" God asked.

Cissy wondered whether or not to ask the

question nipping at her mind. Finally, she whispered, "Am I sick?"

God told her they'd talk later. She tucked Cissy's blanket in around her legs and kissed her forehead. Sleep didn't come easy for Cissy as she wondered if being peculiar was the same as being sick. She also wondered if it was such a good idea to be talking to God at all.

Chapter 15

For most of her childhood, Cissy suspected no one could know for sure if God existed. At St. John's Parochial School, she took every opportunity to question the nuns no matter how many beatings it meant. The point she tried to make to the nuns was, "If God can control everything, why do bad things have to happen?" Of course she was talking about her daddy not having boundaries, but since grown-ups held a special sort of power, she had to keep the details to herself.

Sister Mary Agnes used to beat Cissy when she asserted bad things don't happen just to sinners. Bad things happened to her and she wasn't a sinner. She spent a good number of years receiving beatings from the nuns, but the other kids needn't have felt sorry for her. The physical pain was a comfort, but this wasn't something Cissy could share openly. It'd just make her mama certain she was feeble-minded.

Since Cissy didn't have the regular beatings of the nuns to make her feel alive anymore, she began to use the spring in her ink pen to make small cuts on the inside of her thigh. This gave her a sense of calm whenever she had those moments of pure fright, like the deep, dark place was right behind her.

The nurses made a big commotion when they saw the cuts one morning at bath time. They took away Cissy's pen and notebook, and placed her in a part of the hospital where they could watch her twenty-four hours a day. Squirreling her away in that area wasn't the harsh punishment they intended because the room was as unremarkable as her own sleeping room. She stared at the same white cork ceiling tiles and dingy cinderblock walls, and lay on the same scratchy white sheets. The hardest part was that she'd probably not be allowed to have an ink pen again, at least not one with a spring.

For a week, wide leather wrist straps confined Cissy to the bed, and the shots in her thighs made her body as heavy as cement. There was no explaining to the nurses she posed no danger to herself. It made no sense for her to go and kill her daddy to rid herself of that pain and then go take her own life. And Cissy never heard of anyone killing themselves with an ink pen spring.

There were many people who'd never understand why she did what she did. Freeing herself and her sisters would always be thought of as crazy. And if they couldn't understand it was the exact opposite of crazy, they would never understand why the little cuts made her feel alive and safe.

Dr. Guttman visited almost every day, even if only for a short while. He seemed to understand the why part, but made it clear that it was unacceptable and troubling behavior. He'd made her promise not to do it again, and she'd had to assure him several times before he seemed to believe she understood the ramifications.

While Cissy wasn't allowed any other visitors, God came and went as She pleased because She was God and could do whatever She wanted. Being strapped down gave Cissy nothing to do all day, so God would recite from memory Cissy's favorite passages from *Cotton in My Sack*, which was one of the books her grandmother would read to Cissy and her sisters when they slept over.

She loved hearing the stories of the Hutley family and Joanda, the ten-year-old daughter. The sharecropper life fascinated her in its grittiness and desperation. She identified with Joanda, who spoils her baby sister and loves books. Because Cissy grew up in a family of means, God thought it was important for her to understand how poor people lived.

Her mama was forever telling Cissy and her sisters how lucky they were that their daddy was a respected lawyer and a pillar of the community because it made their lives easier. It seemed to Cissy it would have been hard for her mama to look her in the eye and say that if she knew what he'd done.

While God spoke, Cissy would often close her eyes to listen more closely. Her voice was unlike any human voice. Each word caressed Cissy's brow and slowed her breathing. God's voice wasn't loud, but it had a vibrating quality that masked all other sounds. God could have read the back of a Corn Flakes box and the words would have nurtured Cissy's soul.

"What do you like about this story, Cissy," She asked.

Cissy liked so many things about it she couldn't decide what to choose first. "I guess I love the simplicity of Joanda's life," she said, thinking of how complicated her own life had become. God's presence in her life was one of the larger complications because of the secret nature of their relationship.

With no chairs in the room, God had to lie down on the narrow bed with Cissy, who had to scooch over as best she could to give Her enough space to stretch out. God stayed with her both day and night, leaving when the nurses came to change her bedpan or give her a shot or spoon-feed her bland corn mash the texture of gritty baby food.

God's presence couldn't soothe all of her pains, though. By the fourth or so day of being locked up, Cissy would have sold her soul to Old Scratch to change into a clean nightgown and brush her hair. She longed to eat solid foods with her own fork and go to the bathroom on a real toilet.

"You know, if the hospital gave us fewer shots and more books we'd all be better off," she'd say to each new nurse assigned to watch her. Suggestions like that were never taken seriously, though. The nurses never answered, as if silence was also part of the punishment. It didn't matter. They hadn't given Cissy one reason to believe they had interesting things to say, so the quiet was fine by her.

Talking only to God, though, grew tiresome, and Cissy's attitude grew sassier with each day. God said that a smart mouth would do nothing to change her current circumstances. Hearing those words was like having her grandmother in the room, so she did her best to appear contrite and promised to never hurt herself again.

Cissy couldn't remember when during that week she dreamt her grandmother visited, but it was one of the best dreams of her life. Grandmother's words were almost as soothing as God's, and they talked about the smells of summer and how they occupied a special place in their memories. That evening she slept the soundest she had since being hospitalized. The best part was that she could almost smell her grandmother's perfume and see her yellow suit, even with her eyes closed.

Chapter 16

Self-mutilation. The word itself was horrific. Associating the word—the action—with Cissy seemed nonsensical.

"Mrs. Clayton? Are you all right?"

Janelle looked around the office, but nothing came into focus. Dr. Guttman's voice was too gentle for a grown man's, but she appreciated that its soprano tones could soften even the most devastating news.

"Yes, I'm fine. I . . . I need a moment."

"Cutting is not unusual," he continued, but Janelle could take no more.

"Please. Please no words." She rose and walked to the one window open in the room, directly behind his desk. Proper etiquette dictated she ask permission to invade his personal space, but she'd grown accustomed to a world without rules in the last few weeks. She stood, gloved hands on the sill, coaxing the uncooperative breeze to push through the wire mesh. September was masquerading in July's god-awful heat. Janelle's scalp itched from perspiration mingled with hairspray, but she welcomed the discomfort and its uncanny ability to distract. She counted the seconds she could bear the irritation before scratching, a counting game Cissy would approve of.

The weight of Dr. Guttman's hand on her shoulder was almost imperceptible, just enough to cause her to lose count. She allowed his lapse in decorum because she'd trespassed behind the desk that stood as the sole barrier between him and distraught family members like herself.

"Please sit down so that we can talk further," he said. "May I get you a glass of water?"

She shook her head no and returned to the wooden chair in front of his desk. The dusty sill had left ovals of gray on the fingertips of her white gloves. Janelle felt fingerprinted, so she removed them and put them in her purse.

"Will Cissy try to hurt herself again?" she asked. "Would she take . . ."

"No, I don't believe your granddaughter is suicidal," Dr. Guttman said. "Cissy exhibits a strong sense of self. She's no longer in danger of her father and quite honestly doesn't show much remorse for her actions. I believe she is at peace with her decision to end her father's life."

"Then why did she cut her thighs?" Janelle asked. That she'd resorted to using an ink pen spring alarmed her even more so because it'd escaped the hospital's scrutiny as something dangerous.

"I believe it's just one of the many ways that Cissy soothes her anxieties, much like the counting and list-making," he said. "It's more akin to self-medicating than self-mutilation."

The hospital had isolated Cissy after discovering the cuts, and Janelle was called soon after to meet with Dr. Guttman. He said it was procedure to inform family when a patient was transferred out of the unit and placed in restraints.

"How do you know she'll not do this again?" she asked.

"I've had several conversations with Cissy," he said. "She's well aware her actions brought on the solitary confinement and restriction of the activities she enjoys, like reading and drawing and socializing with other patients. Cissy is extremely intelligent, well beyond her years. I trust she understands the ramifications of her actions."

Janelle had no firsthand experience with psychiatry and so could not trust nor distrust Dr. Guttman's assessment. Their meetings and phone calls left her cheeks stinging with inadequacy and her thoughts jumbled, yet she feigned understanding. She longed to disprove her granddaughter's mental illness but in speaking up, she risked an argument she could never win.

"May I see Cissy?"

"The point of isolation is to allow the patient to reflect on her actions without interruption from normal activities," he said.

"If you weren't going to allow me to see

her, you could have told me all of this over the phone," she said. "Are you so cruel to put me within feet of my granddaughter and not allow me at least a few moments with her?"

Dr. Guttman removed his glasses and rubbed his temples against a headache she seemed to have brought on. Janelle didn't care one lick about his headache, though. She'd gone up against Ruth and Caroline, who railed when she told them of her planned trip to Meridian. Neither spoke to her for two days, and she assumed both were still fuming. Janelle hadn't told them about the cutting, so they assumed it was just a visit to check on Cissy's general welfare.

"I suppose a few minutes couldn't hurt," he said. "But just a few, Mrs. Clayton. Please trust me that I have Cissy's best interests at heart."

Dr. Guttman guided her through the recreation area and down a corridor that led back to the center of the T-shaped building and over to an adjacent wing. The smells of the hospital changed perceptibly between the public and private areas. Janelle could both smell and taste a foulness when they passed through the door into the isolation ward.

"Don't be alarmed," Dr. Guttman said when she placed a handkerchief over her nose and mouth. "Patients must use bedpans because they are restrained to their beds. The bedpans are changed frequently, but the odor is still quite pervasive."

Perhaps his daily contact with such smells had dulled the ability to discern the many scents united in their assault. Yes, urine and feces, but more. Body odor, bleach, pine.

A cry behind one closed door caused Janelle's knees to give way and she stumbled against Dr. Guttman. Throaty and sonorous, yet clearly a girl's pleading. *God in Heaven, please not Cissy.* Her hearing sharpened, and she picked up other muffled cries and soft moans. The hallway proved to be an emotional gauntlet. Dr. Guttman's hold on her elbow drove her forward. When he stopped and reached for his keys, she thought she might weep in relief.

"I have to lock the door behind you, but you'll be safe," he said.

"Dr. Guttman, I am not and have never been afraid of Cissy," she said. "You needn't assure me of my safety."

"I'm sorry, but of course," he mumbled, red-faced. "I'll be back in ten minutes."

The door clanged shut behind her, but Cissy didn't react. She resembled a corpse, covered by a sheet, only her head and her leather-bound wrists and ankles exposed.

"Cissy, are you awake?" Janelle asked, and held her breath.

"God, is that you?" Cissy mumbled, turning her head toward Janelle's voice.

"It's Grandmother."

Cissy's disorientation stunned Janelle so much that she approached cautiously, not wanting to scare her if she was waking from a dream. The room held a chill. Why wasn't she covered with a blanket?

"Grandmother? I didn't think I was allowed visitors."

Matted strands of hair clung to Cissy's forehead and cheeks, so Janelle brushed them out of the way.

"I'm going to insist they bring you a blanket right this instant." She straightened the sheet and pulled it up toward Cissy's face.

"No, Grandmother. I'm fine. Don't ruffle any feathers on my account," she said.

"Demanding proper care is not ruffling feathers."

"No, but insisting wooden stalls be built around toilets is," Cissy said, and smiled.

Janelle hadn't thought to follow up with Mr. Carnell about the project, although her check had cleared and she assumed he'd get to it as soon as he could. She made a mental note to thank him for his expediency. Maybe she'd stop by his office later if she felt up to it.

"Please, Grandmother. Let's just talk. Will you hold my hand?"

Janelle moved the wide band of leather so that she could grasp Cissy's whole palm. With her forefinger, she traced the lines from fingertip to wrist and back again.

"Are you a palm reader, Grandmother?" Her smile dissolved the awkwardness Janelle had carried into the room.

"Actually, yes." She peered more closely. "It says you have a strong spirit that will reach amazing heights in your lifetime. I see much happiness in your future."

"Can you really see that? I wish I could see my palm."

"You'll just have to trust me," Janelle said.

A lone tear escaped the corner of Cissy's eye and disappeared into her hairline. "They don't understand, Grandmother," she said.

"What don't they understand?"

"I wasn't trying to hurt myself. I can't explain why it felt good except that it made things slow down. Everything seemed simple again."

"That doesn't matter, child," she assured her. "As long as you promise not to do it again, everything will be fine." Janelle had become comfortable with making pronouncements as if she'd never be called out on their validity.

"I want to take a bath, Grandmother. And put on a clean nightgown. I don't like the smell in here."

"Dr. Guttman said you have two more full days to go. Be strong, Cissy. I know you can do it."

"Let's talk about other smells, then," Cissy said. "Summer has the best smells, but they're all outdoors and I'm not allowed outside. I'm afraid

I'll forget the smell of the ocean if I stay here much longer."

"Well, let's remember together. Close your eyes, dear."

Only by shutting their eyes did Janelle feel they could escape the grimness of the room and its chalky cinderblock walls. Its distorted shape—narrow in width and depth, yet with towering twelve-foot walls—gave the illusion of being trapped at the bottom of a cracker box.

"The water smells like brine, a salty stew of all the marine life we can't see beneath the surface," Janelle said. She hadn't been to the beach in twenty years and had always refused Caroline's invitation to join her and the girls on their outings. Yet, she could remember the exact scent carried off the Gulf on a hot July day.

"I smell Coppertone and wet straw from my sun hat," Cissy said. "And sometimes a bad fish smell when one has died and washed up on the beach."

"Sunshine has a scent, too, doesn't it?"

"Yes, sunshine is the best smell of all because it stays on your skin and in your clothes," Cissy said. "Then you can remember the day at the beach for a long time."

A key rasped against the lock, so Janelle leaned in to kiss Cissy's forehead, slick with sweat. Her granddaughter wasn't cold after all.

"I'll be back soon, child," she whispered in her ear. "And, Cissy . . . I do understand."

When Janelle turned for the door, Cissy called out. "Grandmother, you have a special smell in my memories, too."

Janelle blew her a kiss and followed Dr. Guttman into the hall.

Chapter 17

Caroline had been curious about her mother's latest visit with Cissy, but had dug in her heels and refused to call. When she couldn't take the silence any longer, she decided to talk to her in person. It was so early that Janelle was sitting on the porch swing, still in her housecoat, and hadn't put on makeup.

"Ruth said you've been feeling stronger lately." Caroline stood on the porch steps, hands tucked in her back pockets.

"Yes, the cooler weather helps my breathing a bit if you can call eighty-five degrees cooler," Janelle said. "I can't remember September ever being so warm."

"And the drive went well?" Caroline asked.

"If you mean, did my visit with your daughter go well, then yes, Cissy's doing fine," Janelle said.

"You could've called to tell me how she was doing," Caroline said. "At least give me some idea of how she's coping."

"I just said she was fine."

Caroline had called Dr. Guttman the day before, hoping he'd divulge some details, but he, too, was vague. Almost too vague. It'd begun to alarm Caroline that they weren't sharing information because they were convinced she didn't care. Her mother's terseness only added to Caroline's worry. She hadn't fought her mother's wishes to become Cissy's guardian all those weeks ago, but in doing so, she'd given up more rights than she imagined.

"I called the hospital to check on her myself," she said.

Her mother stiffened. "And?"

"Her doctor said she's doing well, that your visit meant a lot to her."

"She asks about you and the girls. Speaking of which, how are Lily and Jessie? School should be starting soon."

"It started two weeks ago." Caroline made her way up the stairs and over to the swing at the end of the porch where Janelle sat. Her mother said Ruth had insisted on hosing down the cushions from the wicker rockers this morning and they were still drying in the sun.

"How did they say the first few days went?" Janelle asked.

"Lily gets more taunting than Jessie. I guess Jessie's classmates are a little young to know what happened," she said. "Sister Joseph called to say Lily had pinned down a classmate and given her a bloody nose. Thank God she didn't expel Lily. Probably feels sorry for her."

"Children can be so cruel," Janelle said. "I'm proud of your girls. They'll be fine."

Caroline didn't know that for sure. Nine weeks had passed since Richard's death. Grief had a way of making days so unbearably long you begged God to end your life.

"You look rested, Caroline. Your color is back."

Caroline said she'd had a few nights of sleep uninterrupted by nightmares and it did her some good. She said she was still surprised, though, that she could function at all. Yet each day, Caroline got out of bed, drove her children to school, bought groceries, and paid bills. Life had a way of using mundane matters to propel them forward even when a single step felt impossible.

"I like you without makeup, Mother. I don't think I can recall a day you didn't put your face on, even when staying at home. You're still a beautiful woman." Said aloud, the compliment felt awkward, but it was true.

"Primping has felt like too much trouble lately. And besides, who's looking at an old woman anyway." Janelle touched her face.

"You're not old. Your mother lived to be ninety," Caroline said. "You got a lot of years to cause trouble on this earth."

Caroline lifted her legs straight in front of her and the swing pitched them backward. Her mother raised an eyebrow and pointed at Caroline's toenails, which had been painted with purple glittered polish.

"Oh, that," Caroline said. "The girls wanted pedicures last night so we *all* had pedicures."

Her mother had treated herself to professional manicures and pedicures for most of her life. Caroline couldn't remember ever seeing them chipped or unpolished. Today, Janelle's nails were neatly trimmed and painted with only clear polish. It suited her.

"Mimi wants the house back," Caroline said.

"Wha . . . What do you mean she wants the house back? Who in the goddamn hell does Mimi think she is?"

"Richard and I never owned the house outright. Mimi and Charles kept it in their names, but they said the house was their gift to us. I never thought it'd become an issue." In hindsight, Caroline could admit she didn't want to rock the boat. Mimi planned to leave them a fortune when she passed. She and Richard would not have had to worry about money again.

"Does she care so little for her granddaughters? I'll talk to Mimi and set her straight," Janelle said, fire returning to her cheeks.

"No, Mother, please don't." Caroline couldn't stand the thought of being in the middle of another fight between her mother and mother-in-law. They'd never gotten along, but Richard's death had turned their indifference toward each other into hatred.

"Well, you'll have to move back here, then,"

Janelle said. "There's plenty of room, even for Bess."

"I'd like to see Ruth and Bess living under the same roof," Caroline joked weakly. "Bess is used to having the run of our home."

"No, I guess two housekeepers in one house might be asking too much."

Caroline did concede that she and the girls could move in temporarily, at least until she figured out if they were staying in Mississippi at all. Bess could stay at her brother's home if she decided not to go with them.

"Move? Out of Mississippi?"

"Mother, you had to know I've been thinking about it," she said. "It's hard for the girls. It's hard for me. Maybe we need a fresh start."

Caroline's heart broke, though, at the thought of moving farther away from her mother. Although Janelle hadn't admitted it, Caroline was certain she was more sick than she let on. Ruth wasn't offering up any information either, but maybe Janelle had sworn her to secrecy.

"I can understand you wanting a fresh start," Janelle said. "The day I had the heat stroke I'd been in Rosebuds. The impertinent sales girl and a couple of shoppers started in about Cissy and I couldn't get out of there fast enough. This town has been less than sympathetic."

Caroline nodded her understanding. She'd taken to wearing a scarf and dark sunglasses everywhere she went. The silly disguise rarely worked. "Everyone seems to want to place blame squarely on my shoulders," Caroline said. "It's not fair."

She waited for Janelle to agree or to console, but she sensed her mother fell in the category of people who blamed her as much as Richard for the abuse. Janelle patted Caroline's thigh, but Caroline didn't know what to make of the gesture.

Neither of them had ever been comfortable talking about their emotions. Evasion always seemed easier. They'd instinctively avoided these conversations to spare the hurt that honesty was certain to bring. She wished so deeply that her daddy was still alive. Caroline could talk to him about anything. She'd never doubted his love for her, but had never been certain of her mother's. Ruth had admonished her for these feelings and reminded her that love took many forms. Why couldn't it take the form that Caroline desired most? Why couldn't her mother just say the words? Her daddy said them every day, multiple times a day.

"You blame me, Mother, don't you?" Caroline twisted off her wedding band and stuffed it in a pocket. Why did she even wear it? Her mother might see it as a sign Caroline still loved Richard, believed him incapable of what he'd done.

"Yes," she admitted. "I suppose I do."

Caroline refused to show her mother just how deep a wound she'd just inflicted. Their relationship was probably beyond repair, and that realization hurt as deeply as her mother's answer.

"Will you forgive me one day, Mother?" she asked.

"I hope so," Janelle said.

Caroline didn't meet her mother's eye when she got up and walked toward the car. Perhaps moving away was the only way she'd ever escape the pain. Mimi could have her goddamned house.

Chapter 18

After her time in isolation, Cissy returned to the main ward without much commotion. Martha had told her it was because they were all used to patients being taken away from time to time, and that she'd get used to it, too.

Cissy also returned to her regular sessions with Dr. Guttman. He'd started asking her to talk about how the cutting was related to her daddy's abuse, which made her feel unsafe. She asked God to join her at the next session, but She said that wasn't a good idea.

"But why not?" Cissy pleaded. She didn't expect Her to say anything. She just wanted someone next to her, for support.

God concentrated on the chess board and ignored Cissy for the most part, even when she let out huge sighs and rolled her eyes.

This one-sided conversation reminded Cissy of when she used to pray to a God she didn't know existed and ask for something special. When she didn't get it, her mama would say God knows best and doesn't answer all our prayers. Cissy thought having God right in front of her would give her an advantage over those people kneeling beside their beds.

"You're not real, are you?" Cissy asked, trying to get a rise.

"What if I'm not? Would it matter?"

It wasn't the reply that Cissy expected. God's words usually brought comfort, but today they seemed just plain hateful.

"Why would you say that?" Cissy asked. "I haven't asked you for a lot. Why not just come to one session with me?"

God just shook her head and left.

Cissy's belly was trying to tell her that her next meeting with Dr. Guttman might not go well. She didn't have anything but a hunch, but it was enough to make her sweat strangely and chew her thumbs raw.

Dr. Guttman must have noticed her hesitation in entering his office.

"Cissy, are you well? You're quite pale," he said.

"I'm fine." She sat down in the middle of the sofa instead of the chair by his desk, where she normally sat, and scanned the room from corner to corner. Dr. Guttman asked why she seemed so agitated.

"I'm just fine." She tapped the toes of her right foot—three taps, two taps, three taps. That was the most calming combination this week. Fuzzy slippers, however, didn't make a satisfying sound.

He asked if she would please sit still for a while

because he had something important to discuss. Her belly shouted, "I told you so!" Sometimes, she hated having a good sense about things.

Cissy could count in her head as well as with her feet so it wasn't such a big deal to stop the tapping. Counting and concentrating on Dr. Guttman's words at the same time, though, wasn't so easy anymore. From what she pieced together between the counting, Nurse Edna had reported she'd exhibited signs of isolation, like not talking with the other girls or watching TV as much.

The news hurt because she liked Nurse Edna more than any of the nurses. She was the only black nurse on staff and tall and skinny like Cissy. Her afro shone about her face like a halo. She was the kindest of the nurses, but Cissy sensed her kindness came mostly from pity. You could see that sort of thing in a person's eyes if you paid attention.

It hurt even more to learn Nurse Edna told Dr. Guttman that Cissy had been talking to herself.

"Well, that's just ridiculous!" she said. "Why would she say that about me?"

"So, you don't talk to yourself when you're playing chess?" he asked.

"Ohhhhh," she said, understanding his questioning. "I don't talk to myself. I talk to God when we play chess."

When Dr. Guttman started scratching in his

notebook, she instantly regretted sharing her special secret, which wasn't a secret if the nurses had already been spying on her time with God.

"How long have you been playing chess with God," he asked.

Cissy told him she'd first met Her two weeks after arriving at the hospital. When he asked if God talked back to Cissy, she laughed out loud.

"Why would I talk to someone who wouldn't talk back to me?"

Dr. Guttman and Cissy spent a good half hour just discussing the sorts of topics she and God talked about. He'd never shown himself to be so curious.

"Does God ever ask you to do things," he asked.

"What kinds of things?"

"Does She ever ask you to hurt yourself or others?"

"Why would She do that?" Cissy asked. "You're asking some pretty asinine questions for a smart guy."

"Asinine?"

"I heard Nurse Brown use the word, so I looked it up and wrote it in my notebook. It means stupid or foolish."

"I know what it means, Cissy."

He scratched away some more and she asked why he didn't seem more surprised that God visited her. She thought it was a pretty big deal, especially the revelation that God was a woman.

Dr. Guttman closed his notebook and leaned forward as if ready to tell her a secret.

"Sometimes the patients I work with make up imaginary friends," he said. "It makes them feel better, the way that counting makes you feel safe."

"She's not imaginary. I hate that you don't believe me." She took out her notebook to scribble the sadness he was causing. The fact that Dr. Guttman caused the sadness was the greatest blow of all.

"I believe this woman seems real to you, and that's what is most important."

Maybe having God in the room for the visit wouldn't have helped after all. Cissy might have begged Her to show Herself to Dr. Guttman to prove she wasn't crazy. And if She hadn't done as Cissy asked, it would have been the second thing God had denied her. Cissy didn't think she could take that much hurt in one day.

God seemed unconcerned when Cissy told Her about Dr. Guttman saying She was make-believe.

"Maybe you shouldn't have mentioned me," She said, and took out Cissy's queen with Her knight.

Cissy hated that She could talk and play chess at the same time. Everything about God annoyed her today. Why didn't She ever wear anything else but that blue-green chiffon dress? Even Maria in *The Sound of Music* had day clothes and evening clothes.

Cissy flipped the board off the table and watched the black and white plastic figurines skitter across the floor. Her eyes dared God to get mad, but She just stared the way She always did—Her features as blank as the *Mona Lisa*'s.

The nurse on duty rushed over when she heard the pieces hit the tile. "What happened here?"

Cissy knelt on the floor and began picking up the pieces so she wouldn't have to look the nurse in the eye. "Everything's okay. I accidentally bumped the table."

The nurse hesitated before leaving. Cissy got up only when she saw the nurse had returned to her station.

"People get angry at me all the time," God said. "That doesn't mean I don't still love them. Sometimes anger helps them get to the root of the matter."

"Why do you always talk like that? How much does my brain have to hurt before you talk normal?"

"Pick up the rest of the chess pieces," She said.

"I don't want to play anymore." Cissy leaned back into the chair, arms crossed.

"If Dr. Guttman had believed you, would that have made me more real?"

"You are real to me," she said. "I just wanted

someone else to know that you picked me special to visit."

"Are you worried that believing in God makes you crazy?"

"No, I'm worried other people will think I'm crazy because I *see* you," Cissy said.

"Is Santa Claus real?" She asked.

"Santa isn't real." She grew angry that God was making fun of her. "Our parents put out the presents and pretend to be Santa."

"Do Lily and Jessie believe in Santa Claus?" She asked.

"Of course, they're little kids. Why are we talking about this?"

"Santa is real to millions of children because they believe deep down in their hearts he exists. It doesn't matter what anyone else thinks because that belief is so strong."

God held up Her hand to stop the questions that Cissy wanted to ask.

"Lots of people don't believe in me either," She said. "That doesn't mean I don't exist in the hearts of the millions who do believe. You don't need someone else's validation to make me real to you."

"But I can *see* you. Kids don't see Santa. What if Dr. Guttman thinks I'm crazy talking to you?"

"Like I said, millions of people talk to me every day and they aren't crazy." She touched Cissy's hand. "It's called faith."

The nuns at school had talked a lot about faith. Cissy recalled the martyrs in Bible stories who were put to death because they believed in a God others doubted. Sister Mary Francis relished telling these stories. She'd gnash her teeth like a lion when she told the story of Perpetua, who was torn apart by wild beasts in the Carthage arena. She'd hold her neck protectively when she spoke of poor thirteen-year-old Agnes, who bravely offered her neck to the executioner's sword.

"There has to be a reason I can see you." Cissy's face burned red-hot.

"It's not wrong for you to want me to be real. This is a hard time for you and there's so much for you to process. I'm helping you with that."

Each day seemed harder to slog through. Nothing ever changed. Eat, sleep, read, watch TV, repeat.

Cissy used to badger her mama about how boring summers were, each day merging into the next until school would start up and she'd wondered where those three months had gone. Now the variety of those days unfolded before her: writing plays and performing them with her sisters, catching insects and looking them up in the encyclopedia, baking cookies with Bess and delivering them to the nursing homes, lying in the cool grass of the front yard reading her favorite books, luring crawdads out of their holes with bacon on a string. Now, even the funniest

TV shows brought no more than small smiles, not the hoots Cissy remembered sharing with her baby sisters.

"You're the one thing that keeps me from becoming like everyone else here," Cissy said. "Without you, I'm afraid I'll turn into something I'm not."

"What aren't you?"

"Crazy," she whispered.

God, still wearing the blankest of faces, asked if Cissy wanted to continue the game. She hadn't dispelled Cissy's nighttime fear that she'd risked speaking in the daylight.

Cissy snuffled back her disappointment. She leaned down to pick up the chess pieces from the floor and saw Martha standing at the edge of the recreation room, her lips in a hard line. Without waiting for Cissy to explain, she turned and stomped off down the hall.

Chapter 19

After Janelle returned from the visit with Dr. Guttman, she'd refrained from driving, but not because Caroline demanded it. Her body demanded it. She didn't know if she'd been this tired all along, or if her cells gave up a little after hearing Dr. Stone's diagnosis of cancer. Janelle spent day after day sitting on her front porch, reading books that held no interest, but passed the time. She skipped her weekly wash and set at the beauty parlor, and instead let her hair air-dry after showering. Makeup seemed superfluous, as did wearing anything but dungarees and cotton smocks at home.

Many afternoons, Ruth would join her. She sat in Beau's chair and they played rummy and checkers. Some afternoons, though, they didn't need cards or words. They stared past the scorched brown grass and knotty willows, not focusing on anything in particular, happy to have each other's company. The occasional squeak of their wicker rockers reminded them to get up and refill iced tea glasses or grab a bite to eat. Otherwise, the hours passed comfortably.

Janelle and Ruth had been together longer than she'd been married, and like a marriage, their relationship had good years and bad years. Ruth came from a family of women who took care of other people's households and reared other people's children. Despite their friendship as children, Ruth became a different person when she took over Janelle and Beau's household. She went about her chores with a blank face, never engaging in the conversations Janelle longed to have with her.

Janelle's parents had had money, well at least enough to put on the pretense of having it. When she was young, she didn't see Ruth as being outside her social sphere even though she was the daughter of their housekeeper. Ruth and her mother hadn't lived on the premises. Ruth's father dropped them off each morning at 5 a.m. for a twelve-hour day. The crunch of gravel in the drive would wake Janelle and she'd sprint downstairs, ready to begin the day's adventures. Ruth's wicked sense of humor and knack for mischief sometimes resulted in Janelle's father taking a birch switch to their hides. Neither girl cared. The fun they had far outweighed the punishment. Life seemed so glorious in its simplicity. Not having siblings made Janelle cherish Ruth's friendship all the more.

Ruth, though, felt that childhood friendships were to be outgrown, especially when she became Janelle and Beau's housekeeper.

Their friendship never really went away.

Sometimes it just appeared dormant, like bulbs planted in the fall that must weather a winter before blooming. Over the years, Janelle and Ruth had more than a few arguments when navigating their new roles. Ruth expected to run a household the way her mother and grandmothers had. Janelle wanted things to be more relaxed. She wanted to have talks like they had as children. Ruth had said that it made her uncomfortable to be overly friendly. Soon, Janelle pulled away and the relationship grew formal, almost stilted. After Janelle gave birth to Caroline, Ruth cared less about the hierarchy in the house. That baby mesmerized Ruth, softening the hardest of her edges. She couldn't bear to hear Caroline cry and would cry along with her. Some nights Janelle would find Ruth, tears running down her cheeks, rocking a squalling Caroline and singing a hymn. More than a few mornings, she found them asleep in the nursery rocker, Caroline slumbering across Ruth's sizable bosom. After Caroline's birth, Janelle had miscarried two other pregnancies. Ruth mourned for weeks, heartbroken she'd been deprived of loving two other precious souls as she did Caroline. Janelle accepted the losses for what they were—her body rejecting cells not strong enough to multiply and survive.

When Caroline was growing up, Janelle appreciated that Ruth took the lead in child rearing even if it meant that the two started to develop a bond closer than the one Janelle had with Ruth in their younger years.

It was only since Richard's death, though, that Janelle appreciated Ruth's ability to fill an emptiness in the house she couldn't bear otherwise.

"I love you, Ruth," she said, and patted her forearm. "I don't tell you often enough."

"You've never said it, Mrs. Clayton. Is the heat getting to you again?" She winked.

"Ruth, why can't you call me Janelle now that it's just the two of us?" As soon as she said the words, she wondered why. Lately, her words had declared independence and it proved impossible to stop them.

"I've called you Mrs. Clayton for too long to go changing to your first name." Ruth let out a deep, throaty laugh. "You needn't worry. I know we're friends."

"I haven't always been a good friend," Janelle admitted.

"I didn't need you to be a good friend," Ruth said. "I needed you to understand you had your place and I had mine. It didn't mean we stopped caring for each other."

"I pushed you away more than was necessary." Janelle felt a surge of regret. Sometime after Caroline's third birthday, Janelle decided that if Ruth wanted theirs to be a typical employer–

238

employee relationship, that's what it would be. She'd be Mrs. Clayton. It all seemed so silly now. She and Ruth were in their seventies. There was no one around to judge them if they wanted to recapture some of the lightheartedness they shared as little girls.

"You never mistreated me like your mama mistreated my mama," Ruth said. "I've enjoyed my time here. At least we've not grown tired of each other."

"No, we haven't," Janelle said, chuckling softly. "Although sometimes it seems like we're close to it."

Ruth smiled before her face turned somber. "I know you have the sickness," she said.

"I figured you did."

Ruth didn't ask for details and Janelle offered none. Ruth probably recognized Janelle's decline in the past weeks. At their age, they'd seen many of their contemporaries fall ill to any number of ailments. Death was just a part of life.

"It's getting to be lunchtime," Ruth said, slapping her thighs. "How about some cold fried chicken?"

"That'd be fine."

Ruth's gait had turned into a pained waddle in recent years. Arthritis had laid claim to her hips, and she swung her rigid body from side to side to propel herself forward. Janelle had suggested they get someone younger to help around the house, but Ruth had acted insulted and Janelle dropped the conversation. Still, it pained Janelle to see her ascend the stairs one step at a time or bend over to rest, hands on knees, while hanging the wash on the clothesline out back. In a contest of stubbornness it'd likely be a draw, so neither of them took the challenge.

"There weren't any wings left," Ruth said when she returned, setting down a tray of food between them.

"That's all right. I like wings when they're fresh out of the frying pan. Drumsticks are actually best cold."

"There's only one drumstick left, ma'am, and it's mine." Ruth waited for a reaction, so Janelle glared in mock disappointment. These moments were a precious glimpse into an earlier time.

"There was a bit of cucumber salad left," Ruth said. "I know how much you like it." The salad had been a favorite of Beau's. A dressing of mayonnaise, white vinegar, black pepper, and caraway seeds wilted the thinly sliced cucumbers while allowing just a hint of their crispness to remain.

Janelle hadn't much of an appetite since having the stroke, but meals with Ruth weren't about the food. They were about the space between them that needed tending. Neither of them was pre-pared for a goodbye, and certainly not one of words. Janelle allowed Ruth's caretaking, and

Ruth accepted that allowance as a gift, knowing Janelle's controlling nature.

"You want some pie and coffee?" Ruth asked when they'd finished lunch.

Janelle shook her head no. She'd eaten a few bites of chicken and cucumbers for Ruth's benefit, but sweets disagreed with her stomach more strongly than other foods.

"Dr. Guttman called yesterday," Janelle said, changing the subject.

"Cissy's doctor in Meridian? What about?"

"Seems she's having hallucinations."

"What's hallucinations mean?" Ruth asked, clearing the plates and stacking them on the tray.

"Means she's seeing things that aren't there. He said she believes she talks to God."

"I talk to God," Ruth said. "Every day, in fact."

"Cissy said she *sees* God and that God is a woman."

The noise coming from Ruth started as weak snorts and escalated into brays. Eyes squeezed tight, she pulled her apron up over her face and held it there with both hands.

"Stop it this instance," Janelle chastised. "There's nothing funny about this at all."

As soon as it seemed Ruth would stop her ridiculous laughing, another fit took hold and she put up her hand in apology.

"Ma'am, with all there's to worry about in this hard world, seeing your God doesn't rank as a problem in my opinion," she said, settling down.

"But she's claiming God's a woman. And that they play chess together!"

Ruth reminded Janelle that the Lord had appeared to humans in many forms, including a burning bush, and that a woman made as much sense as any other form. For a few minutes, she went on like a preacher about God's mysteries and a person's duty to keep an open heart and mind, to stand ready to witness miracles.

"I'm a religious woman, Ruth. You needn't remind me of God's wonders. The doctor thinks the hallucinations could be associated with schizophrenia."

"Good Lord in Heaven! Please stop using big medical words for a moment and just listen," Ruth said. "What does your heart tell you? Does fear bubble up first, or is there a bit of relief Cissy has found some comfort in her God?"

"You're an infuriating old woman." Janelle pursed her lips in a tight line.

"There you go with your big words again."

"It means you make me angry and frustrated."

"Nothing new about that," Ruth said, and grabbed her hand. "And I know what infuriating means."

They sat without speaking. Ruth remained tethered to Janelle and never loosened her grip. All she'd wanted was for Ruth to share her deep worry. That Ruth had broken it down so simply should have brought some relief, but instead Janelle feared Cissy's mind had split even further.

She wanted the child to put aside foolish counting games and make-believe even though they'd brought her some comfort these many years. She had to grow up and learn to take care of herself. Depending on when Cissy would be released from the hospital, Janelle would likely be gone, and she was far from certain Caroline would be able to forgive Cissy and take her in again.

"I'll take care of Miss Cissy," Ruth said, breaking their silence. "I mean, after you've passed and all."

Janelle let grateful tears run free without bothering to wipe them. Ruth stood and rested her hand on Janelle's shoulder for a brief second before leaving her to ponder Cissy's friendship with God.

Chapter 20

Art supplies in the recreation area were limited to white butcher paper and crayons most days. On rare occasions, Nurse Brown would waddle out with the glue and construction paper as if she were transporting a delicate plum pudding on Christmas morning, just like Mrs. Cratchit in *A Christmas Carol*.

There was no rhyme or reason to her generosity with supplies, so Cissy gave it little thought except to wonder why someone so mean even bothered to be nice on occasion. However, it perplexed her to no end that patients were given construction paper and glue, but denied scissors.

"Even kids in kindergarten get scissors with the rounded ends," Cissy argued with Nurse Brown. Martha covered her mouth to conceal a grin.

When Nurse Brown scolded that they'd hurt themselves with scissors, Cissy asked if she'd consider letting them use pinking shears because no one in their right minds would hurt themselves with pinking shears.

"That's the point. You girls are not in your right minds," the nurse said with an angry scowl.

Martha and Cissy burst out laughing, which made Nurse Brown's doughy white face go red. To retaliate, she took away the glue and construction paper for a week. That she saw this as punishment made them laugh harder.

Somewhere along the way, Cissy's grandmother had received permission to mail her a pad of thick art paper and a narrow, flat tin of pastels, but she rarely used the supplies outside of her room. She didn't want the other girls to be jealous or to ask if they could borrow the chalky sticks, especially those colors she'd used so much they were just nubs, like blue, green, and yellow.

When the light was exceptionally good in the rec room, though, Cissy couldn't resist dragging a table and chair over to the window. The heavy table legs squawked as she scraped them across the tile, and some of the girls watching TV covered their ears in protest. Morning light cast a golden blanket over most colors, making them appear to seep deeper into the paper. Afternoon shadows sometimes cast a bluish gray tone, making even happy pictures appear somewhat grim.

That morning, she positioned her chair so she faced away from everyone else in the room. She'd hoped that would keep the nosy nellies away from her supplies. Martha, however, ignored Cissy's attempts at setting boundaries and dragged her own chair over, ripped a page from the art pad, and borrowed the azure blue pastel without asking. No one had ever tried anything so bold, but it didn't surprise Cissy that Martha had. Why couldn't Martha just be a normal, polite friend?

To her, Martha was like fire, sometimes mesmerizing and sometimes terrifying. Cissy just didn't know from day to day which type of fire she was walking into.

"Why do you wear that lumpy old sweater every day?" Martha asked.

"Because I'm cold every day. You know that."

"Why don't you wear your dresses much?" Martha asked.

"I like pants better. What's it to you?"

"Were you wearing a dress the day you killed your daddy? Do you still have what you wore?"

She was fishing for something and Cissy refused to take the bait. She tried to ignore Martha and the twisting pain in her gut.

"Why do you put the chalk to your nose?" Martha asked.

"I like knowing how things smell. Is that a crime? And why all the questions today?"

Martha said Cissy was being overly sensitive.

Giving up on the idea of scissors, Cissy began to tear pieces of red construction paper and glue them together to form the petals of a flower. They had gobs of the red sheets, probably left over from the Fourth of July, so she decided to create a poinsettia.

"That's a Christmas flower," Martha chided. "It's just September."

"I can create any flower I want."

"I can create any flower I want," she mimicked.

"You're in a snit," Cissy said. "Don't talk to me until you can be nicer. And why don't you try bathing more often. You smell bad."

"Whatever," she mumbled, and pushed her chair back so that her feet rested on the table. Martha's white socks were dirty from walking around without slippers. She'd decided the rule against wearing street shoes inside was ridiculous and had worn the same pair of socks for the last week trying to make her point. Nurse Brown had called Martha's attitude vexing—a spectacular-sounding word Cissy had to look up right away and capture in her notebook. Martha said her habit of jumping up and running over to the dictionary in the library was irritating. "Vexing," Cissy corrected her.

She worked on the poinsettia for about half an hour while Martha took the pastel in her fist and scribbled angry circles on the expensive art paper.

"Please don't waste my nice paper," Cissy asked after Martha had covered five sheets with blue tornadoes.

"It's abstract art," she said, throwing the pages aside. "What are you making?"

Cissy hadn't noticed God standing at the edge

of the room. She wasn't supposed to appear if Cissy was busy or talking to someone.

"It's a birthday card," Cissy said.

God shook Her head from side to side, so Cissy gave Her a look that said, "Go away."

"Who's it for?" Martha asked.

God put a finger to Her mouth to shush Cissy.

"Lucien," she said. God's eyes went dark and Cissy gulped back a wave of nausea.

Martha's chair came crashing down and she slapped both her palms on the table. "Outstanding!" she shouted. "Just outstanding."

Cissy flinched when Martha grabbed the poinsettia card.

"Isn't this precious? Cissy's making her dear friend Lucien a birthday card. Let's see what it says."

"You're crumpling it." Cissy grabbed for the card that Martha had raised above her head. She stepped on a chair and then onto the table. Martha had the full attention of the room, including Nurse Edna.

"Martha Spencer!" she called out, running from the nurses' station. "Get down right this minute."

Martha jumped from the table to the floor with a muffled, catlike thud and handed Cissy's card to Nurse Edna.

"Look what a sweet card Cissy has made for

Lucien," Martha said. "Did you know they're good friends?"

Cissy used the back of her sweater sleeve to wipe her face, but the wool wouldn't absorb the wetness. "Please stop her," she begged.

Nurse Edna took the card and Martha skipped to the other side of the room, plopping down on the couch in front of the TV set. Nurse Edna's eyes scanned back and forth across the note she had no business reading. Why had Cissy even written it? Lucien had trouble reading and he'd have had to ask his mama for help, that is, if he wasn't too embarrassed to do so.

The nurse pulled the poinsettia off the card and laid it on the table. She then folded the note portion in half and put it in her front pocket.

"Please give it back," Cissy whispered.

"That's a lovely flower," she said, and placed a bony hand on Cissy's shoulder. "I just don't know if it's appropriate for you to give Mr. Thibodeaux a card."

"Yes, ma'am. I didn't mean to do anything inappropriate." She swiped at the pastel dust on her slacks.

"Of course not, child," Nurse Edna whispered. "Let's just have a chat about the visits you and Mr. Thibodeaux have been having. Wipe your nose and come with me, please."

When Cissy scanned the room, she saw that God had gone and Martha was staring at the

TV screen and laughing too loud at a rerun of *Gilligan's Island* that wasn't even funny.

Cissy put the pastels back in their tin and placed the poinsettia under the front flap of her art pad before following Nurse Edna from the room.

Nurse Edna tried to be gentle when explaining appropriate contact between patients and staff, but Cissy realized no one understood the exact nature of her friendship with Lucien. Cissy nodded often to signal she was listening. When Nurse Edna asked her to promise not to meet with Lucien again, she nodded once more, but kept her fingers crossed against this lie. He was too good a friend to give up in a place where friends were hard to come by.

After an appropriate period of looking contrite, Cissy asked if she could go back to the library. Nurse Edna patted her shoulder and said, "Scoot."

The ward's library was just a section of the recreation room set apart by the wall of open bookshelves, but it still seemed like a world apart from the rest of the hospital. Depending on the height of the books in any given row, a person could peer into the other part of the room where patients watched TV or played games. Cissy liked being able to keep an eye on things no matter what side she happened to be on.

The comfiest chair in the room was a black

leather arm chair with a low, wide ottoman, its top cracking with age and its edges studded with brass tacks. Despite the hot breezes that blew through the open windows, the chair always felt cool against her skin. She claimed that chair so often, the other patients didn't sit in it even when Cissy wasn't in the library.

She kept a dictionary open on the ottoman next to her legs so she could look up words that seemed particularly interesting and jot them down. Soon, she'd need a new notebook just for all the strange and mysterious new words that leapt off the pages.

Television couldn't compete with the thrills that came from the worlds Cissy visited in books. She could forget she was plain old Cissy Pickering and imagine herself a dashing swashbuckler on a pirate ship or a sleeping princess waiting for a kiss or the first woman to fly an airplane across the Atlantic.

The book she picked today wasn't technically a reading book but a picture book of paintings by famous artists called the Impressionists. If she squinted her eyes, the colorful spines of the books lining the shelves merged into blurry landscapes like those Monet painted years and years ago in France. It was a technique she hoped to try one day. Maybe she'd ask Grandmother for a set of watercolors for Christmas.

When Cissy opened her eyes, she caught

Martha looking through the bookshelf room divider. Most of her face was obscured, but there was no mistaking those eyes.

"What's up?" Cissy asked.

"You tell me."

"I don't know what you mean," she said, but she did know. The more time Cissy spent with God and with Lucien meant less time spent with Martha and she was jealous. Why else would she do something so mean as to tell Nurse Edna about the card for Lucien?

"Come 'round in here so we can talk privately," Cissy said.

Martha marched around the shelf. The fierceness in her little steps made the books shake and bounce.

"Why don't you like me anymore?" Martha demanded.

"I like you more than anyone here. You're my best friend," Cissy said.

Without stopping to take a breath, Martha wailed about the hours Cissy spent playing chess alone, talking and laughing, pretending someone was playing with her. She claimed Cissy had started to ignore everyone and everything except Lucien.

"You think you're so special because you're Lucien's favorite." Martha's face contorted. "He's nothing but a dumb Cajun who doesn't know how to speak right. He probably likes young girls. How does he show you he likes *you?*"

Her hateful words pelted Cissy like a spray of buckshot.

"You be quiet. What has Lucien ever done to you? He's nice to everyone here."

Martha stood still for a split second, absorbing the words or maybe just taking a good breath before continuing her lashing. "You were the one person I could count on to be normal in this goddamned insane asylum," she said. "Now you're acting just as crazy as every other girl in this joint."

"I'm not crazy, Martha. I swear I'm not. And this is a hospital, not an asylum."

"Oh yeah? A long time ago, this place used to be called the Mississippi Asylum for the Insane. Just ask any of the nurses."

"But it's not anymore," Cissy said. "It's just a hospital now, and people come here to get better." Although, in Cissy's case, she still didn't know what about her needed fixing, or if she was just being punished for shooting her daddy. Yet Martha's words made it seem like they were loonies, locked away for good, and that made Cissy's stomach hurt.

"Some hospital," Martha snorted. "How many girls do you see getting better? You think Olivia, dribbling spit down her chin, will ever go home?"

"Dr. Guttman says that we all have the ability to get better if we work hard," Cissy said.

"Guttman? That weirdo couldn't get a job

anywhere else," Martha railed. "He's just as crazy as you are."

"I'm not crazy! Take it back!"

"Crazy people talk to themselves," Martha yelled.

"I don't talk to myself," Cissy yelled back. "I talk to God."

Nurse Edna popped around the corner to check on the noise. She and Martha clammed up instantly, fearing they'd have TV privileges taken away or worse.

"We'll be quiet. We promise," Cissy said, looking down at her feet.

The nurse eyed them for what seemed an eternity before exiting the rec room and retreating behind the glass wall of the nurses' station. As soon as she was out of sight, Cissy yanked Martha by the hand and forced her onto the ottoman. Her black hair, left uncombed for a week, stuck out in every direction, and her pupils had gone black and menacing. Everything about her seemed darker.

Cissy begged her to calm down; that she'd explain everything. Martha wasn't about to settle down, so Cissy held her wrists. She told her all about God, how beautiful and smart She was, and how She made Cissy think about the world in different ways, at times to the point of making her head hurt. She said she didn't know why God loved chess so much, but it had become something they enjoyed doing together. Cissy thought Martha of all people would understand, but her body just stiffened.

She yanked her hands from Cissy's and scuttled backward to the far corner of the library, putting as much space as possible between them.

"It's just you at the chess board. I see you move the pieces for both players. You're either bat-shit crazy or you're trying to play a trick on me!"

"Don't be scared, Martha." Cissy put her hands up in surrender. "I'll prove it to you that I'm telling the truth. I'll ask God to talk to you, too. One more person knowing shouldn't hurt."

Martha shook her head from side to side, her flushed cheeks shiny and wet.

"Stay away from me! Don't touch me!" she shouted when Cissy rose from the chair, arms outstretched.

Cissy thought if she could just hold her, surely she'd become her Martha again. She took another step, but it was one she'd always regret.

Martha howled. With wide swipes of her skinny arms, she sent books flying off the shelves. She shoved her shoulder into one of the bookcases, which toppled down onto two girls who were listening to the conversation from the other side. Pinned and yelping under the avalanche of books, they incited a frenzy in Martha. She jumped up and down on the ottoman and continued her howling until two orderlies rushed in and dragged her from the room. Cissy huddled in the opposite corner of what had been her safe place, closing her eyes and sheltering her ears.

Chapter 21

The staff doctor, the kind who heals your body and not your mind, expressed concern Cissy had dropped so much weight in the few weeks she'd been at the hospital. He must have phoned her grandmother, who in rapid fashion phoned her. Cissy explained that a bout with stomach flu wasn't a good reason for a seventy-two-year-old woman to drive from Biloxi to Meridian.

"I just don't have an appetite," Cissy said. "I'm not trying to starve myself for Chrissake."

"Don't take the Lord's name in vain, young lady. You've got to put on some weight or they'll start feeding you intravenously or by feeding tube. Do you want me to paint you a picture of how unpleasant that would be?"

To get her off the phone and avoid hearing about those unpleasantries, Cissy had promised to eat more and to take better care of her health. Despite those assurances, she suspected her grandmother would make an in-person visit to see for herself whether or not worry was warranted.

Just as Cissy predicted, her grandmother arrived the next Sunday for the midday meal. Patients who proved they could behave and were not a danger to themselves or others were allowed visitors once a week. With enough notice, family members could eat with the patients. Cissy assumed her grandmother had enough connections and money that she could eat there anytime she pleased. Still, she was glad the visit was on the sanctioned day so it wouldn't appear that Cissy had special privileges.

When her grandmother entered the cafeteria, Cissy ran to embrace her. She was much more stooped than Cissy remembered, so she bent down to get a better grip. While Grandmother usually didn't approve of public displays of affection, she hugged Cissy for longer than what would feel comfortable to normal folks. Not being normal, Cissy hugged her back just as forcefully. Maybe the one good thing to come of this whole mess was her grandmother had learned the importance of showing her love in an outward way.

They walked through the cafeteria line together, although Cissy knew her grandmother would have preferred table service. She watched her wince a bit with each spoonful added to her tray—mashed potatoes, creamed corn, hamburger steak, applesauce. Perhaps having a meal here would convince her that Cissy's lack of appetite was warranted.

"You don't have to eat this if you'd rather not," Cissy whispered. "It takes some getting used to."

The corners of her grandmother's mouth curled with restrained disgust. "I drove more than three hours to dine with my granddaughter and that's what I'm going to do." She took a tentative bite, followed by a large gulp of water.

"You came here to check on my health," Cissy reminded her.

"Well, truthfully, I'm glad I did. You look emaciated. I'm going to talk to the doctor myself."

"I'm just tall. That makes me seem skinnier than I actually am."

"Where's your friend Martha? She usually says hello when I visit."

Cissy used her fork to make a crisscross pattern in her mashed potatoes and shrugged.

"Is there something you'd like to talk about, Cissy?"

There was no simple way to explain how her relationship with Martha had changed. Cissy feared the ugliness had always been a part of Martha and she'd been just too stupid to see it.

"She and I had a fight. It'll blow over soon." Cissy didn't know if her words were lies or just plain old hope.

They ate in silence for most of the meal. Cissy swallowed every last bit of the tasteless beige food. Not just to prove to Grandmother she could eat, but to start putting on weight. She had looked up the word *intravenous* after their last call and the thought of that type of feeding now scared the bejesus out of her.

After the meal, Grandmother removed a gold Estée Lauder lipstick case from her purse and quick as a whip, applied a new coat of lipstick to match the sunshiny orange of her suit. She pressed her paper napkin between her lips and put back on her gloves just as Mr. Carnell, the hospital administrator, approached the table. Cissy put the stained napkin in her sweater pocket so she'd have something of Grandmother for later.

"Why, Mrs. Clayton, what a surprise to see you here today of all days!" Mr. Carnell said in a whiny voice.

Cissy rolled her eyes. Her grandmother shot her a look of consternation as the administrator held out his little man hand for a shake.

"It's truly a lovely surprise, Mr. Carnell," Grandmother said. "And what a coincidence that you happened upon us here in the cafeteria. I have a favor to ask of you."

They stepped away from the table for some privacy, but Cissy still heard snatches of their conversation. Grandmother expected special privileges wherever she went and the Greater Mississippi State Hospital was no exception. She'd convinced Mr. Carnell to allow her to visit with Cissy a little longer, but in the privacy of her room.

A nurse whose name she didn't know led them from the cafeteria, through the locked security area to the ward where she stayed. When they got to Cissy's door, the nurse left it wide open and lingered just a touch too long. As soon as she walked down the hall, Grandmother got up and closed the door.

Cissy showed her the many pictures she'd drawn with the art supplies her grandmother had sent. A gallery of patients and hospital staff lined the white cinderblock walls. She liked drawing faces the best.

"You're a fine artist, Cissy. You capture the eyes perfectly."

"I have lots of time to practice." Cissy beamed with pride and watched her grandmother take a visual inventory of everything in the room, including the books Cissy checked out from the hospital library once a week. It's not like they needed a library card, but for some reason, the nurses wanted to keep track of who had what book in her room. She decided against telling Grandmother about her reading lessons with Lucien, remembering God's advice and Martha's overreaction.

"Are you treated well, Cissy? I'll have any problem straightened out in no time."

Cissy assured her the staff treated her just fine. "Please don't worry, Grandmother. The flu lasted only a short while and I usually stopped throwing up by mid-afternoon. I'll gain back the weight soon."

Her grandmother stared at her for an uncomfortable minute as if she were trying to read her mind. "Cissy, darling, when was the last time you had your monthly visitor?" she asked.

"Maybe the middle of May," Cissy guessed. Didn't she remember they'd talked about this some time ago? Grandmother was the one who suggested Cissy's monthly visitor was irregular because of all the stress she'd been put through.

Her grandmother's blue eyes reminded Cissy of her own. She searched them deeply, confused by the tears now marring her silky, powdered cheeks. Before Cissy could ask what was wrong, her grandmother patted her thigh one last time and said she needed to talk to the hospital administrator.

When Nurse Edna told Cissy she'd have to see the hospital doctor again, she wedged herself under her desk and refused to budge.

"Dear girl, get up off the floor. There's no reason to be so upset." The nurse knelt to look her in the eye.

"You're going to get your white hose dirty," Cissy warned when her long fingers reached in.

"Cissy Pickering, I swear I'll drag you out by your hair," she said, but Cissy knew her favorite nurse was just trying to sound authoritative.

"I'm not sick!" she yelled. "Please leave me alone!"

"Cissy, you will not speak in that tone. This is just a routine checkup and I expect you to cooperate."

Cooperating was the last thing on her mind, so she wasn't surprised when Nurse Possum Eyes arrived with a shot she said would settle Cissy's nerves. A shot wasn't necessary. Nurse Brown had about fifty pounds on her. She could have wrestled her out in no time or lifted the desk off.

"Please, please. I promise I'll go see the doctor. I don't need the shot." Her words didn't reach them before she felt the stinging heat of the drug entering her thigh. She'd had this liquid before—the week she'd been punished for cutting herself—and now melted once again to what she and Martha called the in-between place, not quite asleep and not quite awake.

Nurse Edna led her down the stairs to the infirmary on the first floor. Cissy was grateful she stayed at her side the whole time, a tall and comforting shadow. She was more grateful there was no touching of private parts. The doctor checked her temperature and made her stick out her tongue and say "Ahhh." The shot had made Cissy dizzy and a bit off balance, making it difficult to pee in the small glass jar.

Her hearing went a bit woozy as well, but she heard the doctor advising her to get some rest. Nurse Edna pressed Cissy's head into her shoulder and put an arm around her waist as they walked back to her room. She climbed into bed, not bothering to change into pajamas. When Nurse Edna tucked the blanket around Cissy's legs, the tenderness warmed her. It reminded Cissy of how she used to tuck in Jessie and Lily.

Exhausted, she fell into a strange sleep dotted with memories she wasn't quite sure were her own. She didn't know how long she'd slept when a scraping noise jerked her awake.

"Are you sick?" Martha crouched on the chair next to her desk. "Olivia saw Nurse Edna bringing you back from the infirmary."

"Nah, just a checkup." Cissy sat up and rubbed her head. "But I didn't want to go and they gave me the shot."

Martha didn't frighten Cissy anymore, but a huge sadness hung over her whenever she saw her now. After the outburst in the library, the orderlies took Martha away and Cissy didn't see her for a week. When she returned, Martha wasn't Martha anymore. Large gray circles haunted her eyes and hinted at the horrors she must have endured but refused to talk about. She said it wasn't important anymore, just water under the bridge.

The two girls who had been hit by the falling bookshelf avoided Martha and cried out if she sat anywhere near them at meals or in the rec room. Soon, Martha avoided all patients except Cissy to make it easier on everyone, she said.

Cissy thought back to the old black and white movie *Invasion of the Body Snatchers* that she had snuck downstairs to watch on TV one night when her mama and daddy were out and Grandmother was babysitting. She shuddered to think an alien had taken her friend's place. Could that be any more ridiculous than Olivia's claims that the doctors sometimes shock patients with electricity to make them feel better? Cissy didn't dare ask Martha if that's what happened to her. She wasn't afraid of her reaction; she was afraid Martha would say it was true.

"I hate the shot," Martha said. "Why didn't you want to see the doctor? He's pretty nice."

Cissy didn't know how to explain the complicated feelings she had about doctors, so she just shrugged. She didn't trust this version of Martha to understand her story any longer.

Martha licked one of her palms and smoothed down the pieces of hair around Cissy's face. She flinched, but allowed her touch. Maybe it would mend the awkwardness between them.

"There, you look better," Martha said. "Let's go eat dinner."

To steady herself, Cissy grabbed Martha's hand and they walked to the dining area together. It wasn't until she sat down that she noticed the hum of voices. The whispers faded in and out, and she couldn't hear exactly what the girls were saying.

"They're just gossiping about Lucien," Martha said, and stuffed a spoonful of applesauce into her mouth. She let it drip down her chin without wiping.

"What about Lucien?" Cissy hadn't noticed if he had arrived for work yet. She had just checked out a new book to read to him.

"Two security guards showed up and said he had to leave the building immediately. They took his badge and everything," Martha said. "He put up a fuss and one of the guards hit him on the back of the knee with a little black bat he took off his belt."

Cissy had no words to express her shock.

"Olivia said she heard a nurse say Lucien had gotten one of the patients pregnant and was fired," Martha continued. "I suspect he'll go to jail."

"Lucien wouldn't do that!"

"How do you know? Maybe he's as friendly with other girls as he is with you?" she said, trying to look interested in her food.

"What are you saying?" Cissy's voice cracked and all the girls at the table turned to look at her. "Stop your staring!" she yelled back at them.

"Hush or you'll get another shot," Martha said in a singsong voice.

"Don't tell me to hush. Why don't you like Lucien? He hasn't done anything wrong to anybody."

"I don't know. You've had sex with your own father, why wouldn't you have sex with Lucien? Maybe you're the girl who's pregnant!"

Cissy stumbled from her chair, sending it clanging to the shifting floor. She tried to steady herself against the wall before rushing to the safety of her room, away from the girl who now scared her more than Old Scratch. She buried her face in the quilt until it was soaked with frustrated tears. She cried for Lucien and the lies being told about him. She cried for herself a little, too. Cissy knew how it felt when no one believed you. She knew how it felt when the grass turned blue and the skies turned green.

Chapter 22

For Janelle, faith had required swallowing a good bit of doubt and believing God knew what He was doing. When she'd read about a natural disaster or other tragedy in the newspaper, she'd make the sign of the cross and whisper, "God's will be done." She didn't much care for God's will anymore. In fact, Janelle didn't much care for God. She'd been reared to believe He could be a merciful God, but she'd been misled.

In the several weeks since the shooting, He'd shown not one iota of mercy. Lately, He bordered on cruel. The incest had shaken her foundation and she refused to forgive Him for letting such a horrific thing happen to an innocent. Her nightly prayers had turned into indictments. Ruth said God would never give them more than they could bear. Ruth was wrong.

"Have they told her yet?" Caroline sat forward in the driver's seat, too close to the steering wheel as if she couldn't make out the road through the rain.

"No, Dr. Guttman wanted both of us present," Janelle said.

She'd told Caroline the details of the call several times, yet her daughter asked the same questions over and over, stuck on rewind, pausing only to ensure she'd heard correctly. *Cissy. Pregnant.*

"I don't think I can go through with it," Caroline said. "You'll have to go in alone."

She'd repeated this same line a dozen times during the drive from Biloxi to Meridian, so Janelle didn't bother to answer. Caroline managed to hold on to some semblance of sanity, albeit tenuous, and for that she deserved some credit.

Janelle had not fared as well. Dr. Guttman called the day before yesterday. After she'd hung up the phone, she walked to the garage to get the hedge clippers. She beheaded every rose, zinnia, and poppy in the garden because their beauty disgusted her. She cut them down as Cissy had been cut down. Ruth had grabbed her from behind, but Janelle wrestled free and targeted the wet sheets hanging on the line nearby, shredding them. Exhausted, her arms leaden from wielding the heavy clippers, she sunk to her knees.

Ruth had picked her up and dragged her to the sofa in the sitting room. Janelle waited as Ruth fetched sleeping pills and a shot of bourbon, then made no effort to resist when she put them to her lips. A dead sleep claimed her for eighteen hours and even then, consciousness only came because of Ruth's worried slap to her cheek. She was still in her muddied clothes, but covered with an afghan.

"You're the strongest woman I know, Mrs. Clayton," Ruth had said, helping her up the stairs and into the bathroom. "You can't go losing your senses just yet. Cissy needs you."

Janelle had undressed and Ruth coaxed her into a scalding tub. With a gentle but firm manner, Ruth had washed her hair and dug the soil out from under her nail tips with tweezers. Janelle felt no shame as the hot water trickled over her head and down her back. She had felt nothing.

"After your last visit with Cissy, you suspected she might be pregnant, didn't you?" Ruth had asked.

She remembered she'd been alarmed by her vomiting and weight loss, and had asked about Cissy's monthly visitor. Although the idea may have crept in for a single black moment, it hadn't taken root. Janelle wouldn't allow it. Instead, she had demanded that the hospital physician conduct a physical to discover why Cissy didn't seem well.

"I truly thought I'd jumped to conclusions and even regretted telling you my suspicions," Janelle had said. "We all assumed that the pediatrician who examined Cissy before the hearing would have administered a pregnancy test."

"I prayed to God you were wrong, but he didn't see fit to answer my prayers this time," Ruth had said. "Best get dressed and have a bite to eat. I called Miss Caroline and told her you had to see her right away in person." Ruth left her to sit in the tepid water, a gray scum ringing the edges of the tub and where her skin met the water.

She couldn't remember the exact words she used to tell Caroline that Cissy was pregnant, and she hadn't known how Caroline reacted once home in the privacy of her bedroom. But last night, Caroline stood before her, mute and unyielding, willing to bear the weight of the unbelievable facts Janelle had lain before her. They'd planned the trip to Meridian with few words; just a promise to meet in the morning to drive together. They hadn't embraced. They could manage little more than breathing.

"The Lauderdale County Sheriff will be there to interview Cissy," she reminded Caroline as they pulled into the grounds of the hospital. The rain had stopped and a mist shrouded the building's second story.

"Yes, yes, of course," she mumbled back. "That orderly raped Cissy and needs to be punished. We need the facts."

"That's nonsense. We both know the child is Richard's."

When Caroline slammed both feet on the brake, Janelle's shoulder connected with the dashboard and her head with the windshield.

"Jesus, Mary, and Joseph! Do you want to kill me?" Janelle felt her head for a lump.

Caroline let out a high-pitched scream that

filled the space between them. Janelle shrank back against the passenger door. "The entire world's gone insane! Now you're trying to convince me that my own daughter, my flesh and blood, is pregnant by . . ."

Janelle put a hand on Caroline's shoulder. "I'm sorry. I agree. This all feels insane."

"Mother, why can't you have just a shred of doubt? Why can't you give that to me?" Caroline asked.

Janelle pondered two horrific explanations: Cissy was carrying her father's baby or Cissy had been raped yet again, this time by a hospital employee. How could the latter make Caroline feel any better? Would proving the baby wasn't Richard's make any difference in her ability to live her life, to be a mother to Lily and Jessie? Did her sanity or reputation rest on this one outcome?

"I'm here for you as much as Cissy," Janelle said. "Let's see what Dr. Guttman can tell us."

They made their way up to the women's ward, Caroline taking in every detail. Janelle had forgotten that her daughter had never seen the inside of the hospital. She wondered if the reality of the place matched Caroline's expectations or fears.

Dr. Guttman led them into his office and they took a seat on the sofa while he went to get Cissy.

He said he planned to tell her they were there, but not the reason until everyone was in the same room.

They heard Cissy's excited chatter long before she burst into the office and ran toward them.

Janelle stood first and hugged Cissy with a rocking motion. She wanted to give Caroline time to process what it'd feel like to see her daughter after so long. But Caroline stood almost instantly, arms outstretched. Seeing Caroline and Cissy embrace sent shockwaves through Janelle's limbs. She couldn't imagine what they must be feeling, but the amount of tears being shed surely indicated each had needed the other desperately these past weeks.

It was clear Cissy had no intention of letting go. "Honey, let's sit down," Caroline whispered. "I'm not going anywhere."

Janelle wasn't the only one who noticed that Dr. Guttman struggled with the gravity of the meeting. Cissy instantly called him out on his long face and stooped shoulders. "Why so glum? Fall on your bum?"

The phrase was familiar. Janelle remembered Cissy using it on her a time or two, but when the girl was much younger. Janelle looked down, ashamed that she wanted to be rescued from the room, to be free of them all—Caroline and her rage, Cissy and her sometimes tenuous hold on reality, Dr. Guttman and his talk therapy.

"Cissy, we have something very important to discuss. I need you to be serious." Dr. Guttman motioned for her to sit down between Janelle and Caroline.

A rap at the door caused all four of them to jump. A nurse ushered in a tall man in uniform.

"Sheriff Talbot, this is Cissy Pickering and her mother and grandmother," Dr. Guttman said. "Why don't you pull up a chair for our conversation?"

The man thanked them for coming all the way from Biloxi on such short notice.

"Please, someone tell me what's going on." Cissy seemed to survey the room's occupants. "Is this about me shooting Daddy? Am I going to prison after all?"

Janelle's heart broke to see Cissy frantically trying to understand the true meaning of their visit. She doubted how wise it was to include the sheriff.

"Cissy, you're not going to prison. This is about Lucien," Dr. Guttman said. "He's been accused of hurting you. The hospital suspended him from his position until we can investigate." The doctor's words didn't match the calm behind them. Perhaps it was a technique to keep them all from running from the room, stark raving mad.

"What lies has Martha been telling you? She's not well, Dr. Guttman. You can't believe her lies!" Cissy leapt from the sofa and backed up against the closed door, her hand grasping for the knob and possible escape. Her eyes darted between Caroline's drawn, pained face and the doctor's placid one.

"Dr. Guttman, is this necessary? Perhaps we could meet with Cissy first and then the sheriff could ask his questions." Janelle tried to mimic Dr. Guttman's tone, slowing her speech in an effort to soothe Cissy's agitation. She motioned for Cissy to return to the couch, and her grand-daughter reluctantly obliged.

"Mrs. Clayton, it's the hospital's policy. It can't be helped." Dr. Guttman's words sounded hollow to Janelle as if traveling through a paper towel tube. "Cissy, we have some difficult news to share about your recent checkup. I don't know how to begin. . . ."

The sheriff took out a small spiral notebook that looked a lot like the ones Cissy used. "I can take it from here, Doctor. Young lady, I need to ask you a few personal questions so we can start sorting out this matter. I hope that's okay. I promise to make it quick."

Cissy began humming, soft and low at first, then louder before she started counting—one, two, three, four, one, two, three, four—at the top of her lungs. Although her hands were in her lap, she used an index finger to point at each of them as she counted.

"For God's sake, Cissy, stop that counting," Caroline said. "We just need you to tell us what Lucien did to you. You aren't in any trouble. I promise. The sheriff just needs to know what happened."

"We don't know if this is Lucien's doing," Dr. Guttman replied.

"Doctor, I'd advise you not to jump to any conclusions about the girl's daddy and the pregnancy," the sheriff said. "Mr. Thibodeaux may well have taken advantage of Miss Pickering in her confused mental state. This sort of thing isn't uncommon in mental institutions. We need to look at all possibilities."

Cissy blinked her eyes several times and seemed to sway.

Janelle jumped from her seat and begged everyone to be quiet. "Can't you see you're upsetting Cissy? We agreed to handle this differently."

"Lucien didn't do anything to me. He's my friend," Cissy screamed before going completely slack.

Janelle could tell the exact instant Cissy's brain refused to cooperate further. She had watched in slow motion while Cissy's pupils grew large and murky, and her shoulders slumped, sending her to the floor. The girl hadn't fainted. Her eyes blinked and seemed to follow the shouting around her. Her lips moved as if searching for a lost pacifier.

Caroline, hands balled into peach-sized fists, towered over Dr. Guttman as he loosened Cissy's blouse and listened to her chest.

"You're her goddamned psychiatrist! Why did you and the sheriff just blurt everything out like that? How could you not know she'd react like this?" she screamed.

"Give me some room, Mrs. Pickering," he said, and pushed her away. "Now!"

The sharpness of his order sent Caroline scrambling into a corner of the office, her eyes never leaving Cissy's unresponsive body. Her hands shot to her mouth when two orderlies picked up Cissy by her underarms and led her away. Cissy's feet dragged behind her, useless like a rag doll's cotton-stuffed appendages, so the larger orderly scooped her up in his arms.

"Stay here. I'll be back." Dr. Guttman spoke in Janelle's direction before running after the orderlies and shouting instructions to a nearby nurse.

"Well, ladies, I don't guess you'll be needing me anymore this afternoon," the sheriff mumbled, hat in hand, shifting his weight like he was ready to bolt. The keys on his belt jingled an absurd tune. "That is, unless you can shed some light on the girl's relationship with her daddy. What's the likelihood he's the father of the young lady's unborn child?"

"How dare you!" Caroline pointed a skinny finger at the sheriff. "I won't stand for you to make those kinds of accusations without any proof. Get the hell out of here."

Sheriff Talbot turned to Janelle.

"Yes, please go." She nodded toward the door. As he left, Janelle could see a number of patients and staff standing nearby. They'd obviously seen Cissy being removed from the office. And they'd likely overheard Caroline's tirade.

When they were alone again, her daughter sank to the floor and whimpered. "Let's go, Mother. Please let's go home."

"Shut up, Caroline. Just shut up." Janelle doubted Caroline had heard the impotent order, but no one was going anywhere until they knew more about Cissy's state of mind and where she'd been taken.

Janelle slipped off her shoes and reclined on the leather sofa. Closing her eyes, she could almost convince herself that she and Caroline hadn't left Biloxi yet, that she hadn't received Dr. Guttman's phone call, that Cissy hadn't pulled the trigger that June morning. While Caroline's lack of composure alarmed Janelle somewhat, she envied her ability to make this about her own suffering, to languish in all its grotesqueness. Janelle had felt something similar when she desecrated her garden.

She imagined she could drift off to sleep to escape the incredible fatigue that invaded her body. Was this the cancer at work, or just her inability to absorb what unfolded around her?

They waited close to an hour before Dr. Guttman returned to his office.

"Mrs. Clayton, Mrs. Pickering, I'm sorry for the delay," he said. "I wanted to be sure Cissy was settled and comfortable before I left her."

He told them that she'd been taken to the infirmary. She was awake, but still non-responsive. Janelle and Caroline looked at each other.

"She's in a catatonic state," he clarified. "I like to think of it as her brain's way of shutting down before becoming overloaded."

Caroline joined Janelle on the couch. "Is it permanent?" she asked.

"I can't answer that question just yet," he said. "We'll monitor her closely over the next few days and contact you should there be any improvement."

"I'm staying," Janelle said, and planted her feet on the rug.

"What do you mean you're staying?" Caroline's eyes grew wide and unsure.

Janelle formulated her plan on the fly. "You take the car back. I'll get a hotel room. Have Ruth pack me a suitcase and drive up in my car. She can stay with me."

"You're going to let your housekeeper drive your Cadillac and then share a hotel room with her instead of coming back with me? Don't you care how hard this is for me? *I* need you now."

Dr. Guttman sat perfectly still, allowing the drama to play out.

"As much as you want to make this about you right now, it damn well isn't," Janelle said. "And Ruth has always been more than my housekeeper and you know it."

Caroline looked to Dr. Guttman for support, or possibly to serve as mediator, but he gave her nothing.

"Fine." She grabbed her handbag with an exaggerated yank and moved to the door. "And you're both wrong. I'll get a paternity test."

No words from Caroline or anyone else for that matter could shock Janelle now, but Dr. Guttman paled at the sharp change in Caroline's demeanor.

"Your family might benefit from talking to a counselor," he said after she slammed the door. "You're all under a tremendous amount of stress."

Janelle laughed at his understatement and he shot her a puzzled look.

"Caroline and I won't be talking for a while. I appreciate your concern, though."

He offered to give her a lift to the Howard Johnson, which she gratefully accepted. A strange room and bed held some appeal at the end of this surreal day. She looked forward to slipping into the unfamiliar surroundings and hiding from the realities before her, including how she would arrange an abortion for Cissy.

Chapter 23

Janelle wondered about her motive in asking Lucien to meet her at the Howard Johnson's coffee shop. Maybe she hoped to confirm her belief that he was not the father of Cissy's baby. Maybe she wanted to offer her support knowing he was one of Cissy's few friends at the hospital.

He wore his white uniform as if he'd be heading to work after their meeting. Perhaps it'd become habit to dress in the uniform, or maybe he thought it was more respectable than his street clothes for their meeting. As he raised the cup to his lips, his hands wouldn't cooperate and their tremor threatened to slosh the coffee from its ceramic confines onto the blank canvas of his shirt. He placed his hands under the table, but his body betrayed his nerves. One eye winked in a telling tic every few seconds, and he moved his head from side to side until the bones in his thick neck cracked and popped.

"I would never hurt Miss Cissy, ma'am," he said. "I don't know why you asked me here, but I'd just as soon put that out on the table first."

"I like your bluntness, Mr. Thibodeaux." She spoke quietly so the other diners couldn't hear. "I don't suppose I would've asked to meet you if I suspected you had done what you've been accused of doing. I'm here to help you."

The brown spots dotting her aging hands mocked her. She had forgotten her gloves and felt unmasked in front of this young stranger who waited patiently for her to get to the reason for the visit. The vinyl booth sat so low she could've used a child's booster seat. Janelle had to raise her eyes to meet his. She'd seen those eyes before, reproduced by Cissy's hand in a portrait hanging on the wall of her hospital room alongside portraits of others she cherished.

"Cissy wrote me that you and she were friends. I'm grateful for your kindness to her," she said. "Given those letters and her feelings, it seems far-fetched to think you'd do anything to harm the child."

"Ma'am, I don't understand. What would I have done to harm Miss Cissy? Nothin' changes just 'cause the hospital took away my job. We're still friends. Maybe I can even visit her soon."

Janelle told Lucien she feared more than his job was at risk. Cissy's pregnancy had caused a firestorm of supposition. "Accusing a young man of simple means, one who'd just moved to Mississippi, seems more palatable to law enforcement than admitting a father impregnated his teenage daughter," she said.

Lucien's expression went from shock to alarm. "Miss Cissy is with child?"

"Please forgive me for being so explicit, but the hospital thinks you may have raped Cissy. They've called in the sheriff to investigate. Son, you may be in quite a bit of trouble."

Lucien hadn't grasped that his dismissal could lead to criminal charges. He said he thought he'd been punished for the late-night reading lessons with Cissy and nothing more. "And you think her daddy got her in that way?"

His face distorted, not in anger, but something raw and grotesque. His lower lip, pink and chapped, stuck out over his chin. Janelle glanced around the room, fearing the other patrons had noticed the change in his posture. Lucien now slumped forward, upper arms pressed against the edge of the table, shoulders rising and falling. Fat tears dropped onto the tabletop, but he made no move to wipe them away.

"Mr. Thibodeaux . . . Lucien . . . you mustn't." She pushed a handful of paper napkins toward him. "Get yourself together. I know you're afraid. . . ."

"I ain't afraid, Mrs. Clayton," he blubbered. "My head wants to bust wide open. I can't bear to think about her daddy hurting her in that way. Lord, help me. I wish you'd never put those thoughts there."

His words summed up her mental state so simply. Over the last month she'd been pummeled by one revelation after another, each threatening her sanity in a more concrete way. Her brain cells kneaded the details of Cissy's abuse and left them to rise into an amorphous dough pushing against Janelle's skull. She woke with excruciating headaches and babysat them until sleeping pills coaxed them to leave her for eight blessed hours. Her head had no room to hold the news that the rape had resulted in a pregnancy.

"Lucien, did Cissy tell you she killed her daddy?"

Their coffee cups danced on their saucers when his forearms hit the underside of the table. He sat erect, shocked by the question. Cissy hadn't told him why she'd been committed to the hospital after all.

"The Bible tells us killing is wrong." His voice boomed. "And my mama told me two wrongs don't make a right." Like Cissy, Lucien probably adhered to rules that made his world safer, more straightforward. Gray areas became wide-open terrain with chasms eager to swallow rule-breakers. Janelle had shocked him twice in just these few minutes and he could take no more.

"Yes, son, killing is wrong, but Cissy felt she had no other choice."

"Ma'am, there's always another choice." He shook his head furiously.

Denying this truth made it easier for Janelle to stomach the murder. *Murder*. The word that Cissy had placed on her list of banned words and they'd all followed suit in never speaking it. But for the grace of God, the judge could have felt as Lucien did. He could have withheld mercy, holding her responsible for the very adult act she'd committed.

Janelle reached across the table and touched Lucien's hand. Maybe she calculated her touch could erase whatever judgment pulsed through his mind and heart. Even though Cissy would never know Lucien's reaction, Janelle stood in as proxy and felt the rejection of her friend.

"Cissy's not well," she said.

"What do you mean?"

She explained how the news had been too much for Cissy to comprehend and her mind was sleeping now until she was able to understand all that was happening to her. Lucien's brow creased as he took in this development.

"Well, ma'am, if it's too much for me and you to think about, seems normal that Miss Cissy would suffer from the truth more than anybody. I wonder if there's any way to fix what's broken in her."

Janelle said she didn't know, but planned to stay in Meridian, to be close in case her granddaughter needed her.

"What's going to happen to me?" Lucien whispered as if talking to himself.

"I'm going to stand by you, young man. I won't let you take the blame for something Cissy's father did. I'll handle whatever legal fees you might incur."

"I thank you for your concern, Mrs. Clayton. But I'd just as soon not hear from you again. I can't shut off my brain like Miss Cissy can, but I'd like to try my hardest to never think of this again."

Getting out of the booth, he nearly knocked over the waitress who'd come to refill their cups.

"Ma'am, you all right?" The young woman glared at Lucien's back.

"Yes," Janelle lied. "But could you get me a fresh cup? This one's gone cold."

She and Ruth had been living in the motel room for the better part of a week. They'd not been allowed to visit Cissy, although they showed up every day to the state hospital and sat in the uninviting waiting room. Apparently, patients rarely received visitors, which made the room's purpose moot. It was theirs for the taking.

Ruth brought some knitting to keep her hands and mind occupied. When she grew bored of that, she read aloud her favorite parts of the Bible. After reading the few out-of-date issues of *Time* magazine resting on the coffee table, Janelle just picked a random object to stare at and timed how long it could keep her attention. One day she stared at a dusty leaf on a plastic plant for close to half an hour. Ruth's good humor kept Janelle's temper in check and she became as docile as a lap dog under her housekeeper's care. No use angering the people who held the power, Ruth had said. Before long even the ill-tempered nurse at the front desk melted like butter and began fetching them Styrofoam cups of coffee and toast or saltines from the cafeteria.

"What's different now?" Janelle asked when Dr. Guttman called to say he'd acquiesced.

"Nothing's different now and that's what concerns me," he said. Cissy's condition hadn't changed. They fed her intravenously and changed her position every two hours so she wouldn't develop bedsores. "I originally thought seeing family would be a major stressor and detrimental to her recovery. But you've been the one person to stand by her these past weeks. Perhaps she'll respond to you."

Ruth said she worried Janelle would be disappointed beyond consoling if Cissy didn't speak to her. She was right, as usual. Yet, Janelle would gladly risk the disappointment for the precious minutes she'd have with her granddaughter, a chance to possibly help in her healing.

Diner food at the Howard Johnson's coffee shop lay heavy in their stomachs most mornings, so Ruth decided to go to the store to get fresh fruit they could keep in the motel room. She dropped Janelle off at the hospital with a promise to return in a few hours.

That morning, Janelle had taken an inordinate amount of time primping for a child who'd likely remain in her shut-off world. Still, it calmed her nerves to put on makeup and a nice suit. If anything, Janelle wanted Cissy to recognize her as she'd been before getting sick. The girl needed no other change in her life. When Dr. Guttman descended the stairs of the hospital to greet her, he complimented her appearance and she thanked him for noticing.

The infirmary stood empty except for Cissy's lone bed, tucked in the far corner of the narrow room. It reminded Janelle of wartime hospital wards, where the cot-like iron beds held soldiers trying to heal both physical and emotional injuries—just like Cissy.

A white fabric curtain on ceiling rails enclosed the area around the bed for privacy, although it proved unnecessary on the vacant ward. Dr. Guttman didn't follow Janelle in, but asked that she inform the nurse on duty should Cissy show any signs of awareness. As much as Janelle wanted to see Cissy, the curtain filled her with dread. Her hand shook to think of what lay behind it. "Calm down, Janelle," she whispered. "She's your grandchild."

When she pulled back the curtain, she thought her eyes were playing tricks on her. Cissy looked like a much younger child taking a nap after a summer afternoon of raucous playtime. The nurse had turned Cissy on her side and tucked both hands under her flushed cheek. Had she been posed for Janelle's benefit, or had the woman acted gently, subconsciously, to make Cissy appear as serene on the outside as perhaps she was in her internal world? Janelle pulled up a chair and sat close to the bed, careful not to block the sunlight streaming from the high windows onto her granddaughter. Aside from the freckles amassed across the bridge of her nose, Cissy's face remained flawless. Janelle couldn't remember ever seeing a blemish on her skin. The girl seemed to have escaped that teenage rite of passage while her peer group pricked and popped and squeezed and covered up their acne with Clearasil and Cover Girl. Right beneath Cissy's chin line, though, a thin purplish scar remained from a fall down the stairs as a three-year-old. It'd grown almost as faint as Janelle's memory of Caroline calling her from the emergency room, afraid the stitches would mar her toddler forever. Janelle now thought to herself, *Yes, Caroline, she's marred forever, but only because you did nothing to prevent the damage she's suffered at her father's hand.*

For a short while, Janelle told Cissy about her and Ruth's adventure living together in a cramped motel room. Lord, they'd both become

293

stubborn in their old age. When they'd arrived, they staked out which bed and which side of the vanity they wanted, each desperate to maintain some independence. Janelle didn't feel very independent, though, when Ruth chastised her for keeping the light on too late at night or for not saying prayers before going to bed or for keeping the window AC unit on too cold. Ruth also insisted that the travel-sized shampoo and lotion in the bathroom were hers since she'd packed Janelle an overnight case with her own fancy facial and hair products.

Janelle waited for a weak laugh or a smile from Cissy, or even the rate of her blinking to vary, but nothing changed, even when Janelle pulled one of her hands free to hold.

"Cissy, Cissy. Dear girl, please talk to me. You're not alone. Nothing can separate us but death, and just let that coward try to claim me before you and I can have a good chat again."

She sat with her motionless granddaughter until noon when Ruth showed up with lunch. Janelle met her down in the waiting area. Ruth had bought egg salad and ham salad sandwiches, but apologized they wouldn't be as good as the kind she made. Janelle smiled at her pride.

"At least they used homemade bread," Ruth said, mouth full. "Nowadays everyone's using that gluey white bread. Let me tell you, Mrs. Baird doesn't know a thing about baking."

They ate in relative silence as Janelle had little to share of the morning. Ruth patted her knee a couple of times to let her know she was sorry Cissy hadn't responded.

"I'm going to sit with Cissy until the end of the day, Ruth. If nothing changes, we should go home for a spell. I've grown tired of the Howard Johnson."

Ruth nodded her agreement, but weariness filled her eyes as if she feared Cissy might live in that state indefinitely. While Ruth cleared the leftovers, Janelle asked if she could borrow her Bible. Ruth had one with her wherever she went so as to not waste idle moments with daydreaming or napping. Ruth's eyebrows rose with mock suspicion at the request.

"What? It's for Cissy," Janelle said. "I thought I might read to her a bit."

"It wouldn't hurt you either, Mrs. Clayton," she said, eyes clear and bright again. "Seems you and God have had some words lately and need to have a talk to straighten things out."

"Old woman, best not to step in the middle of the business I have with God. I'll see you back here around five p.m."

"Well, then, I'll just have to pray for you myself." She walked away from Janelle and lifted her arms to the heavens, perhaps already summoning God's attention.

Janelle read to Cissy from the New Testament

because Janelle didn't care much for stories of banishment from paradise, floods and famine, treks into the desert, or parting of seas. Even as a child, she'd thought the Old Testament too full of itself with its exaggerated lessons and heroic and villainous characters. Ruth's Bible told a story of its own: worn and dog-eared pages marking much-loved or much-needed passages, rippled watermarked pages where tears had dropped, her family tree scribbled on the last page and spilling over onto the inside back cover.

Janelle's mouth soon grew cottony from the reading and she asked the nurse to bring some water. As soon as she left the room, Janelle stood on the tips of her toes to look out the window, but the sill remained out of her reach. Confident she was alone, she stood on the wooden chair and took in the views of the hospital lawn and gardens. The skies had turned overcast, but the muted light made the greens seem more vibrant. Janelle peered hungrily as a toddler would, aching to climb over his crib railing and run free.

"I'm tired of Jesus stories for right now. Would you read to me about David and Goliath instead?" Cissy murmured.

Janelle toppled from the chair and landed with a thump on the floor, her mouth still open in surprise. Surely the Lord had intervened because she hadn't broken a bone. Cissy continued to stare straight ahead, not moved enough to comment on her grandmother's indelicate fall, but she *had* spoken.

Janelle pulled the chair back over to the bed. "Let me turn to that page right now."

She read and read about the larger-than-life characters she had once loathed, hoping they'd bring Cissy back to life.

Janelle should've contacted the nurse or Dr. Guttman right away, but she couldn't risk leaving Cissy in that precious moment. If Cissy wanted Old Testament stories, by damn Janelle was going to read them to her. She read long into the afternoon until Cissy's eyes closed and Janelle was confident she slept. Without permission from the nurse, she rolled Cissy to her other side. Cissy may have looked frail in that state, but Janelle found her weight almost too much to move and she puffed from the exertion. After tucking the sheet up around her granddaughter's shoulders, Janelle stood, catching her breath and rubbing her hip and tailbone, sore from the fall.

When she arrived at Dr. Guttman's office, an orderly informed her he was with a patient, so she paced outside the door, too exhilarated to sit still. When his session ended and he caught sight of Janelle, he could tell from her smile that a breakthrough had occurred.

"She spoke!" Janelle strode past him and over to his desk. He hurried behind her to sit down at his notepad.

"Tell me everything," he instructed. He swiped at the wild strands of hair that crept over his glasses and hampered his sight.

She relayed the story, leaving out the bit about tumbling off the chair. She spoke so quickly that twice he had to ask her to slow down and repeat herself. Janelle waited for him to join in celebration, but he remained reserved.

"She just said those two brief sentences? Nothing else?"

"What else did you want? She spoke after being mute for a week. She showed she could hear us, understand what's going on around her."

Dr. Guttman apologized for upsetting her. He'd hoped that Cissy would have had a physical response, moved or asked to be moved, or spoke about where she was and why she was there.

"That's asking a lot, Doctor." Janelle's cheeks burned with anger. "I'll take the miracle I was given and you should, too."

"Yes, it's progress," he said. "If you're sure she said what you said she did."

She imagined Ruth with one hand on her shoulder, which allowed her to bite her tongue, to count to ten instead of lunging across the wide cherry desk and grabbing Dr. Guttman by the hair he seemed unwilling to cut or tame or wash.

"I'm seventy-two, not ninety-two. My hearing's just fine. And yes, I was desperate for her to speak. But I didn't imagine it. Now let's get down to business."

"What business? I don't understand," he said.

"Cissy's not going to carry . . . I won't allow the pregnancy to go forward. I want to arrange for an abortion. Can you help?"

Janelle stared, unblinking and unyielding, until he looked away and coughed.

"I agree that it's not in her best interests to carry the child," he said. "She's physically capable, but I'm concerned about the emotional risks. Her current state is a clear indication of her inability to process what's happened to her."

Janelle sighed with audible gratitude.

"Mrs. Clayton, do you understand what you're asking?"

"I guess I don't by the look on your face. You'd better explain."

"*Roe v. Wade* has galvanized most Mississippians' fervor against abortion," he said. "People have very strong feelings on this subject despite what the government tells them is legal."

"But even in Mississippi, rape and incest seem to be the two exceptions that make abortion more palatable," she said.

"I'd have to take your request to the hospital board," he said. "They're a conservative bunch. It would be a hard fight."

"You could convince them." She steeled her features to mask her doubt.

"The procedure won't guarantee Cissy will get better emotionally."

He needn't have reminded her of that. Janelle's goal was to protect her against nine months of a daily, physical reminder of her father's actions followed by the searing pain of childbirth and the equally painful decision to give up the child. Caroline would never take the child in, and neither of them could risk Cissy actually wanting to keep the baby. The girl's gentle, loving spirit might just be capable of the ultimate act of forgiveness, but the rest of them were not. Janelle was not.

They could rid Cissy's body of those miniscule cells, but they could never rid her of the acts that set those cells multiplying. Dr. Guttman seemed certain Cissy would one day be able to reconcile that the one person who should've been her greatest protector was the person she most needed protection against. He seemed certain that with time and therapy, Cissy could be a happy young woman, capable of love and laughter and a normal life. Janelle hadn't come close to that level of certainty.

"Perhaps after the abortion, she'd be better off somewhere else." She didn't know what she'd meant. The words just spilled out. Everything she said or thought about Cissy came from a primal protective place, a place over which she had no control. If that place said Janelle needed to take Cissy away from there, she'd find a way to do it.

Dr. Guttman appeared perplexed. "What do you mean by somewhere else?"

"Maybe being at a psychiatric hospital reinforces that something is wrong with Cissy," she said. "Maybe she'd get better faster if she were with family."

"Well, the courts have answered that question for you, haven't they? Perhaps you'd best leave me to decide the proper way to approach the hospital board."

"Yes, of course. Please forgive the musings of an old woman." She offered a small smile to mask the resolve building within her.

Chapter 24

After leaving Dr. Guttman's office, Janelle had gone straight to the reception desk to ask for the list of trustees on the hospital board. The nurse gave her a quizzical look, but offered the information quite easily. Janelle's long stays in the hospital waiting room may have softened the woman's doggedness for rules.

When Ruth picked up Janelle that evening, she gloated that the Bible and her God had been the instruments leading to Cissy's breakthrough. Ruth never considered that Janelle's presence and her voice had eased Cissy back to the world, but Janelle let it drop, allowing Ruth to stay in a blissful state of gratitude. Janelle, too, was grateful, but not to God.

Ruth had seemed surprised by the decision to return home to Biloxi considering Cissy finally spoke, but didn't question Janelle's thinking.

"I've work to do," Janelle said, stuffing her belongings into a suitcase. "I'll be back soon enough."

Ruth had no patience with her and butted her out of the way so she could fold the clothing properly. While Ruth organized their departure and prayed aloud, Janelle sat down at the table in the motel room and began making notes on the list the nurse had given her. Six women and three men comprised the board at the Greater Mississippi State Hospital. The women held the power over Cissy's future.

Over the next week, Janelle drove a thousand miles in four days. Ruth knew her itinerary, but had been sullen and unwilling to accompany her. She opposed the idea of abortion, and her convictions overrode the fear that Janelle was not well enough to drive alone.

During her travels, Janelle called on all six women who were quite familiar with Judge Beau Clayton and his family's legacy in Mississippi. Spread across the state, these trustees had graciously accepted her into their homes based on her husband's reputation and allowed her to tell them about a precious girl whose childhood had been stolen away. Five of them were grandmothers themselves, and it took little description of Cissy's situation for them to imagine their own granddaughters in a similar predicament. Janelle carried a photo of Cissy at age twelve, one where she looked away from the camera, no smile, no light in her eyes. All six women had been in tears when she thanked them for their support and bid them goodbye.

When an elated Dr. Guttman called to give her the good news, she let him think his skills of persuasion convinced the trustees that his recommendation for the abortion was sound. As she expected, they'd voted six to three to allow Cissy to be transported to Riley Community Hospital for the procedure. Even the lone Catholic on the board had voted yes, which was a miracle in itself.

"May I be there for her?" Janelle had asked Dr. Guttman.

He had cautioned that they wouldn't know Cissy's mental state, and that perhaps it was best for Janelle to wait to visit until Cissy was transferred back to the psychiatric hospital. Janelle had assured him she wanted to see Cissy right after the procedure.

"I'll let the hospital know you'll be waiting to see Cissy when she's in the recovery room," he had said over the phone. "It should take no more than fifteen to twenty minutes. She'll be able to leave the hospital the same day."

When Janelle told Ruth about the board's decision, she made the sign of the cross and turned back toward the sink and her dishwashing.

"What's that for, old woman?" Janelle asked.

"None of my business, ma'am," she said beneath the clanking of pots and pans.

"Speak your piece."

Ruth turned and stood proud and tall, unafraid to challenge Janelle.

"Why haven't you told Miss Caroline about your plan?" she asked. "Secrets like that cause the deepest type of wound. They'll never heal."

"I'm Cissy's guardian. It's my decision to make," Janelle said. Caroline's reaction wasn't a primary concern, nor was the permanent damage the abortion would likely do to their already strained relationship.

"Hasn't there been enough killing in this family?" Ruth asked. "Taking that baby's life ain't going to punish Mr. Pickering for his sins. He's long dead and will be judged by his Creator. It's not our right to judge the baby."

"I'm not judging the baby. Cissy shouldn't have to carry that monster's child."

"You're not giving Miss Cissy the chance to decide on her own. That baby's soul is pure. It's a miracle from God, a blessing from such a horrible thing."

Janelle let out a guttural cry and took a china dinner plate from the drain board.

"Just what are you going to do with that?" Ruth taunted.

Janelle threw it at the kitchen door, just a foot from Ruth, who didn't flinch. She wiped her hands in the dish towel, leaving the shards where they lay. Although her hair was ghost white, she seemed stronger and more assured than she'd been in her younger years.

"I'm warning you now, Ruth. Don't ever speak of blessings to me. You have your God and your beliefs, but I'll not stand to hear it in my house."

She wanted to run out the back door, to run

and run until her legs gave out. She wanted to lie in the dried hay fields behind the house and disappear. In that moment, Janelle couldn't bear to think she'd somehow crossed a line. Without Ruth's support, Janelle had no one.

"I told you it was none of my business, but you asked anyway," Ruth reminded her.

"Well, I should've listened. Now please clean up this mess for me. I'm going to pack. I want to be there for Cissy tomorrow."

When she reached the bedroom, she slammed the door, confused about what to do first. She needed just a few items for an overnight trip to Meridian: a day's change of clothes and some toiletries. A small carpet bag would do and she dragged it from underneath the bed. It smelled of wool and mothballs. Janelle stood still, breathing deeply of the musty odors and grasping unsuccessfully for memories associated with the scent.

Without thinking, she reached under the bed again and grabbed a smallish suitcase and then a larger one. Soon both lay open on the bed, begging to be filled. Janelle made no effort to resist the plan taking shape.

She rummaged through drawers for late fall and winter outfits to pack. She emptied the contents of her jewelry box into a silk blouse and wrapped it up in a ball, tying the sleeves into a knot around the bundle and tossing it into the small suitcase. Then she loosened a board at the back of the armoire and retrieved ten thousand dollars in cash hidden there. The Depression had taught her that banks weren't always the safest places. Beau had made fun of her secret stash all those years. Now, her foolishness had paid off.

When she'd finished packing, she changed into a nightgown and crawled into bed even though the sun still shone strong in the evening sky. She didn't answer when Ruth knocked softly at the door, asking about supper. Janelle closed her eyes and hoped her nerves wouldn't get the best of her in the morning.

The next day, she made her way down the corridor at Riley Hospital, looking for the door to the recovery room the nurse had described. Cissy should have been resting comfortably by then. The monstrosity that used to reside in her was now just hospital waste and not the precious great-grandchild Ruth hoped they'd have in their lives in a few months.

The plan to rescue Cissy before she could be moved back to the psychiatric hospital now seemed foolhardy. Earlier, she'd decided to trip the fire alarm and hope to get Cissy into a wheelchair and out of the hospital before anyone noticed. There were so many variables including whether she had the physical strength to push the wheelchair into the parking lot. Janelle couldn't know how Cissy would react. If she was confused or belligerent, she'd draw unwanted attention.

Janelle passed a small waiting area and peered in. Her stomach dipped at the sight of the familiar face. "Dr. Guttman? What are you doing here?" she stammered.

"Don't be alarmed, Mrs. Clayton." He rose to shake her hand.

"What makes you think I'm alarmed?" She gripped the wheelchair handles tighter so he wouldn't notice her quaking hands.

"Could we talk?" He gently took the wheelchair from Janelle's grasp and parked it against the wall in the hallway.

The double doors to the recovery area loomed before her, beckoning her away from whatever Guttman had to say. She felt so foolish thinking she had some control over what happened to Cissy or any of them for that matter. She sat down, a child ready to be scolded.

"I can't remember why I even took this job." His words petered out. "How arrogant of me to think I could make a difference."

"I'm not sure what you're saying. . . ."

"Mrs. Clayton, I'm tired. Tired of fighting the nurses and administrators. Tired of believing my degrees or my experience in New York would make a difference."

"I'm sure you have made a difference, young man."

"Young man. Exactly." A bitter snort escaped his lips and he ran both hands through his hair. His glassy eyes held sadness or maybe regret. "I don't belong here and you know it."

She had nothing to offer, so she waited for him to continue.

"I thought I could help Cissy. I *wanted* to help Cissy," he said.

"I'm sure you have helped her."

"The other day, when you insisted you be here for Cissy after the procedure, I suspected you had a plan," he said. "I couldn't guess what, but I thought I could at least help you get her to the car. I have more arm strength than you."

Janelle stared at him, shaken. He wasn't going to stop her from taking Cissy after all. She stifled a cry. Dr. Guttman knelt down next to the chair and took her hand.

"Would you like some water, or a moment alone?" The way he smiled and dropped his shoulders added to her relief.

"No, but thank you. Thank you from the bottom of my heart," she managed.

"Um . . . I brought some of Cissy's things with me just in case I was right about your intentions." He pointed to two crumpled paper sacks. "Her notebooks, art supplies, and some clothes. I couldn't grab much more without arousing suspicion."

"How wonderful. She'll appreciate it so much.

I grabbed a few clothes from her house thinking I'd not get a chance to retrieve anything from the hospital." Janelle peered into one of the bags and then scrunched it closed. "Let's go see Cissy now, shall we?"

He held out his arm and she grabbed the crook of his elbow. After pushing through the doors to the recovery room, he explained to the nurse on duty he was Cissy's psychiatrist from the state hospital and she nodded that they could pass. Dr. Guttman was just a few inches taller than Janelle and they stood almost shoulder to shoulder. She could have never guessed that this unassuming man would turn out to be Cissy's savior.

She let go of his arm and they parted so they could stand on opposite sides of Cissy's hospital bed. Her cheeks held color and she looked peaceful. Janelle leaned in for a kiss.

Cissy's eyes opened. "Grandmother?"

Mute, Janelle looked frantically at Dr. Guttman to explain the situation to her granddaughter.

"Cissy, do you know who I am?" Dr. Guttman rested his hand lightly on hers but didn't squeeze it.

"That's a dumb question. You're Dr. Guttman. Where am I?"

She frowned, but Janelle welcomed her confusion like a belated birthday gift. "You're at the hospital. I mean, a regular hospital. You weren't feeling well."

"My stomach is a little queasy, Grandmother." Cissy tried to sit up, but slumped back, groggy and somewhat frustrated by her fatigue. "Do I have the flu?"

"We'll talk about it later," Janelle said. "What's important is that you'll be fine."

The nurse touched Dr. Guttman on the elbow and whispered something Janelle couldn't make out. He nodded and she walked away.

"The nurse said Cissy is ready to be transported back to the hospital." He motioned for Janelle to follow him so that Cissy couldn't overhear. "She's getting her clothes and some maxi pads. There will be some light bleeding for the next day, but nothing to worry about."

"But how . . . what . . ." she asked.

"The nurse thinks I'm the one who's supposed to transport Cissy," he whispered. "I can't believe our luck."

When the nurse returned to help Cissy dress, Dr. Guttman and Janelle exited to the waiting area to give them privacy. She told him she had something to do and would be back in a few moments. He didn't ask about her mission, although his face held questions.

Janelle walked the full length of the corridor looking for a staff person to help her. Finally, a candy striper delivering flowers directed her to a public phone on the next floor. Her hand shook as she dropped in one coin after another.

312

"Clayton residence." Grace and authority sang out in Ruth's greeting.

"It's me."

After a few seconds of silence, the sorrow in Ruth's words traveled through the phone wires. "I suspect it's done, then."

"She's in the recovery room now, but she talked again. She recognized me." Janelle spoke excitedly, hoping to get a response in kind.

"I guess you got what you wanted." Ruth didn't try to mask her disappointment.

"Oh, Ruth. Please don't start. I'm too tired to fight. I had to do this for Cissy."

"You did it for yourself, ma'am. Don't try to convince me otherwise."

"I'm sorry this has come between us." Janelle's anger had run dry, now replaced with pure sadness. "I'm sorry I didn't make time to speak with you this morning. I wanted to get on the road as early as possible."

Ruth's forgiveness wasn't forthcoming, but Janelle ached for it. Even though she'd have Cissy with her, she knew when they left the hospital she'd feel lonelier than she had her entire life. Janelle would have no confidante, no friend.

"I saw you loading the suitcases into your car," Ruth said without emotion.

"Yes."

Janelle trusted Ruth knew it meant she'd be gone for some time. Ruth coughed, but Janelle didn't know if it camouflaged sadness or anger or both.

"I'll miss you, Ruth."

She wouldn't answer, but Janelle kept the phone to her ear. Half a minute passed and she thought Ruth might have hung up. Then she heard her breath, loud and steady.

"Good luck to you, Mrs. Clayton."

"I love you, Ruth," Janelle said while the dial tone buzzed in her ear.

Chapter 25

The smell of gasoline burned Cissy's nostrils, but, oh, how she loved that burn. Strong smells like gas, oil, and tar were like smelling salts calling a person's brain to attention. Today, though, her brain felt like Rip Van Winkle awaking from a hundred-year nap. She sat up too quickly and fell against the smooth leather of the backseat of Grandmother's car.

"You're up, sleepyhead." Grandmother sat in the front seat and pointed to dirty spots on the windshield of her Caddy she wanted the gas station attendant to wipe.

"Why am I in the backseat of your car?" Cissy asked.

"I thought you should get some rest," Grandmother said.

"No, I mean, why am I not at the hospital anymore?"

"Which hospital?"

"The state hospital. What other hospital is there?"

"I didn't think it was the best place for you," she said, but offered no more explanation.

Cissy looked out her window at the car on the other side of the pump. A little boy with a chocolate smudge on his top lip stared back. He took a big swig of his Yoo-hoo. She stuck out her tongue and he ducked down, continuing the game she started but really didn't want to play. She licked her lips and swallowed hard, thinking how much she wanted a cold drink herself. That is, until her cramping gut called out for attention. Cissy wrapped her arms around her middle to hold in the pain.

"I think I have my monthly visitor, Grandmother," she said, doubling over. "I'm going to see if there's a Kotex machine in the restroom."

"There should be some pads in your toiletry bag on the floorboard. Just take the bag with you."

In the stall, Cissy pulled down her pants to find she already had on a pad, soaked through and bright red. She undid the safety pins that fastened the pad to her underwear, wrapped it in toilet paper, and placed it in the bottom of the trash can.

With her brain lacking so many details, her legs became noodly and unsure. She couldn't remember packing a bag or leaving the hospital, much less putting on a Kotex. The panic circled her like a swarm of bees, mad as blazes, and buzzing in a million different directions. Cissy attached a fresh pad to her underpants and walked over to the stainless-steel sink. She hoped splashing water on her face would jump-start her memory, but the shock of cold just caused goose bumps to shoot up over her whole body.

She rushed out of the bathroom and into the

sun to get warm. Surely the sky had never been so blue. She lifted up her face and drank it in. Grandmother tapped the horn twice to get her attention, so Cissy decided not to ask for a Yoo-hoo after all. She climbed in the front seat and the car took off, sending pea gravel in a spray over the pumps.

"Grandmother, I'm scared. I can't remember how I got here."

"You've just not been yourself lately." Grandmother rested her hand on Cissy's thigh.

"What day is it?" she asked.

"September 26th. Don't worry yourself about anything. You'll be just fine in no time."

Cissy didn't feel fine at all. She felt shivery, like she did when first getting the flu. Her grandmother saying Cissy would be fine wasn't the soothing she hoped for, but her grandmother didn't seem in a mood to share. Cissy asked if they could listen to the radio and she said okay, as long as it wasn't obnoxious rock and roll music. After that comment, finding a station seemed like too much trouble, so Cissy just stared out the window instead.

Nothing looked familiar. The town they'd stopped in had a four-way stop and no traffic lights. The gas station and post office were the only places people seemed to gather. Now, just-plowed fields and leaning wood barns filled her view. "Where are we going?" she asked.

317

"I'm not sure, Cissy." Her grandmother gripped the steering wheel with both hands. They looked ancient and red except where her knuckles were white. She wouldn't look at her and Cissy wondered if that was on purpose.

"Leave your grandmother be for a while." God was reclined in the backseat so that her feet were propped up in the window Cissy had left rolled down. The words didn't come across as chastising so much, but Her voice was firm. "She's still figuring out a plan."

Cissy *was* happy to be out of the hospital. Thinking of going back made her feel as if she were falling down the rabbit hole in *Alice's Adventures in Wonderland*. But not knowing where she was heading made her chest pound. It'd been almost three months since she shot her daddy, but Cissy couldn't account for all of those days. She held a hand over her heart to calm its confusion.

"Does Mama know we're together?" Cissy asked.

"She does by now," Grandmother said.

"Are we running away?" she asked, ignoring God's advice. "Like Bonnie and Clyde?"

"Something like that. But we're not criminals." Grandmother tightened her jaw, which looked hard anyway.

What were they, then? Would Mama or the police or Dr. Guttman come after them? Would

318

Cissy be punished for leaving even though she couldn't remember how she left?

"Grandmother, let's count blue cars," she pleaded.

"There's not enough traffic on this back road. Why don't you just close your eyes and rest a while?"

"Because I'm not tired anymore," Cissy said, but that wasn't exactly the truth. She felt tired through and through, and not just body tired. Her brain didn't feel like working and directed her to obey her grandmother. Sleep, it said. Plenty of time for questions later, it said.

"I'm hungry." Cissy crossed her arms defiantly.

Her grandmother pointed to a crinkled paper sack on the floorboard. Cissy opened it and found three sandwiches wrapped in wax paper plus a big pickle in a plastic sleeve, floating in its juice.

"It's homemade pimento cheese," Grandmother said. "I know that's your favorite."

"And a pickle!"

"Yes, dear, and a pickle," she said, a slight smile emerging.

The gummy cheese and white bread stuck behind Cissy's front teeth, and her tongue pushed against it to loosen it. "This is delicious."

"Dear, don't speak with your mouth full."

Cissy ate two of the three sandwiches and her grandmother didn't stop her. She couldn't remember the last time she ate, but guessed it'd been some hours. Her tummy churned its gladness at being full and her eyes kept suggesting they close for a nap.

"Did you pack my notebook?" She opened the glove compartment to check.

"It's in your suitcase in the trunk," Grandmother said. "When we stop for the night, you can get it then."

"But what if I have to add something to a list? I'm never without my notebook," Cissy protested. "I *need* my notebook."

"Cissy, be patient. You can't hold on to childish things forever."

Her lip trembled and she bit it hard to keep from crying. God was right. Grandmother was doing the best she could. She hadn't explained why Cissy had been allowed to leave the mental hospital or if Grandmother had asked permission at all. Cissy assumed they were running from the law. The judge would be none too happy about her being free. Grandmother had a lot more on her mind than stopping for a notebook.

"Go to sleep," Grandmother and God said almost at the same time. Maybe they were both right. Sleeping might be the best thing for Cissy's nerves, as long as she didn't have bad dreams.

"Don't outlaws move at night and hide out during the day?" Cissy had asked when they pulled into the Whiting Brothers Motor Court.

Grandmother told her in the sternest way she'd be sorry if she used the word *outlaw* again, so Cissy made a mental note to add it to her List of Banned Words once she got her notebooks out of the suitcase. Cissy wasn't as upset as she could have been, considering her grandmother's tone. She was much too excited to be staying at a motel. The best part of family vacations had been exploring the strange new surroundings— the matching bedspreads and drapes, the towels that smelled of chlorine, the in-room coffeepot, the ice machine, the motel stationery Cissy used to make lists of all the exciting things she'd experienced on vacation.

There were just two motels in Okolona where they could stop for the night. Grandmother chose the one that looked freshly painted, or maybe she chose it because it was the one on the right side of the highway. Cissy decided not to ask.

The units were stand-alone miniature houses, each with a little front porch and two metal lawn chairs painted bright red. The air conditioners jutting out from the tiny windows seemed huge in comparison, threatening to tip the little structures to their sides.

"They're the color of the pistachio marsh-mallow salad that Ruth makes for special occasions," Cissy said when they pulled up to the office.

She hoped Grandmother's smile meant she'd

forgiven the outlaw comment. She told Cissy to stay in the car, but that request was downright silly. Where was she to go? She didn't even know where Okolona was except that they were still in Mississippi.

Cissy could see through the large paned window of the office. Grandmother stood at the counter, laughing and chatting with the manager. She withdrew cash from her pocketbook and laid the bills neatly on the counter. The manager looked older than she, maybe in his eighties. Perhaps he was flirting with her. Cissy laughed out loud, not because she didn't believe it could be true, but because it made her happy to think someone thought Grandmother was as pretty as Cissy thought she was.

"She loves you." God crossed her arms and leaned forward on the seat back, speaking into Cissy's ear.

"Sometimes you scare me half to death." Cissy placed a hand over her heart, faking a fainting spell. "Couldn't you ring a bell or warn me somehow before you appear?"

God chuckled and shook Her head as if to tell Cissy she was being nonsensical, which was one of her favorite interesting words to use recently.

"Your grandmother has risked everything to get you away from the hospital," God said. "You should be mindful of that."

She didn't need God to tell her to appreciate her

grandmother, but it worried Cissy to hear how much she'd risked. If they were caught, would Grandmother be the one to pay? Or would they both go to jail? Cissy contemplated whether she'd rather just go back to the hospital and the boring routine to which she'd pretty much grown accustomed. But the thought of Grandmother in jail alone caused a rising panic. Cissy doubted her mother would ask for leniency for either of them.

When Grandmother exited the office, her face held none of her previous gaiety, as if she'd taken off a mask she wore for the manager only.

"We're in unit seven," she said, starting the car. "Last one on the left."

"Seven is a lucky number."

"That's good, child. We need all the luck we can get."

Grandmother looked tired so Cissy offered to unload the suitcases. She'd packed two for herself and one for Cissy, plus two toiletry cases—one for each of them. Cissy carried them in, one at a time, to prolong the experience. Since God had left and there was no one to talk to, Cissy pretended to be a traveling salesperson, stopping for the night and unloading her wares. She couldn't risk keeping them in the car. If they were stolen, she'd lose her livelihood and wouldn't be able to provide for her family, whom she daydreamed she'd left in some faraway town.

The cramping in her gut made it uncomfortable to drag the largest of the suitcases, but Cissy's daydream overshadowed the pain.

Grandmother didn't comment on how long it took Cissy because she'd drifted off, still in her peach linen suit and hose, shoes kicked off by the bedside. She slept soundly, arms crossed on her chest, like the deceased at a viewing. Cissy kept from looking at her because the sight alarmed her so.

The tiny room could hold little more than the bed and two nightstands. To open the suitcases, Cissy would have to line them up between the bed and the wall and lie on the bed to reach their contents. Grandmother probably didn't want her rooting around her things anyway, so Cissy just laid her own suitcase on the bed gently so as to not wake her. She opened it up and gasped at the willy-nilly way that her things had been thrown together. It felt good to have a task. She took everything out to refold her clothes. At the bottom of the suitcase were her notebooks and art pad. Beneath those were portraits she'd drawn—Grandmother on her porch; she, Jessie, and Lily with her mama, but not her daddy; and from the hospital, Dr. Guttman, Nurse Edna, Martha, and, of course, Lucien.

She'd used up almost the entire black pastel coloring Lucien's longish hair and woolly eyebrows, but she thought his portrait was the best of the lot, or at least the closest likeness. Yet, when Cissy picked up the sketch, she had the feeling she'd forgotten something important, something frightening. She let go of the sheet as if it were a hot coal, and it floated down to the carpet. She picked it up by the edges and placed it behind the others in a hidden pocket in the suitcase, its strange power hidden for the time being.

She remembered she was supposed to add *outlaw* to her List of Banned Words, so she looked for the one red spiral notebook among the bunch. Cissy thought choosing a red notebook was particularly clever. Glaring at her, the cover was a stop sign, warning that the contents of those blue-lined pages could be dangerous. Whenever she added a word, she squinted so the pages became just blurry enough to conceal the words already jotted down.

Cissy's tummy growled. The alarm clock on the nightstand said 7 p.m. already. She wanted to wake Grandmother, but worried she needed the rest more than Cissy needed supper. It couldn't hurt to check with the manager. There might be a vending machine with soda or snacks. Or he might be able to recommend a restaurant. Cissy would tell Grandmother when she woke up.

She closed the door but didn't lock it in case Grandmother was still sleeping when she returned.

The gravel in the parking lot radiated heat up Cissy's legs. Funny how the sun could feel so hot late in the evening. Before long, though, it'd set earlier and earlier and they'd all say how much they missed those long, hot evenings of summer and early fall. Folks always seemed to miss what they didn't have at the moment.

The door to the office triggered a tinkling bell and she smiled. That's the exact sort of warning she'd love to have before a visit from God.

"Well, good evening. You're the young miss traveling with Mrs. Johnson?"

"No, sir, I'm with my grandmother. We're in unit seven."

"Why yes, that's Mrs. Johnson."

Seeing his puzzled face, it dawned on her that Grandmother wouldn't have used their real names. They were outlaws even though she wasn't allowed to say the word.

"Oh! Yes, I'm with Mrs. Johnson. She's resting right now. I'm just looking for a vending machine, maybe a soda and some crackers."

"You're in luck, young miss. You'll find both on the far side of this building round back."

She smiled in triumph, knowing she could silence her growling insides. The smile faded just as quickly. Cissy patted her pants pockets. She didn't have any money of her own.

"What's the matter, dear?" The old man reminded her a little of her grandfather, only much shorter and a little softer around the middle. His white eyebrows jutted out shading his eyes, and she imagined his wrinkles were born from a lifetime of smiling, not frowning.

"Um . . . I don't have any money. I'll just wait for supper with Grandmother." Cissy looked back toward their unit, wondering if she could risk looking in Grandmother's purse for spare change.

"I'm happy to lend you a few quarters," the man said, and dug around his front pants pocket. "Here you go."

All the warnings from her mama about accepting things from strangers shouted to her from long ago, but her stomach's pleas grew louder to drown them out.

"Thank you, mister," she said, holding out her palm.

"Please call me Arlen. What's your name?"

"I'm Cissy," she said, shaking his hand. "Thanks so much for the change. I'll be sure to pay you back later."

"No worries, Cissy. Go on now and get yourself some snacks."

She burst through the door with the loot and bounded round back. The Coke machine stood against the back wall, as cherry red as the porch chairs in front of their room. She could already taste the sweetness on her tongue and the acid in her throat.

"Cissy! Cissy!" Grandmother moved across the gravel in her unsteady heels, her hands in fists at her side. Her slow pace seemed to frustrate her all the more. "What the hell do you think you're doing leaving the room?"

"I . . . I was hungry, Grandmother," Cissy shouted to her. "I just wanted a snack."

Waiting for her grandmother to reach her was one of the most uncomfortable minutes of Cissy's life. Grandmother was spitfire mad, and Cissy lost a few inches of height just bracing for the confrontation.

"Where'd you get the money, girl? Did you go through my purse?" Grandmother's face bloomed as red as Cissy's notebook, giving her just as ominous a warning.

"No, ma'am, I promise. The nice man in the office, Mr. Arlen, he gave me the change. But I told him I'd pay him back."

The blush drained from Grandmother's face and was replaced by a colorless pall.

"Did you tell him your name?"

"Well, yes, I introduced myself to be polite."

She grabbed Cissy by the wrist and marched her across the gravel, back toward their little pistachio house.

"Come on, girl. We're leaving this instant. Let's get the suitcases."

Grandmother's rough grip hurt. Cissy looked back to the office to see the manager, his smile now gone, wondering as she did what had gone so terribly wrong.

Cissy almost couldn't bear to see her grandmother crying. She'd only seen her cry a handful of times, and each time Cissy had been the one to cause the heartache. Even worse, she'd hurt others. What would her sisters and mama be thinking? Would they blame Cissy for taking Grandmother from them, too?

"I'm sorry. I don't know what I did wrong."

"Hush, girl." Grandmother shifted in the seat, sitting closer to the steering wheel. Cissy could tell dusk made it hard for her to see the road clearly. She wished she knew how to drive so she could spell Grandmother for a bit.

Since God seemed to appear at times like this, Cissy kept turning her head to the backseat so she wouldn't be startled.

"What in God's name are you looking at?" Grandmother broke the silence. "No one is following us. I've kept an eye out."

"Who'd be following us?"

"The law, of course. How many girls named Cissy with your height and bright red hair are out there? You told the motel manager your name. You're not a girl one would forget."

Cissy suddenly felt a terrible guilt for her physical features and birth name as they marked her as a criminal. She sunk down farther into the seat, legs straining to fit beneath the dashboard. No matter how she tried, she couldn't make herself smaller.

"If you're Mrs. Johnson, what's my name?"

She could've sworn the tenseness in Grandmother's shoulders eased a bit after hearing the question, but the declining light made it harder and harder to see her features.

"Not very original, was it?" Grandmother's voice seemed lighter and Cissy scooted over closer, her head on her grandmother's bony shoulder.

"Well, you can't exactly call yourself Mrs. Butterworth," Cissy said.

Grandmother chuckled just enough to make Cissy's stomach hurt a little less.

She asked what name Cissy would like to use. They tried out different names for the next half hour until they hit Tupelo. Near the city limits stood a little barbecue shack with rusty tin sides and a sign that read BUBBA'S. Strands of Christmas lights hung from the edges of the building to several nearby pecan trees, creating a canopy of red, green, and blue over the three picnic tables in front.

Cissy begged Grandmother to pull over. She said if someone looked up the word *starving* in the dictionary, her picture would be right there proving the point. Grandmother said to stop being so melodramatic, and Cissy wrote the word in her notebook of interesting words because she'd never been called that before. No matter the meaning, Grandmother pulled the Caddy over onto a patch of gravel near the shack and Cissy almost jumped from the car before the engine even stopped.

A black woman, maybe in her early twenties, sat at one table with two little ones, eating brisket off white butcher paper. A loaf of bread in its wrapper sat on each table, probably the only side dish to the meat Bubba barbecued in the smoker fashioned from an oil drum. Well, Cissy assumed it was Bubba because of the wooden plank nailed to the side of the shack, although the paint had flaked off almost completely.

Cissy couldn't stop staring at the young black woman, who wasn't having any of it.

"What you looking at, Carrot Top?" she said with fearsome eyes that made Cissy wilt. If Cissy wasn't showered in the green, blue, and red hues of the Christmas lights, the woman would have seen her beet-red embarrassment.

"I . . . I . . . didn't mean to stare, miss. You're just so pretty and I like your braids," Cissy stammered.

"Well, it ain't good manners to stare so, but thank you for your compliment just the same," she said. "You and your grammy are welcome to sit with me and the kids if you like."

Cissy looked to Grandmother for approval and she nodded, but gave a look that said, "Be careful what you say, girl."

When Bubba, or whoever he was, brought the food to the table, Cissy wrapped up two slices of brisket in a white bread blanket and stuffed the roll into her mouth with the biggest bite she could manage. Her hunger by that time had taken control of her senses and she was forced to appease it. She didn't even stop to wipe the sauce on her face until Grandmother shoved the roll of paper towels on the table toward her.

Grandmother must have been in a better mood because she allowed her to drink two Big Red sodas. Cissy swore Big Red was invented specifically to go along with barbecue. No two tastes together ever seemed so right.

"How do you drink that stuff?" Grandmother's lips pursed as if she were drinking turpentine.

"Because nothing else tastes like it. It's not strawberry. It's not cherry. It's just red."

"Amen, sister!" said the young black woman. "You can keep your Coke or RC Cola. Nothin' is like Red."

They all took big swigs at the same time while Grandmother pinched her nose shut to show her mock disgust, which made them all laugh.

No one else stopped at the shack while they were there, so the owner joined them at the long picnic table. Turned out his name was Leroy. His father, Bubba, had opened the roadside eatery twenty years earlier, which explained the sad shape of the sign. Local folks knew the place, so a freshly painted sign wasn't necessary, Leroy said, but he might get around to repainting it one day.

Before Grandmother got around to choosing their aliases, Cissy introduced her as Mrs. Mae Johnson and herself as Matilda, and felt quite proud of her ability to improvise. She thought it good practice to take the lead if they were going to be on the lam for some time. Grandmother patted her knee, so Cissy assumed she'd done a good job.

Letitia, the young black woman, was Leroy's youngest daughter. When Cissy asked if she was babysitting someone's kids, Letitia let out a hoot so forceful Big Red shot out of her nose. She yelped at the burn of the soda pop in her nostrils.

"No, child, they're my young'uns." She wiped her chin with a paper towel. Her two boys, Damon, five, and Dorian, four, giggled into their hands at Cissy's mistake. Leroy shook his head and smiled.

"You're sure young to have kids of your own," Cissy said.

"Mind your manners." Grandmother pinched her until she yowled.

Letitia assured them she wasn't offended. She'd had Damon when she was just seventeen and Darion the year after. The boys had different daddies who didn't want anything to do with them now, so they mostly just helped Leroy at the barbecue stand while she worked as a nurse at a local hospital.

"How old are you, Matilda?" she asked Cissy.

"Sixteen."

"Well, don't go making the same foolish mistakes I did," she warned. "You're pretty enough to attract the attention of older boys. You finish school and get married before you start laying with boys. It was rough going to community college while caring for babies."

Cissy thought of Martha and her boyfriend, punished for their love, and couldn't imagine a boy caring about her. Especially after what her daddy had done. The one time a boy showed interest in her—sometime in the ninth grade—she ignored him until he called her a snooty rich bitch. She gladly took the insult rather than have him find out she was damaged in mind and body. Now that the secret was out, Cissy would forever be known as the girl who murdered her daddy for touching her. If she moved away from Mississippi, she still couldn't imagine wanting someone's physical attention.

"Could we change the subject, please?" Cissy stuffed more brisket into her mouth.

Letitia didn't seem put out by the request, and they all finished their food without speaking much more than niceties like "Pass the bread, please" or "May I have another paper towel?"

Grandmother asked Leroy if he could recommend a motel for the night, and he removed a pen from his shirt pocket to draw a map on a clean corner of the butcher paper. Letitia asked if Cissy wanted braids like hers. She didn't have to ask twice. Cissy jumped up without a word and straddled the bench in front of her. Letitia's touch was much gentler than Grandmother's when braiding. Cissy rubbed her fingers along the tight, neat rows.

"Quit your touching and let me finish." Letitia slapped Cissy's hand away.

"I like how they feel," she said.

"They're called corn rows 'cause they look like rows in a field," Letitia said.

While she worked her magic, Cissy asked if she'd ever met Elvis, seeing as how they both grew up in Tupelo.

"Not everybody from Tupelo knows Elvis personally," she said with a snort that made Cissy feel silly and uninformed. "Besides, he moved to Memphis a long time ago. All we got now is tourists wanting to see where he was born and where he got his first guitar."

"He got his first guitar here?" Cissy sat in wonder, hoping to hear more about her favorite music star.

"You're not much of a fan if you don't know that, Matilda," she chided.

"Well, tell me, then." Cissy got up to straddle

the bench in the other direction so she could face this interesting and knowledgeable person.

Letitia told her of the day in January 1945 when Elvis's mama brought him to the Tupelo Hardware Store to pick out a present. He wanted a rifle god-awful bad, but his mama said it was too dangerous. Folks who witnessed it said Elvis cried and cried because he wanted that darn rifle so much. The proprietor urged Elvis to try out a guitar instead, and that's the present his mama ended up buying that day.

"Did he show a natural talent at it?" Cissy asked.

"It's not like I was there in the store, girl." Letitia laughed at her ignorance. "I wasn't born until much later."

"Miss Matilda, I'm guessing he showed a natural talent right away," Leroy said, and it made her feel better. "How else would he have become the King of Rock and Roll?"

"Exactly!" Cissy agreed.

"Maybe if you have time on your driving vacation you should head to Memphis and see Graceland in person," Letitia suggested. Cissy whipped around to see Grandmother's reaction.

"The only place we're heading now is a motel," she said, getting up from the table. "Thanks so much for the barbecue and good company."

"Nice to meet you all," Cissy said, and walked over to the car, yawning and wishing she was already tucked beneath the sheets with her head on a pillow.

The Christmas lights had almost made her forget it was just September. She could see them even with her eyes closed as they drove off to find beds for the night.

The next morning, Cissy closed the motel bathroom door softly so she wouldn't wake up Grandmother. She wanted to speak to God in private and this seemed their only option. Cissy asked if She'd prefer to sit on the toilet, but She hunched down in the bathtub, still wearing that darn blue-green chiffon dress.

"Isn't the porcelain cold? Won't you mess up your dress?" Cissy asked, concerned she might be inconveniencing Her. "And why don't you wear anything else?"

"It doesn't matter what I wear. Seems there are other things you should be more concerned about right now."

"Like what?" Cissy worried she'd missed something important in their previous conversations. It's not like they had a lot of privacy with Grandmother around, so she could only speak to God in brief snatches here and there.

"Last night when your grandmother wanted to go to bed, you went on and on about how you wanted to visit Graceland. Don't you realize you're not on vacation?"

"But it's just two hours away!" Cissy said. "We have to drive somewhere anyway. I don't see why it couldn't be in that direction."

God closed Her eyes and Cissy wondered if She was exasperated or bored.

"You're acting a little selfishly right now," She said, stretching out Her legs.

Cissy squirmed on the toilet seat. Its coolness pierced through her thin nightgown, making her wish she'd grabbed the blanket from the bed to wrap around herself. Even though the tone of God's voice didn't come across as judging, Cissy felt ashamed and hurt she'd been called selfish.

"I'm just trying to make the best of the situation." Cissy had been on the road for just a day and had no idea what constituted being selfish. She turned the little motel soap over and over in her hand, wondering why the public couldn't buy miniature soap bars if the motels could.

"Did it occur to you that your grandmother is more than tired?"

"You're scaring me and I don't want to talk to you right now." Cissy got up to brush her teeth at the sink. She rubbed her hair, still trapped in braids, and considered what a time-saver corn rows could be on hectic mornings—although she hadn't had any of those since last school year.

"You need to take care of your grandmother as much as she's taking care of you," God said.

Cissy concentrated on brushing every single tooth, up and down and across, up and down and across. She didn't appreciate God speaking to her as if she were some child who didn't know anything, so she continued to ignore Her. After a few minutes of vigorous brushing, Cissy was relieved to find the tub empty again. God had gone off to wherever She usually went.

"Cissy? Are you okay in there?" Grandmother rapped on the door. She opened it and stood before Cissy, looking like a child in an overly large nightgown, hair sticking straight up from a night of sound sleeping on her left side.

"You slept a long time." Cissy pushed past her to get to her suitcase. Grandmother didn't seem like a grown-up without her hair done and nice clothes on. Cissy couldn't bear to be the adult right now despite what God had told her.

"I can't believe it's nine a.m.," Grandmother said. "You should've woken me."

"You needed the rest. Yesterday was a long day. For both of us."

Grandmother showered while Cissy dressed and repacked her suitcase. Even she tended to muss things up retrieving clean underwear and socks. When Grandmother came out of the bathroom, she laughed to see Cissy sitting on the edge of the bed, dressed and ready to leave.

"Anxious to get on the road?" Her smile didn't hold a trace of fatigue or worry, and Cissy made a mental note to thank God later, just in case She had anything to do with Grandmother feeling better.

"Just thought I should get in a routine if we're going to stay in motels for a while," Cissy said.

Her comment erased any light in Grandmother's smile and seemed to tie cinderblocks to her legs. She took so long to put on her hosiery and shoes, Cissy almost jumped up to give her a hand. Sensing Cissy's frustration, she suggested she turn on the television. *The Price Is Right* had ceased to be Cissy's favorite show. She'd watched reruns so much in the hospital, she'd grown quite good at guessing the prices of appliances and groceries and vacation packages, and it didn't feel like a challenge anymore. Still, it kept her mind somewhat occupied while Grandmother dressed and put on her face.

Because they arrived at the motel after dark the night before, Cissy hadn't noticed the Waffle House just a block away. She looked over at Grandmother, who shook her head no.

"Let's just grab something on the road," she said.

Cissy's eyes screamed please and before she knew it, they were in a bright orange booth sipping hot coffee and planning their day. Cissy remembered breakfasts out with Mama, Lily, and Jessie. She could almost feel her sisters' tiny legs kicking underneath the table.

340

"The waffles here don't even need syrup," Cissy said. "They must use a lot of sugar in the batter, almost like muffin batter, don't you think?"

Grandmother scanned the menu, deaf to the commentary. She ordered the hash browns scattered, smothered, and covered, which meant spread out on the grill to get nice and crispy, and then topped with onions and cheese. That seemed like a pretty sloppy dish for someone so refined, but Cissy didn't comment.

"I can't believe I'm hungry after all the barbecue we ate last night," Grandmother said, taking a breath between bites.

"I'm always hungry. Mama used to say my legs must be hollow to fit all the food I eat."

Grandmother said she'd not had such a robust appetite since right before her stay in the hospital.

In the instant Cissy grasped the meaning of those words, the mug near her mouth clanked against her teeth, sending scalding coffee down her chin. "Hospital? When were you in the hospital?"

Grandmother's expression betrayed her, admitting she'd let an important cat out of the bag. Cissy gave her a stern eye, warning she wanted nothing less than the whole story. So Grandmother described the day she set out to buy the blue sweater, how she felt sick to her stomach and fell asleep in the hot car. She told Cissy about the teenager with tanned skin who found her and took her to the emergency room. She tried to convince Cissy heat stroke wasn't dangerous, but a word like *stroke* demanded to be added to her List of Banned Words.

"Were you scared?" Cissy's teeth chattered like it was the dead of winter. She wanted to stuff napkins in her mouth to stop the noise they made in her head.

"Not really, dear, but for a moment I thought I'd died and gone to heaven. I woke up in the hospital and your mama and sisters and Ruth were standing around me like a hallelujah chorus."

Cissy didn't find her joke funny. Grandmother cleared her throat in apology.

"Seriously, Cissy. There's nothing to be alarmed about. I had a touch of heat stroke. I stayed in the hospital a couple of days and then felt good as new," she said. "Well, except for the appetite part, which appears to be fine now."

Cissy sensed she left out some pretty important details in the retelling of the story. And the tone of her voice seemed plastic and too cheery for such a scary subject. Still, her Grandmother wasn't one to lie.

When their food arrived, Grandmother resorted to small talk to cover up what wasn't being said. Cissy only half listened because she figured a response to the rambling wasn't required.

Instead, Cissy counted the squares in her waffle before cutting them neatly with her knife and munching each row individually. When she'd finished, she asked if she could order another waffle and Grandmother complied. This time, Cissy added butter to every other square so that the waffle resembled a chess board.

"Aren't you a little old to be playing with your food?" Grandmother asked, knife and fork raised upright in each hand, pausing before her next bite.

"Aren't you a little old to be busting a crazy person out of a mental hospital?" Cissy asked, then immediately covered her smart mouth in regret.

Grandmother took the Lord's name in vain and slammed her utensiled fists on the table, causing instant tears in Cissy's heart that she wouldn't allow to escape. The waitress and two other diners looked over at them with admonishing eyes.

"I'm sorry, Grandmother. I don't know why I'd say such an awful thing." She blinked hard several times, keeping her tears confined. She'd made Grandmother cry again, the one person who still cared about her.

"Is your smart remark hiding something you'd really like to talk about?" Grandmother finally asked through the tight lines of her fuchsia lips.

The waffle didn't sit well in Cissy's stomach.

She scanned the restaurant for the restroom just in case she couldn't keep it down.

"I guess I'm scared, Grandmother. Scared you're not telling me something about your hospital stay. Scared about hiding out from the law. Scared I can't remember parts of my life. Maybe scared I'll remember the parts I shouldn't."

"Child, I'm scared, too." Grandmother put down her fork and knife, and offered both her hands to Cissy. "I'm making this up as I go along. I need you to trust I will take care of you."

Cissy nodded until her shaking unleashed the tears she had previously held back. Even when snot nipped at her upper lip, she didn't let go of Grandmother's hands. Something told her that she had nothing else in the world to hold on to.

"Why did you take me from the mental hospital?"

Grandmother hesitated just long enough for Cissy to suspect the answer wouldn't be completely truthful.

"I didn't think you'd get well if you stayed in the hospital. I figured being with family might make the difference." She stared at her half-eaten hash browns as if they were about to speak in tongues when all Cissy wanted was for her to look her in the eyes.

"What makes you think I'm not well? I thought

the hospital was just taking the place of prison because most folks don't understand why I had to kill Daddy." She brought a hand to her belly.

This time, the waffle was coming up for certain. She pulled away from Grandmother and ran for the restroom, both hands over her mouth in a feeble attempt to hold back the dread she'd gulped down with breakfast. She never made it to a stall, and waffle chunks and orange juice and milk sprayed before her. When she looked in the mirror and saw similar pieces on her face and in her hair, Cissy's stomach gave up whatever was left.

The door to the restroom swung open and the waitress stood before her with a mop and yellow bucket on rollers.

"Well, goddamn it." She placed the back of her hand against her nose.

"I'm so sorry," Cissy blubbered. "I . . . I . . . tried to make it to the toilet."

"It's not the first time I've seen waffles in this state," she said. "Ain't your fault. Nobody pays good money for breakfast and wants it to end up like this. Wash your face and go back to your granny. I told the other waitress to bring you some water."

Cissy tried to imagine what made someone take a job at the Waffle House, suffering the heat of the griddles and the strain on the body only to be rewarded with ungrateful tips left by tightfisted vacationers and truckers. From a distance, you'd think she was Cissy's age until you noticed the hardness of life around her eyes and mouth. It shamed Cissy to add to that hardness, but she returned to the table as instructed.

"You all right?" Grandmother asked.

Their plates and glasses had been cleared except for the ice water the waitress had left. She could still see the oily haze of the dishcloth used to wipe up the tabletop.

"I'm not sick. I mean, I'm not sick in the head." Cissy figured she could say scary things out loud now that her stomach was empty.

"Child, you're seeing things that aren't there. That's not well."

Cissy thought about asking her what she meant, but already knew her grandmother meant the conversations with God. No doubt Dr. Guttman had mentioned it since he seemed so certain Cissy's cracked mind had conjured up an imaginary friend instead of believing God could speak to humans in person.

"Don't you believe in God, Grandmother?"

"Of course, I believe in God, but I don't believe He runs around appearing to us," she said with certainty.

"He's a She." Cissy set her jaw as her grandmother had set hers.

"God is not a woman, Cissy. I'll not have you talk crazy around me. I have enough on my mind."

Grandmother closed her eyes and laid both palms on the table as if waiting for anger to pass her by.

"I do see Her."

"Enough already! I don't want you hiding in bathrooms talking to yourself, or looking into the backseat as if somebody is traveling with us. You won't get better until you let go of childish things."

Cissy didn't think she'd been childish to talk to God. But she grew uneasy as more and more people expressed doubt and concern over God's appearances to her. In one of her sessions with Dr. Guttman, he had suggested it was quite normal to have an imaginary friend or guide when a person was experiencing a deep trauma. The person who caused her the most uneasiness was Martha. She'd been the one to tell her that Cissy was moving the chess pieces, and not God. If that was true, why couldn't Cissy remember it? Was it the same as the memories she kept locked away for fear of coming undone?

"Yes, ma'am. I'm sure you're right." She looked down at her hands, clasped in her lap, willing them to stop shaking.

"Drink your water, Cissy."

She lifted the glass with both hands to avoid spilling water. She took in most of it in one long gulp. She needed something in her stomach to fill the pit left by the vomiting and Grandmother's request.

"Where are we going today?" Cissy asked, hoping they could stop talking about God.

"Might as well head to Memphis so you'll hush up about Graceland."

She left a twenty-dollar bill on the table and got up to leave, not asking for any change. Cissy supposed the waitress deserved a big tip for having to clean up her mess in the bathroom.

Chapter 26

Despite Cissy's pleading, Graceland wouldn't allow visitors past the main gate. Janelle stopped at a nearby gas station to buy a picture book about the residence to stop her granddaughter's sobbing. At least the girl would be able to envision what would have been included on a real tour.

"Do you think he's inside the mansion right this very minute or touring in some big city like Las Vegas?" Cissy asked, absorbed with all the details of the brochure, her initial disappointment erased. "Listen to this. Elvis has his own meditation garden. That's where he goes just to think."

Janelle had never known how much Cissy adored her idol. She went on and on about how tired she'd become of people commenting on his weight or how ridiculous he looked in his white jumpsuits now, or that his twenty-three-room mansion was gaudy, or that he took too many drugs.

"Grandmother, they all seem to forget his real contribution—music allows us to escape to a place where nothing bad can touch us. It's like a time-traveling machine we can access almost anytime. Maybe the meditation garden is Elvis's personal time-traveling machine."

When Cissy said the hospital didn't allow music, Janelle found that strange and sad. If anything, the hospital was the most important place for music to break up the heaviness in those girls' long days. She thought it ridiculous no one else came to the same sensible conclusion, particularly Dr. Guttman, since he was so willing to operate outside the rules.

After the quick drive down Elvis Presley Boulevard, Janelle bought ham and olive loaf sandwiches, and found a small park where they could eat at a picnic table in the shade.

"I love how a tree's branches can rescue us from both sunburn and misery," Cissy said in between bites, her cheeks rosy from the heat.

"Cissy, you don't have to eat with so much enthusiasm. Slow down your chewing and act like a lady."

"No one is watching us," she said. "What does it matter?"

"Someone is always watching. And if you practice your manners in private, you're less likely to forget them around proper company."

Cissy sat straighter, crossed her ankles, and placed a paper napkin across her lap. "Now if only I had a knife and fork for my sandwich," she teased.

Janelle pursed her lips in mock annoyance, but was thankful for Cissy's silliness.

"Grandmother, have you ever done something that wasn't proper and polite?"

The question threw Janelle off guard and she thought of dodging it. Secrets seemed pointless at this juncture, though.

"I took one of my granddaddy's cigars and convinced a girlfriend to smoke it with me," she said, not cracking a smile. Cissy's astonished eyes could grow no wider and she leaned forward in anticipation of more details.

Janelle had been just fourteen years old when the foolish idea came over her. Her friend, Madeline, had brought the matches and they met in a creek bottom about a mile from her granddaddy's farm.

"I took the first puffs and Madeline asked how it tasted. Not wanting to seem immature, I lied and told her it was delightful even though I'd never tasted anything so foul," Janelle admitted. "So Madeline took several deep draws herself. I suppose she wasn't about to let me appear more sophisticated than she."

"What happened next?"

"We kept trying to outdo each other by taking puff after puff until Madeline's face turned sour and she threw up over the front of my blouse. I vomited next, but I never knew if it was because of the cigar or because Madeline got sick on me."

"Wow" was all Cissy could manage.

"Close your mouth, child," Janelle said. "It's not that outrageous a story."

Cissy finished her sandwich, smiling wide the whole time. Janelle didn't have the energy to harp at her to keep her mouth closed. More pressing was determining where to head next. Janelle still hadn't decided, so she asked Cissy to run back to the car to get the map.

"You know, Grandmother, I could help with the driving if you would teach me." She looked over Janelle's shoulder, waiting for a reaction.

"You're too young to drive. Case closed."

"I'm sixteen," she challenged. "I'm not a child anymore."

"Yes, you keep reminding me of that." Janelle sighed and looked up at this girl who'd done so much maturing in the last three months. "I don't suppose it could hurt."

Cissy clapped her hands furiously and then plopped back down on the bench after Janelle gave her a stern look.

"Grandmother, it makes good sense that I learn how to drive," she said. "What if you start feeling unwell? I could drive while you rest."

Janelle mulled over this reasoning and agreed to a lesson, although she insisted they find a back road where there'd be no traffic. They drove around for quite some time on two-lane county roads until happening upon a dirt road half hidden by soybean fields.

"Do you think we could get any farther away from civilization?" Cissy asked.

"I know you didn't inherit that mouth from my side of the family," Janelle said.

"Maybe my smart mouth didn't come from anyone. I could just be talented that way."

Janelle relaxed and said a quick prayer that Cissy would not harm their sole means of transportation. Her granddaughter moved the seat back to accommodate her long legs and listened while Janelle gave basic instructions. Cissy fiddled with the knobs on the radio, so Janelle began her instructions all over again, insisting that Cissy pay attention this time.

"It's not like book learning, Grandmother. I have to actually drive to learn." She started the car and pulled the shifter to D. She licked her lips in deep concentration and wiped her palms on her skirt before gripping the wheel again.

"Ten and two. Hands at ten and two," Janelle reminded her as Cissy jammed the accelerator too hard and spun a dark cloud of dust behind them. When Janelle yelled for her to brake, Cissy slammed it just as hard, pitching the whole car forward. They continued the herky-jerky dance until Janelle's patience ran out and her lunch threatened to come up.

"There's a certain finesse to driving, Cissy, just like dancing." She held a hand against her temple. "You've got to have a lighter touch."

Cissy begged to be able to practice just thirty minutes more. "I'm certain I can be a more delicate and refined driver if given the chance."

"Let's try again another day. We have to put some miles on the road before dark."

Janelle could tell her granddaughter thought about pitching a fit. But internal negotiations played out on her face. Janelle smiled at Cissy's struggle with restraint and maturity. She must have remembered who held the power to grant future driving privileges.

Back in Memphis, Janelle pulled the car into a service station for gasoline and to buy Cissy a Yoo-hoo and MoonPie for the road so she'd stop complaining about her growling insides.

"How do you eat so many sweets without gaining an ounce?" Janelle chided.

"Grandmother, you should pay more attention to the wondrous tastes and smells of food instead of fearing your pants won't fit one day."

"That's easy for you to say. You have your daddy's string-bean genes and don't have to worry about your figure."

Cissy turned her head away and looked outside the passenger side window. Janelle hadn't meant to bring up her father. Comparing their physical traits was deplorable.

"Honey, I'm sorry. I didn't mean to mention your daddy." She rested her hand on Cissy's thigh, but her granddaughter scooted even closer to the passenger side door, her head against the glass now.

"Don't worry yourself, Grandmother. It's not like he never enters my thoughts. Let's just get to where we're going."

For the next three hours, Janelle kept her eyes on Cissy instead of on the road where they should've been. The girl had grown so silent, she feared she'd caused Cissy to lapse into a darkness neither of them would be able to lighten.

Janelle was relieved when Cissy asked to stop the car so that she could move to the backseat and lie down for a nap. She wedged herself into a fetal position, legs tucked in because of their length and the narrowness of the car.

"Are you getting enough cool air back there? Do you need something to put under your head?" Janelle asked.

"Please don't worry about me, Grandmother. I'm happy not to have the air conditioner blowing on me. My temperature's just fine," she said without emotion.

The late-afternoon sun soon lulled her into a deep sleep. Janelle listened to her childlike snores while struggling to keep her own eyes open. The sun shone through the canopy of trees, casting a mottled pattern across the windshield. She pictured herself in the middle of a forest of tall pines with Beau. They were young then, before

Caroline was born, and they had their entire lives ahead. Everything was easy. She'd breathe in the smokiness of the needles, dry and sun-bleached on the ground, and he'd place his palms against her flushed cheeks. Sometimes they'd bring a picnic lunch of cold fried chicken and fall asleep, holding hands and watching clouds.

Janelle grew worried that her daydreams were pushing her somewhere below consciousness. She rubbed her eyes and felt the perspiration on her forehead.

Cissy sat up and crossed her elbows on the back of the front seat. "Where are we now, Grandmother?"

"Right outside Nashville. We'll stay here for the night," Janelle whispered through parched lips.

"You don't look all that good."

"I'm just tired, Cissy," she groused. The double center stripe had become four, so Janelle kept the car close to the side of the road to ensure it would stay in the correct lane.

"You look something more than tired."

"Keep your eye out for a motel," Janelle snapped.

"I'm worried about you." Cissy's voice broke and she snuffled back tears. "Tell me how to help."

"Just keep looking. We're bound to find something in the next couple of miles."

Dear Lord, Janelle thought, *don't let me wreck this car after all that's happened to Cissy. Don't make her face more death just yet.*

"Grandmother, look! It's a HoJo's, your favorite." Cissy squealed and pointed to the familiar teal and orange sign.

"I see it, too, Cissy." With shaking arms and legs, she managed to steer into the parking lot.

"Let me help you inside, Grandmother." Cissy grabbed her elbow and steadied her as they entered the motel lobby and paid for a room. She just had to keep it together a moment more.

"My name's Mae Johnson. This is my grand-daughter, Matilda." She kept to the script and handed over cash. The manager eyed her unsure hands, but said nothing.

Since their room was just a few doors down from the office, Janelle asked Cissy to walk her directly there. They could always get their bags later. The room smelled of cigarettes and air freshener, but neither of them commented. Janelle sat on one of the double beds. Cissy lifted her legs onto the mattress so she could curl on her side. Her breathing had become so shallow, Janelle thought to warn Cissy of her illness in case anything should happen.

"Do you want me to cover you with the bedspread, Grandmother?"

"I'm fine, Cissy. I think I'll just sleep for now." The darkness she'd longed for finally came.

Chapter 27

Cissy left the door open as she hurried back and forth to the car, transferring all their belongings into the motel room. A deep and unnamed fear chased her across the parking lot, so she closed the door, turned the deadbolt, and slid the chain into its grooved slot. Even with Grandmother sleeping soundly just a few feet away, Cissy felt truly alone in the world for the first time.

"You're never alone, Cissy." God sat propped up against the headboard of the second bed. Cissy crawled beneath the covers and wished she'd just go away.

"I feel like crying," Cissy whispered so she wouldn't wake Grandmother.

"Then you should cry."

"I don't want to seem like a child. I need to be strong."

"Crying doesn't mean you're weak, Cissy. You're meant to feel emotion. Otherwise you're dead to the world."

Cissy could hear her grandmother's labored breathing, but refused to turn and look at her. Instead, she pulled the bedspread up over her head, which magnified the humming in her ears.

"Why don't you sleep with your grandmother," God suggested.

"I'm too scared."

"I'll be here with you. There's nothing to be afraid of."

When Cissy turned to look, her grandmother slept deeply, her mouth open in a perfect O. Cissy's chest heaved with heartache to think her Grandmother's body wasn't as strong as her spirit. Then Cissy wanted nothing more than to be close to her. She moved to her bed and slid over to the middle so they could share the same pillow. Their faces were so close Cissy could smell the sourness in Grandmother's breath left over from the coffee she'd had with her lunch. Only a trace of her perfume remained after the long travel day, but it was enough to comfort Cissy as she fell asleep.

She didn't think she moved the entire night because her joints seemed locked in place when she woke. Grandmother still slept soundly, but she'd turned over some time in the night and had pulled the covers up over her shoulders. Cissy crept over to the dresser to check the time on the alarm clock. It was only 7 a.m., but they'd skipped dinner the night before and she almost doubled over with hunger. Thankfully, she remembered Grandmother had bought some snacks for the drive when she went into the grocer's to pick up their sandwiches for lunch the day before.

Cissy grabbed the keys to the car and found

the brown paper sack she'd not seen on the floorboard when she got the luggage last night. She didn't bother to return to the room before she dug into the hard salami and saltines. Sitting in the car with the door open, she gnawed small bites of the salami off one end, careful to trim it up straight since she lacked utensils. Still, Grandmother would surely be mortified when she saw her lack of manners.

When Cissy had her fill and locked the car, she returned to the room to grab a few of her notebooks from the suitcase so she could read them by the small swimming pool just steps from the room. It was too nice to stay indoors since the morning air lacked the humidity that typically greeted them each day. She left the door ajar, though, in case Grandmother woke.

The pebbles embedded in the concrete around the pool's edges pricked at her bare feet, but Cissy liked the rough sensation against her skin. The chlorinated water smelled fresh like clean sheets on the clothesline, so she sat down to dangle her feet over the edge. It wasn't the ocean, but it'd do.

She flipped through a couple of the notebooks. Cissy figured now that she was on the road, she'd run across even more interesting and exotic things to add. Biloxi had grown pretty boring, the hospital even more so, and her lists reflected that. She'd never kept a journal before, but perhaps

Grandmother would buy her a new notebook for that purpose. Who knows what adventures awaited them. She'd have a record of her time with Grandmother in case she ended up back at the psychiatric hospital in Meridian.

Even with an excellent imagination, Cissy struggled to envision a future for them. She tried to picture her grandmother buying them a charming house in Charleston, one with columns or with a porch that wrapped clear around the sides. Or, maybe they'd keep traveling to the nation's capital or Boston, and rent an apartment in a brownstone building like the one Dr. Guttman rented in New York City. Sadness washed over Cissy as each daydream evaporated before she could truly latch on to it.

Although late September days could feel as warm as summer, a breeze hinted that fall waited its turn. The pool water started to feel almost too cool with the wind picking up. Cissy lifted her legs back up onto the cement patio. When she stood up to fetch a sweater from the room, a gust blew her skirt up around her waist and sent the notebooks into the water.

They floated like lily pads of all colors and she stared at them dumbfounded. Her fear of their destruction was so great that she jumped into the middle of them in a panicked rescue. Cissy struggled to tread water, her billowing skirt working against her. As she reached for one notebook, her thrashing sent others out of reach. Pool water stifled her cries and she sputtered to keep her mouth free to take a breath.

"Miss! Miss, grab the side of the pool!"

The man's voice sounded hollow and faraway as her ears dipped below the water's surface, but her body sensed his instructions were important. Cissy dog-paddled to the edge of the pool and grabbed his waiting hand. With one strong pull, he yanked her back onto the cement patio.

As she sat and sobbed, he took a mesh net on a long metal pole and retrieved the notebooks, flicking each from the net onto the patio like leaves and debris that had tainted the pristine surface. She clutched them to her wet chest.

"What is going on out here?" Grandmother screeched from the doorway of the room. She'd found both her voice and enough strength to get out of bed. "Cissy? Cissy, are you all right?"

She scuttled over and knelt beside Cissy, stroking her arm, as the man explained what happened. He was a groundskeeper and noticed Cissy had jumped into the pool after the notebooks.

"Miss, you oughtn't be jumping in water if you can't swim," he joked. "You got tangled up in your own arms and long legs."

"I *can* swim!" she stuttered. "I . . . I . . ."

"Her notebooks are very important," Grandmother explained. "She probably panicked.

We're mighty thankful you were so close by to help."

"I've never known a girl to care so much about her schoolwork, especially such a pretty teenager. Shouldn't you be worrying about boys and movies and makeup and such?" The man laughed and shook his head before telling her to be careful around the pool if they were staying a spell.

"Let's go inside and dry you off. Give me those," Grandmother said, and Cissy released the soaking notebooks into her care.

Clammy and cold, Cissy took off all her clothes and crawled beneath the sheets naked, too overcome with sorrow for her lost lists to search out dry clothes. Grandmother hushed her whimpering and said everything would be all right, that Cissy should stay calm. She watched as Grandmother spread towels over the floor of the room and laid out the notebooks to dry. She took great care to dab at their wet pages with a white washcloth that soon picked up blue and black ink stains.

"Thank you, Grandmother."

"Don't give it a second thought," she said. "You can still read what you've written. The pages and covers are just a little warped. Why don't you nap for a while? You're sure to feel better when you wake up."

Her certainty wrapped around Cissy like another

blanket, protecting her from the chattering of her teeth and insides. From the minute she woke in the backseat of Grandmother's car and realized she was no longer at the hospital, each day held perils she'd never faced before. As much as Grandmother loved her, she thought Cissy feeble-minded for talking to God and counting to calm herself. Grandmother would never say such a thing out loud, but her expressions, even the way she held herself, indicated that Cissy tried her patience. Cissy wondered if Grandmother regretted taking her away from Meridian, but couldn't find a way to undo her actions.

Cissy dropped into a fretful sleep, the kind with dreams that shift and turn just enough to make you suspect they're becoming nightmares, yet the boogeyman never appears. When she woke, she wondered if her aching jaws had to do with the dreams or her jump into the pool.

She sat up quickly, forgetting she was naked, and grabbed for the sheets to cover her chest.

"I've seen you naked since you were a little baby. No need to be shy in front of me." Grandmother sat in a chair at the round table in the corner of the room, illuminated by a lamp that hung from the ceiling and cast light straight down on her head. She'd drawn the shades, so Cissy didn't know how long she'd dozed and if it was light or dark out.

"Could you hand me something to wear, Grandmother?"

She reached for the closest thing, which was her own nightgown draped across the other chair, and tossed it over. It smelled of talcum powder and Chanel No. 5. Cissy held it against her face long enough for Grandmother to comment that gowns are for wearing and not for sniffing.

When the tears started rolling down Cissy's cheeks, both of them were confused as to the reason.

"I don't know what's wrong with me, Grandmother. I'm sorry." The deepest sadness Cissy had ever known entered her bones and she hadn't the strength to hide it.

"Don't apologize, child. You've had a rough time. Not just this summer, but your whole life." Grandmother put down the tourist magazine she'd been reading and joined Cissy on the bed. They leaned up against the headboard, and Cissy slumped down so she could place her head on Grandmother's shoulder.

"You and Dr. Guttman and Mama all think I'm sick, but I don't know what you think needs fixing."

"Cissy, I don't think you're sick, but I do think the things your daddy did keep you from living life fully. I want you to know what it's like to fall in love and see the world and have children and be happy."

"Please don't talk about those things, Grandmother."

If Cissy had her wish, no one would mention her daddy again. Each time they did, it got harder and harder for her to keep his memory locked away. A person didn't have to be alive to keep hurting others.

"Maybe talking is exactly what you need to be doing," Grandmother said, and hugged her close. "Sometimes things draw in more power the longer they're hidden."

Cissy hoped the conversation would end if she didn't answer. Grandmother's grip never loosened and Cissy wondered where she found the strength. After all those years Grandmother shied away from touching her granddaughters, she turned out to be the best hugger in the family. Cissy hugged her back with all her might and then slumped down even farther into the bed, hoping to close her eyes and fall asleep again. Facing nightmares seemed easier than facing whatever else Grandmother was going to say.

Grandmother's heartbeat and steady breathing sang to her like the sweetest music she'd ever heard. Cissy imagined how easy it would be to stay wrapped up in her love forever, never leaving the Howard Johnson. When Grandmother pulled away abruptly and refused to look at her, Cissy's stomach lurched.

"Did I do something, Grandmother?" Cissy asked.

"It's not you, dear." She swiped at her cheek. "Give me a minute."

Cissy sat helpless while her grandmother shook her head in a silent conversation. After a couple of minutes, Cissy's discomfort grew so great she moved over to hug her tightly. Grandmother appeared both very old and very young in the same moment. Cissy stroked her white hair until her grandmother turned to face her again.

"When I was thirteen years old, a cousin of my daddy raped me," Grandmother whispered. "I didn't know if I should tell you, but I figured you could handle the truth."

The horror washed over Cissy. She chewed on the revelation until its truth took hold of her heart and threatened to squeeze the life out of her.

"I never told anyone, Cissy. Not my mama or daddy. Not your grandfather. Not even Ruth, who was my best friend at the time," she continued. "I never trusted anyone to say those words out loud, until now."

Cissy had no words to convey the heartbreak she felt. Still more confusing was the relief that lay beneath that heartbreak. Grandmother had held her secret shame for almost sixty years. She understood the very weight Cissy carried in her own heart.

"I want you to know we can survive the bad

people who enter our lives," Grandmother said gently. "I want you to know you'll survive, too. I should have told you sooner and I'm sorry for that."

Cissy thought back to Dr. Guttman's assertion that she could draw comfort from knowing others had gone through what she'd gone through; that she might feel less alone. She had challenged him that day, certain she'd feel no such comfort. Yet, here she was, lighter in heart than she'd been for a long while. A great shame took hold that she could feel better after what Grandmother had said. Cissy rolled over so she could bury her face deep beneath the covers.

"Cissy? Cissy, talk to me." Grandmother's hand rubbed her back through the thick coverlet on the bed.

Cissy's muffled cries sent hot breath into the cocoon she'd made and she had to peek out from beneath the covers just to breathe.

"I'm sorry, Grandmother. About what happened to you. I'm so sorry."

"Don't be, child. I suffered one terrible night while you suffered most of your childhood. Please don't cry for me."

Cissy dug even farther into the covers.

"Do you think you could talk about what happened to you?" Grandmother asked. "You don't have to carry it all alone."

Even though Cissy wanted to jump out of

bed and run from the room, she kicked back the covers. If Grandmother could share such a painful secret, Cissy felt it was wrong to hide her own hurts, no matter how much she didn't want to discuss them.

"When I was very little, I thought that's just what daddies did," she said, measuring her words. "Yet, as the years went on, I convinced myself I was being punished in some way, but could never figure out how to be better."

"It was never your fault, Cissy. I wish you could know that."

"I know that in my head, Grandmother, but my spirit just doesn't believe it."

Since leaving the hospital, a fuller picture of her childhood started coming into focus. Cissy didn't want to worry Grandmother, but each day, a memory would return like a scene from a movie she knew she'd seen but couldn't quite remember. They were just pieces of the whole, but she couldn't deny it was her story any longer.

"Cissy, do you remember being transferred to another hospital?"

"What do you mean by another hospital?" Her racing heart rushed too much blood to her head and she began to feel a little dizzy.

"We can talk about it later, child."

Cissy asked if she could turn on the television and Grandmother nodded, looking almost relieved the conversation had ended. While Cissy didn't remember a second hospital, she knew she left this world in some way because there were days she couldn't quite piece together. She figured there was a mighty good reason her brain wanted to erase that time and she didn't dare challenge it. The knowing knocked patiently, waiting for Cissy at a door she wasn't ready to open. Although the tapping grew fainter at times, it was now always with her, and even reruns of *Big Valley* couldn't drown it out.

They'd fallen asleep, Grandmother still in her clothes and Cissy in her grandmother's nightgown. Cissy stirred first, so she got up and opened the curtains. The intensity of the sun told her they'd slept like the dead while the day had already gotten off to a fine start.

"It's almost noon," she said, and yawned. "Rise and shine."

Grandmother's arm shielded her eyes against the stream of light invading their little tomb.

"I'm feeling poorly, Cissy. I'd like to lie here a while."

Her voice was dry and crackly. Cissy closed the curtain and turned on the lamp on the bedside table. Kneeling on the floor, she rested her head on the mattress next to her grandmother's hand.

"Walk across the parking lot to the Bob's Big Boy. You can fetch some scrambled eggs and coffee to go. You'll be all right," she assured

Cissy. "Just get some money from my purse and hurry back."

This change in attitude about letting Cissy out of her sight alarmed her more than her grandmother's weak voice. She tried to suck in her panic by holding her breath and counting the seconds until she had to breathe again.

"Go now, girl," Grandmother said, and turned over.

She could have slapped Cissy and it wouldn't have felt so dismissive. Cissy held her trembling lips between her thumb and index finger, and chastised herself for feeling so hurt. Just get dressed, she whispered to herself, and grabbed shorts and a T-shirt, pulling them on quickly. She knotted her hair into a bushy ponytail and didn't bother to brush her teeth.

Cissy half ran, half walked across the asphalt that the sun had rendered sticky against the plastic of her sandals. Yesterday's cool breezes had vanished and the oppressive heat had returned. The ice-cold air of the restaurant was merciful and kissed the humidity from her face.

"Sit anywhere you like." A young woman pointed at Cissy with the half-full coffeepot she had in one hand. Three full plates balanced on her other arm and she scurried to a table in the far corner. The red leather swivel stools looked inviting, so Cissy took a seat at one end of the empty counter.

The waitress raced back from her delivery and put a full coffee cup before Cissy even though she hadn't ordered anything yet.

"Do ya know what you want?"

The urgency of the question threw Cissy off guard. "I think just eggs. May I see a menu?"

The waitress stared and then busted out laughing, mouth wide open so Cissy could see the hot-pink bubblegum wad she was chewing.

"I guess you aren't a mind reader. Sorry about that. Don't know what I was thinking, sugar." She placed a laminated one-page menu on the counter. "Take your time."

Cissy had never ordered in a restaurant by herself and felt both giddy and terrified as the choices danced before her. Since Grandmother was likely fast asleep, she decided to eat her breakfast in the restaurant. What could happen in public in broad daylight?

"Miss? I'm ready to order."

"Call me Rita," the waitress offered, and opened her notepad. "Shoot."

Cissy ordered two scrambled eggs, a side of ham steak, one pancake, and a tall glass of milk. She waited for some clue she'd done it correctly, but Rita just commented that Cissy sure was skinny for a girl who could eat so much.

"Yeah, I get that a lot." She blew on the hot coffee she'd decided to drink to be polite. "I'm Matilda."

"Nice to meet ya, Matilda. You a little young to be traveling on your own?"

She explained about Grandmother sleeping in their room, but left out the part about her feeling poorly. Cissy said they were on a road trip, just the two of them, because she was an orphan and Grandmother was her guardian. The words seemed exaggerated and insincere because she didn't have much practice at lying.

"I'm not interrogating you, sugar," Rita joked. "Relax a bit."

"Yes, relax a bit," God said. "You're calling attention to yourself."

Cissy jumped six inches off the stool, knocking the coffee mug on its side.

"Oh, I'm so sorry, Rita!" She took some napkins and dabbed at the hot liquid cascading over the side of the laminate.

"Don't worry your pretty head. I'll take care of it." The cheerful waitress turned around to retrieve a dish towel.

Cissy glared at God while Rita sopped up the wasted coffee. When she left to get a fresh towel, Cissy hissed at God to stop scaring her in public.

"I thought you might need someone to talk to," She said. Her velvety words softened the anger that had bubbled up in Cissy just seconds before.

"It's hard for me to talk in public," Cissy said. "People will stare."

A small part of her didn't care if anyone stared.

She'd grown weary of watching what she said and did, fearful she'd do something wrong. Cissy lived in two different worlds and neither fit quite right.

"Are you scared about your grandmother?" God asked.

"Well, of course I'm scared. She doesn't look well and I know she won't tell me the whole truth so as to protect me somehow," Cissy whispered. "I'm not a child and I can take care of her just as she's taking care of me. We're a team."

"Maybe you could tell her those things."

Cissy thought hard about the fear that welled up when she heard God's words. She'd kept the truth about so many things locked away she didn't feel comfortable speaking them aloud. But she and Grandmother loved each other. Surely you should be able to say anything to those you love.

"I dunno," Cissy said. "I don't want to be a burden to Grandmother."

"When you love someone so deeply, your shared burdens can feel lighter," God said.

Within a minute or two, Rita rounded the corner with breakfast, including a fresh mug of coffee. Cissy wished she had remembered to tell her it wasn't necessary, as now she felt she had to drink it.

"You talking to someone?" Rita grinned in a warm way that told Cissy she wasn't poking fun.

"Sort of." Cissy took her knife and fork to the ham steak. She couldn't look Rita in the eyes and risk any sort of judgment she might be forming.

"I like to talk to myself at times. Clears my head," Rita said.

Nerves had locked Cissy's shoulders to her ears, but Rita's friendliness released all the tension built up since she left the motel room. Her breakfast tasted even better than she imagined it could. While Cissy ate, Rita shared her life story. Cissy listened to it the way she'd pay attention to a good book, not wanting to miss even the smallest detail.

Rita seemed a larger-than-life character. She'd grown up in Dadeville, Alabama, but left home when she was fifteen, hitchhiking to New York, where she hoped to become a stage actress first, maybe off Broadway, then a television star. She didn't make it past Nashville, so she tried her hand at singing country music. While Rita had a strong and clear voice, she'd been told by record company folks it wasn't anything special.

"Did you give up your dream of being an actress?" Cissy hoped she hadn't.

"I'm saving up my money. I'll make it to the Big Apple one day." Rita's face fell just a little, giving Cissy the impression that her dream might be fading with each passing day.

"I heard you singing earlier," Cissy said. "Maybe some big-shot talent scout or agent will drop in to the café to eat a piece of pie. He might offer you his card or ask for an audition."

"Well, Matilda, I guess it doesn't hurt to day-dream. That's why I treat every customer as if he or she could be someone important, my ticket out of here."

"Daydreams are wonderful," Cissy admitted. "I'm thankful our minds are capable of such because we can shape movies of how we'd like our lives to be instead of how they are."

"I like your philosophy. All I have now are my dreams." Rita looked just a little bit sad. Now twenty-four years old, she said she lived in one of the motel rooms with the manager and worked the 5 a.m. to 2 p.m. shift at the restaurant almost every day.

"Honey, when I'm not working, I like to spend every minute by the pool, sunbathing and reading Hollywood magazines. Those movie stars and fashion models are so damn glamorous. It just drips off them."

Cissy thought Rita had star quality and would surely be famous one day. Beauty seemed to come to the waitress naturally. They were both tall, but Rita had curves in places where Cissy was straight as a board. She liked that Rita's nose was crooked and her lips full and bright pink even without lipstick. The mesmerizing thing about her, though, was her mismatched eyes—one brown and one hazel. Too bad she had to wear a uniform the color of canned peas. No one could look like a celebrity in that color.

"Is the manager your boyfriend?" Cissy asked.

Rita snorted. "Not exactly," she said. "We have a deal. He gives me a place to live and I satisfy his needs, if you get my drift."

Cissy's face went hot and her lungs shrunk by half. She dipped a paper napkin in ice water and held it against her cheeks.

"You all right? You look like you've seen a ghost." Rita held a hand to her forehead and Cissy flinched.

The living arrangement with the motel manager gave new life to memories of the bargain Cissy had struck with her daddy to protect Lily and Jessie. No matter how far she and Grandmother got away from Biloxi, her mind came along for the ride, threatening to reveal the past like a mean classmate with a secret.

"I'm okay," Cissy said. "Just feeling a little under the weather. Could you box up my food and add an order of buttered toast and scrambled eggs for my grandmother?"

"Sure thing," Rita said, and the spark returned to those wondrous eyes Cissy had already grown jealous of. "I'll be back in a sec with a box."

Cissy turned her back to the counter and counted the number of chairs in the restaurant, which wasn't as satisfying as getting up and counting floor tiles, but it would have to do. She skipped the benches in the booths because those didn't count. They could fit three regular people across or two fat people. Best not to mess up a perfectly good counting game with ambiguity.

When God appeared again, She commented that Rita seemed like a good person and possibly someone Cissy could trust. Cissy agreed and turned back to sip the coffee, which wasn't half-bad after all with enough sugar added.

By the time Cissy got back to the motel room, Grandmother was sitting up in bed, still in her clothes from the previous day, white hair in all kinds of disarray. She didn't say a word about how long it had taken Cissy to get breakfast.

"Ready for some food?" Cissy held out the Styrofoam to-go box.

"Did you order enough for both of us?"

Cissy explained she'd decided to eat at the restaurant and met a nice lady who worked there. She shrunk back, anticipating a scolding.

"That's nice, Ciss. Put the food on the table and I'll get up to eat."

"You aren't worried I said the wrong thing like accidentally telling someone my real name?" She couldn't believe Grandmother's lack of concern and would have given anything to be reprimanded properly.

"I trust you, girl. You've got a good head on your shoulders."

Cissy sat in the chair opposite Grandmother and watched as she rearranged the dry curds of scrambled eggs with her plastic fork, taking just a bite or two. She'd unfolded the paper napkin and rested it across her lap as if she sat in the finest restaurant. Even feeling unwell, Grandmother acted like a gentle, mannered lady from the South, caring what others thought of her, even if that was only her granddaughter in a sad old motel room.

Cissy thought back to some of the afternoon teas Grandmother would hold for other ladies in society. Her granddaughters would be allowed to arrive at the end of the party, parade around politely in their best Sunday dresses, and then eat leftovers. Cissy never cared much for the cheese straws because Ruth added too much cayenne pepper. The real treat was the little pickle sandwiches lovingly rolled and cut into bite-size pieces. They resembled pigs in a blanket except the inside held a miniature dill pickle wrapped in a piece of flattened white bread. The secret ingredient was the garlic cream cheese spread that held it all together. Ruth added a scant drop of green food color to the cheese to set it apart from the whiteness of the bread, which Cissy thought was genius. She'd devoured dozens over the years. Lily and Jessie gravitated to the sweets first, which meant they had tummy aches before getting around to the good stuff.

Although, whenever divinity was served, Cissy made a beeline for it. Ruth was expert at creating those delicate sugar clouds even in the worst humidity.

"Grandmother, why don't I help you into the shower?" she suggested. "You might feel a little better."

"I rarely take showers, Cissy. I prefer baths."

"Well, let me draw you a tub."

"I'm too weak to get in and out of a tub right now," she countered.

"Well, then, I'll help you."

They went on and on like this until Cissy almost threw the tiny woman over her shoulder and carried her to the bathroom herself. But Cissy vowed to practice some patience, partly as a promise to God and partly as a promise to herself.

Without waiting for Grandmother's permission, Cissy made her way to the tub and turned the hot water faucet as far as it would go. She figured she'd make the water as hot as possible in case it took her a while to convince Grandmother to get in. But when she returned to the room, Grandmother was already unbuttoning her blouse in slow motion. She curled her finger, motioning Cissy over to help her pull off her polyester slacks. When Grandmother rolled off her knee-high hosiery and placed them in her shoes, Cissy urged her to place an arm around her waist.

Together, they took small shuffling steps to the bathroom.

"It's chilly in here," Grandmother remarked.

"You're a naked jaybird. You should be cold."

"I'm not naked, Cissy. I have on underthings."

Cissy kept her chatter upbeat to drown out the sad thoughts forming in her mind about how Grandmother's body had started to let her down. Skin draped over her bones like beige crepe fabric, crisscrossed with blue and green veins around the back on her knees. It was a wonder what clothes could do to cover up a body's secrets.

"You need a pedicure." Cissy lifted one of Grandmother's legs to help her into the tub. She'd insisted on wearing her panties and bra in the water and who was Cissy to argue.

"That's silly. Who's looking at my toes?"

"Well, obviously I am. And they're in sad shape."

Grandmother's halfhearted laugh was a gift. Cissy turned to open a miniature bar of soap and retrieve a washcloth, hoping Grandmother would not notice the tears pricking her eyes.

"You'd think I was a lobster preparing for death considering the temperature of this water," Grandmother said.

"You're a hard woman to please." Cissy's weak laugh did a poor job of hiding the truth of those words. Without asking, she rubbed a washcloth over her grandmother's back and down her arms. She didn't bother to ask permission to wash her hair either. Cissy just squeezed water from the washcloth over her scalp until it was wet enough to lather up with the miniature shampoo the motel also supplied. Working her fingers in circles, Cissy imagined massaging all her pains away.

"Grandmother, do you know how to play chess?"

"Yes, I do, but not very well."

"Why didn't you ever tell me?" Cissy asked, surprised at this hidden talent.

"You never asked."

Cissy told her people would never know much about her if she always waited for them to ask the right questions instead of offering up details that might be interesting. Grandmother said she came from a different time when women were more reserved. It wasn't ladylike to flap your mouth and share yourself with just anyone.

"I'm not just anyone," Cissy said. "So feel free to tell me things you don't think I know about you."

Grandmother's silence should've given her a clue she didn't want to play the get-to-know-you-better game. But Cissy figured since she'd taken liberties to get her in the tub, she could just keep pressing her grandmother until told to stop.

"Okay, let's start off easy," Cissy said. "My

favorite color is purple. Do you have a favorite color?"

Grandmother's back heaved with a sigh, but she answered nonetheless. "The dark green of magnolia leaves."

"Good answer!" Cissy said, as if only one right answer existed, but her excitement got the best of her. "Do you have a favorite food?"

"Fried oysters in cornmeal batter," she said. "How many questions do I have to answer for you to leave me be?"

"My favorite food is coconut cream pie," Cissy said. "How would I know how many questions I have in my brain before asking them? Asking one question can sometimes lead me to think of several others."

"Could you just help me out of the tub and dry me off?"

Grandmother seemed to weigh double after her bath, and Cissy struggled to lift her out in a delicate manner. She didn't say a thing while Cissy set her on the toilet and dried her off the best she could. Cissy brought her some dry underwear and a cotton nightgown, and said she'd wait right outside the door in case she needed help. She respected Grandmother's modesty even though she'd just seen Cissy naked the day before.

When Grandmother had finally dressed, the gown clung to her damp body and outlined exactly what she wanted to hide anyway. Cissy grabbed her under an armpit and they moved as one back to the bed. She wanted to be propped up, so Cissy grabbed pillows off both beds to place behind her. When situated, Grandmother instructed her to roll the wet underthings in a towel to squeeze out some of the moisture and then hang them over the shower rod to dry.

Cissy gladly took care of things. Grandmother had gone against all her upbringing to stand by Cissy these weeks and ultimately free her from a place where her spirit had started to wither. Cissy slipped into the bed beside her and lay flat as a board, not wanting to take any of the pillows.

"I need to ask you something," she said, staring at the popcorn ceiling and noting the brown watermark in the corner.

"Well, isn't that a surprise," Grandmother said.

"I'm being serious," Cissy protested. "When I went looking for your nightgown, I found a big stack of money at the bottom of one of your suitcases. And I'm talking *big*. Plus a whole bunch of jewelry tied up in one of your blouses."

Grandmother explained they'd need money and didn't want her credit card to leave a trail for others to find them. "I wasn't thinking clearly when I packed and headed to Meridian that day. Something in me took hold and I just felt the most important thing was to get you as far away from Mississippi as possible," she said. "I'm feeling mighty foolish right now."

"Your plan was the grandest idea I've ever heard of. I feel more loved than I have in sixteen years." Cissy placed her hand on her grandmother's arm, the skin still warm from the bath. "I know you're not well."

"No, I'm not. I just didn't think I'd be feeling so tired so quickly."

"Do you have cancer?" She held her breath waiting for the answer. The thudding of her heart told her she already knew.

"Afraid so."

Grandmother's shoulders slumped, making Cissy think she was relieved to unburden her secret.

"Do we have to go back to Mississippi?" Cissy shouldn't have spoken the question, but it was like having to peek through your fingers during the scary parts of a movie. It couldn't be helped.

"Not this minute, no. But if I don't start to feel well, we'll have to call your mother."

Cissy started to count the sections of wood paneling lining the walls but gave up before getting halfway around the room. Staying present for this conversation seemed more important.

"Do you think I could live on my own one day?" she asked. "You know, like have my own place and a job?"

"Yes, I do. That's been my hope for you. That

you won't let what your daddy did to you make you give up on life." Grandmother used her palms to sit more upright, but the movement seemed to exhaust her.

"How long after that man hurt you did you start to feel normal again?" Cissy hoped it wasn't wrong to ask questions about the secret, considering Grandmother had kept it to herself for so long.

"The trick is understanding that your idea of normal might have to change a bit," Grandmother said.

Chapter 28

Over the next few days, they led a strange little life at the Howard Johnson. Cissy would fetch meals from the café and they ate most together unless Grandmother was napping. Twice a day, Cissy would walk her around the parking lot, taking baby steps and allowing her to rest often. Building up strength was important, and lying in bed wasn't going to help. Cissy longed to postpone the inevitable return to Mississippi as long as possible.

When Rita and Grandmother met for the first time, they took an instant liking to each other. Cissy guessed that's why Grandmother trusted Cissy to sit in the café and drink coffee while Rita worked. At least she was looked after.

Before long, Cissy trusted Rita enough to confess that Matilda wasn't her real name. Rita was glad to hear it because she said the name didn't suit her. She liked the name Cissy and said her mama had chosen well. Rita was intrigued that the name was not a shortened version of another name like Cecilia or Cecily. Cissy thought Rita was giving her mama too much credit for thinking things through.

Rita taught her that even bad coffee could taste good if you added enough sugar and cream, so

Cissy's daily cup became something to look forward to. Maybe she just associated it with Rita and their talks, and its taste improved because of it. Each day, Rita gave Cissy a slice of pie and refused to take money even when she revealed Grandmother had plenty.

When Rita got off her shift at 2 p.m., they'd sit out by the pool on the lounge chairs and make up stories about the motel guests, where they came from, what they did for a living and such. She treated Cissy like a grown-up, never talking down to her, and Cissy appreciated the respect. She did her best to return it.

"Don't you have a pair of sunglasses?" Rita pulled a lounger out of the shade and into the bright sun.

When Cissy shook her head no, Rita ran to her room to retrieve a spare pair. She kept several, saying it was important to protect the skin around the eyes from premature wrinkles and a lady should never be without her sunglasses, especially in the South. Rita also made it her mission to make sure Cissy slathered Coppertone suntan lotion on every square inch of her body so her fair skin wouldn't burn. Cissy didn't mind because Coppertone was a happy smell, of beaches and the Gulf, and of Lily and Jessie. She missed them, even though she visited with her sisters in her memories almost every day.

"Is your grandmother feeling better?"

"A little stronger every day. Thanks for asking."

"I have to admit I like that you've stayed on so long. I never make any friends 'cause I work every day. And Daryl wouldn't let me go out even if I did find a girlfriend."

Daryl, the motel manager, kept a close eye on them, but not too close. He probably figured Cissy was young enough not to cause any trouble or turn Rita's mind against him. The thing is, Rita's mind had already turned against him. It had the very day he first took a fist to her. She stayed with him because she had nowhere else to go and no money to get there. Somehow her wages never seemed enough to make the first step.

That morning, a guest had left a copy of *New York* magazine in the café, so she brought it out and read to Cissy about Manhattan socialites and their parties, reviews of the latest Broadway plays, and restaurants and the strange foods they served.

"Why would anyone eat a snail?" Cissy asked.

"Suppose it's a delicacy. Rich people eat things that poor folks wouldn't."

Grandmother was rich and Cissy still didn't believe she'd eat a snail. It was a question to ask her sometime.

"Whatcha writing about today?" Rita asked.

Cissy'd grown so comfortable around Rita that she'd bring her notebooks out to the pool.

Although, she made sure to put something heavy on them to keep them from blowing into the water again. Rita never asked to read the notebooks. She was interested without crossing a line of privacy.

"Things to do and see in New York," Cissy said. "May I borrow the magazine so I can write things down correctly?" Deep down, she knew she'd never make it to the sights that Dr. Guttman had described in so much detail, like Central Park, the Statue of Liberty, and the World Trade Center. And, oh, the foods he'd described that she'd never taste, like the poppy-seed bagel from H&H Bagels or pizza from Di Fara's in Brooklyn. Perhaps when she and Grandmother left the motel for good, she'd give Rita the list for when she finally made her move to New York City.

Rita read the latest issue of *Teen Beat* even though she'd long grown out of her teens. Maybe it helped transport her to a happier and safer place and time, the way reading books did for Cissy.

"My psychiatrist is from New York," Cissy admitted, and waited for a reaction.

"Wow. You have a psychiatrist? You get more interesting to me every day," Rita said, and returned to her magazine.

"That's it? You don't want to know why?"

"I figure that's your business," she said.

Like Martha at the hospital, Rita seemed more

interested in the friendship Cissy offered in the present than with the details of her past. In time, she would share parts of her story with Rita, but for now they'd share magazines and suntan lotion.

"You thirsty?" Rita bent over to rummage for some change in the bottom of her canvas bag that held all their magazines and lotions and such.

Rita's T-shirt hiked up, revealing large purple splotches ringed with yellow and green across her lower back and upper hip. The bruises had started to fade, but there was no mistaking she'd been beaten pretty soundly. All the breath left Cissy's lungs.

"What happened to you?" Cissy sat on the edge of Rita's lounger, barely touching her fingertips to the areas of violence. It crushed her to think these weren't the first Rita had hidden, or the last she'd receive.

"Oh, honey, don't you worry about it." She pulled down her T-shirt to cover the marks. "I've had worse."

Rita said she'd convinced him not to hit her in the face or arms because it could hurt her chances for a singing career. He'd also stopped hitting her in the gut when he learned she was pregnant.

"You're having a baby?" Cissy sat in disbelief.

"Yeah, it was a mistake. He promised we'd always use a condom. But one night when he was drunk, he forced himself on me. No matter how much I begged him to stop, it seemed to make him want it more."

Rita seemed so calm and resigned to her condition. Cissy sat with her mouth open until Rita told her she resembled a wide-mouth bass.

In the next second, Cissy stood up and stumbled from the lounger. She fell, landing hard on her tailbone. Her unblinking eyes filled with horror and knowing. Rita shook her shoulders and cried out that Cissy was scaring her.

"Rita," Cissy said as her teeth knocked together, "I was pregnant, too. But I'm not anymore."

Chapter 29

After two full days, Janelle believed Cissy had cried the last tears her body would ever produce. During those desperate hours, she wouldn't speak. Janelle and Rita took turns forgoing sleep and holding Cissy's hands so she'd never go untethered. Daryl had stopped by the first afternoon to protest Rita's absence. After one look at Cissy, he'd left without saying a word.

They couldn't get her to eat anything of substance, but she allowed a spoon or two of hot soup and oatmeal if they forced it. Somewhere along the way Rita brought a milkshake from the diner. Cissy sucked in the sweet, thick liquid, but would gag when she couldn't stop her crying long enough to swallow. Still, those milkshakes kept up her strength.

Rita's presence was a godsend. Janelle couldn't gauge how ill she herself had become and how much longer she'd be able to take care of Cissy. She would have been pretty useless to her granddaughter if she grew any weaker. The waitress's company was sometimes the only thing that kept Janelle sane as they watched Cissy's grief eat away at her, both physically and emotionally.

On that third morning, Cissy woke first. She'd been sandwiched between Janelle and Rita, and now squirmed to free herself. A thin yellow line of sunshine peeked through the drapes and cut across the three women.

"Grandmother? Are you awake?" Cissy's face, still splotched and puffy, was eerily serene, but a welcome sight.

"Oh, Cissy! I knew you'd come through."

But Janelle had known no such thing. Ever since the murder, Janelle feared that when Cissy's demons grew bold enough to show themselves, her mind would be unprepared to process the trauma. No one, not even Dr. Guttman, would be able to put her together again.

"My mind didn't crack, Grandmother." Her sweet voice was pure and confident as if announcing a personal victory.

"You're a strong girl. You're such a strong girl." Janelle patted Cissy's thigh.

Rita listened to the exchange before speaking. "It's just so goddamn unfair what happened to you. I can hardly bear it."

"Oh, Rita, I don't think God is in Heaven dividing up fair and unfair, doling it out willy-nilly until half of us had heartache and half of us didn't. I was just born to the wrong daddy and maybe the wrong mama, but I was given the absolutely correct grandmother."

This declaration triggered an avalanche of

emotion in Janelle, but she refused to cry. Cissy would be okay now. She had to be.

Rita finally glanced at the clock on the nightstand. She said she'd better check on Daryl.

"I hope he's not angry you've stayed with us so long," Janelle said.

"You have enough on your minds than to worry about my sorry life." She left with a reassuring smile after Cissy promised to check in on her at the diner later.

But Janelle did worry. Rita would forever be a part of Cissy's journey back to herself. The thought of that drunkard motel manager punishing Rita for her kindness infuriated Janelle.

"It's time we clean this place up," Janelle said, turning her attention to their room. "And we both could use some tending as well."

She called the front desk of the motel and asked for fresh sheets and towels. They'd kept the DO NOT DISTURB sign on the door for so long, the cleaning staff ignored the room as if it wasn't even there. The morning appeared to be a fresh start on many fronts.

"I'll walk over to the restaurant with you for breakfast. A bit of my strength has returned," Janelle said. "Shall I braid your hair today? I might not do as fine a job as Letitia, but I could try."

Cissy pinched her own arm and yelped.

"Good Lord, girl. What are you doing now?"

"I was afraid this was all a dream, or that I was creating a space in my mind that was peaceful and happy," she said. "I'm so glad you're feeling better."

Janelle hugged Cissy and nudged her toward the bathroom. "Go on now and shower. You'll feel worlds better."

After Cissy had showered and Janelle had bathed, they dressed quickly. Cissy sat on the floor in front of Janelle to have her hair braided. Because it was still wet, Janelle was careful not to pull too hard.

"Put some elbow grease into it, Grandmother. I've never known you to be gentle with my scalp. Why start now?" She let out a high, childlike laugh.

Janelle closed her eyes at its music and considered whether her next question would break a precious spell.

"Ciss, do you need to talk about anything else? I know you've cried out an ocean of grief, but I don't expect you to be strong on my account."

Cissy covered Janelle's hand that now rested on her shoulder.

"Do *you* need to talk, Grandmother?"

"You're a wise girl, Cissy. And I do have something I'd like to say." Janelle helped her up off the floor so they could sit side by side on the bed. She drew in a deep breath.

"Ruth said I did the wrong thing by insisting on the abortion," Janelle said. "I want you to know I had your best interests at heart. It wasn't an easy decision."

Cissy said she couldn't imagine an instance when the decision would be easy for anyone, but she didn't like how abortion sounded when spoken aloud. It sounded as ugly as the things her daddy did and asked that they not speak of it again.

"I know everything you've done is to protect me," Cissy said, gulping. "But when you can't undo a decision, seems the smart thing to do is feel okay about it and move on."

"But, Cissy . . . I need you to forgive me."

She pulled Janelle close. When they pulled apart, Janelle saw heartache in her granddaughter's face and would have done anything to bring back the laughter that filled the room earlier.

"There's not a thing in the world to forgive. But right now, I can't talk about it." Cissy jumped up and turned on the clock radio before plopping back on the floor in front of Janelle.

The rockabilly tune comforted Janelle as she finished braiding Cissy's hair. Janelle experienced a strange glimmer of hope that one day she'd be able to shed her guilt over the abortion, a guilt she'd not confessed to Ruth.

"I'm not afraid anymore," Cissy finally said.

"You can't know how happy that makes me."

Janelle continued to weave Cissy's curls into loose braids, her hands slower than they'd been in the past. The girl sat perfectly still, not saying a word, and Janelle had to resist the urge to check on her mood. After a while, she answered Janelle's unspoken questions.

"You know, Grandmother. Only our minds keep those dark moments alive and breathing, and only our minds can put them to rest."

For the second time that morning, Janelle told her granddaughter how wise she was.

Janelle and Cissy sat in the restaurant much longer than it had taken them to eat. It seemed they both appreciated a break in scenery from the motel room, which had held so much sorrow and sickness in previous days. Besides, they needed to stay gone long enough for house-keeping to change the sheets and tidy the bath-room.

Before they'd left, Janelle instructed Cissy to stand on the bed and put their money and jewelry inside the air-conditioning vent. Cissy didn't understand Janelle's distrust of people—Cissy still insisted most folks were good at heart even after what her daddy had done.

Rita appeared joyful during her shift, and she sang soulful country ballads about long-lost loves and cheating husbands that caused people to let their eggs go cold while they listened. Cissy had once described her voice as angelic, and now Janelle understood that assessment.

"She's quite good," Janelle said. "She could sing professionally."

Cissy related Rita's dream of being a stage actress and that she only considered a singing career after her road trip to New York was cut short because of lack of funds. Janelle took the opportunity to ask if Cissy had dreams for her own future.

"I've always been a live-in-the-present sort of gal and never thought beyond high school, Grandmother."

Everything in the diner seemed to hold her interest except Janelle's questions. When she asked Cissy to pay attention, the girl looked down and to the side, but never in Janelle's direction.

"Is college even an option for someone who's killed another human being? Seems that colleges would have higher standards," Cissy said.

"Truthfully, I don't know the answer, but that doesn't mean you shouldn't try. Think of all the books you could read and all the people you'd meet. You never know what kind of career might strike your fancy until you do some exploring."

"Dr. Guttman said I could be a writer or reporter one day—like at a big New York newspaper. He said my list-making makes me good at details."

Her thoughts seemed to take her a thousand miles away. "Or, maybe I'll just let the future show me my path."

Janelle lifted Cissy's chin so that they could speak eye to eye. "Life doesn't work that way, Cissy. At some point, you have to start envisioning what you want and make it happen."

Squeezing a lifetime of lessons into a minute—or even a day or week or month—was pointless. Yet Janelle feared what would become of this gentle and naïve child if she didn't press her to stand on her own. Janelle's declining health forced her hand.

"If something happened to me, would you know what to do?" Janelle asked point-blank.

"Why do old people always talk about dying?" Her attempt at a joke failed to hide her uneasiness. Janelle suspected her counting would start up any moment.

"Why you gals so serious?" Rita quipped, filling their coffee cups on a break from her concert for the customers.

"We're not being serious," Cissy snapped. "We just don't feel up to chatting."

"Well, excuse me," she huffed. "I'll just come back when you're up for socializing."

Rita turned on her heel and Cissy seemed to want to jump up after her.

"She's mad at me. I can tell. But it seems you and I are having a private conversation right now and I should try to concentrate on what you're saying," Cissy said.

"She won't stay mad, dear. And thank you for understanding what I'm saying is important. Now, back to what . . ."

"Grandmother, if you got sick, I'd know to call for an ambulance. I know how to use a phone."

"And?"

"I suppose I'd call Mama or Ruth, and then Dr. Guttman."

"Everybody faces death. I'm not afraid," Janelle said. "Don't look so grief-stricken just yet."

"How else should I look, Grandmother? I can't bear to be without you. And not just because I'd end up back at the state hospital. I like living with you."

Cissy grabbed her glass of water and downed it in one gulp, ice cubes tumbling onto her upper lip. She wiped her mouth with a paper napkin and returned it to her lap.

"Child, I don't regret my decision to get you out of Mississippi. I knew I was sick when I left. And I knew it'd be difficult for us to stay away indefinitely, but my heart never raised objections because I just wanted you to be with family. I wanted you to be with *me*. These days have been the most meaningful of my life."

"Of your entire life?"

"Yes, my *entire* life."

"I thought I'd cried myself dry, but here I go feeling all weepy again," Cissy said. "But they're happy tears this time."

They talked for almost an hour. Janelle asked her to promise not to panic if she fell ill and needed a doctor. Cissy did her best to have an adult conversation, but would change the subject if Janelle skirted the inevitable.

"Can't we just make the most of each day we have together?" Cissy asked.

Now that Janelle was feeling stronger, she told Cissy they'd be leaving Nashville the next day. She even suggested another driving lesson and searched Cissy's face for an excited reaction.

"What's wrong? I thought you wanted to learn to drive more than anything."

"I do, Grandmother, I really do," she explained. "But I finally made a real friend and I'm sad to think I'll never see her again."

"Rita has been a treasure. I'll be forever grateful that we ran into her," Janelle said. "But, Cissy, you'll make many friends in your life. Some for short periods and some until the day you leave this earth. Both kinds are important."

Cissy said she wanted Rita to be a forever type of friend. Janelle failed to understand her attachment to someone she'd just met two weeks ago. But then again, Rita was present when Cissy confronted the memories she'd buried for so long. Janelle and Rita were the only witnesses to that child confronting her darkest hours and rising above them.

"Well, maybe you two should do something fun today to say your goodbyes," Janelle suggested. "Maybe a matinee? My treat."

She pressed cash into Cissy's palm and folded her fingers over the bills.

"I'm headed back to the room to pack. You joining me?"

Cissy said she'd rather hang out in the diner until Rita's shift was over. She needed time to find the proper words to tell Rita how much she'd meant to her.

Chapter 30

Janelle had instructed Cissy to say her goodbyes to Rita, but was second-guessing her decision. Although she'd felt well enough to have breakfast at the diner earlier, the vertigo had returned and she perspired profusely. Her temples throbbed from a headache that had plagued her for the better part of a week.

Where did Janelle think they'd go next? It wouldn't be long before she'd be forced to end this ill-conceived trip because of her health. She couldn't drive in her current state. Cissy had assured her that she'd know what to do, who to call, should Janelle become incapacitated. Janelle feared that time was near. Better to spare Cissy another traumatic experience and leave now while Janelle could still get them back home. When Cissy returned from the movie, Janelle would tell her it was time to go back to the hospital in Meridian. She hoped she could get through such a conversation without breaking down. She hoped her Cissy would understand.

Janelle had traveled so far from normal, she didn't know how to get back. She wanted her own bed. She wanted to sit in her rocker on the front porch. More than anything, she wanted to die at home, with the people she loved around her, including Ruth.

She sat down on the bed and picked up the phone to make a collect call. Ruth answered on the third ring.

"Mrs. Clayton!" she shouted. "Where are you? Why haven't you called before now?"

"After our last call, I didn't think you'd want to hear from me." Janelle had feared she'd lost Ruth's affection for good after insisting on the abortion for Cissy. And if she had called, what was there to say? Janelle had been more than foolish. She'd been irresponsible.

"I've been worried sick. *We've* been worried sick," Ruth said.

"We?"

Scuffling noises muffled Janelle's question. Then she heard a soft clicking noise.

"Mother? Are you there?" Caroline asked.

"Miss Caroline is with me," Ruth said. "She's on the other line."

The two talked over each other, their words melding into an incoherent jumble. Janelle couldn't make out a complete sentence or question, except that the two of them had been united in their quest to find her and Cissy. She did make out the words "state police."

"You're going to have to speak one at a time and more slowly," Janelle said. The volume of their chatter exacerbated her headache. She wondered how she'd get through a whole conversation with the two of them. Janelle had so much to say, but her thoughts were getting muddled.

"Mother, you've got to come home. Or tell us where you are. We'll come get you and Cissy at once," Caroline said.

"That's why I called," she said. "We're in Nashville at a—"

"Nashville? What were you thinking?" Caroline asked, while Ruth muttered, "Lord have mercy."

Janelle hadn't been thinking. While she didn't regret arranging for Cissy's abortion, she erred in not returning Cissy to the psychiatric hospital. After Cissy's hearing, Mr. Whitney had been confident that she would stay no more than a year under Dr. Guttman's care and would likely come home without any jail time. They all might have returned to some semblance of normalcy with time. Janelle only complicated things by taking Cissy's future into her own hands. Yet, she'd come to know Cissy and love her more over the last two weeks than in the last sixteen years.

Janelle's compassion for Cissy stood in stark contrast to the way she'd treated Caroline since the shooting. She regretted not working harder to bring them all together. Instead, the old divisions between Janelle and her daughter had only widened.

"Mother, the state police have been looking for you. They were going to call the FBI, thinking you'd crossed state lines. You could be in serious legal trouble."

"That doesn't matter now." Janelle didn't fear the police. The cancer would claim her long before she could be tried and convicted for her impetuousness. "I'd like to speak to Ruth alone for a moment. Then Caroline and I will talk. Okay?"

After some protest from Caroline, Ruth spoke softly into the receiver. "How is Cissy?"

"I think she's going to be just fine," Janelle said. "But I don't think I have much time left, Ruth. I'll have to get to a hospital soon. She shouldn't have to deal with the doctors alone."

"You're not going to die just yet, Mrs. Clayton. We have plenty of talks on the front porch ahead of us. And the fall color this year is sure to be something to behold."

Janelle lay back on the bed, the receiver cradled near her ear. Her breath grew ragged. "I'm not afraid, Ruth. I just called to hear your voice; to let you know . . . to tell you that I've been blessed to have you in my life."

Ruth's sobs were audible over the line. "I'm not ready, Mrs. Clayton . . . *Janelle.*"

Janelle longed to comfort her old friend in person, to have one last chance to hug her as they had done freely as children. Vivid memories of those days bubbled up: swimming in the creek, napping in the tall field grasses, playing

Monopoly at the dining table on hot summer afternoons.

"No need for tears yet, Ruth. I'll see you in the next couple of days," Janelle said. "I should give some details to my daughter, if you'd put her on the line."

Ruth handed the phone to Caroline without saying goodbye.

"We're at the Howard Johnson on the south side of Nashville," Janelle said. "I don't think I can drive us back home. Perhaps you could drive out to get us? Or call the authorities—"

"I'm not calling the police," Caroline said. "Of course I'll come get you. Is Cissy there?"

Janelle explained that Cissy was with a friend she'd made. She also relayed parts of their trip and how they ended up in Nashville by way of Memphis. Caroline chuckled at Janelle's description of Cissy's yearning to visit Graceland and the girl's atrocious driving skills.

"She regained her memory," Janelle said. "About the pregnancy and abortion. She'll be okay. Cissy is a strong, brave girl."

"I wish you'd trusted me enough to tell me," Caroline said. "I would have agreed to the abortion. You shouldn't have had to do all this alone."

"I'm sorry, Caroline. About so very much," she said.

"It doesn't matter now, Mother."

"It's always mattered," Janelle said. "I can't explain why things have been so difficult for us or why I didn't do more to change that. You must know I've always loved you."

"I'm going to leave now and be there late tonight." Caroline seemed to struggle to keep her voice from shaking. "We'll figure everything out when we're all together again."

"Why don't you give me and Cissy one last evening together? If you leave first thing in the morning, we'll see you tomorrow afternoon. Will you tell Jessie and Lily that I love them?"

"You can tell them in person," Caroline said, crying freely now.

"Shhh," Janelle whispered. "No tears. Tell Ruth not to cry either. I can hear her bawling in the kitchen."

"I love you, Mother."

"I love you, too." Janelle hung up the phone and turned on her side. She would just close her eyes for a few minutes before resuming packing. Perhaps Cissy could help after the movie.

Chapter 31

Cissy couldn't imagine what it'd be like to leave the comfort of the motel and diner behind. It was her home, and Rita was now part of her family. Until she could get a handle on her emotions, Cissy didn't want to talk to Rita. She moved to the other side of the table so she could stare out at the parking lot instead of back at the counter, where Rita finished up the breakfast shift.

"You snubbing me?" Rita smacked the back of Cissy's head with a menu, but was smiling when she plopped in the chair in front of her.

"No, silly," she said. "I'm just feeling sad. Grandmother said we have to leave tomorrow."

Rita's smile faded and Cissy would have done anything to get it back. She reached across the table to grab her hand, but Rita withdrew it and ran from the diner into the parking lot.

"Don't be mad at me," Cissy said, catching up to her. "I don't want to leave, but it's not my decision."

Rita bit her glossy lower lip to stop its trembling, but gave into what Martha used to call ugly crying. Back at the hospital, she'd explained that actors on television shows and in movies were fake criers because their faces remained too pretty. When people were

413

truly hurting, they contorted their features and grimaced until they were as ugly as the feelings trying to escape them. Rita was not fake crying.

"Can I hug you?" Cissy asked.

"Of course," Rita blubbered. "And you don't ask if you can hug someone. You just do it." She continued to cry, but at least a bit of laughter pierced through it and her lovely face began to emerge again.

"I wish we could be friends forever," Cissy said.

Rita grabbed a wad of paper napkins from her apron pocket and wiped her face with both hands. She blew out her breath in short puffs as if calming herself.

"Why can't we be friends forever?" Rita asked. "You ever hear of writing letters or making phone calls? Just because you're leaving doesn't mean you have to forget me."

"I never said I'd forget you. I said I had to go because of Grandmother. Forgetting you would be impossible."

She asked Cissy not to say anything else so nice because she couldn't afford to cry anymore during her shift; that customers were already staring through the window at them.

"Look at my splotchy face! What will the assistant manager say?" Rita waved her hands in front of her face to cool off the heat in her cheeks. "Whew. I have to get a grip."

"Do you think Daryl would mind if you and I went to the movies this afternoon? Grandmother gave me money for the matinee."

"I'll ask," she said. "I can't make promises, though."

"I wish you'd never met Daryl."

"You and me both, sugar. You and me both. But let's go to the five o'clock feature. We need plenty of time to get you ready."

Cissy didn't even recognize herself after Rita had painted every inch of her face with an artist's palette of cosmetics. Rita scolded her for touching her eyelids, saying she didn't want Cissy to mess up her masterpiece. Cissy had no experience with makeup because her mama didn't allow it, but she knew Grandmother would have a conniption fit if she saw Rita's handiwork. Grandmother had described girls with less makeup as harlots, and Cissy feared she'd crossed some line of Southern lady decorum.

"You worry too much," Rita had said when they left for the movies. They'd taken Rita's rusty VW even though Grandmother had offered up the Cadillac. "You look pretty with makeup on and much older. It'll be easier to get you into an R-rated movie."

Turned out the movie house didn't have any R-rated movies playing so they ended up watching *Bugsy Malone*. Rita griped so much about the story line that Cissy had to tell her to hush up so they could enjoy the show.

"What kind of crime movie has kids playing the role of gangsters? This is ridiculous," she'd muttered. "And they're not even using their own voices for the singing. You can tell they've dubbed in adult voices."

Halfway through the movie Rita left to sit in the lobby. If she thought Cissy was going to miss the rest of the movie, she had another thing coming. Only three other people were in the theater and Cissy relished the time alone in the dark, with a large buttered popcorn and Coke. She couldn't take her eyes off Jodie Foster and wanted to be Tallulah so badly, shooting bad guys with cream pies instead of bullets. They had about the same amount of makeup on and that thought made Cissy laugh out loud, making the few other moviegoers turn around and glare.

When the movie ended, Cissy found Rita in the lobby, a cloud of cigarette smoke obscuring her face. Her slinky halter top and tight knit pants seemed out of place in the daytime, and Cissy was a little embarrassed for her. At least Cissy had insisted on wearing her own clothes when Rita offered to loan her an outfit earlier.

"I thought we were supposed to be doing something together today. You sitting in a theater alone isn't exactly spending time with me." Rita pouted in a way Cissy sensed she'd done a million times to make people feel sorry for her.

"You're the one who left," Cissy reminded her, but tried not to sound defensive. She feared their last hours together were not going well, so Cissy suggested Rita pick something for them to do the remainder of the evening. Cissy was sure Grandmother wouldn't mind. Rita perked right up at the suggestion, but the mischievousness in her eyes made Cissy regret her offer immediately.

"I know what we should do," she squealed, and grabbed Cissy's hand. Rita dragged her, half running, to the VW and they took off like lightning.

Within minutes they pulled up to a brick building painted bright purple, and Cissy doubted it could mean anything but trouble.

"Not if you don't tell anyone." Rita winked and then laughed at the worry she must have seen in Cissy's brow. "Don't fret. You'll have fun."

She'd taken them to a honky-tonk called Tootsie's Orchid Lounge. Rita's friend, Al, worked the bar a few nights a week and used to slip her a free drink or two whenever she went there. Before Daryl turned mean on her, she said they'd gone to Tootsie's together. They hadn't been in weeks because he wouldn't allow her to go to bars or concerts anymore. He said she flirted too much with other men.

"I'm worried what will happen to you if Daryl finds out," Cissy said.

"How will he find out? We're at the movies and dinner, right? We won't stay long anyway."

Despite Cissy's objections, Rita helped her apply a new coat of lipstick because it'd worn off when she ate the popcorn earlier. Rita said it'd make her look older so she could get in. Her friend needn't have worried. The old man at the entrance hugged Rita and shook Cissy's hand until her elbow ached, saying any friend of Rita's was welcome at Tootsie's. His accent revealed he wasn't from Nashville, but its cadence was just as sweet as a Mississippi or Alabama twang. When she questioned him, he said he hailed from the great state of Minnesota, which made Cissy laugh.

It took more than a few minutes for her eyes to adjust to the dark, smoky interior. At 7 p.m., only a dozen or so people sat with drinks in hand, listening to a man play guitar on a dimly lit stage. Sometimes the music sounded like country, sometimes like gospel or rockabilly, but the musician blended it so expertly you couldn't help but want more. He kept his eyes closed most of the time and swayed just enough to make Cissy fear he'd topple from his stool.

"Why are people staring at me, Rita? Do you think they've guessed I'm underage and shouldn't be here?" Cissy shielded her face and turned toward the bar and away from the audience to avoid the stares she'd gotten on her way to the restroom earlier.

"Sugar, they're staring because you're beautiful," Rita said, slapping her back. "Good Lord, you're tall and thin like a model with the best hair I've seen on any living soul. And I did a damn fine job with your makeup tonight. You could have any man in here if you wanted."

Her compliment made Cissy feel self-conscious as if she uttered something shameful that shouldn't be said out loud. When Rita turned to talk to her bartender friend, Cissy wrapped her napkin around the condensation on her glass and then used it to wipe off the rouge and lipstick. At least the darkness of the bar would mask the betrayal of Rita's handiwork until they were back at the motel room in decent lighting.

As the evening progressed, the bartender slipped Rita more than just a couple of free cocktails, all the while teasing Cissy that she hadn't touched hers. He didn't seem inclined to give her something non-alcoholic, so whenever she got thirsty, she just went to the ladies room and cupped her hands beneath the faucet.

"I'm driving, sir," she lied. "I better not drink."

He let out a hoot and slapped the wooden bar top. "Sir? I ain't no sir, baby doll. And drinking don't stop any of these folks from driving."

"May I just have a Coke, please?"

When he set the drink on the bar, she could already smell that more than Coke filled the icy glass. His greasy wink confirmed her suspicion. And while Cissy enjoyed the music and being treated like a grown-up, the night dragged on, and she longed to return to the motel and Grandmother. Rita was so busy catching up with folks she hadn't seen in a while that she almost ignored Cissy. By 9 p.m., she'd had so much to drink that Cissy didn't recognize her friend anymore. Her slurred words and lazy eyes upset Cissy's stomach, which was raw from skipping dinner. She shouted above the music that she had enough money for a cab and they could say their goodbyes in the morning before she and Grandmother checked out. Rita nodded in agreement, but Cissy thought she could've said there was a pink spotted elephant in the parking lot and the response would have been the same.

After ten minutes of Cissy's nonstop begging, Al, the bartender, agreed to call a cab. She wondered if he would have continued his flirting and racy talk if he knew she was just sixteen years old. She half thought about telling him she killed a man so he'd shut up. Using her daddy's death in that way seemed wrong, so Cissy just hummed to drown out Al's observations on her appearance.

Once in the cab, Cissy could breathe easy. She leaned her head up against the window and let the neon lights of downtown Nashville flash across her face on the short ride back to the Howard Johnson. She soaked it all in, knowing that within twelve hours, she and Grandmother would be on their way to the next town. Nashville will have been just a two-week pit stop.

Cissy gave the cab driver more money than she should have, but she had no idea how much to tip and didn't want to seem inexperienced or a cheapskate. He smiled his thanks at the extra cash and told her to have a nice evening.

The scolding she thought she deserved surely loomed just beyond the motel room door. Her shaking hand rested on the doorknob while she summoned the courage to enter and face Grandmother's disappointment. She had promised to be back by 9 p.m. and now it was closer to 10:30. She was angry at Rita for taking her someplace knowing full well Cissy would miss her curfew. Still, Cissy had herself to blame for not calling for a cab sooner. She'd learned some valuable lessons and would be sure to tell Grandmother, hoping to earn some mercy. Surely she'd be impressed that something good came of the irresponsibility.

The creaking door did nothing for Cissy's nerves as she peeked in. The room's air conditioner had been turned off and the air smelled heavy and musty. She called out for Grandmother, hoping she was using the restroom and not out with the police looking for her. Hearing nothing, she walked in and tapped on the closed bathroom door. Her heartbeat grew louder at the silence.

"I'm here," God said, appearing at her side.

Cissy's hand hovered above the doorknob. She resisted touching it as if a raging fire on the other side had heated it up to a thousand degrees.

"I don't want to open the door, do I?" Cissy wished her heart would slow its pace long enough for her to take in a full breath.

"You have to open the door," God said.

"I can't. I need Rita."

If Cissy had eaten dinner, it would have come up by now. Instead, she fought a nausea that caused her ears to ring and the floor to shift. Dry heaves folded her body in half and she rested her forehead against the door.

"You're not alone, Cissy. You're never alone."

Chapter 32

The ambulance men let Cissy ride with her grandmother to the hospital when she explained she couldn't drive herself. Peter, the more talkative of the two EMTs, said scalp lacerations bled like a river, making an injury seem a lot scarier than it actually was. He said Grandmother probably fell and hit her head on the bathtub edge, causing a severe concussion. Cissy asked why she wasn't talking, and he explained she'd knocked herself plum out and her body was sleeping to mend itself.

Cissy stared him straight in the eye. "You'll go to hell if you're lying."

When he smiled, she said there wasn't a goddamn thing to smile about.

"No, ma'am," he said. "You're right. No need for cursing. I apologize."

She regretted using God's name like that and wished she could add the offending curse word to her List of Banned Words, sealing it off from ever being used again. She'd have to remember to apologize to God in person when they spoke next. More than anything, Cissy hoped She'd be waiting for them at the hospital.

Cissy imagined the wheels of the ambulance would squeal as they rounded the corner and pulled up to the emergency room doors, sirens blaring, and that nurses would rush out to meet them like they did in TV dramas. Instead, they pulled up nice and gentle, and the EMTs took their time unloading the gurney holding her sleeping grandmother.

"Why won't you hurry up?" Cissy shouted in their calm faces. "She needs a doctor."

This time, they ignored her and went about their job of handing off the care of Grandmother to two ER nurses who stood ready. They, too, seemed to move in slow motion, walking alongside the gurney and through mysterious doors that were closed to Cissy despite her pleas to be allowed to enter. Another nurse who sat at the ER admissions desk instructed her to stay put in the waiting room. Waiting seemed the absolute hardest thing to do.

"Do you have someone you should call?" the nurse asked.

"No, ma'am. It's just me and my grandmother," Cissy lied. It got easier and easier to create her own version of the truth to protect their time together. But there she was, almost skillful at deceit. Her heart sank at the many ways she'd changed in three months.

The large white clock on the far wall of the waiting room had pitch-black hands and huge numbers that made it easy to count seconds, then minutes, then hours. Cissy stared until her eyelids became sandpaper. At 2 a.m., a doctor finally emerged from the swinging doors her grandmother had entered almost three hours earlier.

"Are you family?" he asked, and sat down across from Cissy.

"Yes, I'm Cissy Pickering. I'm Mrs. Clayton's granddaughter." She'd decided Grandmother's health was important enough to put their aliases aside and face this crisis as their true selves. Telling lies was like digging a hole while someone stood by throwing the dirt back in. There was no way to keep up with them.

His voice, an even but boring baritone, was enough to put a person to sleep and required extra concentration to decipher the seriousness of his message. Grandmother had suffered a stroke and they operated to relieve bleeding in her brain. She lay unconscious in the intensive care unit, and the doctor said they were watching her closely to make sure the swelling subsided.

"Miss, I'm sorry to say that her prognosis isn't good. The nurse said you don't have any other family alive and that you and your grandmother were on vacation when she fell ill. Do you have a family friend to call?"

Cissy said she did. He laid a hand on her knee, yet it seemed as detached and impersonal as his words.

"But may I see her first?" she asked.

He nodded and called over a nurse to lead Cissy to the elevators and up to the fifth floor of the hospital. The ward seemed unusually dark. The strongest light shone on the nurses' station and the lone nurse keeping watch over the loved ones of family members like herself. Her mind went back to her school's catechism books and the many pictures of God's heavenly goodness streaming through dark clouds onto Jesus or a saint or other special person. She sure hoped God looked down on the ICU nurse right now as she looked after Grandmother.

The rooms were situated around the circular station like spokes to a wheel. The faint beeps and buzzes coming from the perimeter assured Cissy the life-giving machines were hard at work while patients slept. She wondered if keeping the temperature so cold helped in the healing as well. She had to rub her arms just to keep her teeth from chattering.

Grandmother appeared to sink into the hospital bed so deeply that the top sheet and blanket rested evenly on the mattress. A large plastic tube snaked into her mouth and distorted her face. Still, Cissy saw her as she was before their trip began, smartly dressed in a fine suit and maybe a summer hat, her white hair just perfect, and her delicate hands wrapped in proper white gloves. Even wearing her sternest face, Grandmother could make Cissy feel loved in the most complete and perfect way.

Cissy pulled up a chair and put her arm through the metal railing so it rested right alongside Grandmother's, their forearms touching. She placed her head against the railing even though the metal was ice cold.

"I need you to get well, Grandmother. I promise I can take care of you. I promise I'll learn how to drive and I'll figure out where we need to go. I know I can do it if you believe in me."

She whispered her wishes aloud, thinking God would be sure to hear and grant them.

The nurse stopped in to check on Grandmother's tubes and wires, so Cissy took the opportunity to ask her a burning question. She needed to know whether a person in a coma could hear the people in the room talking.

"Some people believe that's so," she said, but paid more attention to her busywork than Cissy's yearning.

"What do *you* believe?" Cissy asked.

She stopped what she was doing and looked her straight in the eyes. "I believe she can hear you, sweetie."

The nurse's kindness set off the sorrow Cissy had somehow contained until now. She stood to accept the embrace the nurse offered. Her shoulder soon grew wet from Cissy's tears, but she refused to let go. Every time Cissy lessened her hold, the nurse's grasp grew even tighter. Cissy's cries echoed throughout the quiet ward, but it did no good to try to suffocate the grieving that had already begun.

When the embrace ended, Cissy's body couldn't stand on its own anymore. Her leaden arms and legs ached, and the weight of her head threatened to topple her. She said she had to make a phone call and that she'd be back after resting a spell in the waiting room downstairs. Cissy kissed her grandmother's forehead and whispered that she would be nearby.

She didn't know where else to go, so headed back down to the ER. Cissy decided it was too early to be making phone calls, so she curled up across four armless chairs, folding her arms beneath her chest to stay warm. Her face pressed into the fake leather of the chair and she drifted off. She couldn't remember a night's sleep when she didn't have nightmares or dreams that needed some kind of pondering. Cissy had always felt she lived in two different worlds and never got a chance to sleep in either. Yet, when she woke the next day, she had no recollection of the hours that had passed. Unless someone had moved the hands on the clock as a joke, Cissy had slept for close to five hours. If her full bladder hadn't demanded attention, she might have slept the day away.

After peeing, she stood before the mirror in the hospital restroom that reflected back someone unrecognizable. Black mascara smudges formed a raccoon mask around her bloodshot eyes. Her tangled hair stood out at all angles. She grabbed a paper towel and wet it with liquid soap. The soap stung her eyes and it took some serious scrubbing, but the makeup Rita had applied was finally just a memory. There wasn't an easy fix for the hair, though. All she could do was wet it and work her fingers through the tangles until the squirrel's nest lay down a bit.

Somewhere in the early morning, a different nurse had shown up to staff the admissions desk. Cissy told her a bit of her story and asked to borrow some change for the pay phone. She said Cissy could use the phone at her desk if she was quick about it.

She dialed the number and waited several rings before she heard a familiar voice.

"Lily, it's me."

"Cissy! We've missed you so much!" Lily's euphoria cut through the sadness of the previous night and day, filling Cissy with a long-lost happiness.

"I've missed you all, too," she said.

"Are you coming home? I have so much to tell you about," Lily said, not bothering to breathe between sentences. "I'm already reading books that high school classes are reading. And I remember to look up each word I don't know in the dictionary as you told me."

Cissy smiled at their former reading lessons. Lily had taken to books and words in the same way Cissy had, and they shared endless hours reading to each other. They once vowed to be famous writers one day so they could spread joy to young readers like themselves.

"Is Jessie reading with you?" Cissy asked.

"Aw, you know Jessie. She'd rather be catching crawdads than open a book, but I'm working on her."

In the background Cissy heard her mama insisting that Lily divulge who was on the phone. Lily must have put her hand over the mouthpiece because her answer back was muffled.

"But I'm not finished talking to her!" Lily wailed. Cissy imagined a struggle over the phone in their front hallway.

"Cissy? Cissy?" Lily yelled into the phone.

"Yes, I'm here," she yelled back.

"I believe you."

Cissy didn't have time to sit with the enormity of Lily's declaration because their mama had yanked away the phone and told Lily to go sit in her room.

"I spoke with your grandmother yesterday and she told me where you are. I'm leaving now and will be there soon. Everything will be okay."

Cissy could tell her mama was trying to hold herself together but wasn't doing a very good job of it.

The concern and gentleness in her voice made Cissy's stomach flip-flop. The day Cissy killed her daddy, her mama's anger and hurt had risen up like a tornado that threatened to destroy them all. Sometimes, in the deepest part of night, Cissy convinced herself her mama was lost to her for good. She didn't know what to think of the long-distance conversation they were now having. And she wondered why Grandmother had called Mama yesterday. Did she know she was getting worse?

"Let me speak to your grandmother," her mama said.

"That's why I'm calling. Grandmother fell and hit her head and we're at the hospital right now. The doctor says she had a stroke."

When her mama didn't answer, Cissy thought the line had gone dead.

"Mama? You still there?"

"Yes, Cissy. I'm here. How is she?" If a person could hear panic, that's what came across the telephone wires.

Cissy tried to explain what the doctor and nurses had said, but Mama had more questions than Cissy had answers. When she asked for the address and phone number of the hospital, Cissy handed the phone to the nurse and asked her to relay that information. When Cissy got back on the line, Mama was all business and no crying. She said she'd be there by evening and it'd all be fine.

"Mama? I've been meaning to tell you some things."

"Now's not the time to catch up," she said, and Cissy's heart sank. "I'll see you soon and then we can talk. I promise. Don't worry about anything."

Mama didn't ask about her well-being, but with her own mama dying, there probably wasn't room in her brain for much else to worry about. She never mentioned Cissy leaving the mental hospital or whether the law had been looking for them. Her words held no sharpness or bite. Only after Cissy hung up did she realize how frightened she'd been to make that call. She wondered if her mama had forgiven her.

Cissy also wondered if she and her mama would be staying at the Howard Johnson together while Grandmother recuperated in the hospital. Thinking about that made her sick to her stomach, so she put it out of her mind. She needed food something fierce. She hadn't eaten since the popcorn at the movies the day before and felt close to passing out. Still, she had one more thing to do first.

"Ma'am, may I make another call? It's local."

The nurse nodded, too busy with her paperwork to care.

"Do you have a phone book?" Cissy asked.

She looked irritated at the interruption, but she reached for the bottom drawer of a file cabinet and fished it out. Cissy called the café next to the motel because Rita would have already clocked in for the breakfast shift. One of the other waitresses said Rita had called in sick. She suggested Cissy call the main motel number and ask to be connected to Daryl's room.

The phone rang so many times Cissy figured Rita was too ill to pick up. Or hungover from all the drinks she'd had at Tootsie's. When she mumbled a grouchy "What do you want?" into the phone, Cissy's heart lifted.

"It's me, Cissy. Grandmother's very sick. We're at the hospital."

Over the line, Cissy could hear her thrashing about, trying to roust herself from sleep and out from under the covers.

"Oh, sugar, I'm so sorry," she said. Her weak voice sounded something other than hungover, and Cissy felt ashamed she'd assumed Rita couldn't really be sick.

"Could you come sit with me at the hospital? I'm scared." Cissy figured it was no point in putting up a brave front for Rita. She'd never been so scared and the thought of facing her mama alone crippled her.

When Rita didn't answer right away, Cissy's face burned hot, thinking she'd stepped over a line.

"Let me get ready and I can be there in an hour. Daryl hid the keys to my car so I'll have to take the bus or a cab," she said, still not sounding like herself. "Could I bring you anything?"

Cissy asked her to fetch a change of clothes from the room. Then, without hesitation, she told her about Grandmother's money hidden in the air-conditioning vent. She said she needed some cash and asked if Rita would bring $50. Cissy told her to grab some of the money for her cab fare as well. At this point, Rita was all Cissy had and if she couldn't trust her, she couldn't trust anyone.

While Cissy waited for Rita, she decided to sit with Grandmother a spell if they'd let her. By the time she returned to the ICU, a different nurse was on duty. Cissy wished the kind woman who'd hugged her so sweetly the night before was still working. She regretted not asking her name.

Grandmother looked exactly the same, her chest moving only because a machine willed it so. Cissy placed her palm on her hot forehead, then ran her fingers along Grandmother's arm, which was tethered to a tube and bag full of clear liquid. She moved to the foot of the bed and massaged Grandmother's feet through the thick thermal blanket. Cissy relayed that her mama was on the way and wondered what Grandmother's response would be if she were awake.

"I know I have to go back to the hospital in Meridian." Cissy moved back to the side of the bed so she could stroke the frail arm again. "I'll be okay, Grandmother. And I don't think you'll get in trouble given how sick you are."

She *didn't* know that she'd be okay and she definitely didn't know Grandmother wouldn't get in trouble, but she hoped saying those things aloud over and over again and with some confidence would make them so. Grandmother and Mama often stated things with such surety no one would dare question them. Perhaps it was a trait Cissy had inherited as well.

After an hour had passed, Cissy walked back down to the ER, where she'd asked Rita to meet her. She scanned the room, looking for her familiar face, but she hadn't arrived. When Cissy turned to walk back to the elevator, a woman whose swollen purple face resembled a Halloween mask called out her name. Her stomach rose into her throat when she recognized Rita's voice coming from the mask. With unsure legs, Cissy dropped to the floor.

"Are you all right?" Rita bent down to help her up. "Here. Sit down."

She couldn't find the words to match the horror in her thoughts. Cissy reached for Rita's face and she flinched.

"Don't touch," Rita whispered. "It hurts."

Furious tears spilled from Cissy's eyes at the damage Daryl had done to her beautiful friend. Rita said he'd been so angry with her for going to Tootsie's and staying out late, he didn't care about his earlier promise not to hit her where it would show.

"Did you call the police?"

"Oh, honey, that'd be the last thing I'd do. He said he'd kill me if I did and he's capable of it. I half thought I'd meet my maker this very morning."

Cissy squeezed her hand and they sat together without speaking. Her jaw ached from her clenched teeth. She felt useless in helping Grandmother or Rita. Nothing made sense in her world and God was nowhere to be found. Cissy was convinced more and more that she had dreamt up a God who looked like Julie Andrews, who said the exact right things Cissy needed to hear, over and over again.

"Oh, I forgot. Here's your change of clothes." Rita handed her a paper sack. "And here's your money."

She reached into her purse and handed several bills to Cissy, which she rolled up without counting and slipped into her back pocket.

"Thanks."

"I also brought a couple of your notebooks. I thought they might make you feel better," Rita said. "I brought your favorite pen, too. I know you like things a certain way."

Rita winced when Cissy hugged her, so Cissy let go reluctantly. She wished she had words to express how much she loved Rita in that instance.

"You didn't say your Grandmother had *that* much money," Rita said, breaking the silence. She fished for an explanation to something Cissy didn't know she needed to explain.

"Yeah, I suspect she has a lot more than that. It's what she could get on short notice when she left Biloxi to bust me out of the hospital."

Another person might have worried that Rita would steal Grandmother's money and hit the road, but Cissy had a good feeling about her friend. She believed the rest of the cash was still safe in the motel room.

"She must really love you," Rita said. "I mean, to have left her home and family to be with you."

"Yep," Cissy said. "I'm pretty lucky. But I better go get dressed now. I'll be in the restroom down the hall."

She stayed in the restroom longer than necessary, leaning over the sink breathing through the anger that rose in her against Daryl. She pictured him punching Rita with all his might, as if he were hitting another guy. Even though she closed her eyes, the pictures wouldn't stop coming. His fist colliding with her perfect porcelain face, shattering its beauty until she no longer looked like Rita. Cissy slipped out of the blouse and skirt she'd worn the night before and stuffed them into the trash can. She didn't want a reminder of the day Grandmother had needed her most and she wasn't there.

Rita had brought a pair of white pants, which were Cissy's, and an orange and white striped T-shirt that must have been hers. She'd told Cissy last week it was downright stupid that redheads felt they couldn't wear orange and that she'd grown nauseated by the amount of pink in Cissy's wardrobe. She smiled to think Rita would say "I told you so" when she saw her in the orange shirt.

Cissy jumped when someone pounded on the bathroom door. She opened it quickly to find Rita, breathless and panicked.

"It's your grandmother. The nurse came looking for you." She grabbed Cissy's hand, dragging her down the hall to the elevator. Cissy punched the up button over and over until Rita pushed her hand back and softly said, "Enough." The elevator ride seemed endless. They both jumped when the bell dinged to tell them they'd arrived at the fifth floor ICU.

Cissy ran past the nurses' station and into Grandmother's room, Rita a step behind. The day-shift nurse looked up and shook her head from side to side, a weak, apologetic smile pasted to her face that Cissy wanted to slap right off. She said nothing as she unhooked the wires and tubes that had helped Grandmother cling to life. Cissy wondered why the nurse wouldn't speak it aloud, why she wouldn't say Grandmother was gone.

"Can you take the tube out of her mouth?" Cissy begged.

The nurse nodded and stood between her and the hospital bed so Cissy couldn't see her remove it. A rush of air escaped from Grandmother's lungs, startling Cissy. Rita held her shoulders and cried as deeply as Cissy did. The nurse put down the metal railing and stepped back to let them get closer.

Cissy lowered herself onto Grandmother's chest so that she could nuzzle into her neck. She smelled of warm life, which made Cissy doubt she'd left at all. In that moment, Cissy hated God. If She'd been real, She would have saved the one person who loved Cissy when no one else would. She'd never felt such heartache and wondered how anyone survived the death of someone they loved. Her own grief gave way to the knowing she'd ignored for so long. She'd caused her mama this exact kind of heartache. And that in speaking the truth, Cissy had also destroyed her mama's ability to remember the good in her daddy. She'd taken much more than his life.

Rita bent down next to Cissy so that they almost covered Grandmother's small frame. Their tears fell over her like rain showers to the parched earth. Grandmother's passing split Cissy's heart open; wide enough that she could cry for her daddy, too. She'd taken a life to protect two other lives, but she'd told herself his death didn't

439

matter. It's as if Grandmother's lifeless body became the vessel to hold all the sadness and regret Cissy had locked away to protect herself. Feeling it now didn't destroy her as she feared it would. She could let him go. She had to let both her grandmother and her unborn baby go as well.

Cissy looked up to see God standing near the foot of the bed.

"Rita, could I have a minute with Grandmother alone?" Cissy asked.

Rita kissed her cheek and retreated to the nurses' station.

"I'm sorry about your grandmother," God said.

"I know you're not real," Cissy said, wiping her wet face with the edge of her T-shirt. "I mean, I think God is real. But I think *you're* just here to help me find my way, like Dr. Guttman said."

"Cissy, your Grandmother will always be with you," She said. "You can talk to her whenever you want, just the way you talked to me."

Cissy nodded and closed her eyes. Grandmother had gone on from her earthly body and there was no need to mourn for it. Cissy wanted to believe Grandmother was as stunningly bright as the sun, an angel in the heavens, wings spread wide and strong. Picturing her like that was the only way she could bear to turn her back.

She opened her eyes and walked out into the hallway to get Rita.

"Do you want to wait here at the hospital for

440

your mama, or do you want to take a cab back to the motel?" Rita asked when they were back in the elevator. "Or could you eat something?"

Cissy sighed and used the bottom of her T-shirt to wipe her watery eyes. Now Rita wanted to take care of her.

"I don't know. I guess I should eat. I might think straight if my gut wasn't screaming at me."

"Good, let's go down to the cafeteria," she said, and pushed the button to the lobby.

Before they'd gone down three floors, Cissy looked at her battered friend. "Rita, I have an idea I want to run by you."

Chapter 33

Rita said counting floor tiles and talking to someone others couldn't see didn't make Cissy crazy, but she'd never heard a crazier idea than the one Cissy offered when they got downstairs and stood in the cafeteria line.

"It can't work," Rita said. "Stop talking like a lunatic. The grief over your grandma is clouding your common sense."

Cissy's grief *was* overwhelming, but her common sense had never felt so keen and on target. If Rita would just calm her mind, she might see Cissy's point of view.

Rita shuffled a few paces behind Cissy, tray in hand. Her injuries from Daryl were clearly painful. Cissy waited for her to catch up before choosing a table at the far side of the cafeteria. The thought of eating seemed pointless to Cissy, but she'd ignored her stomach for far too long to argue. Dutifully, she swallowed each bite of the meatloaf special and ate four yeast rolls with butter before she broached the subject again.

"I can't let you go back to Daryl. And it's not charity I'm offering. You'd be helping me as much as I'd be helping you."

Rita's misshapen face turned Cissy's stomach,

but she stared at it because the bruises bolstered her resolve.

"If we wait around until Mama gets here, I'll have to go back to the state hospital," she said, allowing herself to sit with the probability that's where she'd end up by tomorrow.

Rita stared out the large glass windows at the thunderclouds that had blown up in the last half hour. The cafeteria darkened noticeably as if the lights had been dimmed. Soon, the wind howled enough to make the tree limbs scritch against the glass. Goose bumps covered Cissy's whole body.

"Storm's a coming," Rita said, and chewed her nails. Cissy thought to pull her hand away, but that was something her mama would've done. If Rita needed to chew on her fingertips, Cissy sure as heck wasn't going to shame her for it.

Her friend meant they were in for some bad weather, but Cissy wondered if her mama's storm might be much worse. In the back of Cissy's mind, where the scariest thoughts hid, she'd buried a fear that her mama would blame her for Grandmother's death, too. Cissy had killed her mama's husband *and* her mother. She might even want Cissy transferred to a prison to be punished properly. On the phone, she hadn't said she loved Cissy. But then again, Cissy had been too afraid to tell her the same thing. She wouldn't make that mistake with Rita.

As they ate, Cissy told Rita she didn't used to believe much in God or fate, but she couldn't help thinking that something beyond their knowing—something bigger and smarter than their pea brains—was hard at work putting things in motion so they'd know the right decisions to make. There was a reason she and Grandmother wound up in Nashville and that Rita worked at a café just steps from their motel room. Cissy even believed it was necessary for Daryl to be in the picture, or she'd have never thought of asking Rita to drive her to New York.

"There are a gazillion people there. No one would ever find us," Cissy said, thinking back to the travel books she'd read and the stories she'd pried from Dr. Guttman. "And I could help take care of the baby when she's born."

"She, huh?"

"Well, there's a fifty-fifty chance I guessed right," Cissy said.

"But I have a job here," Rita said. "It doesn't make sense."

"You can waitress anywhere. And you won't be a waitress forever. Don't you think we'd have a lot more opportunities in New York?"

Rita pushed her piece of pie toward Cissy after she'd finished her own in four bites. Rita's unwillingness to talk about the option of leaving Nashville, though, planted a seed of despair in Cissy's gut and soured her on a second dessert.

She pushed it away, much to Rita's surprise.

"You don't want to go with me because you think I'm a real crazy person. I guess I can't blame you." Cissy lowered her head.

"Shut your mouth!" Rita hissed. "You're the best thing to happen to me and I won't let you talk about yourself like that. You're not crazy."

"Then why won't you come with me?" she demanded.

"Look at the sorry state I'm in," Rita said, waving her hand around her face to frame the damage Daryl had done. "I don't have a dime to my name and I'm going to have a baby."

Both of them were in a sorry state. Maybe that's why it made such sense to stick together.

"We'll take Grandmother's money and car." The plan grew clearer in Cissy's mind. "It's not stealing. She'd have wanted me to have it."

They sat in silence for a good long time, watching the large splats of rain hit the vast expanse of the cafeteria window. Cissy would catch herself holding her breath, and had to concentrate to make her lungs work. Soon, the drops turned to globs of sleet, sticking to the window before sliding down like big, fat tears. She wondered how cold she'd feel at the state hospital in winter if she'd been so cold there in the summertime. She wondered how the other patients and the nurses would treat her when she returned.

"Fall's not here yet and winter already wants to make a showing," Rita said with a slight frown and went at her nails again, two already gnawed down to bright pink nubs.

"All the more reason to hit the road now." Cissy steadied her shaky voice. She wanted to instill confidence in Rita, to prove to her that the idea was a good one.

When Rita didn't answer, Cissy begged her to consider another option. Rita could take Grandmother's car and money and go by herself, to New York or anywhere far away from Daryl. Cissy just needed bus fare back to Meridian. She'd decided not to stick around to wait for her mama to arrive.

"Sugar, stop talking your damn nonsense," Rita said. "Maybe writing in one of your notebooks will calm you down some and bring you back to your senses."

She retrieved two spiral notebooks from her big, slouchy purse and placed them on the cafeteria table—one with a blue cover that held most of Cissy's general lists, one with a bright red cover that contained her List of Banned Words and the List of Very Sad Things.

Cissy grabbed the red spiral, got up from the table, and walked across the cafeteria until she reached a large garbage can. She began ripping out page after page, crumpling them and dropping them in with the waste from people's unwanted meals. Then she took the red cover and tore it in quarters, then eighths, throwing the pieces on top of the wads of lined paper.

When Cissy got back to the table, Rita sat with wide eyes.

"What did you just do?" she asked.

"I've already lived through some of the greatest sadness I will ever experience in my life," Cissy said. "Why do I need to carry around a written account of that sadness or all those words that used to frighten me beyond all measure? I'm not frightened anymore."

"Oh, sugar, how did I get so lucky to run across such a wise young woman?" Rita asked.

"Luck doesn't have anything to do with it," Cissy reminded her.

"Yeah, yeah, God and fate and all that," Rita said.

"Exactly."

"I guess it's fate that I'm agreeing to go to New York with you even if that's the most asinine plan ever?"

Cissy jumped up, banging her knees against the table in a rush to reach Rita. She hugged her battered body as gently as possible given the magnitude of her joy and relief. Cissy thought about mentioning it was Nurse Possum Eyes who first used the word *asinine* around her, but Cissy was ready to put memories from the hospital in the past.

"I'm going on one condition," Rita said, pulling back from Cissy's embrace.

"You name it!"

"*I'm* driving."

Grandmother wouldn't have had it any other way.

Acknowledgments

Like many authors, I wrote a number of novels before my first book was published. *Forgiveness Road* is my third *published* novel, but its path to publication was circuitous and maybe a bit miraculous. It was the first novel I ever wrote, finished back in 2010. After countless rejections, I thought it'd be one of those manuscripts relegated to the proverbial desk drawer and chalked up as practice. Cissy's complicated story stayed with me, though. My editor at Kensington Publishing, John Scognamiglio, saw promise in the concept. His insights led to a robust rewrite and a much more layered story—one where three generations of women struggle to understand and forgive an unforgivable crime. It is a story of flawed, yet strong women, and one of which I'm very proud. I am blessed that John continues to believe in my stories and my career.

I am fortunate to have JL Stermer as my literary agent and champion in all things publishing. How cool that she is also someone who recognizes the power of a cat gif to celebrate successes or lift spirits. As always, I am indebted to my longtime critique partner, Micki, who has read bits of this story for almost a decade. I hope the two of us have many more years to develop our craft together.

To the community of author friends I've found online, thank you for your support across the miles and multiple social media platforms.

To my husband, Andy, and my amazing circle of family and friends, this journey is all the more meaningful because of you.

To the readers, book clubs, reviewers, bloggers, and booksellers, well . . . you are the true superstars.

Discussion Questions

1. At the beginning of the novel, Cissy tells her grandmother that shooting her daddy wasn't crazy. Later, in the psychiatric hospital, Martha tells Cissy that pulling the trigger was the most courageous thing she would do in her lifetime. What do you think about these statements?

2. Cissy's mother says she is "telling horrible, disgusting lies" and that Cissy has "never been in her right mind." Why is Caroline so reluctant to believe her daughter? Why is Cissy's grandmother, Janelle, so certain she's telling the truth?

3. From the beginning of the novel it's clear that Janelle and her daughter, Caroline, have a strained relationship. How does Cissy's crime strain it further?

4. At her hearing, Cissy's obsessive counting and list-making are described as coping mechanisms. Do you think these behaviors are the result of her father's abuse or personality quirks that are amplified by her trauma? Explain.

5. Dr. Guttman's appearance and unorthodox treatment seem out of place in Mississippi. Why do these differences allow Cissy to trust him?

6. Cissy is terrified that Dr. Guttman will make her confront the deep, dark places in her mind. She thinks, *It could be just dark enough you'd never find your way out again.* In what ways does she prove this to be untrue?

7. Cissy refers to herself as "this side of crazy." How does that help her justify her time in a psychiatric hospital?

8. Cissy believes that God appears to her in the form of a woman who looks like Julie Andrews in *The Sound of Music*. Do you believe this is yet another coping mechanism, or that it is possible she was really speaking to God?

9. Compare and contrast Cissy's friendships with Martha, a fellow patient at the psychiatric hospital, and Rita, the diner waitress in Nashville? What lessons does she learn about herself from having known them?

10. Janelle tells Lucien, an orderly from the psychiatric hospital, that "killing is wrong, but Cissy felt she had no other choice." Lucien tells her there's always another choice. Why does Lucien's remark upset Janelle?

11. How does Janelle and Ruth's relationship change from when they were children to

present day? Do you believe things could have been different given the setting and time period?

12. How does Janelle justify the abortion for Cissy? How does this decision affect the relationship between Janelle and Ruth?

13. Janelle admits to having no plan when she helps Cissy escape from the hospital. Why does she embark on the road trip anyway, especially in light of her own failing health?

14. Janelle tells Cissy that their days together have been the most meaningful of her life. How is that true for Cissy as well?

15. At the end of the novel, Cissy rips up the notebook that contains her List of Very Sad Things. Why does she no longer need it?

16. At one point, Cissy acknowledges that three generations of women—including Janelle's mother—had failed their daughters. In what ways is this true? In what ways is it not?

17. What kind of emotional growth have Janelle, Cissy, and Caroline experienced by the end of the novel?

Books are produced in the United States using U.S.-based materials

Books are printed using a revolutionary new process called THINKtech™ that lowers energy usage by 70% and increases overall quality

Books are durable and flexible because of Smyth-sewing

Paper is sourced using environmentally responsible foresting methods and the paper is acid-free

Center Point Large Print
600 Brooks Road / PO Box 1
Thorndike, ME 04986-0001 USA

(207) 568-3717

US & Canada:
1 800 929-9108
www.centerpointlargeprint.com